UTOPIA UNDONE

OVERWORLD CHRONICLES BOOK FIFTEEN

JOHN CORWIN

ACKNOWLEDGMENTS

To my wonderful support group:
Alana Rock
Karen Stansbury

My amazing editors:
Annetta Ribken
Jennifer Wingard

My awesome cover artist:
Regina Wamba

Thanks so much for all your help and input!

BOOKS BY JOHN CORWIN

THE OVERWORLD CHRONICLES

Sweet Blood of Mine

Dark Light of Mine

Fallen Angel of Mine

Dread Nemesis of Mine

Twisted Sister of Mine

Dearest Mother of Mine

Infernal Father of Mine

Sinister Seraphim of Mine

Wicked War of Mine

Dire Destiny of Ours

Aetherial Annihilation

Baleful Betrayal

Ominous Odyssey

Insidious Insurrection

Utopia Undone

Assignment Zero (An Elyssa Short Story)

OVERWORLD UNDERGROUND

Possessed By You

Demonicus

OVERWORLD ARCANUM

Conrad Edison and the Living Curse

Conrad Edison and the Anchored World

For the latest on new releases, free ebooks, and more, join John Corwin's Newsletter at www.johncorwin.net!

UTOPIA DYSTOPIA

Years after Baal's unsuccessful invasion of Seraphina, a new portal device offers Justin and gang a way back to Eden.

Instead they end up trapped in Utopia, a realm where humans founded a nearly perfect civilization, at least until disaster struck, turning most of the citizens into zombie-like eidolons. The realm is now ruled by a powerful elemental magus named Vokan.

But all is not as it seems. This realm seems to be just another stepping stone for Baal. If Justin can't restore the dystopia back to Utopia, then Baal will add another notch to his belt and be one step closer to supreme leader of all.

CHAPTER 1

D ragons danced in the skies of Seraphina.

They swirled and pirouetted in formation, a dark, dense cloud of claws, teeth, and flames. They were small dragons—drakes, to be precise—but no less dangerous than their larger cousins, the wyverns. They swarmed like piranha, reducing anything in their path to bones. In numbers as great as these, they could flay an entire crew in seconds.

Fire and ice painted the air, an occasional gout of green poison spraying across the blue canvas. The ice attacks hurt less than flame, but the poison ate through flesh, burrowing to the bone. I'd seen people die from the poison alone.

Apprehension weighed my stomach like stones. We had Mzodi ships and flying Seraphim who knew how to fight this threat, but every time we tracked a pod of drakes, I wondered if this would be the battle that ended badly.

"Archangels, flank left," I shouted into my comm badge. Primarion Arturo raised his lightning lance and nearly two hundred Brightlings launched into the air from the deck of the *Evain* and her sister ships.

Sunlight glinted off the crystalline hulls, white as the element of destruction the Brightlings preferred. The *Evain* rotated north to lead the fleet of flying ships into firing position.

"Holy farting fairies, that's a lot of drakes." Harry Shelton eyed the dark swarm. "There's gotta be a thousand!"

"How many more nests could there be?" Adam Nosti pushed a finger up the bridge of his nose even though he no longer wore glasses. "Those damned things breed like rabbits."

"This has to be the last one," I said. "The trail ends here." A chain of rocky black islands dotted the ocean below. I desperately hoped we'd find the last of the drake nests left on Seraphina, because we had about a million other things more important than infestations to deal with.

My dear old grandad, Baal, the grand overlord of Haedaemos, had tried to unleash a dragon army on Seraphina. We'd stopped him, but not before a few hundred drakes had decided to make love, not war. Like an invading organism, they'd spread all over islands in the Castigean Ocean in the year since the failed invasion. Now it was up to us to clean house.

I would've been fine leaving them alone. Larger dragons had lived on Seraphina for thousands of years, but drakes were voracious and deadly. They were stupid, ate everything in sight, and destroyed the environment. Seraphina had no natural predators to deal with them.

Elyssa tapped on an arctablet, tracking the flight of the drakes with a program Adam had written. "They're definitely coming from those islands. This must be the origin for all the smaller nests."

"Sure would be nice to stop playing pest patrol," Adam said.

I tapped my comm pendant. "Daskar, flank right."

The Mzodi ships bearing the Daskar broke off from the center group to form the other end of the pincer that would snuff out the drakes. Darklings in black crystal armor jetted into the sky.

"Ah, shit." Shelton grimaced. "El primero jackass is here."

I didn't have to turn around to know who he meant.

"Why wasn't I informed that we'd engaged?" Tall and delicately thin, Governor Evain of the Brightlings stepped beside me. His long silver hair flowed sideways in the wind. Pointy ears and almond-shaped eyes gave him an elven appearance. "I hope the Darklings"—he spat the word —"will do better this time."

Alysea, my mother, had united two empires with thousands of years of animosity between them, but the Darklings and Brightlings had a long way to go before the word "trust" entered their lexicon.

I counted down from ten in my head. Not because I was angry, but because I was waiting for—

"Is naptime for the children over?" Governor Flava of the Darklings strode from the bow of the *Falcheen*, a condescending smile on her face.

She and I went back a long way—all the way back to the final boss battle with Daelissa and again after Cephus destroyed most of Tarissa. We lost contact when my besties and I decided to overthrow Daelissa's mother, Kaelissa, and take over the world.

Mom decided she was the perfect person to represent the Darkling nation, Pjurna. Unfortunately, Flava lost her sweet disposition after Cephus killed most of her legion and wrecked the city she loved. I didn't know what she hated more—the Brightlings, or the fact that a fellow Darkling was responsible for nearly wiping out their own kind.

Evain, on the other hand, was the former mayor of Zbura, the Brightling capitol at the time my mother became empress. He was a bridge between a distrusting populace and a conquering empress. My mother, Alysea, hoped it was enough to prevent an uprising from angry citizens.

Thankfully, there wasn't enough time for these two to start argument, because the storm of drakes was nearly on top of us.

I tapped my comm pendant. "All ships open fire!"

The *Falcheen* and her sister ships spun broadside. Aether cannons speared white beams into the mass of drakes. Smoking reptiles spiraled into the ocean. The archangels plowed a line through the mass on the left while the Mzodi fleet supported them. The Daskar did the same from their flank. Torrents of destructive energy whittled away at the swarm.

A drake the size of a house cat dropped onto the deck and spouted fire at Shelton's backside. He yelped and threw up a shield just in time to block it. I blasted the mini-dragon off the ship with a burst of Murk.

Dozens more broke through the fire barrage. Shelton whirled his staff and thrust it toward one drake just as it opened its mouth to blast him. Magical bonds wrapped around its muzzle. Fire spurted from the drake's nostrils, but not nearly enough to reach Shelton. Adam swiped his arcphone. A gout of water knocked the invader over the railing.

Elyssa unclipped a notched leather rod from her belt and flicked a switch. The rod unfolded into a curved bow with a beam of light for the string. She pulled back on the string and an arrow of crackling energy formed. She unleashed the arrow and dropped an oncoming drake, turned right and speared another from the air. I kind of envied the light bow she'd gotten from Atlantis, even though I fought with Seraphim magic.

I fired a volley of Murk spheres from my hands, knocking the little monsters out of the air while constant fire from the *Falcheen* took out the bulk of the swarm. Within minutes, our immediate area was clear.

A huge grin broke on Shelton's face. "This never gets old no matter how many times I see it."

"Flying ships, lasers—who could ask for more?" I said.

Elyssa nocked another arrow. "What about laser bows?"

"Hey, don't forget the pirates and dinosaurs," Adam added.

Shelton snorted. "Dragons ain't exactly dinosaurs, but I'll take it."

Slowly but surely, the main swarm thinned. Squads of archangels and Daskar headed toward the islands to burn out the nests.

None of us were prepared for what happened next.

The entire chain of islands shifted and began to rise. Ocean water poured from the rocky spines. The land beneath the islands expanded outward. Fish and other sea creatures flopped helplessly as the water abandoned them.

Shelton's jaw fell open so hard, I thought he was going to drop anchor with it. "What the hell is going on down there?"

Massive wings burst free of the water, creating a small rainstorm. A head the size of an island rose on a long neck and an eye bigger than our ship turned its red glare our way. To say this thing was a giant dragon would have been an understatement of epic proportions. Black as night, eyes burning red, the beast rose in slow motion, not from the power of its wings, but on a glowing cloud of aether.

What we'd thought were islands were craggy protrusions down the length of its spine, naturally worn by the elements. The dragon's back was so broad, lakes of water filled the spaces between the crags.

Shelton gripped my sleeve. "Justin, is this the part where we get the hell out of Dodge?"

I tried to speak, but my throat locked up.

A chorus of other voices rose. Flava, Evain, and Adam spoke at once. Illaena, the captain of the *Falcheen*, stared at the beast, clearly as stunned as the rest of us.

Arturo's voice came through my comm pendant. "Orders, Prince Justin?"

I cringed at my new title. "All forces, fall back!" We didn't have nearly enough firepower to bring down a dragon that size.

"Fall back? We're not cowards!" The voice belonged to Mercuto, the captain of the Brightling flagship, *Evain*. Yes, they'd named it after the governor.

Aside from glaring at us, the dragon didn't seem to want a fight and turned toward the open ocean away from us. "Mercuto, do you really think we can take that thing down?" Another question was, did we really want to? Some dragons were intelligent, especially the bigger ones. I wondered if we could communicate with this one.

"Of course we can." Mercuto sounded supremely confident.

"Do you need glasses?" Shelton said. "Do you see how big that dragon is?"

Mercuto decided to pull an asshole maneuver. "Governor Evain, what are your orders?"

"You do realize I'm in command, right?" I felt like this kid was threatening to take his ball and go home. "Evain answers to me."

"It's true, I'm afraid." Evain's lips peeled back in a grimace. "You must follow the crown prince's orders."

Mercuto let his actions answer instead—a resounding "nah, bro." The *Evain* and the rest of the Brightling fleet accelerated toward the gargantuan dragon, leaving squads of archangels out of range of their carriers. From this distance, the ships looked like white specks against basalt mountains. Beams of Brilliance lanced toward the dragon.

With no more effort than a cow flicking its tail to ward off flies, the dragon's sinuous neck curved back. It opened its maw and huffed. The Brightling ships tumbled through the air, dandelion fluff scattering in the wind.

The *Evain* crashed into one of the spinal protrusions and shattered. The rest of the fleet managed to recover and fled, tails tucked between legs.

"No!" Governor Evain reached out a hand as if he could catch the flagship. "My darling!"

Flava gasped. "What has he done?"

"That idiot!" I tapped my comm pendant. "Arturo, can you reach any survivors?"

Before he could answer, the behemoth opened its mouth and roared. The air visibly rippled, like a stone striking the surface of a pond. Clouds of aether jetted from the dragon's wings. The deck shuddered. Everyone grabbed the railing and held on for dear life as the ship spun and bucked through the sonic storm.

It seemed like an eternity but was probably less than a minute later when the air calmed. I steadied myself and reoriented toward the dragon. It was no longer a half mile off our bow, but at least three or four miles and growing smaller with distance.

Shelton pulled himself off the deck and stared in awe. "How in the hell did that thing move so fast?"

"I've never seen anything like it." Elyssa gripped my hand. "Are you okay?"

I nodded woozily. "Yeah, I think so." I looked where the dragon had been a moment ago and saw archangels diving toward the ocean. I tapped my comm badge. "Primarion Arturo, what's your status?"

"Recovering bodies and survivors from the *Evain*." Even his usual imperious tone was subdued. "We require fleet assistance."

I turned to Illaena. "Rendezvous with the archangels."

"At once." She gave the order and the fiery-headed first mate, Tahlee relayed it to the crew at the top of her lungs.

It was still an odd feeling having Illaena under my command, but Empress Alysea—Mom—had formalized relations with the Mzodi. Xalara, the Muhala Kajeen of the Mzodi, had assigned several of their flying ships to me and ordered the construction of new ones for the Brightlings and Darklings.

The *Frigitis*, now the default flagship for the Brightlings, reached the archangels first, but Arturo glided on blazing wings toward us and landed on the deck. He tore off his ornate helmet and threw it down. "That fool!"

"Does he live?" Evain's face burned red. "I pray he does so I may kill him!"

I didn't need to ask who he was talking about. "Did Mercuto survive?"

Arturo's lips peeled back into a snarl. "Three crewmembers survived, and of course their captain." He took a deep breath and calmed himself. Offered me a curt bow. "Prince Justin, I request the honor of personally executing him."

I threw up my hands. "Will you please stop calling me prince?" I shuddered. "It makes me feel like I'm in a romantic comedy where a poor girl meets a rich prince over the holidays and they fall in love."

"Oh, sounds so romantic!" Elyssa kissed my cheek. "Can I be the poor girl, my little princey-poo?"

Shelton and Adam snorted so hard it sounded like they ruptured their sinuses.

Arturo huffed. "You should treat your office with more decorum, *Prince*. It is unbecoming of someone in your position to act this way."

"My ship is gone and you're making jokes?" Evain clenched his fists. "I want Mercuto's head."

"Hot-headed Brightling." Flava scoffed. "If your people were not so violent and murderous, they would be alive."

"Enough, Flava." I stared her down. "Will you please back off?"

Her hard gaze wilted. She turned and walked to stand next to the rail. I turned to Evain. "You obviously value your namesake ship more than the lives lost. I'll decide Mercuto's fate, not you."

Arturo gave me a grudging nod of respect. "What say you, Prince Justin?"

It still felt incredibly strange having this former nemesis as my ally. He'd led Daelissa's forces against me in the Second Seraphim War. He'd thrown his support behind her mother, Kaelissa, when she took over the Brightling Empire.

Then he'd done a one-eighty and supported my mother's claim to the throne when she challenged Kaelissa.

Arturo wasn't complicated—he just put honor and duty above people. That was exactly why he'd address me as Prince Justin no matter what I said. He would follow protocol to the letter.

As for Mercuto, I really didn't know what to do. The seraph had violated a direct order. Ship destroyed, crew lost. I didn't know what I could do to make his day any worse than that, and I wasn't big on executions. Mercuto hadn't willingly murdered anyone. He'd overestimated his ability to deliver, big time.

I pursed my lips as if I was really deliberating Arturo's request and asked him a question. "What's worse—dying or living with the shame and dishonor Mercuto brought on himself?"

Arturo's brow pinched in surprise, probably because he expected me to start talking about romantic comedies again. "I see your point, Prince. I would ask that Mercuto is demoted to the lowest crew position and forced to remain on duty."

"Like scullery maid?" I didn't really know what the lowest position was. Every Mzodi crewmember was important, from the navigators, to the soldiers, to the gem sorters. The Brightlings probably had their own crew designations.

Arturo scowled. "The lance cleaner."

Shelton scoffed. "Nothing like polishing archangel lances to put life into perspective."

Arturo narrowed his eyes but said nothing. It had been a duel between him and Shelton that gave my mother the throne. Shelton still felt weird around the archangel, but Arturo considered it a matter of honor long settled.

"Permission granted." I'd seen a lot of death in my short life and still hadn't gotten used to it.

Evain made a strangled noise but managed to keep his mouth shut.

I ignored him. "How many souls were on that ship, Primarion Arturo?"

Arturo turned his gaze toward the ocean. "The *Evain* was a troop carrier with five crewmembers. No archangels were aboard since they left us behind. But every loss is a terrible blow."

I nodded somberly. "Mercuto will have a long time to consider his mistake."

"May he suffer for it." Arturo offered me a curt bow.

I took a deep breath and turned to the others. "Now here's the next big question—what in god's name was that dragon?"

CHAPTER 2

N o one answered.

"I've seen wyverns as large as this ship. I've seen earth dragons as large as ten ships. But I've never seen a dragon that size." I looked at Illaena. "Have the Mzodi ever encountered anything like it?"

"I would have to consult with the fleet records," she replied. "We have encountered wyverns nearly the size of the *Uorion*, but nothing approaching that creature's size."

The Mzodi flagship was massive, but even it looked like a ship in a bottle compared to that monster.

Adam had nerded out and made a chart of all the dragons we'd encountered in our time on Seraphina. Drakes were at the small end of the scale. Some were no larger than my hand. Others grew up to six feet long. Wyverns included all the winged dragons we'd seen so far. Those without wings were ley worms, or earth dragons, though Adam and Shelton hoped to come up with a cool name for them without sounding pretentious.

Adam snapped his fingers. "I think I've seen that dragon before." He diddled on his phone until he found what he wanted. A holographic screen projected from his phone so everyone nearby could see a video.

In the video, a massive portal split open to the orange, molten skies of Draxadis, the dragon realm.

"This was recorded before Justin shut down the portal generator and stopped the dragon invasion." Adam put a finger on the hologram and centered on a black shadow near the forefront of the dragon forces. He zoomed in and clarified the subject of his focus.

"That looks just like the behemoth dragon," I said.

"Not only that, but look what's around it." Adam circled the area filled by flocks of drakes.

Shelton took off his wide brimmed hat and scratched his head. "You think this thing got through before Justin shut down the portal generator?"

Adam nodded. "Not only that, but I think the behemoth is the source of the drakes."

Elyssa scoffed. "You think it's their mother?"

"Doubtful." He shrugged. "It's more likely the drakes are somehow attached to the dragon."

"I believe the drakes in Seraphina are now exterminated," Arturo said.

"Hopefully." Adam flicked to another video. "This is today's incident before the dragon surfaced." He zoomed toward the craggy islands that turned out to be part of the dragon. "I don't see any caves or crevices for the drakes to hide in. I think the big dragon might control them, or else it's a symbiotic relationship like sharks and remora fish."

Illaena and Tahlee exchanged confused looks.

"Sharks?" the captain asked. Apparently, Seraphina didn't have sharks.

Adam waved off the question and changed the image to a map marked with red Xs where we'd exterminated drakes. They formed a winding trail through the Castigean Ocean to our current location. "I think the big dragon has been feeding in the waters. Every so often, some of the drakes stayed behind at an island to make babies."

"So we're done, right?" Shelton looked down at the body of an orange drake no one had disposed of. "We saved the environment and all's good."

"Do we just let that monster dragon stay?" Elyssa asked.

"The drakes were the problem," Illaena said. "They infest and consume. I do not think one large dragon will be a problem, but I also believe we should discover if it is intelligent."

I nodded. "It didn't attack us except in self-defense. I think that's a sign of intelligence."

"Yeah, but does it communicate like the earth dragons?" Adam pushed up his non-existent glasses. "Maybe it's as ancient as Altash and Lulu."

Earth dragons resembled monstrous snakes and they breathed aether fire. The smallest I'd seen was the size of a compact car. Altash, on the other hand, had a head size of a city bus. Even he looked like a garden snake compared to this monster.

"Before we say another thing, we need to name this dragon." I smacked the back of my hand into the other palm for emphasis. "I think Gigantor is perfect."

Elyssa groaned. "First of all, you already used that name for Altash before you knew his name. Second, it's still a terrible name."

"Yeah, you always use descriptors for names," Adam said. "If you named your foot, you'd probably call it Walksy."

"Not if I use it to run," I shot back.

Shelton gave me a thumbs down. "Everyone has a weakness, and yours is definitely creative naming."

"Names do not matter," Illaena said. "What matters is that it exists—an enigma that must be solved."

"Oh, I like that!" Elyssa said. "Let's call her Enigma."

Shelton raised an eyebrow. "Her?"

Elyssa scoffed. "Obviously. Even when Mercuto attacked, it showed way too much restraint to be a male."

"Enigma." I said the word a few times. "Yeah, it's okay. Not as good as Gigantress."

"That's practically the same as Gigantor," Elyssa said.

"It's the female version." I let her chew on that.

Adam flicked to his dragon chart. "Well, she flies, so she's a wyvern, but she also swims like a hydra or a sea serpent." He inserted an image of Enigma and tagged it with *sea, air*. "Can you believe that I used to think dragons didn't even exist? Now I'm categorizing them for real!"

"Next thing you know, you'll have your own nature show." Shelton spread his hands grandly. "Nosti's Wild Planet."

Adam nodded eagerly. "I love the sound of that."

Arturo sighed. "Sire, what are your orders?"

With the drakes gone, I was ready to get back to dry land. "All ships return to Cabala." I turned to Illaena. "All except one of the Mzodi ships. Please assign a captain you trust with tracking Enigma and making contact with her."

Illaena nodded. "I will send a ship to track the dragon, but I would also like to send word to Xalara. She may know best how to initiate contact."

"I agree." I turned to Arturo. "I assume you'll be on the *Frigitis*?"

He nodded grimly. "I will distribute the crew and troops from the *Evain* evenly among the rest of the Brightling fleet."

Flava broke her silence. "Shall I order our ships to move out?"

I gave her a thumbs up. "Back to Cabala."

Arturo retrieved his helmet. Blazing white wings formed on his back and thrust him into the air. I couldn't help but feel a bit jealous as I watched him fly to the *Frigitis*. I could channel wings and glide, but actual fast flight had evaded me no matter how much I practiced.

The Daskar, on the other hand, used crystal armor outfitted with special gems that enhanced maneuverability and speed.

Daskar.

The name still made me shudder even though this was a new generation. These were real Darklings who trained with the enhanced armor and not the abominations created by Aerianas. Before Nightliss died, Cephus had stolen fragments of her soul. Aerianas had taken those fragments and combined them with a golem spark in a soul sphere. Using a complex demon summoning pattern, she'd created a body of demon flesh around the sphere, giving birth to a demon golem.

We called them dolems for short.

Most of the original Daskar could have passed as daughters of Nightliss because they were made with her soul fragments. In essence, I'd had to fight an army of beings who bore a haunting resemblance to my dead friend. The only mercy was that they'd worn full-face helmets, so I didn't have to look them in the face and see Nightliss die over and over again.

Dolems were abominations made to subvert everything Nightliss believed in. She'd died in the Crystoid Incident; a plot I'd later discovered was engineered by Victus Edison. Unbeknownst to us, he'd also set in motion another scheme to take over Seraphina, all while pretending to be our ally. His master plan marooned us in this realm, leaving him free to have his way with Eden and the Overworld.

I couldn't wait to get back home and mete some serious justice upside his head.

Elyssa hooked her arm in mine. "You're thinking about Nightliss again, aren't you?"

"Not just her. Everything that bastard, Victus, did to us." I led her to the aft section as the *Falcheen* got underway. "Can you imagine what he's doing to the Overworld without us there to stop him?"

"You're beating a dead horse, Justin." She squeezed my hand. "We have a million reasons to get back to Eden, but until Adam and Shelton figure out how the Fallen made portals, we're stuck."

"It's been nearly three years." I smacked my palm on the railing. "Adam and Shelton haven't had a single breakthrough."

"Probably because they've been gallivanting around fighting drakes with us instead of researching." Elyssa shrugged. "Can't have it both ways."

"Well, Cinder's on the job." I shrugged. "Maybe he's made progress, provided he's not distracted by Issana and Bliss." Both of his lab assistants were dolems. Both had tried to kidnap or kill me before I taught them the error of their ways. I still didn't trust them, but Cinder seemed to think he could reform them.

"Well, with the drake infestation handled, I think it's time to focus on getting home."

Tension melted from her shoulders. "I agree. It's time to go home."

THE TOWERING CRYSTAL cliffs of Cabala rose into view two days after our encounter with Enigma.

The shipyard hummed with activity. Mzodi builders guided construction gems along a frame, molding aether into the crys-

16

talline hull of a flying ship. The organic humps and curves were alien in design, but every detail had a purpose. Wide flat gems studded the bottom. These levitation foils provided lift and thrust. Small turrets directed diamond-shaped gems for maximum firepower.

The crew of each Mzodi ship once powered everything from the levitation foils to the weapons, but during our first foray through Voltis and into Atlantis, we'd discovered super-concentrated aetherite, a solid form of aether. Our resident geniuses, Shelton, Adam, and Cinder, redesigned the circuitry of the *Falcheen* so it drew power from the aetherite instead of the crewmembers.

The Mzodi were integrating this new arcnology into all their flying ships. In exchange for these major improvements, Xalara agreed to build us a fleet of the ships. That agreement, however, didn't include the secrets to ship building, or how to harvest and enchant raw gems.

The finished ships sat on piers behind the city walls. They were small, nimble craft, each one a fully-functional work of art. One bore the shape of a wyvern, wings folded tight to its body as if diving toward its prey. Despite its beauty, it hadn't sacrificed form for utility.

"Wow, that's a beautiful ship." Elyssa wasn't talking about the wyvern ship. I followed her finger. An amber raptor, wings in attack formation beckoned from a distance. Two legs angled forward from the back, talons spread wide to balance the ship perfectly. A wide-open deck expanded from just behind the long neck and encircled an island bridge in the middle.

"Holy dragons and falcons," Shelton muttered. "Those are some hot looking ships."

Adam clicked his tongue. "The Mzodi really know how to craft art."

I loved the *Falcheen*. This ship had taken us to the ends of the world and back. We'd repaired and redesigned it so many times, it was practically a new ship. The crew had become almost a second family to me. Captain

Illaena and her first mate, Tahlee, would never admit they loved us, but I knew deep down inside, they cared.

The *Falcheen* landed on her own specially constructed pad behind the palace. The little ship had saved the world on more than one occasion and deserved some special treatment. Illaena, despite her gruff exterior, enjoyed the prestige.

Grand Empress Alysea, i.e. Mom, waited for us in the courtyard when we disembarked. "Finally, you're home!" She kissed my forehead and gave me a long hug just as Arturo and his elite squad of archangels landed and kneeled.

"C'mon, Mom. Not in front of the archangels." I kissed her forehead and untangled myself. "Things status quo here?"

"Not really." She raised her hand toward the archangels and they rose from their knees. "I will hold council in one hour, Primarion Arturo. I would hear an account of your missions."

"As you say, Empress." Arturo bowed and led his people toward the barracks.

An honor squad of Daskar landed after the archangels cleared the zone. They bowed, full-faced helmets staring with dead eyes toward our feet. The leader, his helmet marked by blue chevrons, touched a gem to remove the faceguard. Trevan's face bore deep scars from battles against the original Daskar. He'd been part of the resistance against Cephus and rose again to fight Aerianas when she took over the Darkling legions with demon clones.

Trevan straightened and met our eyes. "Blessings."

"Blessings to you," Mom said. "We hold council in one hour."

"I shall be there." Trevan spoke with a rasp, probably due to a war injury. "It has been long since we set foot here, Empress. How fares my request for quarters?"

Mom's lips pressed tight. "The separate quarters for the Daskar are complete in the southern sector as requested."

"We are grateful." Trevan bowed again. "I will return for council."

Mom nodded. "Dismissed."

Ultraviolet wings rippled from gems on the backs of the black armor. Aether jetted from gems on the boots and gauntlets, and the Daskar shot into the air, southward bound.

I shuddered. "That dude creeps me out."

Mom pursed her lips. "He's loyal, but as fond of unification as the Brightlings are."

"Not at all, then?" Elyssa looked at the patrolling guards. "Are they all Brightlings?"

"Half and half now." Mom pointed to one patrol bearing purple chevrons. "The Darklings mark their armor so they can tell each other apart."

"That's so stupid." I threw up my hands. "You'd think angels would be more mature about this."

"Some of the riots we've had would indicate otherwise." Mom started walking toward the domed crystal palace. "I tried mixing the guard units, but that only led to infighting. Whenever they dealt with an incident, they'd take sides depending on if it was a Darkling or Brightling in trouble."

"Well, it's only been a year since unification." Elyssa looked at a pair of guards walking the perimeter. "I can't imagine thousands of years of animosity can be fixed overnight, especially since the average lifespan here is three hundred years."

"That's the other problem people want me to solve." Mom's hands balled into fists. "They think I can miraculously fix the damage caused by the Schism."

A few thousand years ago, Daelissa had tried to take over Eden and started the First Seraphim War. During the final battle, the Chalon had been removed from the Grand Nexus causing a tremendous backlash that husked everyone near Alabaster Arches and turned them into soul-sucking parasites of darkness. In Seraphina, the effects hadn't been quite as catastrophic. Instead of husking Seraphim, it had reduced the lifespan of newborns to around three hundred years instead of immortality, give or take a few decades. Only those far removed from the Alabaster Arches had escaped the effects.

"Yeah, sure. I've got a truckload of Flintstones vitamins that'll patch them right up." I rolled my eyes.

"I don't know why anyone would want to be empress," Mom said in a hushed tone. "For every grateful citizen, I have a dozen whiners. Sometimes I wonder if ruling with an iron fist is necessary. But that would mean everything we did to free the nations was for nothing."

Elyssa cracked her knuckles. "Just let me know if you want me to rough up one of the whiners."

Mom laughed. "Careful, or you might earn yourself a new position as my personal enforcer."

The guards at the palace entrance saluted us, fists over chests like the Templars, instead of kneeling as Kaelissa required when she was empress. We walked inside and through a cavernous foyer to reach the personal chambers.

"Are you hungry? I had the cooks prepare you some special snacks." Mom led us to the small private kitchen she preferred to the massive royal dining hall. Plates of hamburgers and pizza steamed on crystal platters.

If I hadn't been hungry before, I certainly was now. I tapped my comm pendant and contacted Shelton. "Where are you?"

"Where are you?" he said back. "You kept telling us how important it is to find a way home, so Adam and I went to talk to Cinder right when we got off the ship."

"Yes, you're right. That's very important, but—"

"But what?" he asked in a suspicious tone.

"Mom has hamburgers and pizza in the kitchen."

"No way!" Shelton sounded like a kid. "Dude, pizza and burgers."

Adam sounded just as excited. "No way! Let's go."

I tapped the gem to end the call.

Shelton and Adam dashed inside moments later.

"Hey, Alysea!" Adam piled French fries on his plate. "Thanks for the burgers."

"You're welcome." Mom munched on a fry. "Thanks to Atlantis, we now have our very own royal herd of cows."

"Oh, man, that's the best news I've heard all day." Shelton dropped into a chair at one of the tables and demolished a slice of pizza.

"The best news all day?" Elyssa raised an eyebrow. "Man, you need to get a life."

"Pizza is life," Shelton said.

Adam shook his head. "I dunno, burgers are life too."

"Harry!" Bella burst into the kitchen, hands on hips. "I haven't seen you in nearly two months and you tell me to meet you in the kitchen?"

"Babe, it's pizza!" He held up a slice as if that explained everything.

She flashed her fangs. "You think pizza is more important than ravishing your wife the moment you return?"

"But, pizza?" Shelton looked worried.

21

Bella stomped a foot. "Harry, put down the pizza and come to our room this instant."

"Fine!" Shelton piled a plate with more slices and flashed a devilish grin. "Pizza and sex. Man, this is gonna be epic."

Adam giggled like a kid. "Maybe for you, but I don't know about Bella."

Bella turned her glowing violet eyes on him. "And where's Meghan, hmm? Have you even told her you're back?"

His grin faded. "She's still on expedition to Sazoris to find local ingredients that can be used in potions."

"I thought she was on her way back," Elyssa said.

"She was, but they found a valley full of promising specimens." Adam shrugged. "At least it's not like we're going anywhere anytime soon."

"Yeah, I'm devoting all my time to portal research." Shelton caught a narrow-eyed glare from Bella and cleared his throat. "And lots of patty-cake with my beautiful wife."

I groaned and threw down a fry. "And now you've ruined my appetite."

Shelton snorted. "Hey, I'll be sure to take pics for you."

"Pics of your hairy ass are exactly what I want." I made a shooing motion. "Now get out of here and make Bella happy."

Shelton saluted. "By your command."

Bella slapped him on the ass and they skedaddled.

Elyssa took a bite out of her burger and moaned. "Oh, this is good. I'm so sick of glurk and panari."

The Mzodi and Darklings stuck to vegetarian diets and viewed killing animals for food as cruel. Ironically, they hadn't had any issues with slaying dragons. Then again, drake extermination was necessary to preserve the environment. Shelton, Adam, and I had tried cooking a drake, but Illaena flipped her lid and made us throw it overboard.

I wonder if it would've tasted like chicken.

The Brightlings, on the other hand, ate meat—lots of it. That was one of the reasons integration between the different cultures proved so tough —well, aside from millennia of Brightlings enslaving Darklings and bullying them around.

The Mzodi were considered a neutral third party with a highly developed culture of their own. They saw no difference between those who channeled Brilliance and those who channeled Murk. Most Mzodi could channel both. Mom had hoped the Mzodi could be a unifying force since both Brightlings and Darklings respected them, but it just hadn't worked out that way.

Elyssa put down the burger and nibbled on a fry. "I'd like to go see my family tomorrow."

I blinked from my thoughts. "Sounds good. I can't wait to see the new Templar compound."

"Nothing can replace the Ranch, but I'm glad they finally found a place to settle for now."

I dipped a fry in ketchup. "It'll be like having a pocket of Eden right here in Seraphina."

Victus had managed to trap the entire Eden army here. Vampires, lycans, felycans, Daemos, Templars, and the kitchen sink too. The Darklings hated hosting us when we lived in their capitol city, Tarissa, because of all the meat-eaters roaming the countryside. The Brightlings were fascinated with us, especially the vampires.

One of the big new attractions in Cabala were the blood bars, where Brightlings willingly let vampires feed off them because it was new and hip. Angel blood supercharged vampires, but without a war to fight, I didn't think it was a good thing. Sometimes, I felt as if our Overworld culture was corrupting this world.

Then again, that was the least of our worries, especially with two big baddies who wanted to rule the universe.

Xanomiel, one of the rulers of old Earth, wanted to recombine the realms back into one world, killing billions in the process. So far, we hadn't heard much from him, but that didn't reassure me a bit. For all we knew, he might be sunning on a beach or searching for the relics that would force the realms back together.

To combine the realms, he needed fragments of the focal point of the Sundering—a female named Saila who died guarding the city of Juranthemon. The Fallen had scattered the Relics of Juranthemon all over the realms to prevent this from happening but I didn't know if that was enough to hinder an Apocryphan.

Baal, the second wannabe dictator, intended to conquer every realm until he ruled them all. We'd stopped his dragon invasion of Seraphina three years ago, but he wasn't done with us. He might have moved on to easier realms, or he might be hatching another dastardly plan. We certainly weren't ready for another war.

The Templars were desperately low on people and supplies. Red Cell, the elite vampire army, was barely two hundred strong now. The Arcane elites, the Blue Cloaks, were down by half, and the lycans had lost two thirds of their pack. Most of the surviving felycans had scattered to the countryside to live their preferred lives of solitude.

In short, the Eden army was running on fumes.

We needed to unify the Seraphim so they could defend themselves. Unfortunately, that wasn't going so well. Ancient hatred threatened to tear apart the fragile alliance between Darklings and Brightlings. Even the threat of the dragon invasion hadn't been enough to unite them.

If Baal or Xanomiel invaded now, we were screwed.

CHAPTER 3

"We did it!" Harry Shelton and Adam Nosti pranced into the royal kitchen the next morning pumping their fists and singing like Dora the Explorer while Elyssa and I cooked pancakes.

"We did it. We did it. We did it, yay!" Adam pushed a wheeled platform ahead of him bearing what looked like a giant magnifying glass with a small orb secured to the lens. "Dude, we can go home!"

"Dude, what?" I nearly spilled pancake batter on myself.

Cinder, our friendly neighborhood golem, walked in after the pair and nodded at us. "Justin and Elyssa, it is good to see you again. I had hoped to speak with you yesterday but determined that everyone was busy catching up with loved ones."

I put down the batter and walked across the room to shake his hand. "No, I'm sorry for not making time to come see you." I waved a hand at the contraption Adam and Shelton fawned over. "Did you have anything to do with this?"

He nodded in his precise way. Despite achieving sentience through a laboratory accident, Cinder still hadn't mastered emotions or human gestures. "I finished this two days ago and ran the final simulations yesterday afternoon. I must caution you that Harry and Adam are overly optimistic about an apparatus that has not been proven in real-world trials."

"Over-optimistic my ass!" Shelton lovingly ran a hand over the lens. "I think Cinder nailed it."

"Technically, Bliss and Issana are the ones who overcame the technical hurdles." Cinder looked out at the hallway. "It is okay if you come in."

Bliss stepped hesitantly inside. She was taller and thicker than Nightliss, but similar enough to haunt me every time I saw her. "Issana had other things to attend to." She looked my way and quickly averted her eyes when I met them.

I swallowed the bitter taste in my mouth and offered her a forced smile. "That's great."

Elyssa flipped a row of pancakes. "Were you able to figure it out from studying Fakor's rift gem?"

"No, his rift gem proved too singular in purpose," Cinder said. "It was coded to open a rift to Draxadis and nowhere else."

"We got lucky," Bliss said. "It really wasn't anything more to it than that."

I lifted an eyebrow. "Explain."

"We searched all over Mount Olympus for the Fallen's portal arcnology but found nothing." She looked up from the floor and slightly to the side to avoid direct eye contact. "I had the scan spell active on Cinder's arcphone when I was going to the observatory in the Fallen's palace and discovered the window was actually a portal lens."

Shelton scratched his head. "Yeah, I could've sworn we scanned that place from top to bottom, but there it was in plain sight."

"This is a window?" I walked around the lens. "Why in the world would the Fallen install a portal lens as a window?"

"Because they likely weren't using it anymore," Adam said. "The portal lens is a gem with a complex set of enchantments we haven't even begun to decipher, but it seems to be an earlier version of whatever arcnology the Fallen use now."

"Yeah, so they retired it and turned it into a window." Shelton sighed. "Wish we'd found the damned thing sooner."

"Bliss's discovery accelerated our project," Cinder said. "All that was necessary was creating a harness for the Chalon."

Adam projected a holographic image of the apparatus from his phone. The title at the top read: *Argus 1.0.* Yellow text labeled the various parts. The Chalon was a universal portal key, but it couldn't open a portal by itself. For that you needed a functional Alabaster Arch, or a portal gem like this.

"Why'd you name it Argus?" I frowned. "It's not very descriptive. What about Portalus? Or Portalizer?"

Elyssa groaned.

"Yeah, that's exactly how I'd name something as fricking amazing as this." Shelton scoffed.

"Portalus is kind of cool," Adam said.

Shelton eye-daggered him then turned back to me. "Now, the only downside to Argus is that it has to be used at just the right place in Voltis, or you'll end up in the Void or Timbuktu."

Adam sighed. "From everything the Fallen's servant told us, we believe they have a device that doesn't require precise positioning."

My forehead tightened. "So how do we know where to go?"

"It's in the slideshow," Shelton said.

Adam flipped to a still image of the massive storm wall of Voltis. Jagged lightning threaded through the gray. Fiery meteors fell toward the ocean alongside giant balls of hail. The place was literally hell on Earth.

"Voltis is surrounded by an aether storm separating Seraphina from Atlantis." Adam flipped to an overhead illustration of the storm wall circling an island of calm in the center. "When the Sundering split Earth into dozens of realms, it left behind an original fragment of Earth surrounded by what is essentially a giant portal."

"But we physically traveled through the storm the first time we reached Atlantis," Elyssa said. "It wasn't like passing through any portal I've used."

"The *Falcheen* and a lot of luck are the only reasons we survived," Shelton said. "What we did was jump through a malfunctioning portal without being torn to shreds."

"We theorize Voltis is caused by the extreme friction between realms." Adam switched to a slide that displayed the giant moon of the Glimmer. "The Anchor Stone holds the realms in place. It's the only reason this original fragment of Earth still exists." He flipped through other slides, each one showing the realms progressively drifting apart. As they did, Atlantis fragmented into another realm and Voltis vanished. "If this happened, there would be no way to travel between realms."

"No way we know of," Cinder clarified. "The Siren builders may possess such knowledge."

Shelton grunted. "This point in space is subject to tremendous pressure and inter-realm friction. That's why Voltis is simultaneously a pathway to Atlantis, and a portal to anywhere in the realmverse."

"Inter-realm? Realmverse?" I examined the final slide. "Are you guys making up new words today?"

"Technically, the realms are not a part of the multiverse," Adam said. "They're different parts of the same dimension. An Earth in another dimension might not even be split into realms like ours is."

"You're getting way out there now." Elyssa piled the pancakes onto a platter. "So you're saying there are multiple dimensions in addition to the multiple realms?"

"Theoretically," Adam said. "But that's science and the realms were created by magic."

"And here I thought you were going to give us the quick version." I pinched the bridge of my nose. "Instead, you're giving me a headache."

"Fine." Shelton threw up his hands. "Go to the last slide."

Adam obliged. This one showed the Anchor Stone with all the realms around it superimposed on Voltis. "Argus can be used to pinpoint specific coordinates in Voltis to open a portal to the corresponding realm. All we need to do is fine-tune the coordinates we found in the enchantment code with some real-world trials."

"So." Shelton looked around expectantly. "Who's up for a trip to Voltis?"

My hand shot up before I even thought about doing it. "Man, I am so ready to see Eden again."

Adam pumped a fist. "And to kick Victus's ass."

"I know you want to get out there right away, but we should really discuss this with my father." Elyssa spared a sobering look for each of us. "Let's take a day to prepare before gallivanting off on another adventure."

"Actually, Shelton and I can take one of the smaller Mzodi ships out to Voltis tomorrow," Adam said. "It's gonna take us a couple days to get there and a few days to calibrate Argus."

"And that's optimistic," Shelton said. "You guys can meet us out there when you're ready. I promise we won't go home without you."

"Better not." I rubbed my hands together, giddy with excitement. "God, I hope this works."

"Me too," Shelton said. "Me too."

Bliss stood in the doorway, a third-party observer despite her timely discovery. A part of me wanted to let her in, maybe offer her a smile of encouragement. But I just couldn't bring myself to like her. It wasn't because she tried to kill me. It wasn't because she'd served Aerianas in her quest to take over Seraphina for Victus.

It was because she reminded me every damned day that a person I loved was dead.

I turned back to the others. "How do we find the right coordinates in Voltis for a portal to Eden?"

"Alignment with the Anchor Stone gives us a good starting point," Adam said. "After that, there's a lot of guesswork involved."

"That's why calibration will take so long," Shelton said. "Even then we won't know exact coordinates for Eden."

"Bliss and I conducted early phase trials," Cinder said. "An Mzodi cruiser took us out to Voltis so we could align the Chalon and open test portals."

My mouth dropped open in surprise. "You actually created portals with this thing? It definitely works?"

"Precisely." Cinder took out his arctablet and projected a video of a portal forming. It wasn't very large, but it was big enough for a human to fit through. In the video, a rock flew through the portal and landed in a puddle of lava on the other side.

Elyssa snorted. "You tested it by tossing rocks through the portal?"

Adam grinned. "Yep! Super scientific."

"Sure as hell ain't gonna stick my neck through a portal before I know it works," Shelton said.

"How did you even know where to start with the coordinates?" I asked. "It's not like we have an alignment chart of the realms and the Anchor Stone lying around."

"Easy." Shelton flicked through the slides projecting from Adam's phone until he reached a wall of dense symbols. "This is the portal enchantment." He scrolled down to something resembling a chart of the solar system. Except the giant green sphere in the center was the Anchor Stone and the multitude of planets orbiting it were the realms.

I leaned closer. "Good lord, all of these tiny spheres are realms?"

"There are hundreds," Cinder said. "Unfortunately, they are not labeled."

"Thus, the guesswork." Shelton grunted. "Wish I knew how they coded in a live-action map of the realms."

"You and me both," Adam said. "This requires incredible knowledge about the very building blocks of the realmverse."

"Guess that's a real word now, huh?" Elyssa gazed at the realm chart. "Good luck deciphering that mess."

"It's easier than you think." Shelton zoomed in on one of the realms, a black sphere broken by molten orange and red. "Don't know which realm this is. Sure as hell don't want to go there. But, you can clearly see it's not Eden."

"Because it's not blue and green?" I said."

Adam snapped his fingers. "Bingo!"

"Yes, bingo," Cinder said.

I noticed the doorway was empty. Bliss left, and it made me feel a little better not having her around. I knew I should thank her for giving us the key to going home, but it actually hurt even thinking of that.

Damn, I have issues.

Even my reservations about Bliss couldn't dampen my excitement. I was practically bursting at the seams to see Argus in action.

A lightbulb flicked on in the recesses of my brain. "I have a great idea."

"Oh, no." Elyssa backed away a step. "Do I want to know?"

"Let's try each blue-green realm one at a time until we find the right one." I waved a hand at the chart. "Not only will it be super cool to see different realms, but we can catalog them while we do it."

Adam held up his hand for a high-five. "Dude, I love it!"

I smacked his hand and turned to Shelton. "Well?"

He didn't leave me hanging. "Man, I am so in. Let's do this!"

"Awesome. We'll hook up with you guys in a few days." I danced in place. "I can't wait!"

AFTER BREAKFAST, Elyssa and I headed to the courtyard where the *Falcheen* docked, but it wasn't there. We tracked down Mom and found her in one of the private gardens.

A holographic version of Dad saw me coming and waved. "There's my kiddo."

"Hey Dad." I waved back. "We're coming down your way today."

"Nice! It's been a real pain in the ass getting Kassallandra settled in. She doesn't want to be too close to the other supers, but not too far away either." He rolled his eyes. "Elitist Daemos are the worst."

"Well, I know how much you love politics."

Dad snorted. "Almost as much as I love hemorrhoids."

Elyssa's nose wrinkled. "Gross."

I sat down next to Mom. "Where's the *Falcheen*?"

"Illaena requested a rendezvous with Xalara. She'll be back by the end of the week." Mom raised an eyebrow. "Why?"

I told her and Dad about our plans with Argus.

"Now that's good news." Dad's grin grew wider. "I'm sick of this place. Are you certain this contraption's gonna work?"

"Crossing our fingers." I held up mine. "I guess we'll ask for one of the new Mzodi ships."

"Sounds good, son. It'll be good to catch up." Shouting echoed from somewhere behind him and he groaned. "Son of a bitch. Damn vampires and lycans fighting again." He winked at Mom. "Maybe you should come down with Justin." His eyes shone like a predator. "I have a lot of catching up I want to do with you."

Mom giggled like a girl. "David, it's only been a couple of days."

"Stop!" I covered my ears. "I don't want to hear another word."

Dad chuckled and waved goodbye.

Mom tapped her comm gem to end the call and patted the bench next to her. Elyssa and I sat down. Mom sighed. "You just got back and you're already heading on another adventure."

"We're so close to opening a portal home, I can almost taste it." I took her hand and squeezed it. "Just think, we won't be stuck here anymore."

"You might not, but I happen to be the empress these days." She slid her hand out of mine and sighed. "It could take centuries to mend the damage done to this realm."

Her words curbed my enthusiasm. "Oh, yeah. Guess I kind of forgot you can't just up and leave."

"Eden will probably need a lot of work as well," Elyssa said. "With Baal and Xanomiel on the loose, we need unification if there's any hope of stopping them."

I cringed at the second name. Daelissa's forces had unleashed massive demons against us, and I'd summoned one equally powerful to fight them. The problem was, I hadn't summoned just any old demon—I'd brought forth one of the original masters of the universe out of the Abyss and unleashed him on the world.

Whatever he did was on me.

"Can we even stop an Apocryphan or the grand overlord of Haedaemos?" Mom pushed a golden lock from her face. "Baal would have us believe he's the champion who can stop Xanomiel from reuniting the realms and killing billions."

"Yeah, because he wants to rule the realms." I thought about my last encounter with dear old Granddaddy. "I think we proved we can stop Baal. He might be able to possess the dolems made with his pattern, but a physical shell limits his powers."

"Perhaps he hasn't shown us his full capabilities." Mom shook her head slowly. "Baal nearly unleashed a storm of dragons on Seraphina. We stopped him this time, but he'll never quit."

"Meanwhile, Xanomiel is doing his own thing," Elyssa said, "and we don't even know what that is."

I held up my index finger. "One problem at a time, babe."

Mom nodded. "Yes, I'm afraid that's all we can do for now."

Elyssa quirked her lips. "Let's just hope it's enough to prevent Armageddon."

CHAPTER 4

After we left Mom, we headed to the shipyard for a loaner.
The Mzodi in charge recognized me, but she didn't seem all
that impressed. "Is there something you need, Prince?"

I almost belted out a couple lines from "Purple Rain, " but figured it
would be wasted on her. "The *Falcheen* is away, so I need another ship to
take me to New Eden."

"You already have extensive experience with our craft, yes?"

I nodded. "Yep."

"Then one of the new scout vessels should suit you." We boarded a
floating cloud and drifted between the new frigates and galleons back to
the smaller ships I'd noticed on the way in.

The amber raptor glinted below us. "Ooh, I really want that one. Can I
have it?"

She raised an eyebrow at my enthusiasm. "Of course."

At fifty feet long and two decks tall, the scout ship was fun sized
compared to the *Falcheen*, but it still looked badass. The moment the

cloudlet settled on the front deck, I ran to the figurehead and examined the weapons turret. I gripped it and turned it to the sides imagining a wave of enemy fighters flying in. "Pew, pew, pew."

"Seriously?" Elyssa sighed and turned to the Mzodi. "How do you fly this thing?"

The bridge perched in the center of the deck. A tap on the domed window opened a portal in the side and the Mzodi stepped through. The bridge spanned about fifteen feet around with plenty of cloud seating available.

A small control stick and lever jutted from the console in front of the captain's chair, giving it the functionality of a cockpit.

The Mzodi tapped the control stick and the ship hummed to life. A holographic map of Seraphina flickered on just below eye level so as not to obstruct the view from the bridge. A blue blip indicated our location. "This is the integrated arcnology your people requested. I do not understand all the functions, so you will have to learn them yourself." She touched a gem on the control stalk. "Please grip the control stick so the gem can imprint you. This will prevent any unauthorized personnel from controlling the ship."

Elyssa went first and then backed away so I could grab the stick.

I felt a gentle zap as the gem took an imprint. "Dude, we're finally in the year two thousand." I scrolled across the map and zoomed in. "I'll bet this has navigation."

"How do I operate the ship?" Elyssa said.

"Quite simply." The Mzodi sat in the captain's chair. "The control stick manages pitch and roll. Twisting it adjusts yaw. Pulling up and pushing down adjusts lift if you are hovering." She tapped the thick-handle of the lever. "And this is propulsion." She moved from the seat. "Perhaps you would like to take it for a test flight."

Elyssa took the vacant seat and pulled up on the stick. The levitation foils hummed and the ship rose straight up. A gentle nudge on the lever propelled us forward. "Easy enough." She shoved the accelerator forward and we zipped out over the ocean, water spraying behind us. I grabbed hold of her seat and held on for dear life.

The Mzodi didn't seem the least bit concerned. "You're quite adept."

Face flushed with excitement, Elyssa couldn't stop grinning. "This is my new favorite thing." She swung in for a smooth landing at the edge of the shipyard. A gangway misted into solid form on the side. "Anything else we should know?"

"Only a few minor items." The Mzodi took us on a tour of the lower deck. Four bedrooms and a galley offered ample living quarters. In the power room, a cube of black aetherite the size of my fist hovered between two metal prongs in a crackling field of electricity. "This will last for two months at normal usage." A recess in the wall held two spare pieces of aetherite. "I suggest you give yourself ample time when you need to change the power source as it takes some time for the system to calibrate."

"Awesome sauce." I rubbed my hands together eagerly. "Is it my turn to fly yet?"

After the Mzodi left the ship, I hopped in the captain's seat and piloted the ship low over the water, weaving between the rocky islands rising off the coast.

"Boys and their toys," Elyssa said.

I grinned. "You just want to pilot it again, don't you?"

"So bad." Her eyes flared. "Can I?"

I reluctantly relinquished the captain's chair and Elyssa slid into the seat. I secured myself in the seat next to hers and tried to remain calm. She threaded a canyon, pulled back on the control stick and took us soaring straight up, whooping with glee.

"I regret my decision!" I shouted. "Slow down, or I'm gonna crap my pants!"

"Hmm, that's not a bad name for this ship." Elyssa leveled out the ship and cast me a sly smile.

"I'm not naming this ship the *Crap My Pants*." I crossed my arms and tried to regain a little dignity. "I'll come up with something awesome soon enough."

In the few hours it took us to reach New Eden, I still hadn't come up with anything. Elyssa glided slowly over new streets and buildings for a look at the rapidly expanding settlement.

Darklings had used gems to construct the buildings out of aether but had adhered to designs that reminded the settlers of home instead of the alien structures they preferred in their cities.

An imposing mansion with peaked turrets and stone gargoyles rose at the edge of town. It hadn't been there when we'd left to go drake hunting, but it didn't take a genius to know it belonged to the vampires. Even the elite vampire soldiers of Red Cell seemed to like Gothic digs.

A rustic lodge overflowing with bombastic conversation and rowdy folk sat on the opposite side of the settlement. I was surprised the lycans hadn't requested construction even further out of town. Though they'd fought side-by-side with the vampires, neither faction usually cared much for each other in peacetime.

Templar headquarters, a square, two-story building squatted sensibly in the center of town. Like that one guy who tries to separate two brawlers and gets the worst of the punches for his troubles, the Templars had physically and symbolically made themselves the Switzerland of New Eden. Stranded in Seraphina without a war to fight, it was only matter of time before convenient alliances dissolved and all hell broke loose.

Elyssa landed the ship in a field behind the Templar compound. A dozen soldiers in dark Nightingale armor surrounded the ship, swords at the ready.

"Did you let anyone know we were coming?" I asked.

Elyssa shook her head. "I wanted to see if our people are still on their toes."

I stepped onto the deck and waved. "Don't stab me. It's just us."

Silver swords slid into sheathes, and the Templars melted back into the trees around the field without a word.

"Nice." Elyssa strode down the gangplank.

A hulking figure of a man strode from the compound, shaking his head. "Trying to start something, Ninjette?"

Elyssa gave her big—and I mean huge—brother, Michael, a hug. "Glad to see you haven't let them slack off."

"Never." He nodded at me. "Justin."

"Howdy, Michael." I shook his hand. He squeezed a bit harder than necessary, as usual.

"Done dragon slaying?" he asked.

"Onto new and grand adventures." I waved a hand at the ship. "Like the new ride?"

"A bird of prey." Michael walked around the talons and ran a hand under the hull. "I like it."

"It's more fun than my Harley," Elyssa said.

"Blasphemy." Michael shook his head. "The commander is inside with the faction leaders." He turned toward the compound. "Things have not been going well."

"Knowing you, that's probably an understatement," I said. "Are the vampires and lycans fighting?"

"The Blue Cloaks and other Arcanes relocated about fifty miles south of here. The felycans scattered into the wilderness. All that's left in town right now are bickering lycans and vampires with the Templars caught in the middle." Michael tapped a gem on the outside wall and a doorway misted open. "We're trying to keep everyone from Eden together, but without a common cause, the army is fragmenting. It won't be long before most of our population is assimilated into Seraphina."

"Is that a bad thing?" Elyssa said. "If we're stuck here, the people might as well be happy."

"I just don't think Brightling society is ready to assimilate humans of any kind." Michael stepped inside and kept walking. "Many of them look down on humans as inferior. Some blame us for the Schism and their loss of immortality even though none of us were alive."

"Well, all our problems are about to be solved." I cleared my throat. "Maybe not all of them, but at least being stuck here."

He spun on a heel, eyes intense. "You found a way home?"

"Shelton and Adam are testing a new device," Elyssa said. "It might be just what we need."

Michael's stony face managed a flicker of excitement. "Let's hope it is."

We rode a levitator to the second floor. Commander Thomas Borathen sat alone in a conference room. A broken table and several upturned chairs indicated his last meeting had gone even worse than Michael said. Despite the furniture carnage, Thomas managed to look as serious and dignified as ever.

"Rough meeting?" Elyssa asked.

Thomas rose to meet his daughter with an embrace. "When did you get back?"

"Yesterday," she said. "I know you hate surprises, which is why I wanted to surprise you with a visit."

The corner of his lips turned up in what I considered a huge grin for someone like Thomas. "Some surprises are better than others." He turned and gripped my hand. "I'm glad you returned. Maybe you'll have better luck unifying the factions again."

My eyebrows hit the roof. "What makes you think I'll do any better than you?"

"You're the one who convinced us to join forces against Daelissa." Thomas set a chair upright. "Many still see you as the real leader of the Eden forces."

"Or the person to blame for getting us all stuck here." I pushed the broken edges of the table back together and channeled Murk into the crack to weld it together. "Besides, who am I supposed to unify them against?"

"Why can't we just all get along even without someone to fight?" Elyssa helped her father straighten the other chairs. "Back in the day it was all about understanding one another despite our differences."

Michael grunted. "I think it was more about Justin wanting to date you."

"Case in point," Elyssa said. "Think about how many times Dad tried to murder Justin just because he's Daemos."

Thomas frowned at her, apparently not thrilled at being called out for his past actions. "We've all changed from those people we were a few years ago. I believe everyone in this alliance has become something more."

"Shelton and Adam are working on something that might unify everyone more than I could," I said. "They found a portal gem in the palace of the Fallen and are on their way to Voltis to calibrate it."

"Recently?" Thomas frowned. "I thought we turned that place upside-down."

"We did," Michael said. "Blue Cloaks scanned every square inch for enchantments. I don't know how they'd miss something like that."

"Where was it?" Thomas asked.

"Bliss found it." I shrugged. "The window in the observatory was actually a portal lens."

"Very odd." Thomas pursed his lips. "I suppose we could have missed it."

"Doubtful, but it is what it is." Michael nodded at me. "Does it work?"

"We'll know soon." I jabbed my thumb west. "Elyssa and I are headed to Voltis after our visit here."

"Excellent." Thomas walked to a window overlooking the town. "The people of this town could use some hope."

"I think we all could," Elyssa said.

I looked out at the rows of quaint houses lining the central street. "On the bright side, the Darklings sure know how to build a pretty town."

Elyssa chuckled. "They've got a real future in construction."

Thomas sat back down at the newly repaired table. "I need a debrief on the drake situation."

The rest of us joined him at the table and I told him about our travels across the Castigean Ocean to rid Seraphina of the infestation. "We believe the drakes are gone, but we haven't heard anything from the ship tracking Enigma."

Thomas leaned forward, elbows on the table. "How did such a large dragon get through the rift without anyone noticing?"

"It's unbelievably fast for something so huge." I wished I had Adams' video to show him. "I was so busy fighting Fakor that Enigma could have slipped through before I noticed it."

"Let's hope there weren't any others that made it through," Thomas said. "And that this giant wyvern isn't looking for trouble."

I shuddered. "I have a feeling that if Enigma wanted trouble, we'd be in for a hell of a fight."

CHAPTER 5

We spent a couple of days in New Eden, hanging out with Elyssa's family and sweet talking the leaders of the various factions. The people were frustrated and tired of being stuck in Seraphina. Nearly all of them expressed a desire to violate Victus in all sorts of terrible ways for trapping us here. I desperately wanted to tell them about Argus but didn't want to give false hope if it turned out to be a bust.

On the morning of the third day, we headed out to sea for a rendezvous with Shelton and the others. I tried contacting them, but our comm gems weren't powerful enough to overcome the distance or the interference from Voltis. Even the *Uorion* and its powerful communications gem couldn't successfully relay our signal.

As the massive storm wall grew on the horizon, I finally got a response.

"Hello, Justin." Cinder's calm voice nearly drowned in a sea of static.

"Finally!" I whooped. "Cinder, where are you guys?"

He sent me coordinates and I used the ship's map to home in on the location.

"What in the world is that thing?" Elyssa peered through a spyglass. "Man, the Mzodi really shafted Shelton with that ugly ship."

I looked through the spyglass and spotted a floating shoebox just outside the storm wall. "What a piece of junk! I've seen shipping containers that look better."

Shelton's mouth dropped open when we pulled up alongside them and docked to their ship. "You gotta be kidding me! I asked for a fancy ship and they gave me this lemon." He banged a hand on the plain hull. "Man, wish I was the prince."

"This ship has been quite adequate for all our needs," Cinder said. "However, the design of Justin's is impressive."

"Looks like a giant falcon or an eagle." Adam sighed. "It's gorgeous."

Shelton snorted. "Did Justin name it *Birdy*?"

Adam laughed. "Or *Flappy Wings*?"

I wished I had some bird poop to fling at them. But this time, the joke was on them. I'd had ample time to think of a name, and more importantly, had asked several people in New Eden what they thought would be a good name. I almost named it the *Falcon*, but that was too close to the *Falcheen*. So I'd chosen something even cooler and saved it for this moment.

Not even Elyssa knew.

"Great names, guys, but no. I have a really awesome name." I let them stew on that moment.

Elyssa raised an eyebrow. "You didn't mention a name to me."

"Oh, I gotta hear this," Shelton said.

"Well, what is it?" Adam asked.

I waved a hand grandly at the ship. "Everyone, meet the *Raptor*."

"Ooh." Shelton shook his head. "Gotta admit, it's a good name with a lot of cool factor."

"Love it." Adam gave me a slow clap. "Great job, Justin."

Elyssa rolled her eyes. "You didn't come up with that did you?"

I elbowed her. "Don't ruin this for me."

"I guess it's hard not to come up with a cool name for a bird ship." Shelton admired the folded wings. "*Talon, Hawk, Blood Eagle*."

I hated to admit it, but I really liked those names. "Yeah, they're okay."

"We didn't give ours a proper name." Adam slapped the hull of their boat. "We just call it the houseboat."

"Yeah, it's a real steaming pile of crap." Shelton ran a hand lovingly along the *Raptor*. "I want one too."

"Enough of the nerdgasms," Elyssa said. "What's the status of Argus?"

"It's calibrated," Cinder said. "We are currently testing coordinates and cataloging realms."

I rubbed my hands together. "Now that's what I'm talking about!"

"Yeah, we just pulled back from the storm wall for some lunch." Shelton pointed to a spread of sandwiches on a nearby table. "Pull up a chair."

I took a seat. "What did you guys find so far?"

Shelton took a big bite of sandwich and looked up at Cinder. "Mmph."

Cinder tilted his head to the side. "Is that your way of asking me to tell them, Harry?"

"Mmph!"

Cinder nodded. "Very well—"

Adam interrupted. "We haven't found anything cool yet. The first portal opened to snow and ice as far as we could see. The next portal opened

45

over water, no land in sight. The one after that looked like god barfed up pizza on a rock and left a fart for the atmosphere."

"I believe that was algae on volcanic rock," Cinder said.

Shelton scoffed. "Puke on a rock."

Elyssa looked back and forth between them. "Three realms? That's it?"

Shelton swallowed another mouthful. "It took us longer than expected to line up with the coordinates. If you're off by more than a few inches, the portal either won't open, or it'll open up to the Void."

"Yikes." Cephus had tried to let the Beast from the Void consume Seraphina. "How many times did you open one to the Void?"

"Twice." Shelton shuddered. "Scariest two seconds of my life."

Adam giggled. "That's what she said."

I turned to Cinder. "Did Bliss open any portals to the Void when you were testing it with her?"

He shook his head. "No, but perhaps we were lucky."

"Luck my ass." Shelton looked around the deck. "Where is she?"

"She is not comfortable around you." Cinder looked at me. "Bliss believes you hate her since she is a dolem."

I didn't have a response for that. "Um, sorry?"

"She's been a big help." Adam projected the Argus code from his arcphone. "I think I finally got the map on my phone aligned with the coordinate system used in the portal lens." He zoomed in on a blue and green realm. It was almost like viewing a planet from space, but through a dirty window. A string of numbers hovered above the image.

I couldn't tell if we were looking at the skies of Eden, or just another similarly colored realm. "What realm is that?"

"Not sure." Adam rotated the image. "I've narrowed the list of possibilities to twenty-three realms that look like Eden."

Elyssa peered at it. "Can you clarify the image any better? It just looks like a blob of colors."

"It would be better if we could figure out the labels," Shelton said. He traced a finger beneath the numbers. "The first twenty digits are coordinates. The last ten are probably something to identify the realm."

"The Fallen likely have a catalog," Cinder said. "But we could not find it."

"How many blue and green realms could there be?" I said. "Let's just look through them until we find the right one."

After lunch, we took the ships back to the storm wall. Lightning raced up and down the roiling gray clouds. Freezing wind swept the deck one minute, then turned hot the next. Shelton turned on the ship's weather shields as he lined up the vessel with the next coordinates.

Bliss hadn't shown herself yet, so I did the honors and channeled into the Chalon. White lines glowed along the surface of the black sphere. Energy crackled and the focusing lens glowed. A curtain of energy flowed from the other side and intersected the storm. The gray clouds flickered and faded. A silver line sliced through the interference and split open into a window to another world.

Pea green fog drifted on the other side, stirred by the winds from Voltis. A humanoid silhouette grew closer. The head looked abnormally large and the torso bent and swayed in a way no human spine could do. The being stepped out of the fog.

It looked like someone had mashed a human together with a raptor and a snake, and the result was terrifying. Forward-facing eyes glowed a mottled green. Scaly humanoid hands reached out toward us. A forked tongue slithered between sharp teeth.

We screamed. The monster let loose a hissing croak then turned tail and ran, vanishing into the fog.

"Close the portal!" Shelton shouted. "Close the portal!"

I was so shocked it took a moment to remember that I was the one supplying it with power. I released it and the portal flicked off. "I think it's safe to say that was not Eden."

"What the hell was that place?" Adam said. "Dinotopia?"

Cinder nodded matter-of-factly. "I will label this one Reptile World. It is a shame we have no ASE devices to scout it with."

All-seeing eyes were a staple of reconnaissance for the Templars, at least on Eden. We'd nearly run out of them here and still hadn't manufactured more.

Elyssa reached into her satchel and withdrew one of the coveted devices. "I have two of them, but they are literally among the last five we have left in this entire world."

"Well, I ain't risking one on that nightmare realm." Shelton shuddered. "That thing looked like a walking snake."

I nodded. "Yeah, we can explore Reptile World at some far point in the future."

"Suppose Xanomiel manages to combine the realms again." Shelton grimaced. "Man, I don't want those things ending up as my neighbors."

"Odds are you'd die along with billions of others before that ever happened," Adam said in a comforting tone. "I mean, the only safe place in any of the realms would probably be in Atlantis, since it's part of old Earth."

"You know, I hadn't thought of that." Shelton tapped a finger on his chin. "Maybe Bella and I ought to move there just in case."

"Hello, Justin."

I turned to face the source of the wary voice. Bliss wore her long black hair up in a ponytail.

Swallowing the grief at seeing the Nightliss lookalike, I forced a smile. "Hello, Bliss. I'm glad you were able to help Cinder."

"Since I was part of an evil plot to take over the world, it was the least I could do." She offered a wan smile. "I think it's what Nightliss would have done."

I didn't like her comparing herself to Nightliss, but I let the comment slide and turned back to Shelton. "Next coordinates, please."

Adam navigated the ship a few feet up and to the left, then spent an inordinate amount of time pinpointing the exact spot and comparing calculations. Just when I was ready to snap him out of it, he gave a thumbs up. "Good to go."

I channeled into the Chalon and Argus opened another portal. Nothing but blue greeted us on the other side.

"Did we open a portal in the sky?" I asked.

Adam shrugged. "Maybe, but it's hard to tell without looking through."

"Is that safe?" Shelton said. "Maybe we should toss in an ASE."

"The portal forms a transition bubble between the two worlds," Adam said. "Right now, I have it set to twenty feet on either side, which means you could poke your head through the portal and not immediately die if the temperature on the other side is a million degrees."

"Good thinking." Shelton chuckled. "Imagine the horror of seeing some-one's head flash-fry."

"And you laugh." Elyssa sighed. "That's awful."

"Awful, but funny." Shelton leaned toward the portal, but it hung ten feet off the bow. "Is it safe to go closer so I can look through it?"

"I'll have to push the nose of the ship through," Adam said. "That way the weather shield can protect us just in case."

"I can pilot it." Bliss went to the bridge in the middle of the deck and the boat slowly drifted forward until the bow penetrated the portal by a couple of feet.

I summoned a sphere of Brilliance and bound it to the Chalon to keep the portal powered for a few minutes, so it wouldn't close and slice us in half.

Shelton, Adam, and I crowded through the portal. The world around me warped and popped like a flexible mirror, and then I stood in another realm. The portal on this side lay flat against a single large thundercloud in a perfectly blue sky. I looked over the railing and saw nothing but blue in all directions.

Adam tapped a finger against his chin. "This thundercloud must be what Voltis looks like in this realm."

"A single cloud?" Shelton said. "Why is it so much smaller here?"

"Of course!" Adam smacked a palm against his forehead. "Voltis is different in every realm depending on the position of that realm in relation to the Anchor Stone."

"Does anyone see land?" I asked.

Elyssa stepped to my side and looked up and down. "I don't think there is any."

"A realm of nothing but sky." Cinder tapped on his arcphone. "Fascinating."

"There might be floating islands of land," Shelton said. "But I ain't looking for them." He waved a hand at the bridge. "Bliss, take us back out."

The ship drifted out of the portal and back to its original position just off Voltis. I unbound the Brilliance sphere powering the Chalon and the portal flicked off.

"That's a neat trick," Shelton said. "How long could you keep a portal powered like that?"

"Depends on how big I make the sphere," I said. "I basically channel Brilliance and encase it in a shell of Stasis to keep it from breaking apart, then bind a channel from it into the Chalon."

Adam waved his hands. "Eureka!" He projected a screen with the portal spell and highlighted the coordinates. "I figured out what these other numbers are. They're intervals."

"Intervals?" Cinder tilted his head.

"Yeah, the interval of time when Voltis and the realm are aligned." Adam displayed the Anchor Stone with the orbiting realms and pointed out black dots on the surface of the green moon. "I didn't know what these were before, but now I realize they're alignment spots for each realm with Voltis."

"That means Voltis isn't always present in a realm," Elyssa said. "If that's the case, you can't open a portal there, right?"

Shelton grunted. "It means you'll open a portal to the Void instead."

"Exactly." Adam shook his head slowly. "This makes things a lot more complicated."

"In other words, we have to check for alignment intervals and coordinates." Elyssa grimaced. "We don't know which of these realms is Eden or what its alignment interval is."

Adam sketched out some calculations. "Thankfully, fifteen of the candidate realms I chose are in alignment. I'll have to calculate the alignment times for the others."

"Then let's get cracking!" Shelton tapped the holographic representation of the next blue-green realm. "This one is about a mile east and a quarter mile lower in altitude."

"I have the spatial coordinates." Adam went into the bridge and took the controls from Bliss. With our ship firmly docked to the side of the houseboat, we sailed for new horizons.

When we reached the new location, I channeled another portal. Far in the distance, great white towers rose next to pyramids and domes. A city unlike any I'd ever seen sparkled like a rare jewel. But something about it seemed off and I couldn't quite place my finger on it.

"Fascinating." Cinder tapped on his arcphone. "The tallest tower in that city is only five feet in height. I wonder how small the denizens are."

I blinked, and my perspective shifted. The city wasn't actually far away, but the buildings, trees, and foliage were so small, my mind interpreted the size as a factor of distance. It was like peering through a toy shop window at a model city.

"Mind blown." Elyssa made an explosion noise and used her hand to simulate her head exploding. "How is this possible?"

"That's kind of a silly question," Adam said. "A magical catastrophe blew the original Earth apart into realms. Some resemble the original geography, while others don't. I can only imagine how it affected physiology."

"Perhaps the denizens were already tiny." Cinder tapped on his arcphone. "I will label this Tiny Town."

"Man, I gotta look closer." Shelton looked back and forth between me and Adam. "Can we go peek?"

"Lets' just use an ASE, okay?" Elyssa took out one of the orbs and tossed it into the air. It hovered in place, then zipped just inside the portal, remaining in the transition zone. The live footage played back on Elyssa's phone. She zoomed in on the city and panned back and forth, but there were no signs of life.

"Let's get a better look around," Adam said.

Elyssa angled up and around for a wider view. The curve of the world was visible from this vantage, revealing just how tiny the entire realm was.

"Holy cow." Shelton gaped. "It's like someone shrank the world down to half size."

"Even less." Adam shook his head. "Man, I'd love to study this place in detail."

"It'll have to wait." Elyssa retrieved the ASE. "We've got to stop a god and the grand overlord of Haedaemos from destroying existence as we know it first."

CHAPTER 6

We moved on to the next candidate and discovered a grassy plain with little else in sight. The ASE scouted around for us and found a herd of unicorns galloping majestically from a thick forest. They were all white, with shiny manes of gold, copper, or silver, and far larger than even the biggest horses in Eden.

Sparks flew from their hooves, and flames shot from their nostrils when they snorted. Cinder named it Fire Breathing Unicorn World.

For the first time, Elyssa desperately want to visit a realm just so she could touch a unicorn.

"Definitely not Eden." Shelton seemed to enjoy turning her down. "Like you said, we don't have time to look."

Elyssa's lips pouted, and her eyes grew huge. "But they're unicorns!"

"We can come back to the unicorns, babe." I hugged her and resisted giving in to that sad face. "I promise, okay?"

She looked down. "Okay."

It took us hours to go through the next several candidates. Nearly every portal opened in the middle of the ocean or on a small island. With the ASE scouting for us, we were able to determine what, if any creatures lived nearby so we could determine if it might be Eden.

One ocean swarmed with giant sea serpents. Another had an island covered by giant mushrooms. The ASE covered distance fast, so we didn't have to wait longer than an hour to find evidence in most cases. Night fell, but with three more candidates to go, we weren't ready to give up just yet.

The next portal opened in a realm where the sun still shone. At first it looked like another open sky realm, but Cinder spotted a dot on the horizon. We used the ASE to zoom in on an island of land rotating slowly in the sky. A snow-capped mountain rose in the middle of thick forest. A huge tree grew at the summit of the mountain, its branches barren. A river ran off the edge of the world and into dense fog below.

"Look, it's smoke." Shelton pointed out a column of smoke rising not far from the edge of the floating island. "That entire place can't be more than ten square miles, and someone lives there?"

"I will name this one Lonely World," Cinder said. "It resembles the skylets here in Seraphina."

Elyssa grimaced. "That's depressing."

"I don't even want to think about it." My chest constricted just thinking about being trapped in such a small realm. "I wonder if the people here want to leave this god-forsaken place."

"How awful a fate." Bliss stared at the island. "Are you certain there are no other skylets like that one?"

"There must be more," Elyssa said. "It's probably like the Glimmer where all the land is broken up."

"Let's take the ASE in for a closer look," Shelton said.

"This definitely isn't Eden, but I'm really curious about it." Elyssa directed the tiny sphere further inside the portal transition zone. A

55

quick look around showed nothing but blue sky overhead, white fog below, and the single skylet with nothing else in sight as far as the ASE could see.

"Maybe we're above the clouds," Adam said. "Why don't you send it lower to see what the ground looks like?"

Elyssa pursed her lips. Nodded. She sent the ASE zipping down into the fog. It traveled for nearly five miles at high speed and entered clear skies. A dot of land appeared far below above a sea of white. As the ASE dropped closer to the island, I realized something.

"Hey, that's the same island." I pointed through the portal to the skylet. "The ASE just traveled in a loop."

"What in the blazes?" Shelton rubbed his eyes. "This place is freaking me out." He jabbed a finger toward the skylet. "Send the ASE there. I want to see who lives here."

Elyssa looked a bit spooked herself. "Something isn't right about this place." Nevertheless, she sent the ASE toward the skylet. It flew over a forest of hardwoods. Birds flew by. A fox ran along the forest floor. Insects whirred and chirped. The place seemed to have a full ecosystem despite its diminutive size.

The ASE found a log cabin near the base of the mountain. A young woman stood outside the cabin, her eyes locked on the surveillance device. She motioned toward it and the ASE swooped down into her hand. Large silver eyes seemed to regard us. Her long green hair coiled and moved as if it had a life of its own. "You promised to leave me be." Her voice was stern and unforgiving. "The relic is safe."

Elyssa touched an icon on her phone. "I'm sorry, but who are you?"

The screen went blank. Suddenly, the woman hovered just on the other side of the portal without the aid of wings or anything else. "You are not the Fallen."

I nearly fell over backward.

"Where did you learn English?" Cinder said.

"I speak in my tongue and your ears hear it as your own." The woman tossed the ASE back through the portal at us. Elyssa caught it. "You will go now."

"Wait." I held up a hand. "Who are you?"

Her forehead pinched. "Eve." She waved a hand. The portal winked off and we were left scratching our heads.

"I'm a little bit afraid," Adam said. "Did we just disturb a goddess?"

"Man, I ain't gonna go back and ask her," Shelton said.

"Eve, as in the original Eve?" Elyssa's eyes widened. "Did we just meet the very first woman ever?"

"Whoa." I stared at the stormy clouds where the portal had been a moment ago. "I thought she was just myth."

"Your parents lived in biblical times." Adam pushed a finger up the bridge of his nose. "Maybe they'd know."

"I'll ask them next time." I turned to Bliss who seemed to be the only person not impressed by what we'd just witnessed.

"What is biblical?" she asked.

Cinder answered before I could. "An adjective used to describe the events and times according to an ancient collection of scrolls that were compiled and sorted into a holy text called the Bible."

Bliss blinked a few times. "Similar to Primogenesis?"

Just thinking about that cultish religion gave me a stomach ache. "We'll send you to Sunday school for an education." I was still shaken by the encounter with Eve. If it was the first woman ever, it meant there were ancient beings scattered among the realms. "Let's move on to the next candidate and pray it's not Adam's hideout."

Adam chuckled. "Maybe he was taking a dump."

"At this point, I'm beginning to think anything is possible." Shelton went to the bridge and steered us to the next coordinates.

"I want to be hopeful, I really do," Elyssa said, "but this is like searching for a needle in a haystack and I'm exhausted."

"Indeed, the probability of finding Eden like this is quite low." Cinder tapped on his arcphone. "We have not even counted how many blue-green realms there are in total, but the ones we have looked at today are merely a fraction."

"How many more could there be?" Shelton said.

"I used to think there were only seven realms total." Adam blew out a breath. "According to the Fallen, there are hundreds. On the upside, we know one of these must be Eden. If we work through them methodically, we'll find it sooner or later."

I really wished we could talk to the Fallen. The former gods of Mount Olympus possessed the magic to travel the realms, but they'd vanished without leaving blueprints behind. We hoped they'd return some day, but it didn't seem likely at this point.

Shelton turned the boat to face Voltis and edged closer to the storm wall. "We're here."

While Adam went through his ritual of confirming the coordinates and aiming the lens at the precise focal point, I crossed over to my ship and grabbed a snack even though I wanted dinner. By the time I returned, Adam was ready for me to channel.

I summoned a sphere of Brilliance in one hand, then wove a thin layer of Murk into the outer edges of the blazing energy to create Stasis. I channeled the sphere into the Chalon and tied it off once the portal blinked open.

My heart raced with excitement at what I saw on the other side—a small house with a concrete driveway. It was not a weird dome house, a medieval cottage, or a crystal cube, but a split-level house with mustard yellow paint on the upper level and red bricks on the base. It was about as human and ordinary as apple pie.

"Am I dreaming?" Shelton rubbed his eyes. "Or is that a house from the nineteen-seventies?"

"Dude, that's a Brady Bunch house." Adam pinched his arm. "I'm awake, and I think we just found home."

Elyssa gasped. "It's like winning the lottery." A tear ran down her cheek. "Home sweet home."

"Something seems odd—"

"Shut up, Cinder!" we shouted at the same time.

Only Bliss remained quiet, apparently confused by our outburst.

"Send an ASE through, just to be safe," Shelton said.

Elyssa activated the one Eve had tossed to her and directed it through the portal to the transition zone. It recorded everything in around it, streaming the footage to Elyssa's phone. The trees were bare, the ground covered in frost. There was no sign of life, but that was probably due to the winter cold. Other nearby houses resembled the one in front of us and the cars looked old, but ordinary.

"This is it!" Adam cavorted like a monkey with diarrhea. "Let's go through and celebrate with burgers and pizza."

"I think we should send a message back to New Eden first," Elyssa said. "Just in case."

I nodded. "She's right. Going through without telling anyone would be risky. What if the portal closed and we couldn't get back through?"

"We should leave Bliss and Cinder on the houseboat and take Justin's ship through," Shelton said. "That way they can open another portal if anything happens."

I turned to the pair. "Is that okay?"

Cinder nodded. "It would be best to have a backup plan just in case."

"I prefer to remain here," Bliss said. "I think you prefer it as well."

"You know what's weird?" Adam said. "Nearly every portal we opened was in the middle of nowhere, but this one is in someone's front yard."

"I guess that's where it aligns in Eden," Shelton said.

Elyssa panned the view around and found the portal exit framed by a dense bank of fog. "That's what Voltis looks like in Eden."

"Disappointing." Adam scratched his head. "I thought it would be bigger."

My stomach grumbled, and I was ready to collapse into a bed. I held up my hands. "Here's the plan. We'll head out to open sea and set up camp far enough away from the storm that we can contact New Eden and give them the scoop."

Shelton tried to speak. "But pizza—"

I stopped him with a glare. "Dude, I'm getting hangry, okay?"

Elyssa recovered the ASE and we sailed a few miles away from Voltis, testing our comm gems every so often. When we got a signal, we contacted the *Uorion* and had them relay the signal to Thomas. His holographic image appeared in our comm room moments later.

Elyssa told him what we'd found and our plans to enter Eden tomorrow.

Thomas's usual stony demeanor betrayed surprise. "After all this time you actually found the way home?"

"That's what it looks like." I tried to repress a grin and failed. "We'll have a full report ready for you tomorrow when we return."

He pressed a fist over his heart. "Excellent work, Templar." The call ended.

Elyssa giggled and clapped her hands. "We're going home tomorrow,

Justin!" She wrapped her arms around my neck and suffocated me with a kiss. "I'm so excited, I don't think I can sleep!"

"Yeah, that won't be a problem for me." I cracked a yawn. "Opening all those portals was exhausting."

We went to the kitchen on Shelton's houseboat where the others had already gathered for spaghetti.

"Thank god for Atlantis," Shelton said. "It's the only place to find normal ingredients around here."

Adam wound pasta around his fork. "What's the first thing you're gonna do when we get back?"

"Oh, man." Shelton took off his wide-brimmed hat and smoothed his short hair. "I'm gonna park my ass in a pizzeria and enjoy a pie and beer."

"I'm going to see all the movies I missed," Adam said.

Elyssa's eyes filled with desire. "Eat chocolate."

All eyes turned to me. "Find my sister. Beat the shit out of Victus."

"Naturally." Shelton clapped a hand on my shoulder. "But let's try to have a little fun first, okay?"

"That's my idea of fun." I stood and stretched. "I'm excited to go back, believe me, but I'm exhausted."

Adam patted my back. "I gotcha. Get some rest and we'll see you in the morning."

Elyssa and I left the others and crossed over to our ship. The distant horizon lit with webs of lightning. A sullen orange glow intensified and faded as if a nuclear bomb had gone off. To anyone who'd never seen Voltis, it looked like the world was ending over and over again and it wasn't far from the truth.

That very storm had raced over Earth during the Sundering, killing millions and breaking the planet into realms. For some reason, it had stopped short of consuming everything and left a tiny pocket untouched. At the heart of Voltis lay Atlantis and Mount Olympus, the only safe place should Xanomiel succeed in recombining the realms.

The thought of Voltis reversing course and sweeping across the realms gave me a stomach ache. Seraphim and Sirens might survive it. Dragons might weather it. The Nazdal that survived would suck in the life force of the dying and become massive monsters. Humans, on the other hand, would be mincemeat. As for Baal and the demons, I had no idea what it would mean for them.

Demons couldn't survive long outside the spirit realm without taking a physical body. It was likely they'd just be evaporated without a spirit realm, unless Baal knew something I didn't.

Combining the realms would be like hitting the reset button on creation. Xanomiel would swoop in and do what he wanted while the rest of the Apocryphan rotted away in the Abyss.

And here we were taking baby steps just to get back to Eden.

Elyssa kissed my cheek and leaned her head on my shoulder. She made me feel better without even saying a word.

I wrapped an arm around her and returned the kiss. "Let's go snuggle."

She smiled. "As you wish."

I JERKED AWAKE. Thunder rumbled in the distance, but that wasn't what woke me. Something felt wrong.

Elyssa's violet eyes glowed in the dark. "Do you feel that too?" she whispered.

I nodded. We slid off the cloud bed and crept through the corridor to the back deck without seeing anything. The rustle of wings drew my attention up. Lightning revealed large dragon silhouettes gliding above.

Humanoid shadows moved around the front of Shelton's boat. I flicked on my night vision, revealing the dark world several feet in front of me. Elyssa and I crawled on our stomachs toward the activity on the other boat until we could make out the faces.

The faces were terribly familiar, but I didn't know a single one.

Shelton's boat had been invaded by Nightliss clones.

CHAPTER 7

Leather wings rustled behind me. I looked up in time to see dragon claws extended to snatch me off the deck.

I abandoned stealth mode and channeled a hard shell of Murk above me. Claws sparked off the barrier and the dragon whooshed past, denied its prey.

Elyssa fired a glowball into the air, basking the area in bright light. I counted ten dolems gathered around Argus, working to unmount the frame from the front of Shelton's boat.

The only male among them offered me a greasy smile. Shaved head, intense eyes, square jaw, and a muscled body, he resembled a dolem we still had in custody—Zero. I knew from the smile on his face that someone else controlled the body.

"Baal." I ground out his name through clenched teeth.

"Perceptive, Justin." Smug condescension filled his voice. "You can go back to sleep and we'll be out of here in a few minutes."

"How about you leave before I blast your host body to bits?" I gathered an inferno of Brilliance around a fist.

Baal shrugged. "Perhaps you're not as perceptive as I thought."

I spun and looked up. Mottled red and black scales flashed. I blasted the dragon before it could breathe fire and knocked it from the air. Dragons weren't easy to kill with magic, so I'd probably just stunned it. Unfortunately, it had a lot of company.

"Fire up the ship weapons," I told Elyssa. "I've got an idea."

She ducked onto the bridge and I did the only logical thing a person can do when being dive-bombed by dragons. I leapt across to the other ship and swung my fists. With me in the middle of their masters, the dragons broke off their attacks. The dolems looked just as surprised by my snap decision as I was. I spun and kicked the first attacker over the railing. Her screams faded in the distance.

The rest of them drew what appeared to be crystal sword hilts. They channeled into them and ultraviolet blades of energy sizzled to life. I didn't have time to think about how cool they looked because an energy blade buzzed toward my neck. I ducked and swept the feet from beneath the nearest attacker.

The close quarters gave me an advantage. They couldn't swing their light swords very easily without hitting each other. I channeled a shield of Murk on my left arm and channeled a white sword of Brilliance in my right hand. I, on the other hand, could swing away.

"What in the blue blazes?" Shelton came onto the deck and yelped when a laser sword nearly took off his arm.

Adam, Cinder, and Bliss flooded out behind him, and all hell broke loose.

Shelton rammed his staff into the stomach of one attacker, then blasted the next with a gout of fire. Adam flicked his wand. Beams of green light turned to slime wherever they hit. Bliss channeled a hail of Murk shards toward the enemy. Cinder punched the nearest dolem and threw her across the deck.

Baal whistled, and a dragon swooped down to retrieve him.

"Running away already?" I said.

"We'll get your portal maker from the wreckage," Baal shouted back.

More dragons dove and snatched the dolems from the deck with their claws. The Nightliss clones lithely swung up onto the backs of the creatures and into saddles. While these dragons weren't huge, they were easily twenty or thirty feet long and heavily armored.

"Watch out for fire!" I channeled a shield. One dragon blasted me with frost. The next barfed up green slime that sizzled and hissed against the crystal deck.

Elyssa opened fire with our ship. Magical lasers knocked dragons off course and stunned them, but the weapons weren't powerful enough to kill them—at least not without me adding my own power to them.

Shelton's ship lurched. The deck cracked. Dragon claws tore a flight gem from the hull and the explosion sent us spinning. Bliss ran inside the bridge and managed to regain control, but the dragons pummeled us relentlessly.

I grabbed Adam's arm. "Detach Argus. I'll get it to the other ship."

He staggered across the shifting deck and tapped his wand against the base frame. The instant the device came loose, a dragon dove in to steal it. I channeled a fist of Murk and slammed the dragon in the face. The creature shrieked and crashed into the deck. The dolem on its back flew off and crashed into the bridge. The awful angle of her neck told me she wasn't getting back up.

I hefted the frame. It was about ten feet tall, including the huge focusing lens, but my demon strength handled it no problem. Elyssa fired over my head, knocking away dragons as they attempted to steal the device.

"Everyone abandon ship!" I manhandled Argus over to the *Raptor* and shoved it inside the lower deck. Adam, Shelton, and Cinder jumped aboard.

"The docking controls are stuck!" Elyssa shouted from above. "We have to undock using the houseboat controls!"

"Are you crazy?" Shelton ducked a gout of fire. "How are we supposed to get back over there?"

Then I saw Bliss run back onto the bridge of the houseboat. Eyes wide, she gave me one last look and slapped a control. With a great cracking sound, the docking clamps tore free. Without the stability provided by my ship, the houseboat veered out of control.

I didn't even stop to think. I fired strands of webbed Murk to the houseboat and held on for dear life. The strain felt as if it might tear my arms from their sockets. The houseboat bucked and swung toward us.

"It's gonna ram us!" Shelton shouted.

Eyes wide with fright, Bliss dove across the gap. I released the binds and reached out a hand. Caught her. Bliss's grip slipped, so I swung down my other hand and grabbed hers.

"I have you." Cinder grabbed my waist and pulled me back before my feet slipped and I fell over the side. I dragged Bliss onto the deck next to me.

Blue fire exploded from the houseboat as it spiraled into the darkness. Our battle shields sprang on and the ship lurched forward. Those of us standing flew backward and landed in a heap on the aft deck.

"Son of a bitch." Shelton held his shoulder and groaned. "Elyssa could have at least told us to hang on!"

Bliss staggered to her feet. "Thank you, Justin."

I jumped to my feet and ran to the bridge without taking time to answer. "What's the situation?" I grabbed Elyssa's chair to steady myself as the ship bounced through turbulent air.

"I was hoping you could tell me!" Elyssa aimed the ship on a course toward Voltis. "We don't exactly have radar to tell us where the dragons are."

I went to the aft turret and channeled into it until the gem glowed white, then fired a huge ball into the air behind us. It lit up the sky like a miniature sun. Dozens of the mid-sized dragons trailed behind us by about half a mile, each one bearing riders.

"How did Baal find us?" I charged the gem again. "Where did that bastard get more dolems?"

"He's had three years to set up a new base of operations," Elyssa said. "There's no telling what he's been up to."

Shelton and the others crowded onto the bridge and strapped themselves into the seats.

"What's the plan?" Shelton said. "Circle around and head back to Cabala?"

"After we came so close to getting back to Eden?" Adam shook his head. "We've only got a few more days before it's not aligned with Voltis anymore."

"How long until the next alignment?" Elyssa asked.

"Four months." Adam shook his head. "Do you really want to wait that long?"

I fired another sunlight pulse. The dragons were even farther back now. "How long will it take to align the ship?"

"Not long since I pinpointed the coordinates and calibrated when we were there earlier." Adam tapped on his arcphone. "I'll need five minutes to extend the transition buffer to accommodate the ship."

"Why bother with that?" Shelton said. "We can just fly through and be done."

"Because the portal generator is on the ship that's going through," Adam said. "As Argus gets closer to the portal, it will narrow the beam and cause it to get smaller. The instant we go through, the portal will snap shut unless I give us a good fifty feet of buffer on both sides."

"Ah." Shelton gripped his chin. "Maybe we should mount Argus on the back of the ship."

Adam shook his head. "No, the narrowest part of the ship needs to go in last just to be safe. Mount Argus on the nose and back the ship through the portal."

"I concur," Cinder said. "The buffer will give us just enough time to slip through before the portal closes."

Adam pulled up the ship map and punched in the coordinates. "Take us here."

Elyssa nodded and adjusted course.

I fired one more light ball behind us. It traveled nearly two miles before revealing the dragons. "Just tell me where you want Argus mounted." I got up and motioned Adam to follow me.

Everyone but Elyssa tagged along. It felt like I was leading a herd down the narrow hallway to the storage room. I slid Argus out onto the back deck and muscled it around the bridge to the stern. Adam did his magic and secured the frame to the very front, then took out his arcphone and got to work.

Blue flames rippled in the darkness behind us and streaked across the night. At first, I thought it might be a reflection from the lightning and flames spewing from Voltis. But as the first fingers of dawn crept into the sky, a massive silhouette formed against the light.

Enigma!

The massive wyvern was closing in fast. Even more wyverns perched on its broad back. Dozens of humanoid forms sat on the smaller wyverns.

"That dragon is like a freaking aircraft carrier!" I grabbed Shelton and spun him around to point out the new threat. "Enigma's working with Baal!"

"This is the wyvern you encountered before?" Cinder said.

"Yeah." I gritted my teeth. "We can't go to Eden. We have to get back out to open ocean and warn Thomas that Enigma is playing for the dark side."

"Just when I thought things couldn't get any weirder." Shelton slapped his cheek as if to wake from a dream. "Demons riding dragons riding a giant wyvern."

"Baal certainly doesn't disappoint." I shook a fist toward the menace. "Leave us alone!"

Shelton held his arcphone toward Enigma. Numbers appeared on the screen. "I hate to say it, but we can't outrun that son of a bitch. If we head to open ocean, it'll catch us."

My jaw went slack. "Enigma is really that fast?"

Shelton grimaced. "If we keep going in a straight line, it'll catch up in twenty minutes."

"Why didn't Baal just use Enigma to capture the ship earlier?" Bliss asked.

"Baal is first and foremost an asshole." My jaw tightened at the thought of what he'd nearly pulled off. "He wanted to pluck Argus off the other ship and spirit it away without us knowing what happened."

"He could've killed us all," Shelton said.

"Like I said, that's not his style. He likes to toy with people." I watched the giant wyvern grow larger. "I'll bet he's having a good laugh right now."

The ship buckled and bounced through turbulence as we entered the outer layers of Voltis. Elyssa slowed so it wouldn't tear apart the ship.

"Enigma will have to slow down too," Shelton said. "But the turbulence won't affect him as much."

I paced back to the front of the ship where Adam still worked, sick to my stomach at the thought of leaving Seraphina without telling Thomas about Baal's connection to Enigma. "We need to get a message to Thomas somehow."

"Look, if we go through a portal before Baal gets here, he won't have a clue where we went." Shelton grabbed the railing for support as Elyssa banked the ship and took it through thick clouds. "We poke around in Eden, confirm Argus works as promised, and then come back. We'll slip back home before Baal figures out where we are."

I looked at the electrified aether clouds drifting around Voltis. "Or we hide out in the clouds like Kirk did in the Mutara Nebula against Khan, circle around, and go home."

"We ain't squaring off against a single spaceship, man." Shelton swept his arm in the general direction of Enigma. "There's a whole fleet of dragons coming for us. Hiding in Eden will kill two birds with one stone."

"And we can get pizza and beer," Adam said. "It's a total win-win."

"I concur," Cinder said. "Hiding in Eden is safer."

"As long as we get in and out during the alignment with Voltis." I looked toward the storm wall. "I don't want to be trapped there for two months."

The ship slowed and rotated so the pointed nose faced away. Adam tapped his comm pendant. "Drop ten feet in altitude."

I met Elyssa's eyes through the large front window. She looked worried but determined.

Adam gave her a thumbs up. "Perfect." He flourished his hands at me. "Your turn, Justin."

I formed a sphere of Brilliance encased in Stasis as I had before and channeled it into the Chalon. Energy crackled and spread through the lens. A much wider portal split the stormy clouds. A translucent bubble extended from the portal and encased the ship. The sound and fury of Voltis faded to the hum of someone shouting underwater and the outside world blurred.

Cinder and Bliss went to the back of the boat and gave the all clear.

"Excellent." Adam held up the flat of his hand and motioned toward the portal. "Full steam, um, backward."

Elyssa reversed the ship through the portal. The vessel slid through and into a bubble on the other side. The house was a blurry smear through the transition bubble, but the sight filled me with hope.

We're in Eden again!

Adam slashed his hand down. "Turn off the portal before Baal comes within visual range."

I cut off the power and banished the energy sphere.

The transition zone shrank in upon itself. As the bubble receded from the stern, the ship shuddered violently. Cinder froze in place. Bliss cried out as the end of the bubble passed over her, mouth agape in a frozen shout.

"What the hell?" Shelton shouted an instant before the bubble receded from us.

My outstretched arms felt as if they were encased in ice. Something was horribly wrong. I shouted in terror as ice seized my entire body.

CHAPTER 8

My yell echoed in the large front yard of the mustard house. I looked at my hands and wiggled my fingers. Cinder and Bliss stared at each other in confusion. Adam and Shelton checked their bodies, as if something might be missing.

"What in the fresh hell happened?" Shelton said. "I thought the transition bubble was supposed to make it smoother."

Adam scratched his head and looked at his phone. "I don't know. Everything worked perfectly."

Shelton looked at his arcphone and scrolled through spell code. "There must be a bug somewhere."

Adam squinted at Shelton's screen and looked back at his own. "Why is my phone a minute behind yours?"

"Huh?" Shelton pulled up the system clock and checked it against Adam's. "They should be in perfect synch."

A section of the bridge window misted away and Elyssa stepped onto the deck next to us. "Can someone tell me why I froze?"

I looked at my arcphone, Nookli, and saw it was several seconds ahead of Shelton's. "Elyssa, what time does your phone have?"

She took it out and showed it to us.

"Two minutes, twenty-three seconds behind." Adam frowned. "There's only one reason this could have happened, but it shouldn't have."

Cinder supplied the answer first. "Logic suggests there is a time differential between Eden and Seraphina, but we know that is not the case."

I looked around. A brown split-level house sat to the right of this one and a brick ranch neighbored the other side. The *Raptor* hovered in plain view for any nom to see. "Can you get the ship into the back yard?"

Elyssa blinked as if suddenly realizing how exposed we were and ran back into the bridge. She guided the ship over the house and into the back yard. Woods bordered the back and tall fences ran along the sides. The ship rose as high as the house so it wasn't well-hidden, but we'd risk hundreds of people seeing it if we tried to fly away in the middle of the day.

"God, I hope nobody's home." Elyssa extended the gangway and disembarked for a quick peek inside the house windows. "I don't see anyone."

"I don't see any activity at the other houses nearby," Cinder said. "I believe everyone is away at work."

Shelton snapped his fingers. "Look, we gotta figure out what happened when the transition bubble receded."

Adam fiddled with his phone for a bit, the creases on his brow deepening with every second. "I have the answer, but it doesn't make any sense."

"Lemme see." Shelton took the phone. An arched brow of confusion turned to slack-jawed surprise. "Oh, shit."

"Yeah." Adam took back his phone. "For some reason, time in Seraphina now flows faster than it does in Eden. This wasn't the case a few years ago." He shrugged. "Unless the laws of the universe somehow changed recently, it shouldn't be possible to change the relative time flow of a realm."

"What about the old gods?" I asked. "The Apocryphan."

"I have no idea. Maybe?" Adam paused. "Even if an Apocryphan could do it, the question is why? Making time flow faster or slower in different realms doesn't serve a purpose."

"Unless you need more time to pull off a caper," Shelton said. "Think about it. If I needed a year to grow an army of dolems, I can make time flow faster in one realm and use it so my enemies in another realm won't have the same amount of time to prepare."

"That is logical." Cinder looked at his own phone. "But I believe there is a more mundane reason for the time differential." He projected the diagram of realms around the Anchor Stone and circled Eden. "We are here." He changed a setting on the filter and superimposed a whirling void hovering near Eden. "This is the Abyss."

Adam gasped. "Our orbit takes us right past it."

"Indeed, and Eden will brush the edge as it passes." Cinder zoomed in. The space near the void seemed to bend around it. "The Abyss was a prison designed to hold the most powerful beings we know of—the Apocryphan. Though I have not studied the Abyss, it bears a resemblance to black holes."

"Space time bends around a black hole." Adam slapped his forehead. "Eden is suffering from gravitational time dilation!"

I blinked a few times, trying to process what they were talking about. Though I'd been a nerd, I hadn't finished high school and was a little behind in theoretical physics. "So a black hole slows down time relative to everything outside in normal space?"

"Exactly." Adam looked at Cinder's diagram. "Superimpose the orbits if you have them."

Cinder changed the view again, and circles formed, intersecting the realms and showing their orbits. Some circled in the same place. Others orbited the Anchor Stone. Eden, it seemed, had an elliptical orbit around the Abyss, meaning it was farther away at some times and closer at others. This just happened to be a time when it was nearly close enough to touch.

"This can't be right." Shelton scrolled on his phone. "Dude, after the war, I went through the Grand Nexus to Seraphina a dozen times or more."

"You did?" Adam raised an eyebrow. "I don't remember you mentioning that to me."

"Yeah, well, it was to take Bella on picnics." Shelton cleared his throat. "She likes that kinda stuff."

Elyssa snorted. "Smart man."

"You're a real Prince Charming." I cut him off before he could make his point. "Long story short—you didn't notice a time shift."

"Nope." He lifted his wide-brimmed hat and scratched his head. "Nada."

"Neither did I." Adam tapped the orbit circle of Eden. "If that's really the correct orbit, then Eden is affected by slow time every two months and three days."

"That would coincide with its alignments to Voltis," Cinder said. "That would mean it suffers from time dilation at one end, the effects lessening after it hits the apex of the Abyssal orbit, and resumes normal time on the outward swing."

"Huh?" Elyssa shook her head. "English anyone?"

"Without all the data, it's hard to calculate." Adam tapped the orbit ring of Eden. "Somewhere in the middle, time returns to normal." He touched the part of the circle nearest the Abyss. "Around here it starts going slower and slower."

"Makes sense." Elyssa rubbed her arm. "Why did it feel like I couldn't move when we got here?"

"The freezing sensation you felt was caused by parts of your body entering a slower time flow from a faster one," Cinder said. "The transition bubble merged the time differential from both realms so the effect was not as noticeable as if you went through the portal with no transition."

"No wonder the ship shuddered so much," Shelton said. "Its molecules were literally slowing down when it exited the transition bubble."

I thought about the difference in times on our phones and tried to calculate how much slower time flowed here relative to Seraphina, but couldn't even hazard a guess. "Any idea how much slower time is here?"

"If the transition bubble was a halfway point, then every day here is roughly two days on Seraphina." Adam grimaced. "The good news is that we only have to wait here for a few hours and nearly twice that time will pass for Baal."

"Meaning he'll give up and we don't have to worry about him waiting out there for us," Shelton said.

"Will this affect the length of time we're aligned with Voltis?" I asked.

Adam shook his head. "I know it sounds strange, but the alignment with Voltis will still last the same amount of time. We have at least two days, maybe three in this time flow before we're stuck here for two months."

"In this time flow?" I said.

"Exactly." He took out his phone and started a countdown. "This is my best guestimate. It could be off by five minutes off or twelve hours. I think we should err on the side of caution, so we don't risk it."

"Two months here equals four months in Seraphina?" Elyssa said.

"Give or take," Adam said. "I think one day here is plenty of time. Baal will probably give up looking for us after a day or two and we can safely go back to Seraphina and get back to Cabala."

I nodded. "Sounds good to me." I turned to Elyssa. "What do you think?"

"We don't have much of a choice." She motioned a hand at the houses. "We do need to find a better parking spot before someone notices the aliens have landed."

Shelton snorted. "Yeah."

Bliss stared with wide eyes up and down the neighborhood. "I have never seen such beautiful architecture. It rivals even Cabala."

"What in the hell have you been smoking?" Shelton said. "It looks like the nineteen-seventies took a big dump all up and down this street."

"Nah, they're gorgeous." Adam sighed with contentment. "I'll take a split-level or ranch any day to those crystal domes they call houses in Seraphina."

"Yeah, fine." Shelton chuckled. "But Bliss needs her eyes checked."

Bliss looked down at her feet. "I am sorry if I said something to offend."

I walked over and with some hesitation, put a hand on her back. "Look, you need to stop walking on eggshells around us. When I met you, you were feisty and determined."

"That was before I discovered I'm not real." She held out her hands and stared at them. "I am but a spark of a beautiful soul you love, not a unique individual."

"More or less," Shelton said in his usual tender-hearted fashion. "But, I guess it's some kind of life."

"That was unnecessary, Harry." Cinder actually sounded hurt and disappointed. "Does that mean I am also living some kind of life?"

"Um." Shelton hemmed and hawed. "You know you're different from Bliss, right, Cinder?"

"Am I, really?" Cinder tilted his head. "She possesses a soul fragment. I have only a simple golem spark."

Elyssa groaned. "Cinder, you're amazing. Bliss, you're alive." She turned to Shelton. "Shelton, you're an ass." She snapped her fingers. "Now, can we find a place to hide the ship while we go get pizza?"

"Yes!" Shelton buried his gaze in his phone.

"What road is this?" Adam said. "The GPS on my phone isn't working."

"Your phone clock has also not synchronized with mine," Cinder said. "Once we were back in Eden, our phones should have detected the aethernet and synchronized with the network."

"I still don't have a signal," Adam said. "The phone is charging on aether, but it hasn't locked onto the magic network."

"Probably just need to reboot the phones," Shelton said. "We probably screwed them up with the homemade network we built on Seraphina."

"True," Cinder said.

Elyssa threw up her hands. "I'll find a place myself." She went back onto the bridge and powered on the ship.

I stood next to her and activated the map. A message popped up on the blank screen: *Location Not Found. Entering Discovery Mode.* "Oh yeah, I guess the shipbuilders didn't install a map of Eden."

The *Raptor* lifted off and rose above the trees. The morning sun reflected off silver skyscrapers on the horizon. Shaped like giant rockets, they towered over the rest of the city.

"What city is that?" I asked.

"No idea, but we've got to get this ship out of sight." Elyssa took the *Raptor* high enough for a better view. She went to the deck and surveyed the area.

"How about there?" Adam pointed out dilapidated brick warehouses.

Weeds grew from cracks in the sun-bleached parking lot. "Doesn't look like anyone is using that place."

Elyssa nodded. "Looks good." She piloted us the short distance and set down in the space between two buildings. "Wish this thing came with camouflage."

"I'll be sure to tell the builders when we get back." I joined Shelton and Adam on the deck.

"Still no damned signal." Shelton looked ready to toss his phone. "I know we tinkered with the phones to get them to work on Seraphina, but we didn't change them that much."

"You're not getting any kind of signal?" I asked.

"Nothing." Adam shoved his arcphone in a back pocket. "It's not that important right now. Let's get some food and relax. I think we deserve it."

"Amen." Shelton put his phone away. "Let's walk to the city. We'll ask around about a pizza joint."

I had something else in mind. "Call me crazy, but I could really go for a taco."

"Taco, pizza, dude, I don't care." Adam nodded toward Bliss. "Wonder if that black unitard will stand out too much."

Shelton pshawed. "Man, you could wear trash bags and the noms these days wouldn't even look twice."

I snorted. "I've got some spare garbage bags if you want to wear them, Shelton."

He tilted his hat up and struck a heroic pose. "The world can't take that much sexy."

Adam laughed. "Harry Shelton, runway model."

Elyssa rolled her eyes. "You guys would sit here and banter all day if someone didn't force you to move."

"Not true," Shelton said. "My stomach wants food, so let's go find some."

Everyone piled down the gangway and headed across the empty parking lot. Bent metal gates hung open to a street covered in weeds and debris. A faded periwinkle blue car sat sideways in the middle of the street, door open as if the driver, gripped with diarrhea, sprinted away for the nearest toilet and never came back.

The boxy design and glass headlights reminded me of Ash's nineteen-seventies Ford he used to drive when we were in high school. The cracked vinyl seats and dashboard looked as if they'd been exposed to the weather for quite some time.

Someone had apparently used this abandoned complex as a dumping area for their broken-down car.

Adam walked around the back and scratched his head. "I'm not terribly familiar with nom cars, but what logo is this?"

I rubbed dirt off a silver emblem shaped like a winged lion on the trunk. "Never seen it. Must be one of those old seventies models they don't make anymore."

"Looks like a gryphon," Shelton said. "I think Ford used to make a car like that."

"I am not familiar with nom car design." Cinder looked inside. "They seem like a rather inefficient mode of transportation."

"I rather like it." Bliss ran a hand over the cracked vinyl and drew in a deep breath. "It smells good."

Shelton grimaced. "If you like the odor of cat barf."

"Priorities, people." Elyssa kept walking. "What's more important— talking about a junk car in the middle of the road, or pizza?"

"Pizza!" Adam said.

I countered his proposal. "Tacos!"

"Damned skippy." Shelton plucked a street weed and tossed it into the wind.

We walked to the end of the block and reached a small crossroads. Square black signs with white circles in the middle occupied each corner. A nearby shop bore a sign with an animated stick figure alternatively guzzling from a beer mug and eating cake. Across the street, a stick figure danced across the brick façade.

"That's cool." Adam inspected the sign. "Man, it doesn't even look like it's a video screen. Wonder if the noms finally perfected organic LEDs."

Shelton ran a finger over the dusty window. "Doesn't look like their fancy sign got 'em enough business to stay open."

Elyssa pointed to several other businesses with stick-figure signs. "What's the deal? Doesn't anyone put words on their signs these days?"

"Icons are an easy way to overcome lingual differences," Cinder said.

"Makes it easier for international visitors." Adam looked up at a stick figure wearing a hat. "We might be in Europe or even Russia."

"Their streets are painted weird too." Shelton scuffed his foot over a solid blue line in the middle of the road. "I thought most countries used yellow and white."

We walked down the sidewalk in the direction of the city for a couple hundred yards before Shelton held up a hand and stopped. "At first, I thought, hey it's a workday, or maybe it's a national holiday and no one is out, but"—he pointed up and down the street—"I haven't seen a single person or moving car the entire time we've been walking."

"That is odd." Adam scratched his head. "Maybe it's Christmas or Kwanza."

"Well, it's chilly enough to be winter." I waved a hand at the bare trees. "So it's possible we popped back in on a major holiday."

"Let's just keep walking," Elyssa said. "I'm sure we'll come across people soon." She pointed down the road. "Looks like a major intersection up there."

We continued on. Empty cars littered the road ahead, doors hanging open as if something frightened the drivers so much they leapt out of their seats and ran. Dust and crud accumulated so thick on the outside, it was evident this hadn't just happened yesterday.

Dark doorways gaped in many of the buildings. Broken windows and black stains in the concrete bore testimony to some long-gone horror that wreaked havoc.

Bliss wandered inside the doorway to a pottery shop. Despite the broken window, the goods remained in one piece. She picked up an urn and traced a finger along the painted designs.

"What the hell happened here?" Shelton knelt next to a dark stain. "Looks like a war broke out while we were gone."

Elyssa examined the nearby building. "I don't see impact damage from bullets or explosions." She traced the stain to the broken window. "I think someone jumped out of the window and cut themselves badly."

"Yep." Shelton grimaced. "They were running from something, but what was it?"

"Since none of this was cleaned up, I'm guessing whatever happened was more widespread than just this neighborhood." Adam cocked an ear. "I don't hear cars, planes, or any sounds of industry."

I closed my eyes. "Just birds and insects."

Cinder offered a stiff nod. "It appears this area is abandoned."

"Why would they just leave all their pottery?" Bliss asked.

"Dollars to dog nuts it wasn't World War Three." Shelton narrowed his eyes. "We left Eden undefended from a maniac and he took full advantage."

Anger burned in Elyssa's eyes. "Victus did this."

"Whoa." I held up my hands. "There's too many missing people to assume that."

"Victus would have attacked with a robot army," Adam said. "I don't see any evidence of that." He patted a car fender. "Aside from being abandoned and unused, there's not another mark on this car."

Bliss held up a vase. "And the pottery is intact."

"You're wrong," Shelton said. "If Victus landed a battalion of battlebots in the middle of the street, people would run in terror. All he had to do was round them up with more troops and bingo-bango, he's done."

"I don't think the nom military would just sit back and do nothing," Adam said. "There would be blood." He jabbed a finger at the stain on the sidewalk. "And a lot more than that."

"Would the time dilation affect how much time he had to do it as well?" I asked.

"Maybe." Adam tapped a finger on his chin. "Taking the elliptical orbit and increasing effects of the Abyss into consideration would require some complex calculations."

"We would need several variables," Cinder said. "I can gather data."

"Probably not worth the time," Adam said.

I climbed onto a car roof and surveyed our surroundings. I only saw more of the same—abandoned cars and otherwise empty streets. "Let's keep going into the city."

"Yeah." Elyssa took my hand. "We need to find survivors and ask what happened."

We passed apartment buildings, neighborhoods, and businesses, but no one responded to our calls. We were still a half mile out from downtown when I stopped. "This is pointless. If an apocalypse happened, nobody's going to care if we show up in a flying ship." I motioned back toward the industrial park. "Let's go get the ship."

"It had to be Victus." Shelton gripped his wand. "No other explanation."

"What if he invented something that just disintegrated people?" Adam shuddered. "I wouldn't put it past him."

Victus or not, someone had obliterated the population of this city.

CHAPTER 9

"Do you think every city is like this?" Elyssa asked as we hurried back toward the ship.

"I hope not." My grip tightened on her hand. "We need to get to Atlanta. I need to find Ivy."

"We don't have time to do that if we're going back to Seraphina," she said. "It'll have to wait."

"It can't wait." I stopped walking and turned to the others. "We can't go back without finding out what happened here."

"Agreed." Shelton cracked his knuckles. "Victus thinks everyone is dead. He'll never expect us to show up."

"If we're stuck here two months, that translates to four months back on Seraphina," Adam said. "Is it really a good idea to leave Thomas hanging without a word from us for that long?"

I blew out a sigh. "No. But I can't go back without knowing if Ivy is okay."

"I will help you find her if you wish," Bliss said.

I couldn't decide if she was being sincere or pandering to get into my good graces.

"Eden got wrecked." Shelton smacked the flat of his fist against a rusting car. "Whatever happened must've happened years ago."

"We've been in Seraphina three years," Adam said. "I'd guess that equals about two years, maybe less here."

Cinder knelt to examine skid marks and a deep dent in a car. "It appears something hit this car and pushed it sideways."

Shelton grunted. "Probably just a wreck when the shit hit the fan."

Cinder pointed to a row of dented cars. It looked as if something had plowed right through them. "It's possible a battlebot did that."

"Yeah, you could be right." Shelton rubbed a hand over the chipped paint and rust. "Doesn't look like another car did this."

"Battlebots are heavy with big metal feet." Adam looked down at the asphalt. "There's no way one could run down the road without leaving cracks or prints."

"Then what did all this?" Shelton kicked a car with his boot. "What made all the people vanish?"

"Here's another thought." Adam nodded toward Bliss. "If Victus could clone anyone with dolems, why attack the populace with battlebots when you could simply take over the governments?"

Elyssa frowned. "Damn. That's a good point. A full-frontal assault doesn't fit Victus's modus operandi."

"Then who did it?" Shelton growled. "Xanomiel? Baal? The Cookie Monster?"

"Good question." Elyssa tapped a finger on her lower lip. "Let's get the ship and look around before whatever did this finds us."

The hairs on the back of my neck pricked, as if I was being watched. "I feel really exposed right now. Let's pick up the pace."

Elyssa glanced furtively around. "I thought I sensed something too."

We sped up to a jog. Shelton huffed and puffed behind us. "Can those of you with super speed just go get the damned ship and pick me up?"

I turned around. "I got you, fam. The rest of you stick together until we get back."

Shelton bent over, hands on knees and wheezing. "Great idea, man."

Adam clapped Shelton on the back. "Someone needs to cut back on the bacon."

"Screw you, Nosti." Shelton took off his hat and wiped sweat. "Bacon is life."

"We will be here waiting," Cinder said.

Bliss cast a worried gaze around but nodded.

Elyssa and I took off at full speed, blurring down the road, dodging between cars or leaping over them. When we reached the warehouses, Elyssa stopped abruptly at the corner of the building where the *Raptor* was parked. I skidded to a stop.

"What's up?"

She put a finger to her lips. "What's that sound?"

I cocked an ear and heard a slight hum from somewhere ahead. "Electricity?"

"It sounds like a transformer that's on the verge of blowing." Elyssa crept silently toward the mouth of the alley. "It's definitely closer now."

"Maybe we left the ship on."

Elyssa shook her head and peered around the corner. I poked out my head next to hers.

Four people stood in front of the ship, staring up at it.

"Oh, crap." I hissed. "Where the hell did they come from?"

"I don't know." Elyssa quirked her lips. "I don't know if I should be happy or irritated that we finally found people."

"One way or the other, we need the ship, and we need answers." I shrugged. "Looks like we can get both in short order."

"I suppose so." We crept around the corner and approached the visitors.

The humming noise grew louder, and I soon found out why.

One of the people stiffened and turned. Blue light glowed where his eyes should have been. Energy crackled across his lips. He opened his mouth to reveal a luminous maw. The electric hum changed in pitch and tone like a robot voice. Except it wasn't using any words I knew.

The other people raced to his side. Two were women, and the fourth, a boy of maybe eleven or twelve years. Like the man, blue light glowed from their eyes and mouths, humming with electrical undertones.

The man wore a brown business suit with abnormally large collars and a thick tie knot. The boy sported a striped T-shirt and bell-bottomed jeans. A light blue dress hung to the knees of the blond woman, and the brunette kept it casual with bell-bottoms and a green polyester button-up.

"Holy mother of god, what happened to you people?" I backed up a step and nearly tripped over Elyssa. "And where did you get those clothes? The Goodwill clearance rack?"

They streaked toward us with inhuman speed. I was so surprised I didn't have time to react before the businessman grabbed me. Electrical impulses speared from his eyes and into mine. My muscles locked up. Every molecule seemed to catch fire. I tried to scream. Tried to fight. But my body wouldn't respond.

Pain exploded in my ribs. I flew through the air and crashed into the brick wall before coming to rest on my face. Control gradually returned to my arms and legs, but I felt sluggish, drunk. I looked up. Elyssa back-handed the boy. He slammed into the *Raptor* and smacked onto the ground. A swift roundhouse flung the blonde across the alley. A punch sent the businessman flying backward.

I staggered upright and saw the second woman coming at me, eyes blazing. Strength and speed abandoned me, so I summoned a shield. She crashed into it at full speed and bounced off. It should have knocked her unconscious, but she leapt back to her feet as if nothing had happened. I channeled a rod of Murk and smacked her upside the head with it. She face-planted in the dirty alley.

"Stay down, bitch!"

Nope. Not a chance. She got right back up and rushed me again, not a bruise or scratch on her. Even her blue dress remained unstained despite lying on the dirty asphalt. Since I apparently couldn't hurt this woman—or whatever she was—I channeled the rod into a club and swung for the fences.

With a mighty crack to the skull, she sailed over the *Raptor* and slammed into a brick wall so hard it left an imprint. Without even a cry of pain, she slid down the wall, turned, toward me, and charged.

Fear sent a charge of adrenalin into my shocked muscles. I ran for Elyssa where she kept the other three people at bay.

"We've got to get out of here!" I said. "I can't hurt these things."

Elyssa grunted and kicked the boy in the chest. He flew backward into the businessman and tumbled along the asphalt. I batted the brunette for a homerun out of the alley, clearing a path to the gangway. We sprinted aboard the ship. Elyssa grabbed the control stick and the systems hummed to life.

As we lurched into the air, I ran outside and looked over the deck railing. I took a quick headcount of the energy people staring up at us to make sure we didn't have any stowaways. Thankfully, none had made it aboard before takeoff.

"Hang on," Elyssa yelled. She rammed propulsion to full, and we jetted forward. I held onto the railing and looked toward the city, trying to find the place where we'd left the others.

It only took us a few seconds to arrive, but our friends were nowhere to be seen. Elyssa hovered the ship over the street.

"Oh, god." I ran around the deck. "Shelton! Adam!"

No answer.

"Where the hell did they go?" Elyssa ran to the other side of the ship. "I know we didn't fly over them."

Just below, the door on the roof of a three-story apartment building burst open. Shelton and the others stumbled out. Adam shut the door and cast a shield spell over it.

"Jesus, Mary, and Joseph, what are those things?" Shelton shouted.

I waved down at them. "We're here!"

He looked up. "Yeah, well get down here and save us!"

Elyssa dropped the ship level with the rooftop. Cinder helped Bliss over the railing, even though she could have handled it easily. Shelton and Adam clambered onboard as if sharks nipped at their heels. The roof door splintered and energy people pressed against the shield. It cracked and shattered. Dozens spilled onto the roof, humming in their cybernetic voices.

I guided the ship up and away from the mob then took that moment I so desperately needed to recover my wits. *What in the hell is going on?* My muscles ached and throbbed from whatever that creature had done to me. I felt like a half-drained battery in need of a recharge.

"Well, at least we know what happened to the people." Adam recorded the rooftop below with his arcphone. "They're mindless eidolons."

"I don't know if they're mindless," Shelton said.

Bliss's face scrunched. "What's an eidolon?"

"A phantom," Adam said. "And these things fit the bill."

"They're organic, but nothing hurts them." Shelton looked at his wand as if it was defective. "I could knock them back, but it didn't even singe their clothing."

Adam nodded. "Like solid ghosts."

Elyssa shuddered. "I still don't know what eidolon means, but it sounds creepy."

Shelton grunted. "From now on it means those things."

I leaned against the railing. The eidolons stood on the rooftop, staring up at us with their creepy glowing eyes, making their creepy humming noises. "Eden got royally screwed while we were gone." I checked the time. "How much longer should we wait before going back to Seraphina?"

"I'd give it a few more hours," Adam said. "We can't risk running into Baal."

I didn't like the thought of going back to Seraphina empty-handed. Was Ivy still alive? Did the rest of the world still exist, or was it all like this? Since we didn't even know where we were, finding Atlanta in a few hours was impossible. The best thing to do right now was gather more information so we could prepare for our return trip.

I stared at the shining skyscrapers. They appeared seamless on the outside, cylindrical with penthouses on top.

"We should find a library or newspaper stand," Adam said. "We can shed some light on what happened here."

"I looked for newspapers while we were walking earlier," Elyssa said, "but I didn't see any stands or kiosks."

"Even China has newspapers." Shelton looked at the eidolons and they stared right back. "Go away, you damned creeps!"

They didn't budge.

"I think I found something." Bliss held the spyglass to her eye. "Someone is standing on the silver tower."

"Huh?" I held out my hand and received the spyglass. I zeroed in where she pointed and spotted a figure standing on the tower to my left. The spyglass didn't offer enough zoom to clarify the features, but it looked like a man standing on the observation deck. A bridge to the right connected that tower with its neighbor. "Elyssa, can you take us closer to the towers?"

She peeked through the lens and grimaced. "Just when I think things can't get any creepier."

"Son of a bitch." Shelton knocked his hat off backward so it hung by the string. "We failed, didn't we? All those times we saved the world were for nothing."

Adam slumped. "Why'd you have to put everything in perspective right this minute?"

A knot of sadness lodged in my throat. *Victus won. We lost.* I tried to be positive. "Look, there's no evidence the entire world is like this. There's still hope."

Elyssa squeezed my hand. "I hope so, babe. I hope so."

Bliss reached out and took Cinder's hand for a brief moment. He looked down and then at her. "Are you okay, Bliss?"

She nodded. "I am now."

That's weird.

Elyssa released my hand and went to the ship controls. "Let's go find some answers."

Before I could voice support, she propelled us toward the silver towers.

As we drew closer to the target, ominous black clouds gathered overhead. The lone figure on the observation deck walked to the center of the bridge.

I used the spyglass for a better look.

A man in a richly embroidered cloak moved his hands through a pattern. Small pulsating spheres, green, sapphire, violet, and orange orbited around his waist. Electrical currents arced between them, growing thicker and brighter with every movement of his hands.

"What in the blazes is he doing?" Shelton recorded with his phone, the camera zoomed in for a closer look.

"I've never seen anything like it." Adam looked up at the thickening clouds. "I think he's altering the weather."

"I've seen spheres like that." It had been a long time ago. Back when I had to choose my affinity to either the dark or the light—Murk or Brilliance. Orbs of power had circled my head, but none of them were these colors. "When I had to make my choice, I saw ultraviolet, white, gray, and clear."

"Maybe it's just for show," Shelton said. Thunder rumbled, and he looked up. "Or maybe not."

"Mr. Gray once told me that there are different ways of using magic." I shook my head. "This dude is way out there."

"Which begs the question—who is this guy?" Adam glanced back up at the sky. "And do we need to be worried about lightning?"

"Only one way to find out." Elyssa turned on the weather shields and slowed the approach to the bridge, stopping a dozen yards from it.

The man closed his fists and pressed them together, as if connecting something invisible. It looked similar to the way I tied off channeled magic. A long mane of silver hair hung past his shoulders. Cheekbones rose high on his narrow face, wide lips fixed in a haughty frown. His eyes glowed soft white, not blue like the energy people. If he had irises or pupils, I couldn't see them.

"We come in peace," I shouted.

The man spoke in a rich, sonorous voice, but I couldn't understand a thing he said.

"I'm sorry, what was that?" I turned to Adam. "Can you bust out that language program you made?"

"Yeah, sure, but it'll take a while to get a baseline for translation."

The man wove his hands back and forth. Lightning danced across the violet sphere. It felt as if the air pressure abruptly changed. Shelton worked his jaw back and forth. Adam dug a finger into his ear.

"Tell me who you are before I snuff your lives like a spark in the might of my storm." The man lifted his hands toward the dark clouds. "For none enter my domain without good reason."

"That was fast," I said.

Adam shook his head. "That wasn't my program." He looked at the man. "I think it was something he did."

Elyssa worked her jaw back and forth like someone trying to pop their ears. "We just arrived from Seraphina. Who are you?"

The man narrowed his glowing eyes. "You are from Seraphina?"

"Yes." She paused. "Are you an Arcane?"

His gaze locked on Cinder. "I can read the others, but you are different. What manner of being are you?"

Cinder tilted his head slightly. "I am a golem. Might I ask what manner of being you are?"

"Those who know not of me are truly not of this world." He pointed to the building on his right. "Dock your vessel. We will speak."

"I don't trust this dude," Shelton whispered. "He thinks his shit doesn't stink, but it reeks to high heaven."

The man pressed his fists together and separated them. The clouds thinned and drifted away, leaving a clear blue sky. "Come now, for my patience is not eternal." He held out a hand and the dancing energy orbs shrank, filled his palm, and vanished.

I turned to Elyssa. "Well, I guess this is the best way to find answers."

She nodded. "Yeah, but let's keep our guards up, okay?"

"Don't have to tell me twice."

I went onto the bridge to dock the ship and found Bliss sitting inside.

"I'm not coming with you," she said. "There's something sinister about that man."

"We don't trust him either," I said. "You don't have to come if you don't want to."

She nodded. "I'll wait here just in case."

It was just another reminder that this dolem was nothing like the person whose soul she possessed. Nightliss would have never left our sides in a potentially dangerous situation. On the other hand, it was probably for the best not having her along.

I guided the ship up to the observation deck on the building and latched on with the mooring clamps. I pointed to the comm badge on my shirt. "Let me know if you see anything suspicious."

"Yes, Justin." Bliss gave me a worried look. "I can come if you want."

I shook my head. "Don't worry about it."

I walked across the gangway to the building. The man crossed the bridge back to us and waited near an arched entrance. With Shelton, Adam, Elyssa, and Cinder at my back, I walked toward him.

"Where is Bliss?" Cinder looked toward the ship.

"She's staying here just in case," I said.

Cinder nodded. "That is a good idea."

I reached the stranger and held out my hand. "I'm Justin."

He raised an eyebrow and looked down at my proffered hand. Met my eyes. "I am Vokan." With a rustle of his fancy cloak, he turned and walked inside the penthouse.

Three tables shaped like equilateral triangles sat in the middle of the room, just close enough to each other to make a larger triangle. A layer of dust covered the tables and chairs. Despite the strange design, it looked more like a conference room in a hotel than what one would expect to find in a penthouse.

Vokan continued through the doors and down a ramp. It wound downward and ended on a deck overlooking a vast atrium. A towering column of blue fire filled a transparent cylinder that spanned from the ceiling all the way down as far as the eye could see, filling the tower core.

A queasy feeling invaded my stomach and my inner demon stirred restlessly, attracted like a fish to a lure. My jaw went slack. "What is that thing?"

"You truly do not know?" Vokan's lips curled into a cruel smile. "It is a cantrap, filled with the souls of the dead."

CHAPTER 10

Elyssa stiffened. Shelton gripped his staff. Adam reached for his wand. Cinder blinked calmly. I watched the man, waiting for any sign of an attack.

Vokan turned and faced the blazing column as if he hadn't just told us it was filled with ghosts. "What brings you to my lands?"

"Might help if we knew what land we were in," Shelton said.

Vokan faced us again. "You are in the city of Solan."

"Solan?" I was flummoxed. "Is that an Asian city?"

"Never heard of it." Shelton blew out a breath. "I knew we should've taken that left turn at Albuquerque."

Adam snapped his fingers. "Man, I should've known. All the weird signs, the cars." He pinched the bridge of his nose. "This place looks haunt-ingly familiar, but I don't think we're in Eden."

"Hang on a minute." Shelton shook his head like a wet dog. "You don't think this is Eden?"

"The preponderance of evidence supports Adam's theory," Cinder said.

"Indeed, for this is Utopia." Vokan clasped his hands together. "What do you know of Eden?"

"Utopia?" Shelton looked incredulous. "Do you even know what that means?"

Vokan raised an eyebrow. "A name, nothing more."

"It's a dystopian nightmare is what it is," Shelton continued.

Shelton was right, but I didn't want him rubbing this man the wrong way, so I answered his question. "We're originally from Eden."

Vokan touched a slender chain around his neck that vanished into his robes. "How did you come by this realm?"

"We thought it was Eden," I said. "We're trying to find our way home."

"Perhaps I can help." Vokan flourished his cloak. "Come."

I hesitated and gave Elyssa a look. She shrugged, so I marched after Vokan. We followed him around the cantrap and into a side corridor. He boarded a levitator and the rest of us piled on. Out of a dozen buttons, he pressed the black one at the bottom. We dropped so fast, my stomach climbed up my throat.

Disco music pounded from the small speakers and I caught Vokan tapping his foot to the beat. It sounded familiar, but I couldn't name the tune. The levitator abruptly slowed and stopped. The doors slid open to a cavernous room filled with books. It rivaled even the great library at Arcane University.

"Jumpin' Jesus on a pogo stick." Shelton took off his hat and ran a hand through his short hair. "You've got the entire Library of Congress in here."

Something else stood out even more than all the books—a silver arch in the center of a golden circle. Vokan held out a hand and summoned his energy spheres. His hands flicked through a pattern so fast I could barely follow them. Lightning crackled between the spheres and the silver arch powered on.

A portal flashed open.

A family of four sat on the other side, eating dinner at a table. The two boys stared mindlessly at their phones, barely looking up to get a spoonful of mashed potatoes. The parents did the same.

The woman scowled and looked up. "I am so sick of Linda's status updates. She can't eat anywhere without taking pictures of her stupid food."

The father burst into laughter. "I love these cat videos."

Cinder took out his phone and recorded. "Fascinating."

Vokan waved his hand and the view shifted to the outside of a house. Another wave zoomed out to take in the entire neighborhood. "This is Eden."

"We can go through right now?" Hope filled Shelton's voice.

"Go through?" Vokan stared at him as if he was stupid then walked over and rapped a fist against an invisible barrier blocking the portal. "It no longer works. I have entertained travelers from other realms, but none have shown me how I might repair this arch or given me the ability to leave on my own."

Elyssa's eyes lit up. "What travelers have been through here?"

"A trio came long ago." Vokan walked to a table and opened a photo album. Three disgruntled people glared at the photographer. On the left stood a tall dark-skinned male. Next to him stood two beautiful females, one with hair of gold, the other of platinum. "Their names are Gallifer, Sithain, and Purah."

"The Fallen!" Adam blurted.

Vokan's eyes narrowed. "You know of them?"

Adam gave him a sheepish shrug. "Never met them, but we know of them."

Cinder walked to a shelf and inspected the books there.

Vokan held out his hand and the energy orbs vanished into his palm again. The silver portal winked off. "Eden taunts me from afar. Though I may watch her all I wish, I cannot reach her."

"Did you build this arch?" I asked.

"No." Vokan stroked the chain on his neck again. "Our people once used it to travel to Eden, but it no longer works. Now it is but a window to that realm." He turned to me. "How did you reach this realm?"

"Our ship," Adam said. "But it doesn't work as well as we'd like."

Shelton grimaced and elbowed him.

Adam scowled. "What was that for?"

"Damn it, Nosti." Shelton rolled his eyes. "We don't know this guy."

I changed the subject to avoid revealing much more about ourselves to this stranger. "What did the Fallen want?"

"They visited our people long ago." Vokan seemed to look into the distance, though it was hard to tell since the glow in his eyes concealed his pupils and irises. "They left us a powerful relic for safekeeping, and thusly have we served."

Elyssa raised an eyebrow. "What does the relic do?"

He shrugged. "I know not. It is called the Child of Jura." Vokan paused as if for dramatic effect. "They warned me it is cursed."

"Whoa, a Relic of Juranthemon." Adam rubbed his hands together. "Where is it? Can I see it?"

"No, you may not." Vokan touched the chain on his neck. "As I said, it is cursed." He looked at me. "Tell me more of your story and how you came here."

I figured it couldn't hurt to give him a little information about ourselves despite my misgivings. "We used to travel the realms through special arches. We went to Seraphina but were trapped when someone sabotaged the arch that would take us home."

Vokan raised an eyebrow. "Go on."

I held out my hands in a shrug. "That's basically it."

"I see."

He didn't sound convinced, so I asked him a question of my own. "Why does Utopia look so much like Eden?"

"Our people once traveled freely to Eden. Our society was more advanced, our magic and science, superior." Vokan scowled. "Our leaders believed it our duty to guide our sister realm into enlightenment, but it was a fool's errand."

"Sister realm?" Shelton held up a hand. "Whoa, you're saying Eden copied Utopia?"

"In many ways, yes." Vokan's lips curled up slightly. "Does this offend you?"

"I find it hard to believe, is all." Shelton frowned. "I thought we figured out things on our own."

"Sure would explain why this place looks so much like Eden," Adam said. "What I want to know is what happened to the people."

"War," Vokan said in a low voice. "Our realm was once governed by the Magus Council. Their leader, Imogen, desired absolute rule. She tried to use the Child of Jura to grant her infinite power. Instead, she drained the citizens of their soul force and turned them into mindless monsters."

"Those are the souls of citizens in the cantrap?" I asked.

His hand wandered to the necklace again. "We joined forces with the other three cities to defeat her, but the city of Camelyn betrayed us and sided with Imogen. Many thousands were lost. Were it not for my elemental mastery, all might have been lost."

This guy has an ego bigger than a dinosaur turd. "Where are the survivors?"

Vokan held out his hands. "I am all that is left of Solan. The other cities suffered greatly, except for Camelyn. The traitors still hide behind her walls, even decades later."

"Decades?" Adam scratched his head. "How old are you?"

Vokan pursed his lips. "I am just into my fourth century."

I blew out a breath. "In Eden, most humans don't live to be a hundred."

"Arcanes live longer than most," Shelton said, "but I don't know about four hundred years."

"Only great masters live so long," Vokan said. "I was the greatest of the Magi even before the war." He stated it as fact, like water is wet and sand chafes your ass crack.

"Okay," I said slowly. "Since you obviously know a lot, is there a way to release the souls of the people and save them?"

"No," Vokan replied simply. "Their bodies are empty vessels, animated only by the foul magic of the relic."

"I'd like to study the relic," Adam said. "Maybe we can figure it out."

"Doubt we have time," Shelton said.

"It is out of the question." Vokan clasped his hands over his stomach. "The relic is off limits. I will not risk it being used again." Energy orbs orbited above his palm.

Adam held up his hands. "Hey, we don't want any trouble. It was just a suggestion."

Shelton didn't look concerned. "What kind of hocus pocus is that?" He nodded at the orbs. "Are those just for show?"

"For show?" Vokan clenched his fist and snuffed the spheres. "I hold in my hand the mastery of the elements. None before me have ever mastered more than two. Most are barely adequate with one."

Shelton shrugged. "Sure, if you say so. Looks like a fancy light show to me."

Vokan looked down at the wand in Shelton's holster. "You say this, and yet you use crude instruments which barely scratch the surface of magic."

"We focus our spells through wands and staffs," Shelton said. "There's nothing crude about it, it's just different."

"Ah, casting." Vokan smiled as if he thought that was cute. "You use only the fifth element, aether, weaving it into crude spells."

Shelton's face turned red. "Yeah, well how do you do it?"

"It is rather complicated." Vokan looked bored. "Let me simplify. There are four primary elements—earth, air, water, and fire." An orb flickered to life in his palm as he listed them, green, violet, sapphire, and orange. "The fifth, aether, bridges them." Electrical currents flashed between the four orbs. "Mastery over a primary element requires years for most."

"That's not a big deal." Shelton scoffed. "I can shoot fire out of my wand. I can freeze water with a spell. For all your fancy talk, I doubt you could do much better than me."

Vokan stiffened. "Perhaps you would like to test your theory."

I intervened with a question to head off a duel. "Is aether necessary to use an element?"

"Without aether, an element is constrained to its primary form," Vokan said. "Aether unlocks limitless possibilities and combinations."

"Fascinating." Adam tapped on his phone screen. "I didn't realize you could control elements on such a granular level."

"Indeed." Vokan spread his hands and the orbs reappeared. "I have barely scratched the surface of what is possible."

"Earth, air, water, and fire aren't even elements," Shelton said.

"Scientifically, no," Vokan said. "Magically, yes."

"Can you teach me some basics?" Adam looked enthralled. "It could revolutionize magic on Eden."

Shelton broached the question the rest of us had been too polite to ask. "What's with your eyes?"

Vokan raised a silver eyebrow. "Elemental mastery opens one's eyes far beyond the human spectrum."

Adam chimed in. "It's a side effect?"

"Precisely." Vokan didn't offer further explanation.

I really wanted to dig further into the way this guy did magic, but that would have to wait. We had to get back to Seraphina and tell Thomas this trip was a bust. "Thank you for your hospitality, Vokan, but we have to get back to Seraphina."

Vokan stared at me for a moment. "Tell me more of your ship."

Adam gave me an uneasy look. "We're testing a new apparatus."

"Yeah, the darn thing nearly blew us up," I said. "You're welcome to come with us to Seraphina while we test it out. Maybe we'll finally find Eden."

"That would be sufficient." Vokan headed back toward the elevator. "There is little left for me here." He touched the slender chain on his neck again, as if seeking comfort.

"What's with your fancy necklace?" Shelton blurted.

Vokan looked down, seemingly surprised that he touched it. "A reminder of days long past. It offers me comfort."

I expected him to pull it out of his robes and show us a pendant with a picture of a deceased loved one, but he went to the elevator instead. Once we boarded, the doors slid shut. Instead of rising, the elevator shifted to the left.

I steadied myself against the wall. "Where is this thing going?"

Vokan gave me a sideways look. "I must stop by my quarters for traveling attire."

"Got any cloaks I can borrow?" Shelton said. "I want to spruce up a bit."

"Should you ever master the elements, you will earn a cloak such as mine." Vokan traced a finger down the rich embroidery. "I wove this cloth myself with the skills of the magi."

Shelton groaned. "Man, you are—"

Adam hurriedly interrupted him. "Are we headed to the other building?"

"Yes." Vokan clasped his hands together and remained quiet. After a moment, the elevator stopped, and he stepped out.

I'd expected his quarters to be palatial, but the midnight-blue shag carpet and puce floral wallpaper left a lot to be desired.

Elyssa gasped. "You live here?"

Vokan hesitated, as if embarrassed to admit it. "If suffices."

"Who's your interior decorator?" Shelton bent down and ran a hand through the carpet. "Their color choices make me want to bleach my eyeballs."

Adam elbowed Shelton. "It looks very, um, vintage."

Vokan motioned us to follow him and walked down the hallway. He stopped outside a family room furnished with a wood-cabinet television and a vinyl couch. "Please wait here. I will return momentarily." He walked to the end of the hall and entered a room.

"Something ain't right with this joker." Shelton grunted. "Vokan wouldn't get a joke if it farted in his face."

"For real." Adam spoke in a hushed voice. "He takes himself way too seriously."

"I find this experience fascinating," Cinder said. "This world suffered a cataclysmic war. I would like to utilize the library if we have time."

Shelton scoffed. "Are you kidding me? I don't like this realm, and I sure as hell don't like Vokan."

"Me either." Elyssa eyed Vokan's bedroom door for a moment. "Let's go wait on the elevator."

Shelton grunted. "I say we take it back up to the roof. Vokan can find us in the ship when he's ready."

"Would it be wise to rankle him?" Cinder said. "He is already quite surly."

"Rankle?" Shelton snorted. "Did you pull that word out of your ass?"

Cinder tilted his head slightly. "If you are attempting to rankle me, Harry, it will not work."

Adam guffawed. "Nice one, Cinder."

Elyssa sighed loudly. "Elevator, okay?"

I went to the bedroom door and knocked on it. "Vokan, we'll take the elevator up and meet you on the roof, okay?" He didn't answer me, but he might also be dropping a deuce before the trip. I twisted the door handle and it clicked open. I peered into a bedroom with an awful floral theme but didn't see Vokan inside.

The elevator doors dinged at the other end of the hall. We spun around. Vokan stood in the elevator. His lips curled into a sneer. "Baal sends his regards, Justin Slade."

Before I could even register what he said, the elevator door slid shut.

CHAPTER 11

Without thinking, I sprinted to the elevator and slammed against the doors with all my might. The impact should have demolished them. Instead, I rebounded off the doors as if they were made of rubber. I flew backward, bowling over Elyssa and rolling to a stop.

"Son of a bitch!" Shelton took out his staff and hurled a fireball at it. The door absorbed the energy.

"Wait!" Adam grabbed Shelton's staff before he cast another spell. "Is that diamond fiber?"

Elyssa groaned and pushed to her feet. "Doesn't look like it."

Cinder pressed his fingers to a door. "It does not feel like diamond fiber."

Adam activated a divining spell on his phone and scanned the material. He sucked in a breath when he checked the results. "This isn't diamond fiber, but it's similar. It absorbs energy, magical or kinetic, and discharges it once it reaches a threshold."

I pounded a fist on the wall and felt it kick right back. "I don't understand! How does Baal know Vokan? How would Baal even know we'd come here?"

Elyssa pried at the crack where the elevator doors met in the middle but couldn't wedge her fingers inside. Her sword wouldn't penetrate the crack either. She huffed and backed away. "Can you try, Justin?"

I gave it a shot. No matter how hard I pressed, I couldn't force the doors apart. "Son of a biscuit eater!" Anger heated my face. My inner demon licked his chops. *Fine. You try.* I opened the window of my soul and let the caged beast lunge for control.

Destroy!

Muscles coiled around my arms, my legs, and bulged against my clothes. My fingernails sharpened to black claws. I kicked off my shoes as my toenails followed suit. Since I didn't have spare clothing on hand, I held my demon in check so I wouldn't rip my pants and shirt to shreds. He thrashed against my will, but finally relented.

"Let's see how this door holds up now," I said in an unnaturally deep voice. I jammed my claws into the crack—or tried to. No matter how I strained or roared in frustration, I couldn't pry open the crack. I raked my claws down the metal to no effect. When I pounded it with a fist, the energy kicked back and sent me spinning.

Destroy! Destroy!

My demon was not having a good time.

I tested the walls, the ceiling, the floor, but they were all built of the same material.

"Baal, you jackass!" I raised a demonic fist and shook it toward the ceiling. "I'm going to pound you to hamburger." I slammed the demon back into its cage and shrank back to normal size. "Split up and test every square inch of this place for a weakness."

Shelton snapped a salute. "Yes, sir."

Adam stared at the door. "This is bad. Really bad."

I agreed.

Adam modified his divining spell to scan wider sections and we covered most of the bunker within a couple of hours. We found no weaknesses in the walls, floors, or ceilings. The only thing we could break were the furnishings.

Wool turtlenecks, bellbottom jeans, and polyester shirts hung in the bedroom closets. My neck itched just looking at them. Unless there was a way to clean our clothes, we'd be sporting seventies attire in a few days.

Shelton tugged open the door to a utility closet we hadn't scanned. He shouted and nearly tripped over his own feet.

"What in the actual hell is a skeleton doing in here?"

The rest of us peered inside. A human skeleton hung from a peg on the wall right next to the mop and broom.

Elyssa popped around the corner to a chorus of our surprised shouts. She backed away. "What's wrong with you people?"

"Skeletons in closets." I showed her the Halloween surprise.

"Weird." She blew out a breath. "I found the secret tunnel Vokan used to sneak back to the elevator. I couldn't find any other hidden passages."

"Why a skeleton?" Adam shook his head. "Man, Baal goes all out when he messes with people's minds."

"No telling what else is in store for us." I walked into the last room we needed to scan. The kitchen looked every bit as gut-wrenching as the rest of the house: orange laminate countertops, brown vinyl flooring, and wallpaper that looked as if someone vomited green flowers on it before highlighting random areas with baby shit gold.

The mustard-yellow oven boasted old-school radiant heat coils, and a large woodgrain metal box turned out to be a microwave, activated with a giant time dial on the front. A bright green KitchenAid mixer and matching blender seemed to expect a lot more food preparation than any of us were prepared to do.

The puce fridge was fully stocked with frozen Totino's pizzas and a variety of microwave dinners. The crisper held raw veggies. Milk, eggs, and butter sat on the other shelves.

Shelton noticed the one critical omission. "There's no bacon." He dropped to his knees, hands held to his head in despair. "That rat-bastard trapped us without bacon!"

Elyssa looked in the cabinets. "No tea. Only Taster's Choice instant coffee." She slammed the door. "Pure evil."

I sniffed an apple to make sure it was real, then bit into it and gagged. "Damn, this thing is mealy."

Elyssa looked with despair at the instant coffee. "Is it possible Baal staged an entire city just to draw us in and trap us?"

Adam scratched his head. "I don't know about an entire city, but I wouldn't put anything past him."

"That's a lot of work, even for someone like Baal." Shelton grunted. "Then again, what are the odds of finding a realm that looks just like nineteen-seventies Eden?"

"The odds are not infinitesimal," Cinder said. "When Earth split into realms, I theorize that not all Seraphim ended up in Seraphina, just as not all Sirens went to Aquilis. Given the preponderance of humans, it is far likelier their species propagated to multiple realms."

"Agreed," Adam said. "The population across species was a fraction of what it is today, but humans were scattered all over the world."

Elyssa pursed her lips. "Let's say Vokan told us the truth—that Eden was heavily influenced by Utopia. Then why is Utopia stuck in the seventies?"

"Probably the apocalypse," Adam said. "Utopia stopped evolving while Eden kept advancing."

"Did you see the look on Vokan's face when he brought us here?" I said. "It was the one time he looked ashamed."

"Probably because he had to pretend this was where he lived." Shelton snorted. "Hard to swallow pride when you're a narcissist."

Cinder assumed a professorial tone. "Vokan exhibits classic narcissism."

"Let's walk through this," Elyssa said. "First of all, Baal had to find Utopia. Then he had to let us discover it. Then he had to get us to come here so Vokan could trap us. I know that sounds simple, but it's not."

Adam held out his hands "I agree, but here we are."

"We could overthink this all day long and still not figure it out." I blew out a breath. "Baal has ways of travelling the realms without an arch. I suspect he can go anywhere he can possess a human, so finding this realm wouldn't be impossible."

"I'll bet he staged stealing Argus and then herded us back to Voltis, knowing we'd try to escape to the realm we thought was Eden." Shelton sighed. "But how did he know we'd found Utopia?"

"He probably spied on us the entire time we were out there." Adam slumped. "Baal sure knows how to make a person feel stupid."

"We have a whole lot of ifs and none of it really matters." I tossed the mealy apple into the garbage. "No matter how elaborate the plan, we're trapped, Vokan is in cahoots with Baal, and we only have two days max before this realm passes out of alignment with Voltis."

"Bliss is still in the ship," Elyssa said. "Maybe she'll realize something is wrong before too much longer."

"And do what, precisely?" Shelton groaned. "It's not like she'll know where to find us."

"She can't use the ship," Adam said. "I locked the controls to only respond to the five of us. Even Bliss isn't authorized."

Cinder snapped his gaze to Adam. "Why would you exclude Bliss?"

Adam gave him a sheepish grin. "Uh, I didn't think Justin would want her to have access. It's not exactly a secret that he doesn't trust her."

"Why is this my fault?" I said. "I never said to lock Bliss out of the ship's controls."

Cinder turned his gray eyes to me but didn't say anything. His look was enough to make me feel like I'd just kicked a small child in the head and taken his candy.

"Great." Shelton squeezed his eyes shut for a moment as if warding off a headache. "So the ship is stuck, Bliss is stuck, we're all stuck!"

"What does Vokan get out of all this?" I said. "If he's a narcissist, what could Baal offer him?"

"That's easy." Elyssa gave a mirthless laugh. "He wants the ability to travel between realms, so Baal offered him our ship."

"Then we have leverage." I scowled. "He won't go anywhere without our help."

Cinder stepped into the hallway and looked toward the elevator. "I hope Bliss is okay."

"Maybe she'll kick Vokan's ass and force him to release us," Adam said.

"Someone's mighty optimistic," Shelton said. "I expect to see Bliss tossed out of the elevator door any minute now." He opened the pantry and found a case of beer. "Freaking ass taters in a vegan salad." He held up the case. "Baal left us horse piss to drink."

Cinder tilted his head. "But it claims to be 'Milwaukee's Best.'"

"Yeah, the best they could drain out of a urinal." Shelton tore off the pull tab and examined it with disgust. "Man, this thing even predates the environmentally friendly pop tabs." He tasted the beer and grimaced. "It's warm and disgusting, but I guess it'll do."

Adam took the rest of the case and put it in the refrigerator. "Maybe it'll taste better cold."

"I don't know about the rest of you, but I saw a TV in the middle room. Let's go see what's on." Shelton belched and walked out of the kitchen.

Lacking anything better to do, we followed him. A plaid cloth couch sat in front of the nineteen-inch color TV. There was no remote, so Shelton pulled the on switch and turned the clunky dial through several channels of white noise.

The last channel was the only one with a signal. Actors in polyester bell-bottoms and turtlenecks watched a paramedic crew attempt to save the life of a kid next to a mangled bicycle.

"Oh, man, this show is awful." Shelton took another swig of beer. "I don't know what it's called, but I remember seeing reruns of it when I was a kid. Something about firefighter paramedics and ambulances."

"Baal has outdone himself," Adam said. "I can't think of anything worse than being trapped with crappy food and ancient TV shows while he hatches whatever nefarious plans he has in store for Seraphina."

The television flickered. White noise filled the screen and was almost immediately replaced by Vokan sitting in an ornate chair. "Ah, you are all here."

"Where else would we be?" Shelton burped again. "Thanks for the crappy beer, by the way."

"Baal is the one responsible for your accommodations." Vokan's white eyes and resting bitch face didn't look the least bit amused by our predicament. "I was promised your portal technology."

Elyssa snapped her fingers. "Called it!"

"Good luck using it." Adam stepped into view of the TV. "We're the only ones who can operate it."

"So I have discovered." Vokan steepled his fingers. "I would rather you tell me how to operate it than be forced to resort to unpleasant means."

"We'd be more than happy to take you with us to Seraphina." I held out a hand. "Just let us go and you can come with us. We're still discovering how the portal generator works, but we'll eventually find Eden."

"Unacceptable." Vokan frowned. "My agreement with Baal precludes your freedom."

"Well, ain't that just peachy?" Shelton took another swig of beer. "You're an honest kidnapper."

The magus nodded. "Once Vokan gives his word, he keeps it."

"Yeah, well once Justin is kidnapped he gets really cranky." I leaned forward. "Let us go."

Vokan gave me a steely stare. "No."

"How did you meet Baal?" Elyssa asked. "How did he know we'd come here?"

"Where there are humans, there are demons," Vokan said. "The demon lord knew of Utopia and contacted me some time ago to propose a deal. He said this world so closely resembled Eden, that it would provide a perfect trap to deal with a nuisance."

"Wow, that's harsh." I leaned back on the couch. "We're just a nuisance?"

"For someone of my power, yes." Vokan narrowed his eyes. "Now, tell me what I must do to use your ship and the portal maker."

"How about you kiss my hairy ass?" Shelton said. "Better yet, come down here and I'll show you how much of a nuisance I can be."

"You can't hold us forever," I said. "I don't know what Baal told you about us, but we'll escape and make you pay." I put on a tough-guy face. "Let us go and we can all be friends. Last chance."

"The bunker is designed to resist all magical and physical attacks. It survived everything my enemies threw at it during the war." Vokan didn't even crack an overconfident smile. He just stared at us. "You will remain there until Baal decides your fate."

I didn't know what else to say, so I tossed out an insult. "Well, it's an ugly bunker!"

The TV flickered and resumed its regularly scheduled program.

"Dude, I'm pissed." Adam smacked a fist into his palm. "Vokan doesn't know who he's messing with. If there's a way into a place, there's a way out."

"Hell yeah!" Shelton threw the empty beer can across the room. "Let's crack this bitch, Nosti."

They went through an elaborate handshake that ended with them pretending to take a hit and snuffing imaginary joints on the floor. Then they stared at each other.

"You don't know what to do, do you?" I said.

They shook their heads.

"No." Adam frowned. "But it felt good to decide to do something about it."

Elyssa chuckled. "Boys and their overconfidence." She walked around behind the television and pulled a plug. The TV turned off. "Everything I've observed indicates this world operates a lot like ours. They use electricity. They have levitators."

"And polyester," Adam said.

Elyssa pointed to the power outlet. "Find out what makes that thing tick. Is it science or magic?" She redirected her finger to the hall. "The levitator button in the hallway might be the way out of here. I happen to know some very good hackers who might be able to crack it."

Adam already knelt at the power outlet, phone extended. "The power is a combination of aether and electricity." He turned his phone toward the television. "Interesting. It's almost identical to the TVs we have in Eden, just a lot older."

"Where's the signal coming from?" I asked.

Shelton scanned the room with his phone. "I don't detect any airwave signals."

Adam tugged on another cord. "Coax cable." He traced it to a wall panel. "The other end of the cable must connect to a device playing the TV shows. That's also how Vokan just communicated with us."

"Well, two mysteries down." Shelton bobbed his head toward the hall-way. "Let's go check out the elevator."

"I would like to inspect the signal cable," Cinder said. "Perhaps I can find the source."

"Sure," Shelton shrugged. "See if they have some nineties sitcoms we can watch later. I hate seventies shows."

While Cinder remained in the family room, the rest of us filed into the hallway and marched to the elevator. Adam pressed the button a few times, as if it would magically work now. When it didn't he took out his phone and ran the divining spell. After a moment, the phone projected a wall of dense code.

"What the hell is that?" Shelton zoomed in on a section. "Doesn't look like Cyrinthian to me."

"It's not." Adam frowned. "Magic is so different in this realm that they don't use Cyrinthian as a base language. This is something else. Might even be encrypted."

"Foreign programming language. Hyper encryption." Shelton shrugged. "Easy peasy."

Adam scoffed. "This is gonna take a while."

Elyssa and I sat down and watched them work for about an hour before we started to fall asleep from boredom. I jerked awake for the umpteenth time and stood. "We're gonna get a snack."

"Uh huh." Adam didn't even look away from the code.

"Grab me a beer?" Shelton said.

"Sure." I took Elyssa's hand and we went to the kitchen.

I opened the fridge, but the beer wasn't in there anymore. It was back in the pantry. The garbage can where I'd tossed the terrible apple was empty.

Elyssa raised an eyebrow. "None of us would dare move the beer from the fridge."

"Which means someone else did." I stared at her. She looked back at me.

Someone else was in the bunker with us.

CHAPTER 12

Elyssa and I searched high and low in the kitchen for any signs of a secret entrance but came up empty. She headed for another room, but I stopped her.

"We're going about this the wrong way." I put the beer in the fridge and tossed another apple in the garbage can. I whispered in her ear. "Let's make them come to us."

Her eyes brightened. "Ooh, I like that idea."

We left the kitchen to deliver a beer to Shelton. He took a sip, grimaced, and promptly went back to his hacks. Elyssa and I sneaked back to the kitchen and hid just outside in the hallway. I had grand visions of catching Vokan himself sneaking in here through a hidden door and taking the beer out of the fridge just to mess with us.

We didn't have to wait long. The door to the utility closet down the hallway opened and out stepped a white, lanky figure—the skeleton. It clinked as it walked right past us and into the kitchen. It removed the beer from the fridge and put it back in the pantry, then took the apple I'd tossed in the garbage and put it back with the rest of the fruit.

"Gross!" I got in front of the skeleton. "Are you a golem?"

It stopped and stared at me with glowing eye sockets. "I am Bonehead." The jawbones didn't move, but a rich voice emanated from somewhere inside that empty head. For the first time, I noticed fine lines carved into the skull—enchantment symbols, perhaps.

"Okay, Bonehead." I resisted the urge to tap the skull with a fingertip. "Why did you move the beer to the pantry?"

"I am here to keep the bunker in order. I was instructed to keep the beer warm, and stock the kitchen with food that is not unpleasant, but also not good."

"By Baal, right?"

The skull bobbed a nod. "By Baal."

Elyssa groaned. "Baal is one evil bastard."

"Is Baal your master?"

The skull shook his head. "Vokan is my master."

I went back to my first question. "Are you a golem, Bonehead?"

"I am a sprite bound to this human skeleton by Vokan." He stepped past me.

"Wait."

Bonehead paused and turned. "Yes?"

"What's a sprite?"

"A spirit of nature." He started to walk away again.

"Why do you keep walking away from me?"

"Is it annoying?" Bonehead asked.

"Extremely!"

"That is good. Perhaps I won't be punished."

I hesitantly touched his arm to keep him in place. "Can we request things from you?"

"I am instructed to perform any requests in an unsatisfactory manner."

"Like walking away when I'm trying to talk to you?"

He nodded. "Exactly."

Elyssa groaned. "Well, that doesn't help. How did you end up here?"

Bonehead turned to her. "I was put in the closet."

She groaned. "No, I mean, how did you end up in a skeleton?"

"Sprites are routinely used as servants," he said. "Many are given malleable forms, but Baal specifically requested this one."

Elyssa scowled. "You're a slave."

"How can anyone force a spirit to work for them?" I asked.

"Magic, of course." Bonehead slipped from my grasp. "I cannot continue to answer your questions, or I'll violate my terms. Unless you wish to see me tortured, you will let me go."

I held up my hands in surrender. "For what it's worth, I'm sorry."

Bonehead tilted his skull to the side. "Wonderful." He turned and walked away.

"Wow, I feel sorry for the, uh, spirit guy." Elyssa frowned. "You know, we don't have sprites in Eden, at least not as far as I know."

"Well, we didn't really have angels either." I shrugged. "Considering we found a realm with unicorns, it seems the possibilities of what exists might be endless."

"You may be right." She quirked her lips. "Sounds like sprites don't have it too good in Utopia."

"You can say that again."

Elyssa tapped a finger on her chin. "I don't suppose you could summon any demons to help us break out."

I sighed. "If we couldn't smash or blow our way out of here, I don't know of any demons that could." I reached through the window in my soul and concentrated on the floor while reaching for a suitable spirit in Haedaemos. I found an entity and willed it to take form. A puddle of oily pitch formed, and a figure struggled against the mass. I released the spirit and the floor returned to normal.

Elyssa gave me a puzzled look. "What was that about?"

"Just making sure I can summon here." I shrugged. "For all I knew, the magic proof material might not allow it."

"True." Elyssa sighed. "I guess all our hopes rest on Adam and Shelton."

"Wouldn't be the first time."

"You're right. I should have more faith." She cast a doubtful look toward the hallway.

"I wonder if we could trick Bonehead into helping us." I grinned. "He has to perform our requests in an unsatisfactory manner, right?"

Elyssa frowned. "Yeah, so?"

"How about I tell him to make sure we're completely locked in here with no way out?"

She groaned. "And since he's supposed to be half-assed about it, he'll leave us a way out?"

I snapped my fingers. "Bingo!"

"That is probably the dumbest plan yet." Elyssa marched down the hall. "Let's go try it."

We stopped outside the closet. "Let me work on phrasing." I thought about it for a moment, then formulated it into a sentence.

Bonehead hung inside as he had before, so I addressed him. "Bonehead, I need something."

His eye sockets flickered on and the skeleton pulled itself off the wall rack. "What do you need?"

"I need you to make absolutely certain we don't know about any secret ways out of this bunker."

"There are none."

I was disappointed with his quick answer, so I tried another tact. "Make sure the elevator door does not open for us."

"I am unable to operate the elevator door, or through any attempts of reverse psychology, to help you escape." Bonehead reached behind him and jerked himself back up to hook his skull onto the rack. The light in his eye sockets faded and the skeleton went limp.

"Well, that went about as well as expected." Elyssa sighed. "What now?"

I yawned so hard I couldn't answer. When I finally had control of my mouth again, I said, "We could get some sleep."

She nodded. "I like that idea."

We went to the first room on the left and closed the door. It had no locks, of course.

Elyssa stared at the knob. "So much for privacy."

I brought her in for a kiss. "Hanky panky time?"

"What if Vokan is watching?"

"Wow, that really killed the mood."

Her lips pressed into a thin line. "Yeah. It seems like something Baal would really enjoy knowing."

"I wouldn't doubt if he's recording everything so he can enjoy it later."

Elyssa shrugged. "Oh, he probably has a live stream he can access anytime he wants."

"Yeah? Well, I have a brilliant idea to foil his plan." I grabbed her and pulled her under the covers with me then took my time undressing every gorgeous inch of her body. "Unless he has x-ray vision, he can't see through the sheets."

"Yeah, but Vokan will probably still watch and do pervy things."

I scoffed. "Let him."

Needless to say, we enjoyed ourselves and then it was night-night beddy-bye time.

SOMETHING PRODDED MY ASS. I opened my eyes and shouted in alarm.

Cinder hovered inches from my face. "Hello, Justin. I hope you do not mind me waking you so early."

"Can you back off a little?"

Elyssa giggled from under the covers. "He stood there for about five minutes before deciding to poke your butt."

I grimaced. "Phrasing!"

She laughed harder.

I sat up and saw my underwear lying far out of reach on the floor. "Um, can you give us a moment to get dressed?"

Cinder nodded. "Yes. Harry does not like it when I walk in on him naked and try to talk, although it makes no difference to me. Are we not all naked beneath our clothes?"

"That is so deep, Cinder." Elyssa slow-clapped. "Now, will you get out of here? Because I am not parading naked in front of you or anyone else but Justin."

"I enjoy parades whether the participants are clothed or naked, but I will do as you request." Cinder left the room and closed the door behind him.

Elyssa slipped out of bed and had bra and panties on before I'd even grabbed my boxers off the floor. She looked so delicious, I just wanted to get in another half hour of aerobics with her before talking to Cinder.

The dressers held some clean underwear, but they were polyester tighty-whities. A quick sniff told me my underwear was passable for another day.

Elyssa grimaced. "Gross."

"Yeah, well you didn't even sniff test your underwear before putting it on."

"Because I'm always clean, Justin." She went into the bathroom. "Besides, we can wash our clothes in the sink."

"That sounds fun." I pulled on my jeans. "Let's see what Cinder wants."

Cinder waited across the hall, staring blankly at our door. "Hello, Justin."

"What did you need to talk to me about?" I asked.

"I tried to wake Harry, but he told me to go away. Adam blocked his doorway with something, and I did not want to force my way in." Cinder offered a mechanical shrug. "I discovered something very interesting."

My interest piqued. "Oh?"

Elyssa came out of the room. "Well, let's get the show on the road."

Cinder gave her a deadpan stare, seemed to realize it was one of our strange idioms, and headed for the family room without further comment. The cable outlet lay on the floor and several feet of coaxial cable hung from the wall. Cinder held his arcphone next to the cable and turned on the screen. Green text appeared before a blinking cursor.

"The magical computer system is quite primitive." He tapped in some text and hit enter. A view of Vokan's empty throne appeared on the TV screen. "Through trial and error, I have compiled a small list of commands."

"Whoa, you hacked the system!" I held up my hand for a high-five.

Cinder recognized the offer and responded with a stiff slap. "Thank you, bro dude."

I shook my head. "Just dude or bro, but not both."

"Thank you, dude." Cinder held out a fist.

I gave him a bro-fist and made the asteroid explosion. "What else have you found?"

"The surveillance system is extensive." Cinder typed in *List Cameras* and hit enter. A long list trailed up the screen. "The bunker we are in does not have any cameras. There are one hundred twenty-three in the complex."

"That's odd," I said.

"Not really." Elyssa tapped a finger on her chin. "This bunker was made to keep Vokan safe. He wouldn't want any enemies spying on him from a control room in the towers."

"Oh yeah." I rolled the coax cable between my fingers. "Vokan put cameras in the towers in case an enemy controlled them."

"That would explain why the system was not difficult to hack," Cinder said. "It took me several hours to realize the cable connected to a centralized computer. Once I did, it was a matter of divining the operating system commands. I still have more to discover but decided this was important enough to wake you."

"Oh, it was." I clapped him on the back. "Can you make it do anything else?"

Cinder hit the backspace key on his virtual keyboard to clear the screen.

He typed in *Search Library.* The cursor changed from an arrow to a blinking colon. "It will search for whatever I enter."

"Type in Vokan," I said.

Cinder did as requested. A long list of news headlines appeared.

Vokan Declares Martial Law

Vokan Defeats A-aron

Vokan: Civil Unrest Is Treason

"Can we read these?" Elyssa asked.

Cinder tapped the number of the first article. There was a loud hiss and a thump behind us. I spun toward the bookshelf. On the empty shelf above one lined with romance novels sat a newspaper in a stiff binder, like the kind they used at public libraries.

"Where did it come from?" I asked.

"Send another one," Elyssa said.

Cinder did as requested. A thin slot opened behind the shelf and regurgitated another bound newspaper. It snapped shut, leaving no trace it was even there. Not that it mattered—there was no way we could fit inside it if we tried.

I set the first newspaper on the table and read the main story aloud. "Degenerates and lawbreakers have driven Grand Magus Vokan to invoke martial law. He encourages law-abiding citizens to report insurgents. The sooner they are arrested, the sooner we may return to normal life."

Elyssa scoffed. "Good old propaganda."

"There are also history texts in the library." Cinder tapped on his screen and the slot in the wall admitted several leather-bound tomes. He gathered them and started flicking through the pages. "This text appears to be fact-based, unlike the newspaper."

"Maybe we can find books about the computer system," I said.

"That is a good idea." Cinder searched again and sent two books. A man with a bowl cut and thick glasses grinned from the cover of the first. The other showed a family in full polyester regalia looking at a twelve-inch monochrome computer screen.

"Man, they are behind the times here." I shuddered. "Must be the time lag."

Elyssa frowned. "How is it we can read this language? It looks like English to me, but I'm pretty sure it isn't."

"It is not English," Cinder said. "The language spell Vokan used allows us to perceive it as English in the same way we understand his language. Since my consciousness operates differently from yours, I am able to turn off this perception and see it in the native tongue."

"What about the computer code Shelton and Adam found?" Elyssa said.

"Native computer code is not the same as Vokan's language, so the spell does not translate it." Cinder shook his head stiffly. "This is why Adam and Harry were unable to break the encryption on the elevator button last night."

I pinched the bridge of my nose. "Man, talk about confusing."

Elyssa nodded. "What say we get some breakfast while we read?"

"Sounds good."

Cinder turned back to the history books. "I would like to research. Perhaps books will offer useful insight."

"Anything is helpful at this point," I said. "I'd also like to use that surveillance system to spy on Vokan."

Cinder nodded. "I will activate it and keep watch."

Elyssa and I made eggs and toast and lamented the absence of bacon. There was no butter, but our evil host gifted us with margarine. The computer books were elementary, but useful. Apparently, the computer systems of Utopia resembled technology from Eden in the seventies, but the operating systems used magic code, much like arcnology-based computers in the Overworld.

It was all text based, but when we tried to dig into the actual coding part, the programming language looked like gibberish since the translation spell ignored it.

Elyssa pressed hands to her temples. "Ugh, talk about a headache. It'll take forever to learn this stuff."

"Let's hope we're not stuck here that long." I closed the book and took a sip of the bland instant coffee.

We returned to the family room. Vokan was on TV, standing on the deck of our ship and scowling. It made me feel pretty good to see he was every bit as frustrated as me.

"Any sign of Bliss?" I asked Cinder.

He shook his head. "I used the cameras to search for her before I went to wake you but was unsuccessful."

"Damn, I wonder where she is." I nodded at the history books. "Find anything interesting?"

"Yes." He flicked through the last few pages of one and turned to us. "Nearly everything Vokan told us about his history is a lie."

CHAPTER 13

"Why am I not surprised?" Elyssa said. "Dish."

Cinder stared at her. "Is that an idiom?"

"Yes, it means tell us what you found."

"Ah." Cinder looked behind us. "Hello, Harry."

A bleary-eyed Shelton stood in the doorway. "What in the Sam Hill is going on in here?"

"Better go get Adam first," I said. "Cinder hit the jackpot."

Shelton grunted and vanished. A fist pounding on a door echoed down the hallway. "Open the damned door, Nosti!"

A few minutes later, an exhausted looking Adam joined the party.

Adam yawned and rubbed red eyes. "You hit the hackpot?"

"Jackpot," Elyssa corrected.

Shelton snorted. "Nice play on words, nerd."

Elyssa sighed. "Just tell us what you found, Cinder."

Cinder told Shelton and Adam about the security system.

"Whoo!" Shelton clapped his hands and spun in a circle. "You struck gold!"

"Indeed." Cinder switched through several cameras and stopped on Vokan slouched in a chair, drinking wine from an oversized goblet. "It appears Vokan was unable to operate the ship."

"Dude, this is awesome." Adam looked at the camera menu. "I wonder how much more there is to this system."

"A great deal more, I imagine." Cinder told them about the library and the history he'd uncovered. "Though Utopia and Eden evolved similarly, religion never took root here. Magic and science formed a symbiotic, instead of adversarial, relationship. Many of the mythical creatures described in Eden lore exist here but not in our realm."

"Interesting," Adam said. "Sounds like a better society already."

"It was superior in many ways," Cinder said. "Three councils governed most of the realm: A Magus Council, a Citizen Council, and the Science Council. One random magus, scientist and ordinary citizen were randomly selected each year to serve from the five cities."

"So five people on each council," Adam said.

"Yes. This prevented ties, and political maneuvering was frowned upon."

"Wow, that's kind of cool," I said. "But what about vampires, lycans, Daemos, and all the other magic-based factions?"

"They do not exist here." Cinder shrugged as if apologizing. "Vampires were created by Daelissa's attempts to make slaves when she wished to rule Eden. Daemos were created by Baal to fight the original Seraphim war on Eden. The lycans and felycans evolved naturally in Eden, but not here."

"Interesting." With all our similarities, our cultures seemed very different. "But they have other mythical beasts we don't?"

"It would seem so." Cinder nodded. "I did not study the specifics since it would not help us escape."

Adam grunted. "I'm surprised they aren't way more advanced than us without religion hindering them."

"That is because Eden mirrored Utopia." Cinder tried to look apologetic and failed. "Utopia magic and technology were centuries ahead. Utopian observers traveled regularly back and forth to Eden. They directly influenced our progression at times, and even tried to quash religion."

"Too bad they failed," Elyssa said. "I guess that explains why our technology is so similar to theirs."

"Yeah, except now we're way ahead." Shelton looked with disgust at the room. "Looks like the Utopian apocalypse struck them when polyester and shag carpet were still in fashion."

"Accurately stated, Harry." Cinder managed a somber expression. "Even our calendar was derived from Utopia."

"So our dates match?" I said.

"The last date a newspaper was published without propaganda was Triptan the eighth in the year three thousand seventy-two." Cinder wrote the date on a holographic screen. "Triptan is the third month."

"Holy smokes." Shelton slapped his face as if to wake up. "It really was the seventies even in another realm."

"Yeah, the three-thousand seventies." Adam whistled. "It's amazing how much that decade in Eden resembled this one."

"Explains all those wacky road signs too," Shelton said. "They used icons instead of text for just about everything, though with only five cities, I don't think language would be a problem."

"All five cities are on this continent," Cinder said. "They all share the same language. I did not research why they prefer icons to text-based signage as it seemed irrelevant."

"What's the geography like?" Adam asked.

"Ah, another fascinating point." Cinder projected a slowly rotating globe from his arcphone. The largest continent, Utopia, stretched from pole to pole. A narrow isthmus connected it to the arctic. Further south the landmass bulged outward, growing wider until just above the equator where it narrowed and skewed diagonally. A long chain of islands reached all the way to a small mass resembling Antarctica.

A circular continent labeled Anatopia dominated the other side of the globe both north and south of the equator but stopped thousands of miles from touching either pole. Where Utopia had five major cities, Anatopia had only one on the east coast.

Utopia's city of Hevia sat to the far north and Camelyn to the south, but still well above the equator. Ganalon occupied the west coast and Boranon the east. Solan sat nearly dead center. Despite all the elbow room on the continent, the cities looked no further apart than the span of the United States. A long range of mountains separated Camelyn from the north, and large lakes nearly the size of inland seas ate up swaths of land in the west. There was literally nothing in between—no towns, villages, or listed settlements of any kind, just nature unin- terrupted.

"Utopia and Anatopia are both continents and nations," Cinder said.

I tried to make sense of the map. "Why so few cities on such a large continent?"

"An interesting question," Cinder said. "The last census claims under two hundred thousand citizens in all of Utopia. Average lifespan is just over two hundred years, and the last war was several thousand years ago. With such long lifespans, procreation is probably not a priority."

"Explains why Vokan is so old," Shelton said. "What's the deal with Anatopia?"

Cinder rotated to the other landmass. "I found very little in the way of documentation about Anatopia, except that the last great war was between it and Utopia, and humans are not the dominant or ruling species there."

"Wow." Adam spun the globe back to Anatopia. "Who rules it then?"

"Unknown," Cinder said. "The war apparently started because Utopia wished to establish formal relations, but Anatopia regarded it as an act of human aggression."

"Color me intrigued." Adam peered at the globe. "I'd love to dig into some history texts."

"Fascinating as all this is, it doesn't do squat to get us out of this mess." Shelton slumped onto the plaid couch. "Maybe we should concentrate on that instead of history lessons."

"Shelton's right," I said. "But we need to know who we're up against. What's Vokan's story? What weaknesses can we exploit?"

"This is where it gets quite interesting." Cinder dismissed the globe and changed it to an image of our favorite Grand Magus. "Vokan was not mentioned in any history texts. In fact, the only mention of him from his earlier years are in disciplinary records at magi school." Cinder displayed the photo of a young Vokan with long brown hair and pale blue eyes. "Vokan had no commendations on his record but over twenty reprimands. He was faulted for attempting unauthorized magic, for stealing advanced texts, and even illegal demon studies. He was eventually dismissed from school for subversion of Eden culture and forbidden from studying magic."

"Subversion?" Adam raised an eyebrow. "I thought our cousins from Utopia routinely influenced us."

"They did. Apparently, Vokan sneaked into Eden and proclaimed himself emperor of a civilization in South America." Cinder shook his head in an approximation of disappointment. "His short rule resulted in a catastrophic war which destroyed what the Utopians considered a very promising secular civilization."

Shelton grunted. "How'd he go from chump to champ?"

Cinder approximated a shrug. "There is little information except that Vokan was later caught engaging in illegal demon studies and banished from the cities for ten years."

"You've brought up illegal demon studies twice," Adam said. "What exactly does that mean?"

"Demon magic is forbidden in Utopia," Cinder said. "I do not know why."

"I think I see a big old dot to connect." Shelton grunted. "You got Vokan, a magus willing to do anything for power on the one hand, and illegal demon studies on the other. I'll bet that's how he and Baal met."

"Your logic is sound, Harry." Cinder switched to a holographic notebook and typed in the details before continuing. "Vokan appeared in Solan fifty years and one day after his banishment. Where he had been just an apprentice before, he was somehow a master of all elements even without formal training. According to the magic texts I surveyed, mastering even two elements requires decades of study and practice."

"In other words, he had outside help." Shelton pursed his lips. "Baal."

"How could Baal possibly help Vokan master elemental magic?" I asked.

"Unknown." Cinder retrieved a news story. *Dark Realm Discovered.* "During Vokan's banishment, the silver arch began to malfunction. A joint effort between scientists and magi discovered that Utopia was caught in the gravity of the Abyss, which they termed the Dark Realm. It pulled Utopia out of alignment, thus ending their abilities to traverse to Eden. Dozens were stranded in Eden, where they apparently continued to exert influence."

"Explains how Eden didn't go off the rails," Shelton said.

"Indeed." Cinder switched to a video. "When Vokan returned, he was immediately arrested and put on trial for breaking his banishment. This is the last newsreel before he took power."

In the grainy video, Vokan stood in a large meeting chamber while an unseen newscaster described the scene. "The three councils called Vokan before them today to decide his fate. His crimes were extensive and grave: practicing forbidden demon magic and subverting Eden culture. Though he was formally banished from the five cities decades ago, he has broken his oath and returned. We now go live to the scene in the Grand Chamber."

Three triangular tables occupied the front of the large chamber, arranged so one sat above the others to form a larger triangle. It looked identical to the one atop Vokan's tower, but larger. Five mages in blue robes occupied the head table. An equal number of scientists in black coats occupied the one to their left, and citizens in street clothes sat to the right. Nearly all of them were female except for one male scientist and citizen.

Judging from the dominant position of the head table, the Magus Council took precedence over the other two.

The scene could have passed for something from a low-budget science fiction movie. Polyester clothes, lamb chop sideburns, mullets, and the funky mage robes made for a sickening view to anyone with a lick of fashion sense. It was hard to believe this wasn't some old film from Eden.

"Vokan, you stand accused of violating the terms of your dismissal from magus school by studying magic and by breaking your oath to banishment." The woman didn't look angry, just very disappointed. "How do you plead?"

Vokan sneered at her. "Oh, Imogen, you always thought yourself superior to me during our schooling. Even this day your arrogance overshadows the cruel truth." He summoned the familiar spheres in his palm and laughed. "I am your superior. Should not the greatest among us hold the seat of the Grand Magus? Let us dismantle this foolish form of government and allow the powerful to rule."

"You are not my superior, scoundrel." Imogen pounded a fist on the table. "Whether your claim of mastery is truth, you acquired it illegally. The sentence for such a crime is permanent banishment from the five cities."

Vokan reared back his head and laughed. "Dearest Imogen, your seat is mine."

Imogen stood. "No, it is not." She stabbed a finger toward the door. "The people will not accept such illegitimacy." She controlled her trembling hand and sat back down. "I call a vote."

"Seconded," said a scientist.

"Thirded," said a citizen.

"Shall Vokan hereby be stripped of citizenship, banished from our lands for all eternity, cast adrift in the ocean, never to be heard from again?" Imogen glared at Vokan. "All in favor on the Magus Council, say aye."

All five voted yes. "Might does not make right," Imogen said.

The Science Council broke rank, three voting against, and two for the sentence. Their apparent leader made a statement. "We would like to study how Vokan mastered the elements without formal training."

A dissenter stood. "Power gained by illegitimate means is not worthy of scientific review."

The Citizens Council voted yes by four to one. "We see no value allowing one who consorts with demons to foul our fair lands." No dissenter stood to make a statement.

"Two councils for, one against. The ayes have it." Imogen pounded a fist on the table. "Vokan, you are permanently banished from Utopia. May you find peace wherever you go."

Police in blue uniforms moved toward the prisoner. Vokan's hand went to his neck. He tugged on something and brilliant light flashed. The video flickered. Distorted audio turned screams into warped shrieks. White noise filled the holographic screen.

"Holy farting fairies." Shelton's mouth hung open. "What in the hell just happened?"

"Unknown." Cinder turned off the video. "Somehow, Vokan defeated them."

"Somehow?" Shelton threw up his hands. "That's all you know?"

"I'm afraid I could find no records showing what happened after that moment." Cinder shook his head. "Either nothing was recorded, or Vokan destroyed the evidence."

"What year was it in Eden when this happened?" Adam asked Cinder.

"The silver arch became impassible in the late seventeen-hundreds in Eden, so this video occurred in the early eighteen-hundreds."

"Damn. They had seventies tech when we were still in industrial diapers," Shelton said. "Just how old is Vokan?"

Cinder paused a moment. "Perhaps over four hundred years old in the regular time flow."

"Put that video up again," Elyssa said. "Go to the last minute." Cinder did as asked, and Elyssa zoomed in on Vokan's face. "His eyes aren't glowing."

I grunted. "I thought he said mastering the elements did that."

"Then why ain't they glowing?" Shelton said. "Another lie."

Elyssa went frame-by-frame to the point Vokan reached into his robes.

"I have a feeling that whatever is on the end of that chain isn't good for our health."

"Was there any mention of the Fallen in any records?" Adam asked. "If they really brought a relic here, it seems like that would be big news."

"It occurred while Vokan was an apprentice." Cinder flicked through several images before stopping on a document. "This secret memo details the visit from three otherworldly travelers, and the importance of guarding a dangerous relic. Only the top council members at the time were privy to this information. Apparently, the Fallen gave them the history of the Apocryphan and explained that the relics must be kept as far from each other as possible. The three councils agreed to keep it a secret and stored the relic in a hidden vault."

"Wonder where that vault is," Shelton said.

Cinder displayed another memo. "According to this, it's inside the towers."

Shelton pointed a finger at the ceiling. "As in the towers above us?"

"The very same." Cinder displayed a layout of the towers. "The private council chambers are in the top of the right tower, the Grand Chamber is in the bottom, and in between are private quarters for council members and visiting members of the general public when they were in session. The left tower was designed as an elemental atrium, used by the council members to manipulate weather favorably."

"That's really cool." Adam peered at the diagrams. "That explains why the left tower is hollow."

Shelton grunted. "I take it that big column of souls wasn't part of the original design."

"No, it appears Vokan altered the atrium to suit his purposes." Cinder switched to a picture of the inside. A giant crystal filled the hollow core of the building. "This is the original design. I suspect Vokan adapted the crystal."

"I don't know." Elyssa frowned. "The cantrap didn't look like a crystal when I saw it."

"Just damn." Shelton blew out a breath. "Baal really got us good this time."

"You make it sound like a practical joke, Shelton." Elyssa threw up her hands. "We're flying by the seats of our pants, boys, and Baal perfectly executed a years-long con to trap us in another realm so he can have his way with Seraphina."

"Well, when you put it like that, it does sound kinda bad." Shelton sank into the plaid couch. "Guess we're royally screwed."

"We beat Baal in his first attempt at taking over Seraphina about three years ago," Adam said. "Think about it—it took him three years to come up with this trap."

"Why would he have even plotted this trap three years ago?" I said. "We didn't know the observation window was a portal lens, and had no way of opening portals to other realms."

"Son of a biscuit eater." Shelton grabbed a couch cushion and flung it across the room. "That's because the observation window wasn't a portal lens." He took out his arcphone and tapped on it furiously. "Yep, here it is."

"Here what is?" Adam looked at the screen. "Oh. You scanned the observation window nearly two years ago when we did our first big sweep of Olympus."

"Yep, and it wasn't a portal lens." Shelton burst into crazed laughter. "Baal swapped out the old window for this one but we didn't realize it until two years later when Bliss accidentally stumbles across it."

Adam shook his head. "I can't even."

"Can't even what?" Shelton said.

"I just can't!" Adam looked distraught. "I thought we were large and in charge, man. I thought we were so smart. But we've been running through Baal's maze all this time and didn't even realize it."

"So Baal's just been hanging out, waiting for us to stumble upon that window," I said. "Two whole years he waited while we exterminated drakes."

"The more I think about it, the more I think the drakes were just a ploy to keep us occupied until he was ready to lead us to the real bait," Elyssa said. "Drakes breed like rabbits, so Baal scattered a few nests around Seraphina and we spent years tracking and exterminating them."

"Then he showed us that huge dragon which made us scurry home right about the time Cinder discovered the observation window." Baal's twisted jigsaw puzzle snapped together in my mind. "He staged the theft of Argus once we discovered Utopia, then chased us through the portal."

"Ain't the first time we've been played, but it still stings every time." Shelton huffed. "Maybe he won this round, but we've got the rest of the bout ahead of us."

"Exactly." I tried to sound confident but felt broken on the inside. I was just a kid playing in a sandbox filled with cat turds, and Baal was the one who put them there. "We need to take this one step at a time. First, we get ourselves out of this bunker. We'll worry about what else Baal's got in store for us after."

Adam held up the timer on his phone. "We only have a few more hours before the Voltis alignment ends here. Somehow, we have to escape the bunker, get past Vokan, and get our ship back before time runs out."

Shelton snorted. "When you put it like that, it sounds easy."

I looked at Adam. "What's the status of the elevator hack?"

"The code is completely alien and encrypted." Adam shrugged. "My translation program is working on deciphering the code, but that's just so I can decrypt it. The first part might be done in a couple of hours, but there's no telling how long decryption will take."

"Why is their arcnology so different from ours?" I asked.

"For starters, they don't use Cyrinthian as a base language." Adam's fists clenched. "Their magic system is also very different. Add encryption on top of an alien programming language, and you've got a puzzle anyone would struggle with!"

I held up my hands. "Don't get upset. I'm just asking, not blaming."

"Well, it feels like everyone expects a miracle." Adam shoved his hands in his pockets. "I thought Cyrinthian was the universal language of magic, but apparently I was wrong and now we might be screwed." He spun and stormed toward the door.

"Adam, wait." Cinder put a hand on Adam's shoulder. "There are educational texts with their programming language. Perhaps your arcphone can collate enough data to give you a working knowledge of the system."

Adam nodded somberly. "Yeah, maybe it'll help." He gazed forlornly toward the hallway. "I'll take anything at this point."

The weight of our despair was crushing. For the first time in a while, I didn't think we were going to win.

Elyssa took my hand. "I wonder if that security console Cinder found has controls to open the elevator. Maybe there's more to it."

I perked up a little. "Yeah, that's true. Vokan wouldn't want his enemies having control of the elevator if he was in here."

Elyssa turned to Cinder. "Send anything you can find on programming from the library to help Adam and Shelton. Then I want you to spend every waking moment on that computer console. Find out if there are commands for the elevator." She paused for a moment. "Please."

"I am on it, boss," Cinder said in a deadpan tone.

We shared a laugh, and for a moment, the clouds lifted.

We can do this! It was hard to believe at that moment, but I was determined to fake it and make it.

Moments later, Cinder dumped a load of magic programming books on the table. Adam and Shelton began importing the alien programming language into their arcphones. I picked up an elementary magic text and started reading, and Elyssa followed suit.

This felt right. I had a feeling that in no time, we'd hack ourselves right out of this place.

Naturally, that was when Bonehead walked around the corner and started shooting lasers from his eyes.

CHAPTER 14

Adam and Shelton fell like rag dolls.

"Shelton!" I shouted. Rage boiled in my veins. *That bastard killed them!*

Cinder looked down at them, his expression blank as usual. Bonehead hit him with a blast, but it didn't so much as singe his gray shirt. "Justin, I believe he is trying to stun, not kill us."

Cinder saved Bonehead from absolute destruction. Instead of hitting him with Brilliance, I encased the skeleton in Murk. "What are you doing?" I shouted.

"Escape is not permitted," Bonehead replied, his voice muffled by the shield.

Cold fingers raked my spine. "Did you tell Vokan what we're up to?"

"I cannot give you that information." The lack of air inside the shield didn't seem to stop Bonehead from speaking. Then again, he was just a skeleton.

"Doubtful," Cinder said. "I believe this television is the only means of communication since the walls block magical means."

"You're rather smart for a block of wood," Bonehead said.

"I am not wood." Cinder pinched a hand as if testing. "Golems are constructed from many different materials."

"Not important right now." I knelt next to Shelton and Adam and confirmed they had pulses. "How long will they be asleep?"

"Quite some time," Bonehead replied in a matter-of-fact voice. "I must warn you I'm under very strong compulsion to report your activities to Vokan."

"You're his slave, right?"

"Sadly, yes." The glow in his eyes turned dark blue. "Now, kindly release me so I can render you all unconscious."

"This guy is going to be an issue." Elyssa released a long sigh. "Bonehead, is there anything we can do to free you from the compulsion spell?"

"I am not allowed to discuss it," he said. "Again, I cannot resist asking you to release me so I can subdue you."

"Sorry, but not gonna happen." I lifted the shield and Bonehead with it, then deposited him in one of the bedrooms. As he pleaded for release, I wove strands of Brilliance into the Murk, converting it bit-by-bit into Stasis. As hoped, it froze him, effectively rendering him unconscious instead of us. I tied off the weave, giving it enough juice to last for the foreseeable future and brushed my hands together.

"I have to admit, that's the first time I've seen a skeleton shooting lasers out of its skull," Elyssa said. "Really shook me up at first."

"You and me both." I tried to wake Shelton with a gentle slap, but he kept snoring. Elyssa poured water on Adam's face, but he didn't even stir.

"They're down for the count." Elyssa groaned. "Right when we need them the most."

"Well, I guess I should get them off the floor." I grabbed Shelton and Adam and piled them into the same bed.

"That's a rookie move." Elyssa rolled her eyes. "You should put them in a spooning position."

I burst into laughter. "And that's why I love you." I put them on their sides and made Adam the spoon. It looked hilarious, but it was hard to enjoy the moment. Our hackers were down and out, and we were up the creek without a paddle.

We went back into the family room where Cinder tinkered with the bunker menu. "Any luck?" I asked.

He shook his head. "Admittedly, I am unfamiliar with this sort of computer system. It doesn't use arcnology as I first assumed."

I bit my lower lip. "So the system isn't even magic based?"

"Not that I can see," Cinder said. "It appears to be a very basic nom operating system." He looked up from his screen. "Should I divert my efforts to hacking the elevator?"

I pondered the question. "Which do you think has a better chance of getting us out of here?"

"The elevator button," Cinder said. "Since Vokan controls the lift with a button, I think it is unlikely he would have elevator controls built into the camera system."

"Or maybe he has all the security controls in the nom system," Elyssa said. "I think the security computer is the one we should concentrate on."

I looked at the countdown on my phone. Either option would eat up the few hours we had left, so I couldn't afford to put our only talent on the wrong task. On the one hand, hacking the elevator would definitely get us out of here, but deciphering the encryption might take days. On the other hand, the security console might have a command for unlocking the elevator that we could find relatively quickly. If it didn't, the wasted time might be the reason we missed our window to escape this realm.

I held out a hand for Cinder's phone. "Can I take a look at the operating system?"

"Of course."

I stared at the blinking green cursor on the screen. Something seemed awfully familiar about it. "Utopia shared their technology with us, so the odds are this operating system is probably similar to the ones we used in the seventies."

"A logical assumption," Cinder said. "As I stated earlier, I am not familiar with nom computer systems."

"I had to take computer classes in high school, so maybe, just maybe..." I typed in *dir* and hit enter. A list of directories and files appeared. "Bingo!"

Elyssa clapped me on the back. "Score one for the nerds."

Cinder raised an eyebrow. "How did you do that?"

"I used an abbreviation for *directory*."

"Interesting. I tried that word, but nothing happened."

I tested the full word and an error message blinked on the screen. "Strange." I typed in a forward slash and hit enter. The green cursor turned into a blinking sideways arrow. I entered *dir* again. A long list scrolled down the screen. "I think this command interface is where DOS came from."

"DOS?" Cinder tilted his head. "I am unfamiliar with that term."

"Disk operating system." I grunted. "So much for IBM and Bill Gates inventing it." I tapped a finger on the blinking arrow cursor. "DOS displays a hard drive letter and the directory, but this system just changes the cursor to an arrow when you're in the root directory. It seems really rudimentary."

"What?" Elyssa blinked a few times. "Less nerd speak, please."

"Oh, sorry. DOS is the operating system we used on old computers in Eden." I shrugged. "I'm surprised Shelton and Adam didn't recognize it."

"You didn't recognize it earlier," Elyssa said.

"It didn't even occur to me until now. All our talk about Utopia giving Eden technology helped me connect the dots." I entered a question mark on the screen and a long list of commands appeared. "This is insane. I can't believe how much tech in Eden isn't even ours."

Elyssa pointed to a file called *cmdlist*. "That looks promising."

I tried it and got an error. *File Not Found*. "Great. It's not working."

"Did you enter it right?" She studied the screen. "Try it again."

I did, but it didn't work. "I hope he didn't disable the commands."

"Why would he do that and still leave the camera commands working?"

"Or…" I tapped a finger on my chin. "Maybe the working command is in another directory. Problem is, there's hundreds of them. I don't remember how to search all directories at once."

Elyssa wrinkled her nose. "How do you know so much about something so old?"

"Because I was a big nerd in high school." I shrugged. "Before I knew about angels and demons, I thought about being a programmer. Prerequisite courses required a basic knowledge of DOS and other operating systems." I sighed. "Hard to believe I'm just a high school dropout without a diploma."

Elyssa flashed a grin. "A diploma won't help you save the world."

"True that." I finally remembered how to find specific help topics and entered *dir ?*. A list of commands scrolled down the screen. "Ah, yeah. I need to add a wildcard."

"Um, sure." Elyssa frowned. "Whatever that means."

I typed in *dir cmdlist* /s* to search all directories for that name, hit enter, and watched the magic happen. It found the file buried three levels down in a directory called *CmdFiles*. "The terminal that usually runs this operating system must have a batch file that automatically pulls up the proper menus."

Elyssa pursed her lips and nodded. "Exactly what I was thinking."

"I find this disk operating system somewhat perplexing," Cinder said. "It is quite basic compared to the magical operating systems I am familiar with."

"Oh, it's super basic and confusing." I navigated to the directory and entered the command. Six menu items appeared, but there was only one I cared about: *3. Call Elevator.*

I whooped. "Bingo!"

Elyssa kissed my cheek and hugged me. "My genius!"

"Don't celebrate too hard just yet." I hovered a finger above the corresponding number. "God, I hope this works." I entered the number and almost hit enter, when I decided to do something uncharacteristic and consider the options. "What if Vokan realizes we activated the elevator? Adam and Shelton are still knocked out. If we have to fight our way free, we can't do it with them slung over our shoulders."

Elyssa looked impressed. "Wait, are you saying you want to think this through before barging forward?"

I nodded uneasily. "Yeah. It feels weird, but what you said earlier is right."

"And that is?"

"We're flying by the seat of our pants." I shrugged. "Right now, we need planning, and you're the planner."

"True." Elyssa tapped a finger on her lower lip. "Let's see if we can wake Shelton and Adam. Then we tell them the good news and hope the elevator door opens."

I frowned. "That's the plan? I was expecting something more complex."

Elyssa shrugged. "Simple is usually better. In this case, we run for all we're worth." She paused. "Maybe we should make sure Vokan isn't hanging out near the ship when we make a run for it. Let's use the security camera to keep an eye on him while we wait for Adam and Shelton to wake up."

"An excellent idea," Cinder said. "I would also like to find Bliss. I'm worried about her."

I hated to admit it, but I'd nearly forgotten about her. "Um, yeah." I put a hand on Cinder's shoulder. "If we don't find her, we might have to leave her behind."

Something seemed to flash in Cinder's gray eyes. "You do not value her life because she is a dolem."

Oh, god, here we go again. How could I admit that it wouldn't bother me a bit to leave her behind? I felt horrible for even thinking about it, but I just didn't consider the life of a dolem even remotely close in value to Cinder's even though he was a golem. *Does that make me a horrible person?*

"It has nothing to do with that." I held out my hands helplessly. "If we have a chance to escape, we've got to take it." I showed him my phone screen with the countdown. "We're running out of time, and our allies have to be warned about Baal."

"Baal trapped us here for a reason," Elyssa said. "He must be up to something major back in Seraphina."

"Your reasoning is sound." Cinder blinked and looked away from me— an all-too-human reaction from someone who struggled to understand emotion. "I will do what is best for the group." He took his phone back from me and started perusing camera feeds.

Elyssa took my arm and led me into the hallway. "Are you really okay leaving Bliss behind?"

"It wouldn't break my heart," I said.

"Because you don't know her well, or because of what she is?"

"Maybe both? I don't know." I groaned and ran a hand down my face. "Look, I don't want to leave her behind. I just won't sacrifice getting out of here—the greater good, I might add—to risk being stuck here for two months while Baal has his way with Seraphina."

"Your mother has an army to fight Baal." Elyssa pointed toward the family room. "What if Shelton was the one missing? Or Adam? Would you sacrifice them for the greater good?"

I didn't like her logic, so I deflected. "Do *you* think it's worth sacrificing the mission for Bliss?"

"I'm not judging, Justin." Elyssa's gaze softened. "I know you better than anyone. You've done selfless things for complete strangers, but you're ready to leave Bliss behind and I don't think it bothers you a bit." Her forehead pinched. "That's just not like you."

I took a long breath so I could ponder my feelings. It wasn't hard to identify why I didn't care. "I loved Nightliss." Just saying it brought tears to my eyes. "I miss her every single day."

A tear sparkled in Elyssa's eye. She wiped it away. Nodded. "Me too."

"She sacrificed herself to save thousands." My sadness turned to anger. "Then Victus used a beautiful soul to build evil things. Dolems like Bliss."

"Bliss can't help how she was made, Justin." Elyssa blinked, and another tear rolled down her fair cheek. "I remember a guy who made me believe that it didn't matter what you were, but what you did that counted. He united enemies and made them friends, because what counts is right here." She pressed a hand to my heart.

I swallowed the lump in my throat. "I had a lot of help."

"Yes, you did." Elyssa wiped her cheeks. "Victus had a hand in making Bliss, but remember that even if she's made of demon flesh, she still carries a part of Nightliss in her."

"I don't know if that's enough to ever make her anything more than a cheap copy."

"Maybe not." She took my hand. "I just don't want you to regret leaving someone behind. I think Seraphina can survive a few months without us. I'm not so sure Bliss can."

"Look, I'll probably never come to terms with my feelings about dolems." I bit my lip and looked down. "But you're right. Bliss is part of the team. We should do whatever we can to bring her back with us."

I just hoped it wouldn't cost us dearly.

CHAPTER 15

"Justin, you son of a bitch!" Shelton stormed into the family room about an hour after I'd put him to bed.

Adam's laughter echoed down the hallway. "Aw, come on, buddy. I thought you liked being spooned."

"By my hot wife!" Shelton glowered at me. "We're trapped in a bunker by a madman, time ticking away, and Justin decides to play games."

"You're the one playing games." Adam put his hands on Shelton's shoulders. "With my heart."

Elyssa burst into laughter and leaned against the plaid couch for support. "Well, at least we have good news for you lovebirds."

I grinned. "Yep, we found a command to open the elevator!"

"Woot!" Adam pumped a fist.

Shelton grunted. "I still don't forgive you for that joke."

"I also have good news." Cinder drew our attention to the television. "I found Bliss."

I looked up from the history books I'd been reading. Bliss sat on a bed in a large bedroom, eyes gazing forlornly at the floor. Orange flowers seemed to be the motif. Everything from the wallpaper to the curtains to the bedspread boasted the unearthly bloom, while the shag carpet viciously fought back with eye-bleeding red.

Shelton sucked in a breath. "Holy shit, that place looks like hell."

Adam grimaced. "The interior decorator needs to be beaten with a wooden spatula."

"What room is that?" I asked.

"The camera is labeled ninety-one dash B twenty-two." Cinder shook his head. "I am not certain where that is."

"Probably the floor and room number," Adam said.

"I mean, we gotta hope, right?" Shelton blew out a breath. "If we have to search every floor, there's no way we'll make it back to Voltis in time."

I glanced at my phone. "Just under three hours left. Let's hope it's enough."

I nodded at the TV. "Where's Vokan?"

"Inside the ship." Cinder switched cameras. Vokan stood on the bridge, zapping the control stick. "It seems he is no closer to accessing the controls."

"What if we activate the elevator and there's an alarm?" Shelton said. "Do we still search for Bliss?"

"Yeah." I didn't want to belabor the point in case Shelton disagreed, so I immediately turned to Cinder. "Pull up the menu and let's do this."

Cinder held my gaze for a moment. "Thank you, Justin."

I looked away. "She's part of the team."

"She wants nothing more than to be helpful." Cinder turned to the menu.

154

Elyssa flashed across the room and through the door. She grunted, and it sounded like she'd rammed into a Jenga tower.

"Let me go. I must stop you from escaping."

"Not this time, bitch!"

I ran into the hallway and found Elyssa wrapping a puke green curtain around Bonehead's skull. She grabbed another curtain and bundled him up like a skeleton burrito in a spinach tortilla.

I grimaced. "I forgot about him."

Bonehead struggled. "Please do not make me angry. You won't like me when I'm angry." Despite his bony frame, the curtains began to tear.

"Need something stouter," Shelton said.

"Hold him still for a moment." Elyssa dashed away, leaving me to bind Bonehead with Murk. She returned with her satchel and took out a pair of sleeper cuffs. "I hope these work on him." She zipped them tight around the skeletal arms and Bonehead went limp.

"That would've been swell if he'd knocked us out again." Shelton took off his wide-brimmed hat and ran a hand through his hair.

"I feel sorry for him," Elyssa said. "Vokan stuffed him in a skeleton and made him a slave."

I looked down at our skeletal attacker and actually felt worse for him than I did for Bliss. *Man, I am messed up.* "Well, since we're saving Bliss, why don't we take Bonehead with us too?"

"Normally I'd call you crazy, but it would really piss off Vokan to break out and save this guy." Shelton chuckled. "Man, I'd love to kick Vokan in his elemental nuts right now."

"He's not heavy." Adam hefted Bonehead with ease. "Let's blow this joint."

We went back into the family room. Cinder looked from me to the

Bonehead curtain burrito but didn't remark on it. He held out his phone with the command menu already up. "Are you ready?"

I typed in the number three. "Pray this works." I hit enter. Nothing happened.

Shelton whooped from the hallway. "The elevator light came on!"

I dashed through the doorway and clapped my hands at the glorious sight. "Let's pray Vokan doesn't find out about it."

We huddled before the elevator, all eyes glued to the door with anticipation. Every second felt like an eternity, but the elevator wasn't in any hurry to get here. It took nearly two minutes before it dinged and the doors slid open, disco music thumping from the crappy speakers. I half-expected to find Vokan glowering on the other side. But it was empty.

I hadn't paid much attention to the buttons before, but I did now. Four columns of numbers went from one to one hundred and thirteen. The row below that offered four buttons labeled SL, A, S, and B.

"SL must mean sublevel," Adam said. "The others are for buildings A and B with the safe room in the middle."

"Building B is the one with Bliss," Cinder said. "The room designation makes more sense with this information."

"Our ship is docked at the top of the other tower." Shelton stroked his chin. "If Vokan is still there, we might have to fight our way across the bridge."

Elyssa hit button B. "Let's go. We don't know if a silent alarm went off."

The doors slid shut, but the elevator didn't move.

Adam nudged Cinder. "What floor is Bliss on?"

"Ninety-one," the golem replied.

Adam hit the corresponding number and the levitator jolted sideways. He gave Elyssa a shrug. "Guess you need the building and number."

The levitator slowed to a stop, then shot upward so fast, Shelton stumbled into Adam.

"Sorry, not in the mood right now, Harry." Adam smirked.

Shelton growled and shot him a few eye daggers. "You're never gonna let me live this down, are you?"

Adam snorted. "Nope."

I resisted the urge to fan the flames and got down to business. "I recommend everyone wait outside the levitator while Elyssa and I fetch Bliss." I held up a thumb. "Got it?"

"I would like to come," Cinder said.

"I'd prefer you guard our backs." I pointed in the general direction of the other building. "If Vokan knows we're on the move, he might try to get the jump on us."

Cinder nodded. "Very well." The levitator stopped, and the doors slid open. "Good luck."

I stepped into the hallway and found room twenty-two staring us in the face. "Huh?" I tested the door knob, and it clicked open. "It can't be this easy."

"Yeah, normally everything is hard as hell." Shelton stood in the hallway. "Well, is she in there?"

I opened the door and found Bliss asleep on the bed. I walked up to her and shook her. She screamed and leapt to the opposite side. Eyes blinking with confusion, she seemed to realize it was me. "Justin?"

"Yup." I motioned toward the door. "Want to get out of here?"

"Where have you been? I looked everywhere."

"Trapped in an underground bunker." I sighed. "It took us a while to spring ourselves."

"I couldn't figure out what Vokan did with you, but I knew when he

157

came back to the ship by himself that he must have done something." Bliss shuddered. "It was awful not knowing."

Seeing her distressed reminded me that despite her demon flesh and golem spark, she felt emotion. If we'd abandoned her here, it would have absolutely broken her. A little bit of ice around my heart thawed, but I wasn't quite to the point of getting over my Nightliss issues.

"Let's go. We have to get to the ship."

She nodded and followed me out of the room.

"Man, that was too easy." Shelton looked up and down the hallway. "I keep expecting something terrible to happen to make up for this convenience."

Bliss embraced Cinder and kissed his cheek. "I'm so glad you're okay."

Elyssa and I exchanged surprised looks.

"I am happy to see you, Bliss." Cinder awkwardly patted her shoulder. "What happened after we left?"

Elyssa hit the levitator button and the doors opened. "Tell us on the way."

We piled inside and Bliss gave us a brief account. "I stayed in the ship a little while after you left, then I went inside the building after you and saw that it was hollow except for the column of electricity." She shrugged. "I went back outside and across the bridge to the other building and looked around while I waited on you to return. When you didn't, I started looking everywhere, but there are so many rooms."

The levitator stopped, and the doors opened to a huge chamber of marble and ornately carved wood like the one in the other building. As with the other chamber, three triangular tables sat near each other—probably where the three councils used to meet. Wide windows granted a panoramic view of the city.

I briefly wondered why they needed two of them but returned to the matter at hand.

I shushed everyone and peered through one of the windows. I couldn't tell if Vokan still stood on the bridge of the ship. I crouched so the outer wall would shield me from the window and crept to the arched doorway leading to the sky bridge.

The sun glared off the ship, making it impossible to see inside.

"I can't see a thing," Elyssa said. "Maybe we should take the levitator back down and around to the other building."

"I don't want to take a chance of Vokan trapping us in that thing with the ship so close." I balled a fist. "Besides, I can probably take whatever he throws at us."

"I don't think his magic is like the Arcanes from Eden, Justin." Elyssa put a hand on my arm. "Let's think this through a little."

"Probably a good idea." I peered out at the sky bridge. "If we stay low, the sides of the bridge will keep us hidden until we're almost to the other side." I tried to gauge the distance, but it was pretty far. Over a hundred yards at least. "If Vokan is there, I'll distract him while you power on the ship. I'll disable him if I can, then jump on the ship. We'll fly over here and pick up the others."

"Sounds like a plan." Elyssa unfolded her light bow. "I'll watch your back."

The others crouch-walked to our position, Adam awkwardly holding Bonehead under one arm. "What's the plan?" Shelton asked.

I told him.

"Man, I'd really like to punch that smug asshole in the face." Shelton pressed his lips into a thin line. "Guess it'll have to wait."

"Yeah, until never," Adam said. "I don't plan on coming back here."

"Not even to learn more about their magic?" Shelton grunted. "I think it'd be worth it just to figure out some of that elemental stuff."

"We're going," I told the others. "Wish us luck."

Elyssa and I ducked and crept across the bridge. When we reached the other side, I peeked around the wall and got a clear view of the bridge of the ship. It was empty.

"We're in the clear."

"Wow, two easy missions in a row." Elyssa made a thoughtful noise. "I guess the universe felt sorry for us."

"Impossible!" Vokan stepped onto the terrace a few feet from us, elemental orbs dancing around his torso. "How did you escape?"

Damn it universe, couldn't you have given us one more easy out?

Elyssa darted for the ship. Vokan fired a bolt of lightning at her, but it splashed off the shield I channeled to give her safe passage.

He turned to me. "You have no elements and yet you have magic." Vokan raised an eyebrow. "Baal warned me about you, but I have never faced my equal."

"Yeah, well, let us go, or you'll face your superior."

Vokan scoffed. "Doubtful. Arcanes are pitiful compared to even the weakest of the magi."

"Just so happens, I'm not an Arcane." I channeled a sizzling orb of Brilliance. "I'm an angel, bitch."

"I have never heard of an angel bitch, but I am eager to test you in a duel." Energy arced between the elemental orbs. "Face me, boy."

"Maybe later." I threw up a shield and ran for the ship.

A gust of wind caught me and slammed me into my own shield. I staggered back just in time for another gust to sweep my feet from beneath me and toss me toward the edge of the building. I cast another barrier to keep me from falling over the edge and smacked into it.

"You are but a fly in a storm," Vokan said. "Soon to have its wings plucked."

I threw up barriers to either side of me and the wind abated. I made a mad dash for the ship, but the wind funneled between my shields and swept my feet out from under me. I channeled a rope of energy and snagged the arched doorway. Wind howled past my ears, tossing me up and down as I held on for dear life.

"Go!" I shouted to Elyssa. "Get the others!"

Vokan spun toward the ship and lightning speared from a dark cloud overhead. Hail the size of watermelons slammed into the vessel with little effect.

"That thing was made to withstand Voltis!" I tried to stand, but the wind tore at my feet. "You won't put a scratch on it!"

It didn't stop him from trying. The *Raptor* pulled away from the roof and jetted over to building B where Shelton and the others waited. The clouds and hail followed. Bliss channeled a shield to protect the others. Adam ran aboard with Bonehead. Shelton, Cinder, and Bliss made it to safety.

The *Raptor* spun toward me.

Vokan snarled and returned his full attention to the fly. "You will not leave here alive." Lightning danced along the rooftop. Thunder rumbled, and the smell of ozone tickled my nose. I couldn't run because of the wind. I couldn't remain, or I'd be roasted like a chicken. So I did the only thing I could.

I let go.

The wind flung me like a rag doll out over the edge. Out into the void.

I fell.

CHAPTER 16

I 'd hoped Elyssa could catch me with the ship, but I reached terminal velocity in about two seconds. The *Raptor* was nowhere to be seen. I concentrated on my back. Felt the itch between my shoulder blades. Red-hot pain sliced through my skin. I screamed. An ultraviolet wing blazed from my left, a white one from my right. I spread my wings and caught air.

"Yes!" I pumped a fist.

A gust of wind spun me sideways and I smacked into the side of the building. Stunned, I barely had an instant to channel a rope of Murk to secure me to the building before I became acquainted with gravity again.

My comm badge crackled. "Justin, where are you?"

I cleared my head. "I fell off the building. I'm on the other side."

I heard a roar and looked up. Claws of energy raked the sky.

"Can't get through!" Elyssa shouted. "There's a lightning shield blocking us."

"Loop around the side!" I said.

The entire sky lit up. Two giant hands made of pure energy grasped at something. I saw the *Raptor* darting around the side of the building. One of the hands grabbed it and held it in place.

"How freaking powerful is Vokan?" I could barely make out Elyssa's determined face through the bridge windows, but the ship struggled in the grasp of the giant hand. I waved her off. "Just leave me! Get back to Seraphina!"

"No, Justin, I won't leave you behind!"

More energy hands moved in from all sides. Despite the *Raptor's* excellent design, it wouldn't last against all that.

"Dammit, Elyssa, just go." I waved furiously with my free hand. "Go before Vokan catches you!"

Bliss cast Stasis at the energy hand and it lost its grip. The *Raptor* dodged between the other hands and sped away. Another gust of wind slammed me into the building. Dust and debris swirled around me. The comm badge fell off my shirt and vanished.

"No!" Vokan shouted. "No!"

I imagined him howling at the skies in rage. I felt like doing the same thing myself. I was stuck in a strange realm with a raging madman and I'd lost my only means of communication. Elyssa and the others had gotten away, but I was still in trouble. Thankfully, the wind died down and the crazy weather subsided. I wasn't the best at flying, but I could glide, and it would be a lot faster than climbing my way down.

"You!"

I looked up and saw Vokan about fifty stories above, lips peeled back in a snarl.

"Yep. Me!" I shoved off the side of the building, rolled and spread my wings. I wished I could fly faster, but despite all the practice in the world, I'd never gotten as good as Arturo and the archangels.

The middle of my back tingled, as if I was being targeted. I held out a hand and thrust myself sideways with a burst of Brilliance just as one of those big energy hands came for me.

"Son of a bitch!" I folded my wings and aimed for the ground. Another swipe missed me. I unfurled my wings at the last possible instant and made a running landing. By now I was hundreds of yards from Vokan's building, but the giant hand in the sky still came for me.

How in the hell can he cast magic from that far away? I sprinted away at top speed, dodging between stopped cars, cutting through alleys, and slipping down side streets. When I stopped to catch my breath, I didn't see the hand anywhere and the twin skyscrapers of doom were about a mile away.

The streets were deserted, the chirp of birds and hum of insects the only signs of life. I didn't let that fool me, though. Those eidolons were probably prowling the streets. I stared at the distant horizon and bit back the bitter taste of defeat. It seemed ironic that I was the one left behind while Bliss got to go back.

I tapped my comm badge to let Elyssa know I was coming one way or the other, but of course it wasn't on my shirt anymore. I tried my phone and got a no signal error just like earlier. Somehow I had to reach the alignment zone before she and the others left.

Two months. It was going to be a long wait if I didn't hurry.

The countdown on my phone showed twenty minutes left. If I ran straight down the street between the skyscrapers and back to the neighborhood, I might be able to make it by the deadline. But jagged bolts of lightning still webbed the area around the buildings, and it didn't look safe to traverse.

That left me with only one alternative.

I sprinted two blocks over and cut a hard left at the next intersection. The four-lane road ran straight through the heart of the city and in the direction I needed to go. I'd gone barely ten feet when a shriek jerked my attention up and to my left. An eidolon leapt from a two-story building, hands spread, claws of electricity crackling from its fingers.

A quick dive and roll saved me from getting pounced. Another eidolon, this one built like a brick shithouse on steroids, pounded around the corner. It slammed a shoulder into a car and sent it spinning across the street. Behind it came a horde.

"Where in the hell did you come from?"

The pouncing eidolon growled, crawling like an animal on all fours. Electricity crackled from its fingers, claws of pure energy. I knew what would happen if that thing got close—if any of them touched me. I'd be a deer in the headlights. Dead meat.

I kept a wary eye on the pouncing eidolon and backed away. Not a chance in hell I could make it past the horde. I dashed to my right, down a perpendicular street, but monsters clogged the next road. I reversed course and went several blocks down, but eidolons burst from buildings, leapt from rooftops, and just generally made a nuisance of themselves.

"This is bad." I looked for a way out of the rapidly closing tide of soul-sucking death. "Really bad."

Another pouncer leapt from a building. I channeled a king-sized bat of Murk and hit a homerun. Its shrieks faded with distance. More of the king-sized eidolons slammed through the mass of their relatively normal kin.

Apparently, there were categories to these freaks. *What do I call the big ones? Ramalons? Big boys?* My bowels were ready to abandon ship, but here I was coming up with names. *The big ones are rammers, and the normal ones are stalkers.* I was pretty damned proud of myself for coming up with names under pressure.

Unfortunately, no one would ever hear these awesome names because I had nowhere to run. Eidolons charged from all directions. The only way to go was up, except I still couldn't fly.

I did the next best thing and fired a web of Murk at the top of a square brick building. It latched on and I willed the strand to shorten in a fraction of an instant, flinging me up like a slingshot. I landed on the roof and looked around. The birds-eye view froze my heart.

Hundreds of glowing eyes regarded me with the hunger of a million suns. Pouncers swarmed nearby rooftops. Rammers slammed against the building I stood on. There were enough of them that I reckoned they could bring down the entire structure given enough time.

"Ain't nobody got time for that." I set my sights on the direction I needed to go and gritted my teeth. "You can do this. Just concentrate."

I highlighted the course in my mind. Most of the buildings were just tall enough for what I had in mind. I got a running start and fired off a Murk web at the building across the street while jumping at an angle. The strand caught. I swung around the building, gathering speed. At the last second, I willed the web to snap short and flung myself high into the air. Just high enough and far enough to hit the next building with another web.

Wind whistled in my ears until it felt as if I was swinging at a hundred miles an hour. I flung myself up again. Fired another web. Swung.

"Whoo-hoo!" It was a dream come true. I never could have gotten away with this in Eden—at least not without revealing magic to the noms.

I sailed over the heads of the eidolon horde and kept on swinging. I ran out of buildings tall enough to keep me going and opened my wings to glide. By now, most of the eidolons were well behind me, but I spotted bodies lying in the street. I angled my wings back as the street rushed to meet me and came in for a mostly smooth landing near one of the still forms.

A woman lay in the fetal position, eyes staring blindly, smoke rising from her ears, nose, and mouth. "What in the hell happened to you?" It looked like one of the eidolons had run out of juice and keeled over. I spotted another body with identical symptoms.

I didn't have time to inspect them further. The silver towers loomed behind me and clear streets waited ahead. I broke into a dead run straight toward the neighborhood where I prayed Elyssa waited until the last minute before leaving. I glanced at my phone and all the hope drained out of me.

3

2

1

0

I was out of time.

"No!" I raised a fist to the heavens. "I am so screwed."

I remembered what Adam told us when he set the timers. *This won't be entirely accurate. I might be five minutes off, or even an hour.* "Maybe Voltis is still aligned." This tiny spark of hope reignited my drive. I sprinted forward again, racing around a building.

Dozens of eidolons blocked my path, glowing swords humming in their grips. I skidded to a stop and backed away. The creatures looked back at me with normal eyes.

"Wait, are you eidolons?"

A young woman stepped forward. "Who are you, and why were you in Vokan's tower?" She brandished her laser sword threateningly.

Another time I would've pelted them with a million questions, but I couldn't waste another second. "Look, people, I've got a boat to catch." I channeled a shield. "So get out of my way and no one gets hurt."

"Capture him," the woman ordered. Her people came for me.

I hadn't let a horde of eidolons stop me and I sure as hell wasn't going to let this bunch keep me from getting back to Elyssa. I curved the shield around me and rammed through. Grunts, cries, and curses rang out as I sent people flying. I blurred forward at full speed and left them behind.

After another few minutes, I finally reached the neighborhood. Huffing and puffing, I ran to the right address—222 Dilling Street. But the *Raptor* wasn't there and neither was Voltis. *I'm trapped!*

Exhausted, I sank to my knees and tried not to cry. I half-expected Elyssa to jump from behind a tree and surprise me. "Hey, baby, I couldn't leave without you, so I made the others go ahead."

Nope.

Gone, baby, gone.

Two whole months without Elyssa. I could hardly believe it. I got up and looked around, but there wasn't much to see. On another note, I was starving, both literally and demonically. I'd burned up a lot of energy to get here, and somehow, I needed to recoup it.

The Voltis house seemed like a good place to start.

The front door wasn't locked so I waltzed inside. The inside of the house was sparkling clean—not a hint of dust or cobwebs. The fridge was fully stocked and the food looked suspiciously fresh, considering the previous homeowners had probably been turned to eidolons decades ago. The pantry yielded cans of soup and something resembling franks and beans. I took out a can and screamed when I turned around.

A porcelain clown leered at me, its hand outstretched.

"Don't kill me!"

"Would you like me to open that?" it said.

The fact that it stood only four feet tall freaked me out even more.

"W-what?"

"I am here to serve." It spoke in a calm, reassuring voice that absolutely didn't match its frightening face.

"What are you?"

"I am the sprite assigned to this home," it said. "Are you okay?"

"You're a freaking clown!" I shouted.

"I can assume another form if that would be more pleasing."

"For god's sake, please." I shuddered. "I hate clowns."

The porcelain cracked and crunched. The clown screamed and his entire body went rigid. The pointy hat fell off. Clumps of red hair drifted to the floor. His face cracked.

I shouted in alarm and jumped back "What in the hell are you doing?"

Voice trembling in agony, the clown answered. "Changing physical forms is tremendously painful." He screamed again.

"Oh my god, I can't take it! You don't have to change!"

He fell over backward. The face turned to mush, swirling until the colors blended to beige. The clown rolled over and went still as death.

I shuddered. "Did I kill you, little fella?"

The clown's head rotated a hundred and eighty degrees. A porcelain boy with a maniacal grin stared at me.

I cried out in alarm. "Jesus, that's even worse!"

"Shall I change again?" His voice quavered with apprehension.

"No, absolutely not!" I took a breath to calm my pounding heart.

"Would you like some food?"

"Yes." I held up a can. "Is this stuff still okay to eat?"

"The magical preservation seal is not broken, so it should be fine." The porcelain boy took the can. A cabinet door opened, and a bowl drifted down. He traced a finger around the top of the can and it popped off.

"You can do magic?" I asked.

"Sprites are allowed limited magic." He dumped the frank and beans into the bowl and it drifted up to something resembling a microwave. Within a few seconds, I had a steaming bowl in front of me.

I wolfed it down. "Thank you, um, dude."

"I am Gob."

"Thanks, Gob."

He bowed. "It is my duty to serve."

"Are you a slave or something?" I asked.

Gob stared at me with his painted-on eyes. "I am not permitted to indulge in such conversations."

"Huh?" He reminded me of Bonehead. "Where do you come from?"

"I do not remember." It was creepy the way he spoke without the doll mouth moving.

"What's your natural form?" I said.

"I do not remember, but my owners once watched a documentary on sprites. Apparently, we resemble orbs of light." Gob stared at me with his unblinking eyes. "Would you like a drink?"

"Sure. Water is fine."

A floating cup fetched water from the refrigerator fountain.

"Thank you." I gulped it down. The food in my belly helped, but my demon side wanted more. Unfortunately, the only source of soul essence around here was probably those people I'd encountered earlier. The eidolons might work, but they were too dangerous to mess with. "What happened to all the people in this city?"

"I do not venture outside, so I do not know what you mean." Gob held up his tiny hands in a shrug. "I am required to be inactive when no one is here, so long as the house is maintained."

"Can you leave the house?" I asked.

"Not without the master's permission." Gob sounded sad. "Perhaps when he returns from work you can ask him."

"I don't know how to say this, but I think your master is dead."

"Dead?" Gob sounded shocked. "If my master died, I would not be bound to this physical form or this house." His porcelain head shook. "Unfortunately, I am still unable to shed it."

"Man, I thought Utopia was enlightened." I shuddered. "Sounds like a freaking nightmare if you're sprite." I waved a hand around. "Do all the houses have sprites?"

"I believe so. According to the documentary, my kind is widely used within this city."

"That sucks." I held up my hands helplessly. "If I knew how to free you, I would."

"According to the documentary, sprites are captured and processed in an enchantment facility which binds us to a physical form." Gob flexed his tiny fingers. "Sprites are capable of mimicking many forms, but the binding spell makes it quite painful."

"So the way to free you might be in an enchantment factory?" I asked.

"I do not know."

"Can I take you out of the house?"

He backed away from me, tiny hands held out defensively. "Please do not. If I leave the yard, I will be stricken with unending agony until I return."

I felt awful for poor Gob. He didn't know much about this realm and he

171

was trapped like me, though admittedly his situation sucked way more than mine.

If I wanted to survive this world for two months, I needed knowledge and help. Those people I'd encountered could probably provide useful information and maybe even protection, if they didn't kill me first. Having witnessed the eidolon horde in action, it seemed they were coordinated, probably by Vokan. That meant they could be searching for me this very moment.

Unless I found help, I wouldn't survive until Elyssa returned.

CHAPTER 17

I polished off another can of beans, then looked around the house for anything useful. The furnishing, carpets, everything looked hauntingly familiar, but there was just enough weirdness to dispel the notion this place was Eden. Magnets held pictures and kid's drawings on the pea-green fridge. Little Suzy had gotten a Q in her basic skills class and a ZZ on her sociology attenuation exam.

I had no idea what those grades meant, or what the classes were, but they were on the fridge, so it had meant something special to the people who once lived here.

The family photos looked normal—a short, thin woman with long blond hair stood next to a tall man with a thick porn 'stache and long, stringy hair. Suzy was a little girl with curly blond hair. All wore matching brown polyester shirts and corduroy pants.

Oh, the humanity!

More family portraits hung on the wall—a wedding photo, pictures of old people, children playing outside, and other people I didn't recognize. They even had pictures with dogs and cats and something that looked like a rabbit with wings.

The television looked a lot like the one from the bunker. I turned the dial, but all thirteen channels played nothing but Vokan propaganda.

I preferred the seventies shows.

It was as if this world had reached the most awful point in fashion possible, and just given up. Somehow, Eden had survived polyester pants, turtlenecks, mullets, shag carpets, and floral wallpaper. I wondered if the influencers had guided nom culture or if Eden had finally come into her own.

I didn't feel safe staying in the house. It wouldn't take much for eidolons to trap me here, and I wouldn't have the option of web-slinging my way out of the mess this time.

"Gob, I'm leaving."

The doll looked up at me with its painted-on smile. "Do you require anything for your travels?"

I felt awful leaving the enslaved sprite, but there was nothing I could do. "Maybe some water."

He fetched me a bottled water. "Earlier you said my master was dead. What happened to him?"

I realized I'd dropped a bomb without giving him the details, so I explained what I knew about the people of this city turning into eidolons.

"How ironic," Gob said. "Now they are trapped souls just like me."

"I don't understand how people can still enslave sentient beings. I thought Utopians were supposed to be better than that." I patted the top of his porcelain head. "If I can free you, I will."

Gob looked up at me. "I would appreciate that, sir."

"Justin," I said. "You can call me Justin."

"Thank you, Justin." Gob stood in the doorway and watched me leave.

When the door shut, I imagined he went to a nook somewhere to wait for someone who was never coming home. It was so sad, it made my insides hurt.

With my belly full of beans and regret, I turned toward the city. At least there were other normal humans left in this world, and maybe they could provide some answers. I set off for the place I'd last seen them. It didn't take me long to find the laser sword people. Apparently, they'd tracked me and were searching the neighborhood about a mile from the Voltis house. I waved at them from afar, hesitant to go any closer.

"Stop there," the woman from earlier said.

"You stop," I shouted back.

They didn't.

"Look, I'm a stranger in a strange land. I'm not here to hurt anyone unless they try to hurt me first." I held out my empty hands. "Can we talk without the laser swords and the threats?"

The woman scowled. She held up a hand to stop her followers and approached me alone, though her hand lingered near the sword hilt. Without the glow, I realized the sword was actually made of metal, and not pure energy as I'd thought.

I held out a hand. "I'm Justin."

She looked down at my hand and frowned. Then reached out and grasped it. "I am Ki of the Southlands, keeper of the word, defender of law, servant of Utopia."

"Well, if you put it that way, I'm Justin of the dude-bros, keeper of the pizza, defender of tacos, servant of juicy hamburgers."

Ki's eyebrows shot up. "I know nothing of pizza, tacos, or hamburgers."

"Your loss."

"Perhaps." The top of Ki's head barely reached my shoulder. A perky nose and big round eyes gave her an innocent look. But there was an intensity in her gaze that cautioned me not to underestimate her. "Why were you in Vokan's towers?"

"It's kind of a long story, but I'll give you the short version." I thought about trying to feed my demon from her aura, but stopped myself. She might have defenses against that and it would irrevocably destroy this fragile trust.

She nodded. "Proceed."

I didn't know how far back to go, so I kept it as simple as possible. "My friends and I are originally from Eden, but we've been trapped in Seraphina for years. We thought we'd found the way home, but we mistook Utopia for Eden."

Her eyes lit at the mention of Eden. "You're from our sister land?"

"Yeah." I frowned. "Have you been there?"

Ki blinked. "Of course not. The way across became blocked long ago. Continue your story."

"Oh, yeah." I tapped my chin. "So, we came here on a flying ship and parked it nearby. But we ran into those people with the glowy eyes, or eidolons, as we call them. To be safe, we came back to get the ship. We flew it to the city and saw Vokan standing outside on his towers." I told her how he'd tricked and trapped us, about our escape and how I was now stranded.

"I would not believe you, except you used strange magic on us earlier and ran at incredible speeds." Ki looked me up and down. "What manner of magus are you?"

"That's quite a can of worms."

Her lip peeled up. "What do worms have to do with this?"

"It's an expression." I sighed and launched into an explanation about my odd genealogy. "So I'm part demon spawn and part angel, but all heart."

Her eyes grew guarded. "You practice demon magic?"

"No. I'm Daemos. It's a kind of magical creature from Eden."

She nodded. "Ah, a Daemos. I have read of them."

"Utopia banned demon magic. Do you think Daemos are all bad?"

"Of course not. We banned necromancy, possession, and other harmful demon magic when we learned of it millennia ago." Ki peered into my eyes. "I will reserve judgment until I know you better."

That's refreshing. "Given that I'm a stranger in a strange land, I feel a little lost. Did Vokan really turn all the people everywhere into eidolons?"

"Not everyone." She looked toward the towers rising in the distance. "The citizens of Solan were turned nearly thirty years ago. The other cities were spared, so long as they bent the knee."

"The other four cities are still okay, then?"

"Not even remotely so." Ki's gaze grew unfocused. "The initial war took many lives. Some joined Vokan of their own free will. Vokan used demon magic on others to force them to his will. All the cities suffered, some more than others."

"What sort of elemental magic allowed Vokan to turn people into eidolons?"

Ki scoffed. "It was no ordinary magic. Vokan possessed a relic of great power to rip souls from bodies. He stores them in his cantrap in the Solan tower, leaving empty human shells for him to control."

"If they don't have souls, what's that energy glowing inside them?" I asked.

"I don't know," she said. "Our magi believe it is pure magical energy. It preserves everything physical at the instant of the soul rip, making them impossible to kill."

"When I escaped from Vokan, I saw bodies in the streets. Were those your people?"

Ki shook her head. "Those are the consumed."

I blinked a couple of times. "What does that mean?"

"Vokan draws upon the souls in the cantrap for even greater power. When he burns through a soul, the body dies." Ki shrugged. "We have observed that only a few eidolons, as you call them, die per year. We believe this is because Vokan consumes their soul force for longevity. If you saw many bodies, it means he must have used considerable power in his attempts to stop you."

I thought back to all the crazy lightning and energy hands. "Yeah, I think he did." I suddenly felt guilty. "Does that mean I caused those people to die?"

Ki's eyes narrowed. "You sound concerned."

"Yeah, I'm not a fan of bullies, and Vokan sounds like a major asshole to me." My fist clenched. "He killed people trying to catch me, and I don't like that one little bit."

"Those people are already dead, Justin." Ki tilted her head slightly, as if seeing me in a different light. "I think that release is a mercy for them."

I scowled. "Look, I'm stuck here for two months until this realm aligns with Voltis again. Maybe we can team up and kick Vokan's ass."

Her eyes flared. "You already admitted to losing a battle with Vokan and fleeing. What makes you think you could win another encounter?"

I shrugged. "Because I've faced plenty of bad guys who looked unstoppable and won." I felt sad that I didn't have Elyssa or my friends with me, but I tried not to let it show. "Also, it turns out another bad guy named Baal is backing Vokan. Anything I can do to put a crimp in his plans is fine by me."

"It seems we have a great deal to talk about." Ki looked back at her people. They stared at us expectantly. "Would you come with us?"

"Well, as long as you don't kidnap me."

She frowned. "I believe we can be allies. Come be our guest."

I wanted to trust her, but this world had really leveled up my skepticism. Unfortunately, I didn't have much of a choice. At some point, I had to tell her that I needed to feed my demon and hope they were cool with me borrowing a little soul essence. It sounded a lot like what Vokan did even though it wasn't.

Somehow, I had to explain that without anyone freaking.

I also needed to replenish my Seraphim side. While it wasn't necessary for survival, it amplified my power exponentially. Vokan had tossed me around like a plastic bag in a windy parking lot. I needed all the magical steroids I could handle if I planned on beating him.

Ki went through the ritual of assuring her compadres that I wasn't Vokan's friend and hadn't meant to be a complete asshole when I barged through them. She told me all twelve names, but I only remembered a few.

Kek was a big burly guy sporting a hipster beard and a longsword. He wore a red shirt, so I figured he'd be the first to die in a fight. Patch was a curly-haired young man with a weasel nose and a belt full of daggers. Gemma, a Viking-sized woman, towered over everyone and carried two broadswords on her back. The rest weren't as memorable, but I figured I'd learn their names eventually—just in time to forget them in two months' time.

Gemma was the only one in the group determined not to like me. Apparently, I'd bowled her over in my mad dash to escape them. "I would test him again." She looked down at me as we marched through the streets. "He is so tiny."

"Look, I had to catch up to my friends before they left me behind." I threw up my hands. "I didn't have time to ask nicely."

She scoffed. "You fear me."

"Um, can we get over the bruised ego and talk about Vokan?"

Gemma scowled. "Fight me if you wish to prove your worth."

I decided to ignore her and turned back to Ki. "What do you know about Vokan's soul-ripper relic?"

"Not much," she said. "After he defeated the Magus Council, he televised their draining." Ki shuddered. "I have watched the recordings, and they're awful."

"I can imagine."

"Oh, it was," Kek said. "I was a kid when it happened, but it's seared into my brain forever."

Murmurs of assent rose from others in the group.

"When the citizens rebelled, Vokan unleashed the soul-ripped magi. The eidolons, as you call them, claimed the soul force from those they fought."

"Do they siphon it into the relic?" I asked.

Ki shrugged. "I don't know."

"The entire inside of one tower is filled with the cantrap." The true horror of what that represented became clear in light of what Vokan told us when we first arrived. "That thing must be full to bursting with souls."

Ki grimaced. "Tens of thousands."

Kek bared his teeth and looked toward the towers. "All those trapped souls, and not a thing we can do about it."

"We'll have to do something." Gemma growled. "Before this plague marches south again."

"By plague, do you mean the eidolons?" I asked.

"Of course, you fool." Gemma spat on the ground. "Vokan controls them like puppets. He threw them against Ganalon to the north and Hevia to the east. Boranon is nothing but ash. All that remains is Camelyn."

I frowned. "That's the city Vokan claims betrayed him. Then again, he also said someone named Imogen is the one who sucked the souls out of everyone."

"Lies." Gemma spat again. I hoped it wasn't what she did every time she felt strong emotions.

"The traitor, Imogen, is a common theme in Vokan's propaganda films." Kek scoffed. "He transmits that garbage constantly to keep the other cities in line and to wear us down."

"If Vokan conquered all the cities, where did you come from?"

"Camelyn remains free." Kek puffed out his chest. "He tried to defeat us years ago, but we stopped his monsters."

Ki shook her head. "He sieged our walls for months, but the eidolons, as you call them, could not penetrate the enchantments. We feared Vokan himself would come, but instead, his forces retreated. Why, we do not know."

"How long ago was that?" I asked.

"Perhaps eight years ago." Ki looked into the distance. "We do not know if he plots against us, or if he has turned his sights elsewhere."

"Where else is there?" Gemma said. "He cannot travel to other realms."

"Well, he almost had that ability." I described Argus to them. "If he'd been successful, Vokan might have moved on to other worlds."

"And yet you escaped?" Gemma looked me up and down with a scowl. "You're a runt. How did Vokan not squash you like a fly?"

"Dudette, what's your freaking problem?" I looked up at her in disbelief. "Are you really that pissed about earlier?" I waved off the question. "You know what? It doesn't matter." I looked back at Ki. "Why are you all wandering around this city instead of safely tucked behind your walls?"

"We can never rest, so long as Vokan might attack. We keep a constant vigil so we might have advance warning." Ki waved a hand at the towers.

"The hive might awaken and come for us again. For now, Vokan seems content to let his loyalists hound us."

"Tell me more about these loyalists."

Ki folded her arms over her stomach. "They are few but lead an army of slaves."

"Seems to be a common theme around here," I said.

"The head loyalist, Askot, despises us for our freedom." Ki's face flushed. "He wishes to bring us to our knees himself. He has scorched the lands outside our walls and attacks our fishing vessels when we send them out to sea."

I stared at the silver towers. "I wonder if Vokan controls the eidolons with the relic."

"Likely." Gemma stomped a boot on a bug. "Let us destroy the relic and crush Vokan."

I scoffed. "You can't destroy a Relic of Jura."

Kek scratched his head. "Relic of what?"

"Juranthemon." I sighed. "Look, there's like a zillion years of info I need to dump on you guys to get you up to speed on the state of the realms. I can do it now, or you can take me to your leader and we can talk about it in Camelyn."

"Camelyn is a day's ride due south," Ki said. "You will have plenty of time to tell us along the way."

"Better yet, you can answer my questions about Utopia." I looked around. "Did you get here in a car?" From the grimaces and glares, I figured out that wasn't the case. "Um, horses?"

"Horses?" Patch and the others shared a laugh. "It'd take us a week to get back and forth on horseback."

I threw up my hands. "Fine. What do the citizens of Camelyn use for transportation these days? Unicorns?"

"Why would we anger unicorns by using them as steeds?" Gemma said. "The few who live here already distrust humans, thanks to the technological greed of Solan."

"Huh?" Her comment flabbergasted me. A low growl tickled my sensitive ears. I looked up and saw a dark form lurking on a nearby building. Ki and the others stopped and looked around. Shrieks echoed through the concrete jungle.

The hive had found us.

CHAPTER 18

Four pouncers jumped two people in the back of the group. Another half dozen leapt from a building to our right just as a line of rammers rushed around the corner.

"Activate armor!" Ki held up a fist. "Swords out!"

Her people touched silver bands at their throats. Armor flowed over their clothes like liquid mercury. Laser swords hummed.

Gemma and Kek tried to fight off the pouncers behind us, but the creatures dragged away their prey before we could help. Ki and the others jumped back to avoid attacks from the sides.

"We're surrounded!" Gemma said. "We should enter a building."

"And trap ourselves even more?" Ki shook her head. Her eyes locked onto something. "Their east flank is weak. We break through there." Without pausing, she raced toward a group of stalkers while the rammers ate up the ground behind us.

Just as we neared the target, a pair of female eidolons lit up from head to toe, eyes glowing like miniature suns. Their heads reared back, and hideous screams shattered the air.

"Wraiths!" Gemma shouted.

Kek skidded to a halt. "We're doomed!"

"My ears!" I couldn't stand the noise.

The wraiths blurred forward at incredible speed.

I channeled two walls of Murk and slammed them down between us and the witches. I thrust them back then scooped them apart. The eidolons piled into each other as if a bulldozer just plowed into them. The screaming only intensified, but at least we had a hole. "Run!"

We dashed through, but it wasn't over yet. More pouncers leapt from roof to roof, following us overhead. Rammers slammed through cars, racing after us. The stalker horde ran after them, slower, but still plenty fast for the mostly human group.

Normally, the eidolons wouldn't have had a chance keeping up with me, but my demon side was already starving from the earlier physical demands, so I paced the rest of the group. At least Ki and her people weren't slouches when it came to running, speeding along faster than any humans I knew.

A pouncer landed in front of Gemma. Her broadswords hummed to life. "Die, beast!" She parried strikes from the energy claws and drove her blade at the creature's face. Sparks flew. Electricity hummed and crack-led. The creature shrieked like a cat pooping out spicy Indian food. It thrashed, fell to the ground, and went still.

I channeled a war hammer of Murk and batted away another of its comrades. "Did you actually kill it?"

"No, it is only temporarily drained." Gemma short-circuited a stalker that came from the side.

"Then why did you tell it to die?"

She bared her teeth. "Because it satisfies me to do so."

A rammer thudded out of an alley and creamed another one of Ki's comrades. We were already down to eight and it hadn't even been five minutes.

"Kevin!" Patch tried to go after him, but Ki jerked him back into formation.

"It's too late!" she jabbed a finger ahead. "We're almost there."

"Almost where?" I asked. Two more rammers sprinted at us, charging us like bulls. I had a sudden inspiration. "Keep going. I got this."

"They're coming straight at us," Gemma said. "Do you mean to make us fly?"

"Quite the opposite." I flashed a grin and channeled a translucent platform of Murk on the road ahead. The instant the pounders stepped on it, I willed my makeshift levitator to shoot up about ten feet in half a second. With their forward momentum combined with the lift, they flew over us, arms and legs flailing comically. They plowed through the horde, tossing eidolons like bowling pins.

I pumped a fist. "Strike!"

"Wow!" Patch nearly tripped over his own feet. "What sort of magus are you?"

"I'm not." I channeled several smaller shields about ankle height and tied off the weaves as we ran. They formed a minefield of invisible stumbling blocks to trip up anyone in a hurry.

We dodged a roadblock of rusting cars, ran past derelict buildings, over crumbling bridges, and through a park overgrown with weeds. Grass sprouted from the roadways and sidewalks. Rust and dust covered everything. Bones of dead people and animals lay where they'd fallen long ago. An eerie feeling sat heavy in my stomach, as if I were in a post-apocalyptic version of Atlanta, and everyone I knew and loved was dead.

Utopia sat somewhere in between. The citizens weren't dead or alive. A lone man had achieved world domination. Vokan would've made

Daelissa proud. It was a glimpse at an alternate future for Eden had we not won the war. It also hinted at what lay in store if we failed to defeat Baal and Xanomiel. Billions would die, and the resulting Earth would be a wasteland, ruled by ancient gods.

One of my favorite video games used to be a zombie shooter where the player had to survive each day by scrounging for supplies and keeping the safe house maintained so zombies didn't break in. Survival horror video games were fun. In real life it sucked big time.

Solan wasn't nearly as large as Atlanta, and the neat grid layout of the streets allowed us to make good time, especially with the eidolons far behind us. It took us about twenty minutes at a jog to make it to the outskirts. Civilization seemed to end right at the last street, aside from a four-lane highway running into the distance.

I wiped sweat off my forehead and slowed to catch my breath. My inner demon clawed at my stomach, furious and starving. "Are we there yet?"

Ki nodded. "Almost." She pointed to a thick forest a few hundred yards ahead. "We just have to reach the trees."

I pushed back the demon, but it was getting harder and harder to keep him at bay. Rather than risk losing control and rampaging, I broached the awkward subject. "I, um, need to ask your permission for something a little strange."

Ki didn't bat an eyelash. "Of course."

"I gain my strength from feeding on psychic energy."

This time she batted an eyelash. "You what?"

I tried to think of the best way to phrase it. "I promise it doesn't hurt, and it won't harm anyone."

Gemma scowled. "What sorcery is this?"

"It's not sorcery." I tried to think of a better way to describe it without it sounding monstrous, and failed. "You won't even know I'm there."

Ki gave me a dubious look. "Does it involve inappropriate touching?"

I snorted. "No, absolutely not." Back in the day it certainly had, but I'd gotten a lot better at it.

"Very well." She nodded. "Proceed."

I switched to demon vision. Ghostly halos of psychic energy floated around her and the other party members. Seraphim auras generally glowed bright white or ultraviolet. Humans tended to be dimmer and yellow. The Utopians were somewhere in between. I didn't know if they were just hardier stock of humans, or more evolved. I sent a ghostly tendril to Ki and gently latched on.

Her eyes widened and her pupils dilated. "What was that?"

"It's me." I really hated asking strangers, because it was super awkward. I kept my emotions neutral to avoid arousing her and sipped on the sweet nectar my demon loved.

"It is not unpleasant." Ki looked around my head, as if expecting to see the connection. "Now I don't feel you."

It seemed she didn't have any protections against this sort of intrusion, but I felt better for having asked even though Gemma, Patch, and the others regarded me like some sort of molester.

Gemma scoffed. "You are strange."

"Yup." I started walking. The others took it as a cue to continue onward. By the time we reached the forest, I felt right as rain. With the old psychic fuel tank topped off, I felt ready to conquer the world again.

A deep rumbling noise reached my ears. I stopped and cocked my head. "There's something ahead of us."

Ki didn't seem concerned. "Yes, there is." She tapped her throat and the armor retracted to a choker band. "Armor off."

The others followed suit.

We passed through the trees to a small clearing. Giant beaked heads with pointy feline ears popped up from a pile of golden bodies. My eyes and brain seemed to disconnect, unsure what to make of this sight. One of the beasts stood and walked over to Ki. It stopped to scratch behind an ear with a feline hind leg.

White feathers ruffled in the breeze. The eagle head swiveled to me, and the creature screeched softly. Ki stroked the feline lower body, and a low purr rumbled in the beast's chest. It scratched at the ground with the forelegs of a bird, but its hind legs were those of a lion. Golden wings unfurled and stretched. A long tail lashed the air.

Words failed me. "Is—is that a bird cat?"

Kek snorted. "It's a gryphon."

"Head of an eagle, body of a lion?" I reached out tentatively and stroked the feathers, afraid it might snap off a finger with the sharp beak. It purred louder.

"We don't ride horses as they did in Eden," Patch said. "It would take us quite some time to get anywhere."

Ki looked sadly at her comrades. "Kevin, Jan, Lott, and Belvedere are gone." She raised her sword. "May they always be remembered."

The others thrust their swords straight up and shouted, "Always remember!"

I'd been in so many battles. Lost so many good people. I couldn't even begin to remember them all. As always, Nightliss haunted me. I thought of Vallaena, my father's sister who died in a battle at the Grand Nexus. The glowing eyes of a thousand ghosts I'd never known peered at me from the dark vault of death. So many had followed me to their dooms.

Ki sheathed her sword. "You look troubled, Justin."

I sighed. "I'm very sorry about your people."

189

"I knew we shouldn't have gone into the city," Gemma growled. "We lost four people." She held up her fingers. "Four!"

"I can count, soldier." Ki narrowed her eyes. "They died in the line of duty."

"To find this stranger?" Gemma spat. "Their lives weren't worth it."

Ki stiffened, and her voice went cold as ice. "Are you questioning me?" She wasn't nearly as tall as the other woman, but Gemma backed up a step, cowed.

"No, commander." She looked down. "I wasn't questioning you."

Gemma's claim sparked my curiosity. "You were looking for me?"

"We saw your ship at Vokan's tower," Ki said. "Vokan rarely leaves his towers so it was vital we investigate."

It made sense.

Ki touched a black band that circled her gryphon's neck. A saddle of dark honeycomb material spread across the golden back. Though she wasn't even tall enough to touch the top of the saddle, Ki gripped a knob on the side and lithely swung herself up. She pointed to a silver-furred gryphon. "That was Belvedere's. Take it, Justin."

I mimicked what she'd done to the circlet on its neck, and a saddle unfolded. It reminded me of Templar Nightingale armor—a commodity we no longer had back on Seraphina due to manufacturing issues. I mounted the gryphon.

Wings unfurled from the gryphon's shoulders and flapped. Wind gusted past my face. Ki's gryphon turned in a circle, but I couldn't see how she controlled it. Her mount leapt into the air. Its huge wings thrust it higher. The other gryphons took off. Mine screeched and took off after them as did the ones without riders. I gripped the saddle horn and held on for dear life as the gryphon skimmed low over the trees.

Without any direction from me, my mount joined in a neat V formation and gathered speed with every beat of giant wings. Wind blew back my hair and roared in my ears. The ground blurred past.

"Well, so much for conversation," I muttered.

"We can hear you just fine," Ki said in my ear.

I nearly jumped out of the saddle. She rode four gryphons down from me, but it sounded like she stood right next to me. "How?"

Ki patted her saddle horn. "The armor allows us to communicate. If you wish to quiet the noise of the wind, simply think about it. You may also control the gryphon in the same way."

"Really?" *Hey, gryphon, climb higher.* We rose higher. I willed it to go side-to-side and it did. "Dude, that's so cool!"

"Dude?" Gemma's grouchy voice grated in my ears.

"Why didn't you fly into town on your gryphons instead of hoofing it through eidolon-infested streets?" I asked.

"Vokan could strike us from the skies," Ki said. "You witnessed his elemental control."

"Yeah, I guess you're right." I wondered just how far the magus could reach with his powers. "Do the other cities look like Solan?"

"Solan relied on technology and eschewed magic," Ki said. "Its citizens valued their automobiles and televisions. They lost touch with the land, choosing to cover it in concrete and asphalt. Though they built roads to the other cities, cars are not as prevalent elsewhere."

"Television is everywhere, though," Patch said. "The farmers up in Ganalon loved watching their shows during the winter months before Vokan ruined everything."

"Tell me about Camelyn," I said.

"Mostly agrarian," Ki said. "With the other cities conquered by Vokan, we support ourselves with limited resources."

"Does Vokan keep eidolons in all the conquered cities?"

"No," Kek said. "The eidolons only go where Vokan goes."

"He can control them anywhere in the world?" I asked.

"We don't know," Ki said. "When his flying citadel first laid siege to Camelyn, it brought Vokan and thousands of eidolons. Perhaps he must be nearby to control them."

Another question bugged me. "How did the stalkers mutate into pouncers, wraiths, and rammers?"

"Pouncers and rammers?" Kek scratched his head. "Do you mean the jumping ones and the big ones?"

"Yeah. You had a term for the wraiths, so I assume you came up with something for the others." I didn't think it would be better than my names, but I was curious to find out.

"We called the eidolons the soulless," Kek said. "The wraiths were magi before they were turned. Before today I never saw a pouncer or rammer."

"They must be new mutations," Ki said. "Perhaps Vokan changed them with the relic."

"The eidolons are legion and they are indestructible." Patch slumped in his saddle. "No force in this world can defeat Vokan."

CHAPTER 19

I didn't like Patch's defeatist talk. "You stopped Vokan before. You can do it again."

"We didn't stop him, he stopped himself." Ki gave me one of those *you just don't understand* looks. "The eidolons, as you call them, cannot be killed."

I wanted to kick her off her gryphon. "Yes, I call them eidolons and it's a lot better than soulless. Why do you keep saying, 'as you call them' over and over again?"

"The word eidolon sounds like nonsense," Ki said. "I have never heard anything like it."

I realized the translation spell must not have an equivalent meaning in their language. "Eidolons are basically ghosts or phantoms in physical form."

Gemma spat. "Ghosts do not take physical form."

I didn't feel like engaging her negative energy and forged ahead with another question. "So you've never once managed to kill an eidolon?"

"Our enchanted blades can temporarily drain and immobilize them, but they recover." Ki shook her head solemnly. "Even then, our blades still cannot pierce their skin."

"I fought some of them earlier and couldn't even stain their clothes." It was quite a puzzle—one that I really wished Cinder and the others were here to help me with. "It's almost like they're protected by shields. Somehow, your laser swords short-circuit their energy, but it doesn't disable their defenses." I looked at the sword on Patch's back. "How do you make swords like that?"

"A blacksmith forges them, and our magi infuse them with elemental magic." Kek unsheathed a dagger. The blade glowed bright blue. "Air and heat create an electrical current that interferes with the magic protecting the eidolons." He turned off the blade and slid it back into place. "We've tried increasing the power, but it still doesn't harm them."

The eidolons reminded me uncomfortably of creatures that once plagued parts of the Overworld. Cherubs, infantile creatures black as pitch, tried to drain any who came near of their life force. Null cubes were the only thing that kept them inactive. I wondered if they might work for eidolons.

Unfortunately, I didn't exactly have a blueprint for building them. Another option might be to build a huge box made from diamond fiber since that blocked magic altogether. As with null cubes, I had no idea how to manufacture the stuff. There was, however, a bunker full of magic resistant walls that might offer clues.

"The way I see it the eidolons are connected to the cantrap. Maybe severing that connection will make them vulnerable."

Ki nodded. "Perhaps."

"The walls in Vokan's bunker are made of something that might do the trick. It absorbs magic and fires it back at you."

"The walls of Camelyn are likewise enchanted," Ki said. "The enchantment is intensive and requires weeks to infuse stone or concrete."

"We can't build a prison large enough for fifty thousand." Gemma scoffed. "Much less enchant every square inch."

I blinked. "Fifty thousand?" I hadn't even considered the scale of the eidolon problem. "What was the population of Solan?"

"Around forty-eight thousand," Ki said. "No city is allowed to exceed a population of fifty thousand. Our founders determined this to be an ideal balance between humanity and nature."

Holy crap! There's nearly fifty thousand eidolons. I had trouble imagining a solution for that many creatures. Then again, it could have been much worse. Without population controls, there might be millions of monsters. I strained my brain for a solution.

"Are there any large sports stadiums in Solan?" I asked.

"We don't share Eden's obsession with spectator sports," Kek said. "But the Solan Theatre holds twenty thousand bodies."

"What?" I drew out the word in disbelief. "What kind of movie theatre holds that many people?"

"It's not a movie theatre," Kek said. "It's for plays."

"Oh." I felt stupid. "Makes sense."

"It would be impossible to enchant a building that size," Gemma said. "Why do you even entertain such foolishness?"

"It's called brainstorming." I almost stuck out my tongue. "Sometimes if you throw around enough ideas, one will stick."

"Sticky ideas?" Ki looked perplexed. "This must be one of your idioms."

"It means if we collaborate and express ideas, no matter how crazy, we might figure out something that works." I shrugged. "It's worked in the past."

Patch pursed his lips. "You'd have to replace all the doors with concrete. Wood can't bear the anti-magic enchantment."

"Even if you treated every square inch of the building and trapped twenty thousand eidolons inside, we still have more left outside." Gemma looked like she wanted to spit again, but she didn't. "It's a useless idea."

I did my best to ignore her. "Well, it's better than doing nothing."

"Not dying for a useless plan is better than doing something," Gemma shot back.

"I am willing to entertain any ideas that might remove Vokan's yoke of oppression." Ki's eyes saddened. "Life was good until I was ten. Since then I have known nothing but fear and war."

"Do the eidolons grow any weaker with distance from Solan?" I asked.

"Not that I know of," Ki said. "They overran Ganalon hundreds of miles to the north and Hevia over a thousand miles west."

"Did they march there, or come in Vokan's flying citadel?" I asked.

"The citadel, of course." Gemma scoffed. "Why march them across land when they can fly?"

"How many can the citadel carry?"

Gemma went silent, but Kek picked up the slack. "Maybe two thousand."

"Damn, that thing must be huge." It was hard to imagine anything that flew carrying two thousand people.

"The citadel stands five stories high and sits on a flat platform about a hundred yards in diameter." Patch counted his fingers as if doing some quick math. "I suspect you could fit far more than two thousand on the platform."

"If the eidolons come, Vokan is always there," Ki said. "Perhaps he does need to be within range to control them."

"He rarely leaves Solan these days," Kek said. "Askot does most of his dirty work, keeping the populace under control."

I frowned. "Askot is the head loyalist you mentioned earlier?"

"Yes." Ki pointed to a mountain range on the horizon. "Once we reach the Falgur Mountains, we must be vigilant not to cross paths with Askot's patrols."

"Have you tried taking in refugees from the other cities?" I asked.

"We did," Ki replied. "It nearly cost us the city."

"There were loyalists and slaves among them." Gemma made a spitting noise but didn't actually spit. "They tried to open the gates and let in the eidolons."

"Who in the world would willingly work for Vokan?" I said. "The dude's a monster!"

"There are few who willingly do," Ki said. "Only the loyalists seem to relish their power."

"Fear and intimidation work on the rest." Patch sighed. "We have tried to help the other cities and it cost us dearly."

"Have you ever asked Anatopia for help?"

Ki's forehead wrinkled. "The animal kingdom has never opened diplomatic relations with us. Every emissary we send is turned back before they even reach land."

"Animal kingdom?" I imagined Simba lording it over the jackals. "Like lions and elephants?"

"Sentient beasts," Patch said. "We know little about them. Past attempts to establish relations did not go well."

"Like the war a few thousand years ago?"

"Precisely." Patch shrugged. "Most of the records were destroyed so what little information we had was lost."

A woman whose name I didn't know spoke. "It is said the humans lost.

Destroying the records and expunging all information of Anatopia was required, lest we face total destruction."

"Sounds hardcore." It sounded like Anatopia could kick Vokan's ass if they wanted to, but even if I could get there without the *Raptor*, history told me I had no chance of convincing them.

Considering the current state of affairs, it seemed Vokan didn't much care about staying in Utopia anyway. He'd struck his Faustian bargain with Baal to lure us here and steal our ship. I suspected Baal didn't really care if Vokan got out of Utopia or not. He probably just wanted to get me out of the way for a time.

Maybe Baal counted on getting Vokan and his eidolons out of Utopia so he could deploy them in Seraphina. Just the thought of turning Seraphim into eidolons sent a shock down my spine. They'd be unstoppable.

Could that be the plan?

Baal might not want Vokan controlling such a powerful army, or he might know a weakness so he could take out Vokan at any time. There were too many terrifying possibilities and not enough clues leading me to the right answers.

That diverted my train of thought back to the cantrap. *What if I could cut off Vokan from his soul battery?* The Grand Magus proved I was no match for him, but maybe that was because he had access to a hell of a lot more power than me.

Manipulating weather on a large scale took tremendous power. I'd summoned tornadoes with the help of Fjoeruss and it had been exhausting. I couldn't go toe to toe with Vokan without extra power. The only way to do that required pulling a page from Daelissa's playbook and completely draining the soul essence from humans.

But I couldn't possibly condone something so heinous. Surely there had to be another way.

Precision will always defeat brute force. Fjoeruss told me that when he helped me make my first tornado. It seemed I had no choice but to look for a sneakier way to take down Vokan so he didn't open another family-sized can of whoop-ass on me.

For starters, I didn't even have a rudimentary knowledge of elemental magic. It might be helpful to understand how Vokan controlled the weather if I wanted to search for weaknesses.

"Are any of you a magus?" I asked.

Ki answered immediately. "No. The few skilled magi we have remain safely behind the wall."

"Smart." I wished I'd brought along the magic textbooks from Vokan's library. I probably could have learned something during the long trip.

Rolling forest hills grew into small mountains and valleys. We soared over the lower peaks, headed for a pass between snow-covered mountains in the distance.

We had traveled for nearly an hour in silence when Patch broached another question. "What sort of magus are you?"

I knew I'd end up repeating myself once we got back to Camelyn, but story time might make the journey less boring. "I'm not a magus. I'm part demon spawn and part Seraphim."

"So you said earlier," Gemma said dryly.

I gave her a sardonic smirk and returned to my story. "Magic users in Eden are called Arcanes. They have a magic well where they store aether so they can cast spells."

"Yes, I've read about them," Ki said. "They must use instruments to focus their magic."

"Seraphim are different from Arcanes. They don't cast spells, they channel them without the use of wands or staffs." I described Murk, Brilliance, Stasis, and Clarity, and told them how Seraphim fed by

199

splaying their fingers. One of the riders whose name I didn't remember volunteered so I could demonstrate.

She guided her gryphon close to mine, their wings inches above and below each other's, and stretched out her hand. Her eyes glazed over when I made the connection. "It feels amazing."

Kek stared dubiously at the energy crossing from the woman's fingers and into mine. "Are you draining her?"

"Only a little," I said. "The soul repairs itself within hours."

"You are fools!" Gemma scoffed. "I would never let this boy near my soul force."

I couldn't hold my tongue any longer. "Well, you're an asshole."

Kek belted a laugh. "Do you mean the anus?"

Patch grinned. "She certainly emits foul-smelling barbs at everyone."

"Yes, the anus." I groaned. *These people don't get our best idioms!* "An asshole is someone who's obnoxious like Gemma."

A chorus of agreement went up from the other riders.

"Yes, she is rather obnoxious at times," the woman I fed from said.

"Unnecessarily rude," said another.

"Very impolite."

A man regarded Gemma with apprehension. "She means well, but her attitude is toxic."

"You people are way too polite about this." I wondered if Utopia had been founded by Canadians.

Ki nodded. "That is because we are not like Gemma."

Gemma glared at the others. "I am a warrior, not a coddler. Do you think Askot will politely ask to take your head? No, he takes what he wants!"

I shrugged. "It seems like I've been fighting nonstop for years, but I haven't let that turn me into an asshole." I didn't know these people, but I needed to earn their trust, even Gemma's, if I wanted their help, so I started my story in the painful past. "I was bullied a lot in school."

"Bullied?" Patch looked me up and down. "You don't look like someone who could be bullied."

"I didn't have this physique. I was shorter, fatter, and nerdier." Remembering my story was almost like looking back at someone who wasn't me. "Although my mother is a Seraphim and my father a Daemos, I hadn't developed any powers. It wasn't until one fateful night in the gym parking lot that things started to happen."

I didn't get far before the first barrage of questions.

"What's a Daemos?"

"Felycan? I've never heard of it."

"What in the world is a Templar?"

By the time I finished describing the Overworld, my throat was parched. Though Utopians had extensive information on normal humans in Eden, the secretive nature of the Overworld prevented them from discovering as much about the supernatural.

"It amazes me how many types of supernatural humans Eden has." Ki shook her head. "Vampires, felycans, dhampyrs—I can barely keep them all straight."

"Our nom culture celebrates the supernatural." I shrugged. "Believe it or not, books about vampires are always popular."

"I wonder how it is we never had vampires or lycans here." Kek touched his teeth, as if imagining fangs.

"Vampires were created by Seraphim as a way to reward their servants way back in the bad old days." I swallowed with difficulty since my throat was so dry. "I have no idea how lycans and felycans came to be.

Some people think shifting is an extension of Arcane abilities, but no one's ever come up with a good explanation."

Patch handed me a canteen of water. "You sound thirsty."

I gulped it down and sighed. "Thanks. I really needed that."

He opened his mouth to reply when his eyes darted to my right and behind me. I followed his gaze but only saw mountains and trees.

Patch held up a fist. "We're being shadowed."

Ki's eyes flared. "One of Vokan's patrols?"

He shook his head. "I only caught a glimpse of something."

"Let's take no chances." Ki pointed to a valley east of us. "We'll take the eastern pass. It's a longer journey, but—"

She didn't have a chance to finish. The trees below us trembled. Giant wings beat the air and black-furred monsters rose from the forest, each bearing armed riders. We were surrounded.

CHAPTER 20

"Ki Sotoro." A brawny man on creature that looked half-bat, half-panther flashed a confident grin. "Must be my lucky day."

Even though we stopped moving, the gryphons weren't bothered by gravity or physics. An occasional beat of the wings kept them hovering in place. It probably wasn't the first thing I should have noticed. Elyssa would've had a complete count of the enemy, their strengths, weaknesses, and a way out. I tore my eyes from the strange bat creatures and let the drama pull me in.

Ki unsheathed her sword. It hummed to life, glowing bright blue. "Or perhaps your unlucky day, Askot." Gemma's and the other's swords hummed to life.

So that's Askot.

Askot waved a hand around at his comrades. "Anyone who can count would see you're far outnumbered."

Ki bared her teeth. "Numbers mean little when there's no skill behind them."

Askot chuckled and snapped his fingers. Two dozen crossbows aimed for our hearts. "Who needs skill with these? Unless you're very good at dodging, I think it best you surrender."

I tuned out their banter and studied the enemy. Their black-furred steeds flew on webbed wings, as if someone tossed a bat and a panther in a blender then baked it in the oven for an hour at four hundred degrees. Their tails ended in sharp horns, and all four feet bore long, hooked claws. *What in the hell are these things? Bat gryphons? Byphons?* For the first time in a while, I had trouble coming up with a cool name.

Askot and three other riders wore dark red armor with spiffy shoulder pads. Askot's open-faced helmet bore two long horns curling up and back, while the others sported smaller, pointy nubs. I assumed it had something to do with rank and compensating for their miniscule man parts.

The bulk of the riders stared blankly at us, eyes glazed over like someone who just woke up from a drug-fueled night of nonstop partying. Their filthy gray tunics looked incapable of stopping anything stronger than the dirt all over them. They had to be the slaves Ki mentioned, and those in armor were likely the loyalists.

Their weapons looked conventional. No glowing swords, no laser crossbows, and no guns. Vokan apparently didn't want his underlings to have anything more powerful in case they got greedy for power.

Bullets or arrows—it didn't make much difference to me. I could shield myself and some of the others, but I wouldn't be able to save us all. There were eight of us and nearly thirty of them.

I processed all that within a couple of seconds. Just enough time for Ki to circle the proverbial wagons and ready her people for their last stand. "I would rather die than allow Vokan to devour my eternal soul." She stroked the fur of her gryphon as if giving it a final farewell before Askot's forces turned us to pincushions.

I wasn't quite ready to give up the ghost. I could survive. I could shield myself and run. Use a few Arcane tricks to camouflage myself and vanish into the forest. But I'd be letting a lot of good people die if I played the coward.

Sometimes when you're outnumbered and outgunned, the best thing to do is pretend you've got the biggest gun of them all. I channeled a shield just in case of twitchy trigger fingers and stood on my gryphon's back.

"Do you know who I am?" I magically amplified my voice to thunder all around us.

Askot's loyalists shouted in alarm at the sudden noise. The slaves didn't even react. When Askot realized it was me, his gaze turned steely.

They're too accustomed to magic to be frightened.

I flared my blazing wings. "I am not of this world, Askot." Brilliance formed a crackling white sword nearly ten feet in length in my right hand. "Attack my comrades and I will smite thee down!" My speech sounded awfully familiar, and then I realized I'd used it during a Kings and Castles tournament just before we assaulted a fort and were mowed down like weeds.

Kinda wish I hadn't remembered that.

Askot laughed. "Your light show doesn't scare me, boy. What are you, a fledgling magus I've never heard of?"

It was really frustrating trying to frighten people who'd grown up with magic, especially when I didn't want to actually fight them. "I'm not a magus. I'm a Seraphim, a being from another realm."

"He speaks the truth, Askot." Ki stiffened her shoulders. "Attack us at your own peril."

"No, dear, my peril lies in not attacking you." Askot sighed as if the weight of the world settled on his shoulders. "My peril is Vokan's wrath."

"You use the usurper as a shield to hide the truth, Askot." Ki summoned an angry glare. "Even before he took power, you asked to lead an army to Anatopia. You craved war and power. This is why Vokan put you in command. He knows your truth."

Gemma held up her sword. "Attack us, Askot. We will show you the meaning of futility."

For once, I kind of liked the woman.

Askot sighed and nodded at one of his armored loyalists on the bat panther next to him. "Show them true futility."

The other man raised a small brass horn to his lips and blew. A dark cloud lifted from the forest about a quarter of a mile south and came our way. "As you can see, our gepheron forces have grown."

Ki blanched. "This isn't possible."

"Oh, it's quite possible." Askot gave her another oily smile. "Now, surrender, or die."

"Death before surrender!" Gemma bared her sword.

Kek thrust his sword into the air. "Death before surrender!"

Patch and the rest of Ki's people followed their example.

Ki's face darkened. "The people have spoken, Askot. Today we die."

I calculated about ten minutes before the rest of Askot's forces reached us. As outnumbered as we were now, I'd take these odds any day over the hundred-to-one force that was about to bitch slap us out of the sky. I took aim at the asshole leader first and fired a blast of Brilliance at Askot.

His eyes grew wide as urinal drains, but he recovered quickly. His steed dropped ten feet in a split instant, easily dodging my strike. I blocked a dozen arrows with a shield and fired another blast at the nearest person holding a bow. Fear showed in his eyes, but it was as if he couldn't stop himself from reloading the crossbow even as heat struck him in the chest. He cried out once and tumbled into the forest far below.

Gemma charged, screaming like a warrior princess, slashing arrows from the air with her sword. She cut the head off a bat panther and impaled the rider of another. An arrow slammed into her right shoulder blade and bounced off the armor. She flung up her left hand. An arrow pierced it instead of her face. She didn't even cry out in pain.

"I'll boil your bones in your blood!" Gemma roared and streaked toward the guilty bowman. Like the one I'd hit, he stared death in the face with fear, but went through the motions of reloading his weapon until struck down by her blade.

Ki and the others held their own, but it wouldn't last for long. Patch gurgled and toppled off his steed, an arrow in his throat. I caught him with a strand of Murk and bound him to his gryphon.

They're just slaves!

I fired a volley of Murk spheres at the enemy, cracking and breaking as many crossbows as I could without actually killing anyone. "We've got to retreat!"

Askot was a step ahead of me. His people circled around from the other side, giving us nowhere to go.

Something glinted above. I looked up and saw a giant bird of prey streaking down at us, the sun shining gloriously at its back.

Lasers tore through armor and flesh. Panther bats screeched in pain. Askot looked like he'd soiled his pants. The *Raptor* flashed past, weapons blazing. Harry Shelton himself stood at the stern, firing spells from his staff. "Get wrecked, you bastards!"

Bliss manned the front turret. Bolts of Murk smashed into slaves, destroying weapons and knocking them unconscious.

A laser winged Askot's gepheron. Bugle boy blasted a few panicked notes and the bad guys retreated back to the bulk of their oncoming forces.

The *Raptor* pulled up even with us. I caught a glimpse of Elyssa's huge eyes through the bridge windows. I didn't have time to blow her a kiss, though. Shelton shouted at us. "Get your asses moving, people! We can't handle the shit storm coming this way."

"They're my friends," I said. "Let's go."

Ki shook her head as if clearing confusion. "Let's go, now."

Our gryphons paced the ship. Bliss looked with alarm at Patch's slumped form. "He's injured! Bring him closer."

Kek gasped as if just realizing his comrade hung on by a thread both literally and figuratively. The gryphon angled for the ship. I unbound Patch and Bliss brought him onboard. Blood pooled from the wound in his throat.

"Is he dead?" I asked.

Bliss didn't answer. She ran inside and returned with healing gems.

I abandoned formation and took my gryphon to the ship. I leapt ten feet to the deck and ran to the bridge. Elyssa released the control stick and nearly crushed my ribs with a hug. "You're alive!"

"You didn't leave me!" I kissed her lips, her cheeks. Still holding onto her, I leaned back and gave her a serious look. "Why didn't you go back to Seraphina?"

"We got into a huge argument about whether to go or not and before we made up our minds, Voltis vanished." Elyssa wiped a tear from her eye. "All I wanted to do was go back and look for you. When we got back to the city, there were hordes of eidolons racing through the streets and another one of those energy hands came for us."

"They were probably chasing me," I said.

"We saw those"—she stared at the gryphons—"creatures flying in the distance and realized people rode them. We didn't realize you were with them until an hour ago. Then we got into another argument about whether or not you were a prisoner and how to rescue you. Then those assholes on bat monsters showed up."

I chuckled. "So you guys did nothing but argue without me around to keep the peace?"

Shelton clapped my back. "You son of a bitch! I thought we'd left you for dead." He gave me a hug then abruptly backed off and acted nonchalant. "Good thing we stuck around to save your ass."

"Woot!" Adam ran onto the bridge and punched me in the shoulder. "Man, am I glad to see you. We thought you were toast."

Cinder came in behind him. "Yes, we thought for sure you had perished."

"Rumors of my death were greatly exaggerated." I finally let go of Elyssa. "The bad news is we're all trapped here for two months. The good news is we might have a place to stay." I waved a hand toward the gryphon riders. "Provided we can escape the bad guys behind us."

"Just who are these new buddies of yours?" Shelton asked.

I briefly brought them up to date on my adventures and the state of affairs in Utopia. "Camelyn is the last bastion of free humanity. Vokan controls the other three cities with eidolons and that army of flying bat panthers."

"Man, those gryphons sure are magnificent." Adam gazed longingly at them. "Can you imagine what other mythical beasts live in this realm?"

"More than you know." I went onto the deck and knelt next to Patch. His bleeding had stopped. Thankfully, his breathing had not.

He looked up at me and smiled weakly. "You saved me with that web thing of yours. Thanks."

I patted his arm. "No problem." I got up and waved at Ki. She steered her steed closer. "How far to Camelyn?"

"It should be five hundred miles, but Askot's forces block our primary route through Morgan's Pass." Her finger wandered southwest. "Mor-

JOHN CORWIN

gan's Crossing and another pass are another hundred miles out of the way, but we may have no choice."

"I agree. There's no way we can get through that blockade."

"We cannot continue much longer without resting the gryphons." Ki looked up at the sky. "We have already flown them too long without food and water."

I hadn't even thought of that. "This ship can go a lot faster. Why don't you all get onboard and leave the gryphons behind?"

Ki's eyes flared. Her hand reflexively stroked her steed. "I would never abandon Algernon. He is my friend and companion. I would rather die."

I held up my hands. "Okay, okay, I got it." I looked at the dark cloud behind us. "What are those things?

"Unnatural creatures." Ki stroked the mane of her gryphon as if to calm herself. "Vokan took gryphon stock and mixed it with other species since gryphons are so difficult to breed. When that failed, he tested other species until he found success."

"They look like a cross between a bat and a panther."

"Yes, they do." A shudder passed through her shoulders. "Vokan named them *gepheron*, gryphon killers."

"Well, that's just mean." I blew out a breath. "Damn, there must be three hundred of them."

Ki's brow furrowed. "I don't understand how their entire army blocked the pass without our knowledge. Our scouts should have seen them coming."

Elyssa joined me. "Hey, I'm Elyssa."

"I am Ki."

My mouth dropped open. "Whatever happened to 'I am Ki of the South-

210

lands, keeper of the word, defender of law, servant of Utopia' and all that jazz?"

She ignored me. "Justin told us about you. He said you were a great warrior."

"I'm not too bad." Elyssa's eyes wandered to the gryphon. "Is it okay if I pet him or her?"

"Of course! Algernon loves having his mane rubbed."

Elyssa stroked the golden mane. "Oh, he's so fluffy!"

"Isn't he though?" Ki grinned.

"Well, I'm glad to see you're bonding." I jabbed a finger behind us. "But maybe we should concentrate on surviving first."

Ki's smiled faded. "Yes."

"I overheard you say Askot doesn't usually attack in such numbers," Elyssa said.

Ki nodded. "He hounds us with raiding parties to prevent us from utilizing outlying lands and to prevent us from hunting. I have never seen so many gepheron riders in one place."

"Probably because Vokan summoned him," I said. "If Vokan controls the eidolons, he knows I'm with you guys. He probably told Askot to track us down."

"Agreed." Elyssa pursed her lips. "And now they know the *Raptor* didn't go back to Seraphina."

Shelton came up next to us. "Vokan's got a real hard-on for Argus. Dollars to dog nuts he's gonna come at us with everything he's got."

"Dollars and dog nuts?" Ki's brow furrowed. "What is a hard-on?"

"Damn it, Shelton." Elyssa pushed him away. "Keep it PG for once, okay?"

He backed off. "That is PG!"

Adam snorted. "Hosting guests for five minutes and Shelton's already talking about hard-ons."

Shelton grunted. "I know how to entertain."

Hard-ons or not, Shelton hit the nail on the head. Askot would relentlessly chase us until every last gryphon fell from the sky.

CHAPTER 21

Overwhelming odds or not, I wasn't ready to admit defeat. "Let's get everyone involved." I waved Cinder and Bliss over and introduced them.

"Can I pet the gryphon?" Adam asked.

I rolled my eyes. "It can wait. The gryphons need rest or else they'll start dropping dead. I would suggest we try luring Askot away with the *Raptor*, but he'd probably just split his forces and chase them down anyway."

"True," Elyssa said. "Splitting up isn't an option, and the ship can't hold more than one or two gryphons at a time."

"So we rest them up in rotations," Shelton said. "Simple."

"They need sleep and food," Ki said. "They cannot simply take a five-minute nap and be restored."

"You're making it way too easy." Shelton grunted. "Let's add more impossible conditions so it's a challenge."

"I believe it is difficult already, Harry." Cinder shook his head. "Please do not make it harder."

Ki raised an eyebrow. "He was being sarcastic."

Cinder paused. "Ah, yes. Though I've improved my human interaction skills, Harry often confuses me."

"He's a confused individual," Adam said.

I clapped my hands to get their attention. "Look, can we skip the banter and brainstorm a way out of this?"

"Our first problem is line of sight." Elyssa held her arm straight out as if gauging our surroundings. "There are several hills we can duck behind, but we can't clear enough distance before the swarm sees us again."

Shelton pointed south. "What about flying over the mountains?"

"They cannot fly that high," Ki said. "The oxygen is too thin."

"Thin air also affects the levitation foils," Adam said. "They lose lift and thrust the higher you go."

I looked ahead. "We could duck into the forest on the other side of a hill and camouflage."

Adam held out his hands as if measuring the ship and the gryphons. "Dude, it'd take us ten minutes to set up a net big enough."

"Yeah, plus it'd be super obvious where we were hiding." Shelton looked around at the clear blue skies. "Man, what I'd give for some haze or fog right about now."

"Unlike Vokan, I can't just summon a thunderstorm." The last time—the only time—had been years ago, a battle at Thunder Rock. I'd channeled Murk into a gust of wind and Fjoeruss had threaded Brilliance through it to form a tornado. I hadn't practiced weather control since then.

I channeled a gust of wind that blew Shelton's hat off. The stampede string caught around his neck.

"What the hell?" He looked toward the stern as if the weather shields had suddenly failed, then back to me. "Did you make wind?"

Adam grinned. "We call it farting, Shelton."

I ignored them. "I might be able to manufacture some bad weather, but I can't do it while we're flying."

"What do you mean?" Elyssa said.

"It means I need to get enough distance between me and the enemy so I can stir up a storm."

"Like you did in the Battle of Thunder Rock?" Shelton ran a hand through his hair. "You had Fjoeruss helping you. Do you have enough juice to pull it off on your own?"

"I can help." Bliss stiffened her shoulders as if expecting resistance. "I may not be powerful, but every little bit helps."

It just might work. "Then let's do it." I pointed to a mountain peak a few hundred feet higher than the other small ones around it. "Get us there."

Elyssa turned to Ki. "We'll have to fly ahead. If Justin is successful, you'll need to go around his storm."

Ki frowned at me. "You are not a magus, but you can create a storm?"

I shrugged. "Maybe, maybe not. I've done it before, so let's see if I can pull it off again."

"Very well." She reached across and clasped Elyssa's hand. "Good luck."

Elyssa ran to the bridge and urged the *Raptor* to full speed. We jetted forward, leaving the gryphons in the proverbial dust and reached the distant mountain peak moments later.

"Why are you doing this from the ground?" Adam said. "Wouldn't it be more effective to take the ship into the sky and make clouds?"

"I don't know how to do it that way," I said. "Fjoeruss and I made a tornado and that caused a thunderstorm."

Adam wet a finger and held it up. "The air is fairly humid already. I don't know much about changing the weather, but I can tell you that you'll need to suck up as much moisture as possible."

"I'm not sure how to do that, but I'll try."

"You need to create two separate wind masses—one as hot as possible, the other cold." Adam held his hands apart and brought them together. "That should fuel the first funnel. From there, it's about ramming more and more air together."

I imagined what he meant. Nodded. "That sounds doable."

"If you give it enough fuel, the tornado will take over and do the rest." He shrugged. "I hope."

"If this doesn't work, we'll have to abandon the gryphons," Shelton said.

I shook my head. "Ki will die before she does that."

"Perspective changes when death is at the door." Shelton activated the gangway as we landed. "I think she'll choose to live."

Bliss and I ran down the gangway and across the plateau. The view of the mountains and valleys was breathtaking from here. The blue sky looked vast and endless. How was a small, insignificant speck like me supposed to have an impact?

If Vokan did it, so can I.

I summoned a sphere of Murk.

I turned to Bliss. "I'll create a funnel of cold wind. You create the hot funnel and we'll ram them together on my signal."

Her right hand crackled with power. "I'm ready."

I formed cold Murk into a cone and willed it into motion. It stood no taller than me and the wind barely tousled my hair. Bliss threaded an even amount of Brilliance into its own funnel. A hot breeze brushed against my face. I nodded.

We slammed the two funnels together.

Lightning crackled. Thunder rumbled. The sonic blast sent us stumbling backward. The tornado lifted dirt and debris and flung it in all directions. It was only twenty feet tall, but our baby had quite the temper. The cone wobbled and began to shrink.

"Keep channeling," I shouted over the wind.

Bliss hit it with more hot air while I streamed in the cold. The wind roared louder and louder. The funnel soared higher. Sweat trickled down my forehead. Bliss's faced burned bright red. But despite our efforts, we just weren't doing it. The tornado wobbled like a drunken ostrich around the plateau, but it wasn't nearly tall enough. I needed it to reach hundreds of feet into the sky to stand a chance at starting a storm.

"Maybe I don't understand how this works at all." I slashed my hand down and stopped channeling. "It's not working."

"Come here quick." Adam waved at us from the ship. "I've got an idea!"

We left our baby tornado all on its lonesome and joined Adam. He removed the Chalon from Argus and aimed it at our little monster. "The focusing gem is designed to amplify magic." He pointed to the tornado. "Try hitting it now before it runs out of gas."

The tornado was already shrinking and slowing, so I quickly channeled through the gem. Bliss crossed her hot stream with mine and we hit the tornado together. It was like mixing steroids with rocket fuel. Baby tornado soared fifty feet high and doubled in girth. Adam swiveled the gem to keep up with the erratic movements of the growing twister.

The funnel sucked the moisture out of the air. It went from hazy white to dark gray in a matter of seconds. Hot, humid air clashed with cold. Wind roared past my ears. The *Raptor* shook. Dirt pelted the deck. Bushes uprooted and vanished into the funnel. The suction was so fierce my feet began to lose their grip.

Adam gripped the railing for support. "Turn on the weather shield!"

The air shimmered and the roar of the wind abated. Debris bounced and slid off the shield. "I think baby is almost ready to walk!"

Bliss gave me a confused look.

Ki led her gryphons wide around the growing storm. Elyssa motioned them to keep on going. One of the magnificent creatures wobbled and spiraled to the ground.

"No!" Elyssa cried. The riderless gryphon smashed onto the plateau and skidded off the side.

We didn't have much time before more fell. I redoubled my efforts, straining with every last ounce I had. The tornado rewarded me by surging higher. Bliss staggered back, unable to keep channeling. Exhausted, I dropped my hands and groaned.

"Please work." I offered a prayer to the weather gods and hoped they heard me.

Freed from its chains, the tornado ripped across the plateau and down into the trees, growing taller and wider with every passing second. It plowed a furrow a hundred yards long as its destructive journey began. The only problem? It was headed in the wrong direction.

"No, not north!" I shouted. "Go west, you idiot!"

It meandered northeast, completely ignoring me.

"You're the fruit of my loins, and you do this to me?" I sank to the deck. "We're screwed."

"Maybe not." Adam pointed up. Lightning threaded the black skies. Thick fog rose from the forests. I stepped outside the protection of the shields. Hot air tore at my clothes one minute. Freezing cold raked me the next. Nimbus clouds darkened the world to twilight. A thin funnel dropped from the sky and ripped through the trees. Another twister formed, and another. Before long, half a dozen tornados ravished the terrain.

A gust of wind nearly ripped me off the deck. I gripped the rail and pulled myself back inside the weather shields. "I think we overdid it!"

Shelton belted a laugh. "It's a twister, Aunty Em!"

Hail pelted the shields and the ground shook. Giant tornados rampaged across the land. Dust, debris, and rain obscured the horizon. We might have unleashed a disaster, but at least Askot couldn't see us.

"Mission accomplished?" I said in a weak voice.

Elyssa stared at the destruction with wide eyes. "Thank god we're in the middle of nowhere."

"Well, we've got our cover," Adam said. "Where do we go from here?"

"Let's catch up with Ki and find out." Elyssa went back to the bridge and hauled back on the control stick. The *Raptor* lifted off and spun around to pursue the gryphons.

The creatures were fast, despite their exhaustion, so it took us a moment to catch up. Ki had already pinpointed a valley, so we followed her until it narrowed into a canyon. The ship fit inside a small clearing. Shelton and Adam camouflaged the top to blend in with the treetops while the gryphons took shelter beneath the trees.

The great beasts gathered in a tight circle except for a single gap. They screeched softly to each other.

"What are they doing?" Adam asked.

"They're mourning," Ki said. "Moranth was Balana's mate."

"Moranth is the gryphon who went down?" I asked.

Ki bit her lower lip. Nodded. "He was already upset that his rider died in the city. I think in the end, he just gave up."

Adam grimaced. "I didn't realize they were so intelligent."

"Before Vokan, all children of Camelyn were bonded with a young gryphon when they were ten years of age." Ki's eyes seemed to gaze into the past. "When a rider or gryphon dies, it often leads to depression for the survivor."

"Seems kind of cruel," Shelton said. "Creating an emotional dependency like that."

"It's a bond, not a dependency," Ki said. "Most gryphons who survive their riders still lead happy lives and can even befriend other riders."

"So it's like losing a pet." Shelton nodded. "I can see that."

Ki narrowed her eyes. "Gryphons are not pets."

"Semantics." Shelton narrowed his eyes back at her. "They're smart animals, but they're still just animals."

Adam clapped Shelton hard on the shoulder. "Now's not exactly the time to be an ass about it. They lost comrades and friends, man."

Shelton looked down, somewhat abashed. "Yeah, you're right. Being an asshole is how I cope."

I snorted. "Ain't that the truth."

"We need a plan." Arcphone in hand, Elyssa tapped on the screen. "Cinder scanned several maps from Vokan's library." She cast a hologram between us. Red X's marked the location of several mountain passes. Thin lines traversed the rough terrain.

Gasps rose from the gryphon riders. "What sorcery is this?" Ki examined the arcphone curiously. "Even at the height of our technological prowess, we never had anything like this."

Shelton snorted. "Because you never made it past the seventies."

"It's called an arcphone. It's basically a portable magical computer." Elyssa drew attention back to the map. "Ki, can you tell me which of these mountain passes are viable?"

A smiled touched Ki's lips. "You must be a military leader."

Elyssa blinked. "Um, sort of. My father is the Templar commander. Why?"

"You have the mind of a tactician." Ki stood next to Elyssa and circled two of the X's. "These valleys end in impassible terrain." She pointed to the one we'd originally intended to use. "Morgan's Pass is the easiest route, but Askot stands between us and it. The other two are very narrow and easily blocked by the enemy." She traced a finger to the edge of the map. "Morgan's Crossing is southwest of here, but it will take us far out of our way."

"Hey, if it gets us to Camelyn, then I'm all for a detour," Shelton said.

Elyssa traced the line of Morgan's Crossing. "It intersects Morgan's Pass." She bit her lower lip. "If Askot sends his forces in we'll almost certainly run into them."

"I'm certain he's deduced that we're going to Camelyn," Ki said. "The next pass is another hundred miles past Morgan's Crossing. By the time we cross through, Askot will have blockaded the city and we will be trapped outside."

CHAPTER 22

"Don't assume Askot will guess our move," Elyssa said. "He may not even think to send troops through Morgan's Pass and choose to mindlessly pursue us instead."

"He's got enough people that he could split off a hundred and send them through," Shelton said. "The only good thing is that we dragged them about halfway to Morgan's Crossing, so his people will have to backtrack about eighty miles or more."

"So there's a chance we could beat him through. Gryphons are faster and more resilient than gepheron." Ki pursed her lips. "Somehow we must calculate the odds of making it through first."

"Easy," Adam said. "If a train leaves Atlanta going fifty miles an hour, how long until it meets the train from Nashville going sixty?"

"Oh god." Elyssa groaned. "I hate these kinds of math problems."

"Let's fill in the variables," I said. "How fast can a gepheron fly?"

Ki look up, as if searching for the answer. "Perhaps a hundred and fifty knots at top speed, but only for short bursts. They can cruise easily at a hundred knots."

"A knot is one point fifteen miles per hour." Adam fiddled with his arcphone. "How about a gryphon?"

I noticed a lone figure sitting on the ship railing. It wasn't hard to guess who it was. As Adam continued his math lesson, I excused myself and walked up the gangway.

Bliss got down off the railing and started to walk away.

"Wait."

She turned slowly. "Yes?"

"I never got a chance to thank you." I looked up at the apocalyptic storm clouds. "I couldn't have done that without you."

She shrugged and looked down. "You're powerful enough that I think you could have."

I touched her shoulder. "Bliss, look at me."

Her eyes rose hesitantly.

I held her gaze for a moment. "Thank you. I really couldn't have done it without you."

"I'm glad I could help." A tear rolled down her cheek.

"Why are you crying?"

Bliss blinked and more tears fell. She wiped her eyes. "I'm just a tiny piece of a legendary war hero. Nightliss saved thousands of lives and touched thousands more. She was the Templar Clarion and one of your best friends." Bliss swallowed hard. "I might carry part of Nightliss inside me, but I'm not her and I never will be."

"You don't have to be like Nightliss." I squeezed her shoulder. "It's okay to just be you."

"I'm just a demon construct." Bliss backed away. "No matter how hard I try, I'll always be a fake." She turned and went below deck before I even knew what to say.

I felt horrible. I'd mistreated her and never given her a chance just because of what she was. Bliss was no better or worse than any of us. She'd been made for bad reasons but overcame her original conditioning to be something better.

It was hard—so damned hard—to see past the Nightliss in her. I would never have my friend back, but part of her precious soul lived inside Bliss. No matter how difficult it was, I needed to make her feel welcome. Make her feel like part of the team.

Make her feel loved.

I rejoined the others. Bliss needed her alone time, and I didn't want to force anything. Faking my emotions would just make things worse.

Adam stood in front of the holographic map, his calculations drawn in red at the bottom. He saw me coming and nodded at the map. "We've got some scenarios."

Elyssa took over the briefing. "Ki and I suspect Askot will send part of his force to block us off from Camelyn while others hunt us down and drive us toward their trap."

"That's a lot of assuming," I said. "We could just keep going west and foil his plans."

Elyssa nodded. "We could, but I think going to Camelyn is our best option to weather out the next two months."

I couldn't disagree. "Even if we get there before Askot, can't the gepheron just fly over the city walls?" I asked.

"We have defenses against aerial assaults, but I don't know if they can hold back nearly a thousand gepheron." Ki's forehead scrunched. "The addition of your ship might be enough to hold them back."

Shelton grunted. "Problem is, there's no way we'll beat him through the pass."

"Shelton's right," Elyssa said. "If Askot sends his forces through Morgan's

Pass, then we'll run into them if we use Morgan's Crossing." She scrolled further west. "The only other option is the Irdan Pass, but it's two hundred miles away."

The line took a meandering path between the mountains before finding its way to the other side.

"Is there a solution here somewhere?" I asked. "Because all I see are more problems."

"Simple," Elyssa said. "We're going to slip right past Askot's nose and into Morgan's Pass."

My jaw went slack. "How in the world will we manage that? The gryphons aren't fast enough."

"No, but the *Raptor* is." Elyssa flashed a grin. "Ki will come with us on the ship while the others take the gryphons to the Irdan Pass and connect with us later."

"I will not be left behind." Gemma scowled. "Kek and the others can take the gryphons. I won't miss this fight."

Ki shook her head. "You will stay with the others. They'll need your sword if you get into any trouble."

"What if the city is under siege when they get there?" I asked. "Won't they be stuck outside?"

"We can deal with that when the time comes," Elyssa said.

Adam frowned. "Should we expect Vokan and the eidolons?"

Ki nodded. "If Vokan wants your ship as badly as you said he does, he will stop at nothing to acquire it."

"Why don't we just take the *Raptor* out of the equation?" Shelton said. "Let's take off and hide for a couple of months."

"Vokan might take out his wrath on Camelyn," Ki said. "We don't have enough gryphons to stop a legion of gepheron. He might even be so bold as to fly his citadel into the city and drop the eidolons on us."

"What's kept him from doing that all this time?" Shelton said. "If it was that easy, it seems he would've done it before."

"Because he never had so many gepheron," Ki said. "We scout Vokan's forces constantly, including his hatcheries. Our last reports indicated a total of three hundred gepheron under Askot's command."

"I'll bet Askot knew you were watching." Elyssa zoomed out the map. "He probably found a remote area and hid some hatcheries. Then it was just a matter of conscripting more slaves to fly them."

"I'll bet Vokan meant to assault Camelyn with his new forces at some point in the near future," Adam said, "but then the *Raptor* and Argus came along and caught his eye."

"Vokan's got a real hard-on for Eden," Shelton said. "I guarantee you finding a way there would be his first priority."

"Man, you are really overusing that term," Adam said.

"Fine, I'll switch it up," Shelton said. "Vokan's got a king-sized erection for Eden."

I snorted. "You have an unhealthy obsession with penises, Shelton."

"Enough with the penises," Elyssa said. "We have bigger things to worry about."

"Or do we?" I waggled my eyebrows.

She face-palmed and groaned.

"But seriously." Adam struggled to keep a straight face. "We've got a lot to plan."

His words sobered me. "I'd like to skewer Askot on our way to the pass tomorrow."

"Might be kind of hard," Adam said. "Considering the swarm of gepheron around him."

"What is it with these small-time bullies we keep running into?" I said. "Don't they realize we have bigger fish to fry?"

"That's the point," Shelton said. "Baal keeps tossing tin pot dictators in our faces while he focuses on his own agenda."

"And what's Xanomiel been doing this entire time?" Elyssa bit her lower lip. "With Baal trying to take over entire realms, why haven't we heard a peep from his main competition?"

"Excellent question," Cinder said. "The realmverse is rather vast. Perhaps our paths simply haven't crossed."

"Well, we have been stuck in Seraphina for years," Shelton said. "Ain't no telling what he's up to. He might be raising an army of Nazdal for all we know."

I shuddered at the thought.

"And here I thought our problems were big." Ki looked a little frightened. "If we cannot even defeat Vokan, how can we hope to survive titans?"

"Good question." I looked up at the dark sky and wondered if Askot still hunted us or if he'd hunkered down for the storm. "I guess now's a good a time as any to tell you everything."

I started my story way back in time when the Apocryphan ruled the Earth. They'd started a war and ended up sundering the world into dozens or even hundreds of realms. The Sirens trapped the Apocryphan in the Abyss, a great black hole of a place that Utopia now orbited. I gave them the short version of the two Seraphim wars, and everything that led up to us being trapped in Seraphina.

Then I got to the meat of the problem—Baal and his aspirations to stop Xanomiel from recombining the realms and killing billions. Except we knew Baal wasn't in this to save the realms. He wanted to keep them separate but rule them.

If Ki had been unsettled earlier, she was downright disturbed now. "How in the world does one defeat a god?"

"With steel and will." Gemma bared her sword. "Just show me this god, and I'll show him mortality."

I chuckled. "It might almost be amusing to see you trying to attack Xanomiel or Baal." I imagined her flailing fists while held at arm's length by the target. "Baal is a spirit, the most powerful demon in Haedaemos. You can't stick him with a sword." I thought back to the time Xanomiel ate two giant demons. "An Apocryphan would just squash you like a bug."

"Then what hope is there?" Kek's voice filled with despair. "How could we defeat either of them?"

I pounded a fist into my palm. "Because we've overcome impossible odds before and we can do it again." I held my arms wide to encompass the entire realm. "This world is just one of many with warriors who can help us fight evil minions."

"Minions." Adam chuckled. "I love that word."

"If the Sirens trapped the Apocryphan once, there's no reason to think they can't do it again." I waved a hand. "But first, let's overcome Vokan. Then we can talk about Baal and Xanomiel."

"The problem with Vokan is his source of power." Shelton sat on a small boulder. "We need to know more about that relic he uses and if we can sever the connection."

"I found very little information about the cantrap," Cinder said. "Since his library is physical and not digital, I couldn't download the information. The only way to find out more about the cantrap is to study it."

"I noticed he touched that chain around his neck a lot," Elyssa said. "It's like he's making sure something dear to him is still there."

Shelton grunted. "It ain't a family photo, that's for sure."

"Unless Vokan's got a personal diary hidden under his pillow, we'd have to spy on him for information." Adam shook his head. "That's a very tall order."

"We'd have to sneak through a city infested by eidolons, get into the towers, then hide in his bedroom closet." Shelton shrugged. "Easy as pie."

"I believe Harry is being sarcastic," Cinder said. "Hiding in Vokan's closet would not be advantageous."

"What about the bunker and all those spy cams?" I said. "Maybe we could get back into the bunker and watch Vokan from there."

"Getting back inside would be very risky." Adam pushed a finger up the bridge of his nose. "For all we know, he's undone everything we did by now."

Bliss stepped from the darkness and stood next to Cinder. "I don't know a lot about computers, but maybe you could tap into the cameras from one of the other rooms."

"Yeah." Adam held up a finger. "I'll bet we could piggyback the signal from a camera cable."

"Or put a tap on the main console in the bunker," Shelton said. "Then we could remote in using a phone and not have to risk staying in the building."

"I really like that plan," Elyssa said. "What are the odds we could use the piggyback method instead of tapping the bunker console?"

Adam shrugged. "No way to say until we try."

"I should point out a problem," Cinder said. "We are about to enter a city that will soon come under siege, possibly even from Vokan himself. That will make travel back to Solan difficult."

"Good point." Shelton frowned. "If Vokan thinks we're heading to

Camelyn, then maybe he'll take his eidolons with him. The cantrap will be undefended and we can see what makes it tick."

"You would abandon Camelyn?" Ki held out her hands, pleading. "We need your help to withstand Askot's forces."

"Yeah, but there's no guarantee the *Raptor* is enough to make a difference." Shelton shook his head. "Let's study the cantrap and destroy it. Maybe that'll bring Vokan down a few notches."

Bliss gripped Cinder's arm and spoke into his ear. He listened, nodded. "Perhaps Bliss and I can return to the city on gryphons and infiltrate the towers. I can determine the best way to tap into the security cameras."

Adam and Shelton looked at each other. Elyssa gazed thoughtfully at Cinder. She looked at me and nodded.

To say I felt apprehensive was an understatement. "Cinder, can you be sneaky enough?"

"I used to be a spy, remember?" Bliss let go of Cinder's arm. "I can get us in, I'm sure of it."

"My programming as a gray man prepared me for tactical operations," Cinder said. "I also have the technical expertise to tap into the system."

"You'll need an extra arcphone to do a remote tap," Shelton said. "Adam has a spare we can load all our best hacks onto in case you need them."

"If we are successful, we will return to Camelyn and sneak in." Cinder turned to me. "Do you approve, Justin?"

"You have to be extra careful, Cinder." I resisted the urge to walk over and grab his shoulders like a parent who's trying to beat something into a kid's head. "There are eidolons who pounce from buildings, and others who can ram down walls. Vokan can strike gryphons out of the sky with his lightning so you'll have to risk walking through very dangerous streets. If the eidolons spot you, Vokan will know you're there. If that happens, you have to leave."

"There's also no guarantee Vokan will go to Camelyn," Elyssa said. "I need you to let us know if he's coming or staying in Solan."

"How?" Shelton tapped his com badge. "These things don't have the range, and there's no communications network for the arcphones."

"I will send Bliss," Cinder said.

Bliss shook her head. "I won't leave you."

He touched her shoulder. "You must if it is for the greater good."

"You'll be the messenger." Elyssa held onto her gaze. "We have to know if Vokan is coming or not."

Bliss sighed. "I will do what I must."

Fear knotted my insides. It was the same kind of fear I felt every time I had to send someone into danger. Then again, Cinder and Bliss might stand more of a chance than those of us going on to Camelyn.

We could take the Raptor and hide. Vokan would never find us, and my friends would survive. *But that's not who we are.*

I hardened myself against the fear. Steeled my resolve as I'd done a hundred times before. Cinder and Bliss were more than capable of doing this. I just had to have faith in their abilities.

"Good luck." I touched her shoulder. "I have faith in you."

Bliss's shoulders loosened. Unreadable emotion flashed behind her eyes. It might have been gratitude or sadness. Or maybe she just had indigestion. Whatever it was, I hoped it was enough to get her and Cinder back to us safely.

CHAPTER 23

The storm grew more violent, wind howling through the trees until they bent sideways. We were safe aboard the *Raptor*, but I worried about a tornado ripping through the gryphons.

"Well, at least we know Askot won't be poking around in weather like this," Shelton said with a grin. He sat in the galley, sipping whiskey and reading one of the books about magic he'd liberated from Vokan's library.

Adam sat across from him, thoroughly engrossed in a text. I stole a sip of his whiskey and let it burn down my throat. It wasn't exactly pleasant, but it wasn't terrible either. I had yet to discover an affinity to booze. Probably because I had too many worries to ever drink away, and no time to drink anyway.

"Learn anything useful?" I asked.

"As a matter of fact, yes." Shelton put down the book. "The Utopians don't use Cyrinthian for anything. It's almost like they didn't even know it existed until they started traveling to Eden."

"What do they use?" I glanced at Adam, but he was immersed in his reading.

"They call it Faeric." Shelton thumbed through the pages. "Says they discovered the magical language in caves thousands of years ago, but no one knows where it came from."

"In caves? Like caveman drawings?"

"Yeah. Their historians figured it was left there intentionally for humans to discover." Shelton grunted. "I'd really like to know who and why."

"Is it similar to Cyrinthian?"

"Not at all." Shelton turned the book so I could see a table of symbols. "Everything is based on the four elements and nature-based magic, whereas Arcane spell casting is centered around bending magic to human will."

I peered at the chart. "I don't get it."

"It's hard to explain, but you allow the elements to flow through you, and then bridge them with aether to achieve different effects." Shelton took his hat off and set it on the table. "I'd like to learn it, but I'd have to rewire my brain first."

"Seems so much easier to use willpower and focus," I said.

"There's a lot more to it too." He turned to a page with even more symbols. "These represent base elements and all the combinations required to achieve specific outcomes."

"Like elements in chemistry." I said.

He nodded. "Yep. That's why it takes years to master this stuff."

It gave me a headache just looking at it. "Well, good luck with that. I'm heading to bed."

"Later." Shelton settled back into his chair and started reading again.

I walked down the narrow hall to the bedroom. Elyssa was still in a planning session with Ki, but I was too exhausted to stay up any longer. Making tornados had taken a lot out of me. I heard a knock on the door and slid it open. Bliss stood in the hallway, eyes uncertain.

"Is everything okay?" I asked.

She nodded. "What you said earlier meant a lot to me." Bliss looked down. "It makes me proud knowing you have faith in me. I promise I won't let you down."

"Bliss, look at me." I waited until her eyes wandered back up to meet mine. "I do have faith in you. I also know you care for Cinder and won't let anything bad happen to him."

She stiffened. "He's my best friend. I love him."

Those simple words choked me up for a moment and I didn't even know why. "Cinder isn't the best with emotions, but in his own way, I think he loves you too."

Bliss nodded. "I hope so." She backed up a step. "Good night, Justin."

"Good night." I closed the door and stood there reflecting on the moment. Worry and confidence warred in my heart. Despite all of Cinder's and Bliss's skills, Vokan's defenses were formidable. I'd worry about them until I knew they were safe.

THE NEXT MORNING, we said our goodbyes to Cinder and Bliss.

I gave Cinder an awkwardly long hug and backed away. "Don't take any unnecessary risks, okay?"

Shelton snorted. "Yes, mother."

"I will be very careful, Justin." Cinder climbed into the saddle of a gryphon. "I will also enjoy every moment of flying."

The gryphon purred and screeched gently.

"Morly likes you," Ki said. "It is rare for a gryphon to like a stranger."

Cinder nodded. "I must thank Harry for teaching me to be such a good person."

Adam burst into laughter. "I think Cinder just made a joke."

I snickered. "Yeah, Shelton teaching someone to be good is like a rabid dog teaching someone not to bite."

"Hey now!" Shelton scowled at us. "I'll have you know I'm a beacon of kindness and caring."

Adam and I laughed even harder.

Elyssa shook her head and groaned. "And these are the same people who are supposed to save the world."

Ki smiled. "Perhaps this is how they cope with the specter of doom hanging over all creation."

Elyssa blinked. "I guess that's one way to look at it." She swung her finger in a circle to round everyone up. "Let's get this show on the road."

Cinder and Bliss rose above the trees on their gryphons and headed west so they could skirt wide around Askot's army. Ki bade goodbye to her companions and boarded the *Raptor*. Gemma hopped on her gryphon and belted out orders to the others as they made ready to fly further west to the Irdan Pass."

Ki took a deep breath. "I hope they make it to Camelyn."

"I think they'll be okay," Elyssa said.

Ki took her hand and squeezed it. "Thank you for all your help."

Elyssa smiled back. "My pleasure." She let go of the other woman's hand and went to the bridge. "Time for liftoff."

The levitation foils hummed, and the *Raptor* rose above the canyon giving us a bird's eye view of the destruction.

Giant furrows scarred the forests. Mudslides left dark channels on hills and mountains. Dark storm clouds hovered low overhead and thunder rumbled in the distance. Despite the mess, it felt like the perfect morning—cool air against my face, the sweet scent of greenery in my nostrils.

The weather shield blinked on and the breeze vanished. Shelton grumbled under his breath and pointed to another dark cloud on the horizon. "Looks like Askot is the early bird."

A swarm of gepheron funneled toward Morgan's Pass. I left the front deck and stood next to Elyssa on the bridge. "Can we beat them inside?"

"Let's hope so." She thrust the accelerator forward and the *Raptor* lurched ahead.

I gripped the back of the captain's seat to keep from stumbling backward. The rear flank of the massive army shifted toward us. At this speed, their flank would never intercept us, but their lead elements were already entering the pass.

We streaked past the flank. Shelton flipped off the distant riders. "Eat my dust, assholes!"

Elyssa sighed. "Is he thirty or thirteen?"

"A little bit of both." I couldn't take my eyes off Morgan's Pass and the swarm of gepheron racing us there. The bottom of the pass narrowed to a V, barely wide enough for anyone on foot or horse to walk single file. The canyon walls angled to about a hundred-foot span before continuing straight up and vanishing into the clouds.

"Can fly into the clouds?" I said. "Or is that too high for the levitation foils?"

"We could, but it'll slow us down a lot." Elyssa's face tensed. "It's better if we beat them inside and outrun them."

"Whatever you say, captain." I charged the weapons gems and went onto the deck. "Everyone grab a turret. We're going in."

Shelton went to the starboard turret and test-fired it by pressing the ruby-red gem on the handle. A solid white beam speared into the dark sky, dissipating a little over a hundred feet from the ship. "These things are weak sauce without Seraphim powers boosting them."

"I could increase the range," Adam said, "but it'd burn through the power gem in half the time. Speaking of which, we should switch from beam fire."

I rotated the gem on his turret so it was half red and half green. "Try it again."

Shelton pressed the gem and a flurry of white spheres exploded from the turret. He nodded. "Yeah, that's better."

"Saves energy." Adam stared at the swarm. "We're gonna need every last drop of juice to fight them."

The swarm resolved into individual gepheron and their riders. "We're almost there. Get ready." I manned the front turret and Adam took the one to port. "What can I do?" Ki said.

"There's another turret aft." I showed her how to operate it. "Target anything on our backside."

"Affirmative." She ran to her station.

It quickly became obvious we had to pass through the front of the swarm, a dark spike of enemies only yards away from entering the pass. Once they reached it, we'd have to blast our way through a narrow space. The enemy seemed to realize this and surged toward the canyon mouth.

"Not good!" Shelton shouted. "Can't this thing go any faster?"

"No," Elyssa shouted back. "Battle mode activated!" The shields flickered and hummed with extra power and the gems on the turrets brightened. "Here we go!"

We were flying so fast, I barely had a chance to open fire before we were right on the enemy. Volleys of sizzling energy spheres pierced wings and burned flesh. Gepheron shrieked and fell from the skies with their screaming riders. Enemy crossbows fired back. The bolts simply bounced off the shields and hull, doing no harm.

Mercilessly, we pounded them, but they didn't retreat. Despite the fear and desperation in their eyes, these slaves had no control of their actions. Any sane person would have called a retreat. Driven by their loyalist masters, the slave riders flew kamikaze right at us.

Gepheron claws had no better luck finding purchase than crossbow bolts. The giant bat creatures bounced off the shields and spun out of control to the ground far below.

"Suck it!" Shelton took down three fliers in the space of a minute.

I shuddered at the slaughter. The slaves' faces filled with despair, pushed into the grinder by merciless masters.

"Stop firing!" I shouted. "We've killed enough."

Adam had stopped firing long before I did, his face twisted with disgust.

One man sprang off his gepheron and managed to grab the fin above the bridge. He held on for dear life, futilely stabbing a knife against the hull. We zipped inside Morgan's Pass, scant yards ahead of the swarm and quickly outdistanced pursuit. I looked up and saw the man still trying to get in.

I got Elyssa's attention. "Slow down and turn off the shields."

She nodded and the ship slowed. The man shouted in alarm and slid forward just as the shields cut off. He thudded to the deck, moaning and shivering.

Ki rounded the corner at a run and skidded to a stop. "Who is this?"

"One of the enemy soldiers." I leaned down and narrowly avoided getting face stabbed. I gripped the man's wrist and wrenched the knife away.

"No!" He tried to grab the knife, but Elyssa twisted his arm behind his back and held him down.

She raised an eyebrow. "What are we supposed to do with him?"

"Tie him up for now." I looked in the man's eyes and sensed something else lurking behind his frightened face. "He's under compulsion."

Elyssa pursed her lips. "Yeah, I see what you mean."

I procured some sleeper cuffs and put them on the slave. It reminded me of someone else. "Hey, what happened to Bonehead?"

Elyssa blinked. "Oh, shit." She grimaced. "I completely forgot about him."

"He's in the hold in sleeper cuffs," Adam said. "I'd forgotten about him too."

"Let's keep him that way," Shelton said. "Damned skeleton is crazy."

"He's not crazy, just compelled to obey like the gepheron riders." Elyssa went back to the bridge and engaged the thrusters, hurling us down the narrow canyon before the swarm caught up. She waved at Ki. "Is there anything else I need to know about the pass?"

Ki stood by her side. "There are some narrow areas, but nothing your ship can't fit through."

"Good." Elyssa stared ahead. "I've had about enough of living dangerously for one day."

"Yet you remain calm. A true warrior." Ki rested a hand on Elyssa's. "I would like to know you better."

Elyssa blinked a few times and looked down at Ki's hand. "Well, we're the guardians of the Overworld."

Shelton smirked. "Looks like Ki has the hots for Elyssa."

"I thought the same thing too." Adam flashed a grin. "Looks like Justin has some competition."

I stared at Ki. Her body language said a lot more than what came out of her mouth, and I hadn't even realized it. Elyssa looked a little stiff, probably because she'd figured it out too. "Awkward," I said in a sing-song voice.

"Maybe's she's down for something crazy." Adam nudged me. "If you know what I mean. Nudge, nudge. Wink, wink."

I snorted. "Sorry, but no." My gaze lingered on the pair for a moment, but Elyssa wore her big-girl panties full time these days and could handle things herself. I knelt next to the captured soldier and peeled back his eyes. I shielded his eyes with a cupped hand and noticed a faint glow in the pupils.

"Do you see this?" I motioned Adam and Shelton to take a look.

Shelton frowned and cupped his hand on the other side. "There's something in there."

"Weird." Adam grunted. "Let's get him inside the healing ward. Maybe there's something we can examine him with."

I waved a hand at Elyssa. "We're taking this guy inside."

She nodded. "Let me know what you find."

I hefted the guy on a shoulder and carried him below decks to the tiny healing ward. Adam took out his arcphone and ran a few scans.

"I detect a faint demonic presence, but it's not the same as possession." He switched to another diving spell. "I don't detect any mind control spells, but there's an anomaly my program can't identify."

I plucked a gem off the wall and channeled Murk into it. It ran a deep scan and projected a hologram of the man's insides, all the way down to his soul essence. The same anomaly twinkled like a pinpoint of light in the man's head.

"It's not a chip, and it's not a spell." Shelton pressed his lips together. "It's definitely not an organism."

"Wait here. I'll be right back." I went down the hallway and ducked down a ramp into the cargo hold. I located Bonehead wedged between food crates that had shifted during flight and pulled him out. I took him back to the healing ward and put him on the floor since there wasn't enough room on the narrow bed. "Scan him."

Adam repeated the process and I used the gem. We found an identical anomaly inside his head.

Shelton whistled. "They've got the same thing inside them."

"Yeah." Adam's forehead pinched with worry. "A sprite. Vokan is using sprites to mind control people."

CHAPTER 24

"I'm officially creeped the hell out." Shelton shuddered. "Are you saying those sprites can control our minds anytime they want?"

"Sprites are servants—no, slaves—in this realm." I stared at the stricken man on the table. "It's as if Vokan took an enslaved sprite and made it take control of a human host."

"Isn't that like demonic possession?" Shelton said. "Sprites are spirit beings, right?"

"Possession is a matter of the soul," Adam said. "This is more like compulsion. The sprite is positioned in the brain, so it pulls the strings like a puppeteer."

"A puppeteer with a puppeteer." Shelton huffed. "Man, this is spooky shit. Does this mean Vokan could send sprites to take over our bodies too?"

"That's a good question." I walked out the door. "I think I know who can answer it."

I marched upstairs and found Ki. "Why do Utopians enslave sprites?"

Her eyes flared. "The enslavement of any entity is unlawful." Ki's face hardened. "In their greed for technology, the Solanites adopted the practice even before Vokan came so they could have factory workers. Our representatives on the councils demanded they cease and desist, but the other cities did not allow a vote."

"Was the practice already illegal?" I asked.

"Yes, of course." She held out her hands helplessly. "Thousands of years ago, sprites were kept as pets. That was before we knew they were sentient beings. At the Great Founding, our people laid down laws that protected all beings, even those that were not sentient. That was why it was such a shock when Solan broke the code."

"I'd bet my left nut Baal had a hand in it." Shelton grimaced. "He has a way of making people do bad things."

"Maybe so," I said, "but we can worry about that later." I felt better knowing Ki didn't condone slavery. I just hoped she knew the answer to my next question. "How are sprites enslaved?"

"I do not know. The enchantments for such things are forbidden."

"Why didn't Vokan just directly mind control the humans?" Shelton said.

Ki shook her head. "I do not know that either."

I put on my thinking cap. "How do you free a sprite? When I escaped Vokan, I ran into a house sprite. He said unless his master was dead, he couldn't be freed."

"Anything that can be done can be undone," Ki said. "There are magi in the city that may know."

Elyssa raised an eyebrow. "Is this about the slave?"

"Yep." I jabbed a thumb over my shoulder. "That soldier is being controlled by an enslaved sprite."

"Impossible." Ki's mouth dropped open. "I've never heard of such a thing."

"Well, believe it, sister." Shelton scoffed. "Looks like Vokan's got some tricks up his sleeve."

"And up his pants legs too," Adam added.

"Gross." Elyssa wrinkled her nose. "I don't want to know what tricks he has up his pants."

Ki recovered her wits. "Are you saying Vokan's gepheron soldiers are all under the control of sprites?"

"Probably a mix," I said. "Askot and his loyalists are firmly on Vokan's side. Many of the gepheron riders are slaves, but I noticed a few who were able to retreat from us. They might be fighting to protect loved ones."

Elyssa shuddered. "Sinister but effective."

I looked down the seemingly endless canyon. "Are we there yet?"

"No, but I need a break." Elyssa stepped away from the controls and put Adam behind the control stick.

Adam looked hurt. "Not even a please?"

She smiled sweetly. "Will you please fly the ship?"

He rolled his eyes. "My pleasure."

Ki touched Elyssa's hand. "Where are you going, Elyssa?"

Elyssa gave her a look I'd seen a million times before. It meant she'd reached a decision about something and decided to nip it in the bud before it got out of hand. "Ki, come outside with me, please." Elyssa's violet eyes locked onto me before I could take a step. "Justin, wait here."

"But—"

"No." She waggled a finger. "Stay." Then she took Ki's hand and led her outside.

"Oh man." Shelton rubbed his hands together. "They're gonna kiss, aren't they?"

I glared at him. "I will knock you to the moon if you don't shut up."

Shelton and Adam giggled like schoolboys.

Elyssa returned a few moments later without Ki. She grabbed my hand and pulled me downstairs with her.

"Um, so what happened?" I asked.

Elyssa pulled me into our room and closed the door. "I told Ki she was an amazing leader, and beautiful, but that I already had a lover."

"I'm just a lover to you?" I feigned a hurt look. "Harsh."

"Ki's sad that I'm taken." Elyssa pulled off my shirt and shoved me onto the bed.

I grinned. "Well, I'm glad you didn't leave me."

"Never." Elyssa stripped down to bra and panties and crawled on top of me like a prowling panther. She bit my ear lobe and traced her tongue up my neck. Raven hair cascaded down her fair shoulders and tickled my nose.

I shivered in delight. "Please, do go on."

Elyssa caressed my cheek. "I thought I'd lost you back in Solan. I thought I'd have to leave you in this god forsaken realm."

"But you didn't." I kissed her soft lips. "Why didn't you tell me this last night?"

"I was too exhausted physically and emotionally." A tear glistened in her eye. "I didn't want to admit the truth."

My curiosity perked. "The truth?"

She averted her eyes. "I fully planned to go back to Seraphina and leave you here."

"But you said—"

Her finger pressed to my lips. "Justin, I love you more than life itself, but I had to do my duty. I had to warn Seraphina about Baal and Enigma. Shelton and Adam didn't want to go, but they knew we had to." Tears ran down her cheeks. "It was Bliss who stopped us."

"Bliss?" I thought back to our conversation last night. "How did she stop you?"

"She told us that our duty was to friends and loved ones. That abandoning you was a betrayal to duty."

"What?" I shook my head. "That doesn't make any sense."

"It makes all the sense in the world." Elyssa kissed my forehead. "Leaving you meant abandoning my heart, my soul." She kissed me again. "I couldn't do it, Justin."

"But what about Seraphina?"

"Our parents survived centuries before we existed. They won an impossible war, and I expect them to be fine without us now." Elyssa traced a fingernail along my chest. "Besides, it would've broken Shelton's heart to leave you."

I chuckled. "Really?"

"He wanted to stay." She rolled her eyes. "On foot, of all things. He wouldn't have lasted a day with the eidolons."

"Well, I'm not going to complain." I sighed. "I feel awful about suggesting we leave Bliss behind now. Cinder must think I'm a bastard."

"Cinder understands why you feel the way you do about the dolems." Elyssa rested her chin on my chest. "He knows Bliss threatened to kill you for a bloodstone."

"Issana threatened to kill us too, remember?" I pshawed. "That was after she told us she was Nightliss's daughter."

"People can change." Elyssa quirked an eyebrow like a shrug. "Maybe dolems can too."

"Probably because they've hung out with Cinder so much." I frowned. "I wonder if they're all—"

Elyssa put a finger on my lips. "Please, dear god, don't go down that road."

I snickered. "I was going to say close friends. What did you think I was going to say?"

She shuddered. "Don't play games. You were definitely going there."

I rolled her over beneath me and kissed her long and hard. "You mean there?"

Elyssa shut me up with another kiss. And then we definitely went *there*.

WE RETURNED to the bridge after a nice long nap to find Shelton piloting the *Raptor* down the narrow canyon. He apparently didn't hear us come up behind him, because he made *pew-pew* noises and talked to himself. "Stay on target. Stay on target."

I barely held in my laughter. "Use the Force, Luke."

Shelton spun around, face scarlet. "What the hell?"

I summoned my worst British accent. "You're a wizard 'arry!" Shelton looked so mortified, I lost it and burst into hysterical laughter.

Adam came in from the outside, a concerned look in his face. "Damn, I thought someone was dying in here."

"About to be," Shelton growled.

Elyssa looked confused. "Did I miss a reference?"

I told Adam and he lost it too. "Oh, god. This is too good."

Elyssa threw up her hands. "Still don't get it."

Shelton tried to look angry but couldn't hide a grin.

"Hey, I think we're near the end." Elyssa took the controls from Shelton and pointed to a break in the seemingly endless rock face.

A few moments later, we burst from the canyon mouth and into a river valley bordered by rolling hills. Elyssa projected the map from her phone. "A couple more hours and we'll finally be there."

Shelton groaned. "God, can you imagine how long this trip must take on gryphons?"

"It takes about a day to get from Solan to Camelyn," I said.

"Yeah." He scoffed. "Way too long."

The river valley wended past forest and grasslands. The hills turned to cliffs of pure white stone and then back to rolling green hills again. The blackened remains of razed farms dotted the countryside. Herds of horses, cows, sheep, and other livestock roamed wild. Ki joined us on the bridge. Even Patch was recovered enough to leave his room and join us on the deck.

"Did Askot destroy all those farms?" Adam asked.

"Yes." Ki's eyes turned sad. "We took all the livestock we could manage inside the city walls."

"Beautiful country." Adam leaned on the railing and pointed to a water-fall in the distance. "It's too bad you've got an asshole ruining it for everyone."

"Always somebody," Shelton grumbled.

Far in the distance, a tall line of gray rose above the trees.

"The walls of Camelyn," Ki said in a tone that sounded proud and sad at the same time. The wall started at a cliff face on the east side of the city and curved outward. It dipped in the middle, forming a bowl along the front before curving back out and around on the west side where it intersected more cliffs.

Patch pressed a hand to his heart. "Long may they stand."

"Big walls, but they ain't much use against flying enemies." Shelton pursed his lips. "You have shields?"

"Nothing like the ones on your ship," Ki said. "Our magi create a storm wall of lightning and wind to keep out flying enemies."

"Sounds effective," I said. "Maybe that'll be enough to keep out the gepheron."

"The strain of maintaining such a huge shield is considerable," Ki said. "If Askot throws slaves at the shield, our magi will be unable to hold it for long."

"You don't have aether generators?" Adam said.

Ki's forehead scrunched. "I've never heard of such a thing."

Shelton snapped his fingers. "Well, I'll be. Looks like we've got something over our superior Utopian cousins at last."

"Finally." Adam sighed. "All I could think about was how much better their magic seems than ours. I was starting to feel pretty insecure."

Elyssa cleared her throat. "We don't have an aether generator with us." She stared at the massive wall. "Even if we did, it wouldn't be nearly powerful enough to make a shield that big."

Adam's shoulders slumped. "Oh. I didn't think of that."

Shelton scowled. "How many magi does it take to make that shield?"

"All of them," Ki said. "We have fifty-three."

"Hot damn, that's a lot." Shelton ticked off his fingers. "But it's not undoable."

I raised both my eyebrows. "What's not undoable?"

"We can make some aether generators to help maintain the shield." Shelton tapped on his arcphone. "I've got schematics. We'd need a precision metalworking shop, diamonds, and gasoline."

"We can provide you with all those things," Ki said.

"You think you can really build an ICE-based aether generator?" Elyssa said. "That I'd like to see."

Ki blinked. "What's ICE?"

"Internal combustion engine," Adam said. "It's old-school, but it works." He tapped a finger on his chin and looked into the distance. "We just have to hope the generators are compatible with their magic."

"Aether is aether," Shelton said. "If they can tie off a spell, then the generators can power it."

Elyssa looked skeptical. "I've torn down motorcycle engines and rebuilt them with my brother. It takes very precise measurements to make cylinders fit and fire correctly."

"That's why we'll make molds," Adam said. "Once we get those done, it's just a matter of pumping out the parts."

"Yeah, if this metalworking shop is up to snuff." Shelton turned to Ki. "Can we do molds there?"

"Well, of course," she said. "Our alchemists can make anything."

Adam's eyes widened. "Wait, you have actual alchemists?"

Ki puffed out her chest. "Yes, our earth magi are exceptional at metalworking."

"Son of a bitch." Shelton smacked the railing. "Now I understand how Jan felt about Marcia."

"Marcia, Marcia, Marcia," Adam grumbled. "Always better at everything."

"Well, maybe it's time you learned some new tricks," Elyssa said. "Because if you don't, even Marcia won't survive what's coming."

Shelton looked back toward the mountains and shuddered. "Let's hope Jan can save the Brady Bunch."

CHAPTER 25

 squad of gryphons met us halfway to the wall. The riders kept their distance, faces screwed up with comical confusion when Ki waved to them from the deck.

"What is this thing?" The commander of the group shouted.

"A flying ship," Ki shouted back. "Clear us for entry. We must speak to the council."

The soldier directed his gryphon closer and examined Ki. "You're not under duress, are you?"

Shelton made a raspberry. "Do you really think she'd answer that honestly if she was?"

The soldier didn't even blink. "I would hope so."

Ki shook her head. "I act of free will, squad leader."

He tapped a badge that looked a lot like a Templar com badges and spoke into it. "One flying ship cleared for entry."

"Thank you, sir." Ki turned to Elyssa. "Follow the river into the city."

JOHN CORWIN

The river went all the way to the wall where it flowed through grates designed to keep out invaders while allowing water through. Elyssa directed the ship up and over the wall. The concrete looked at least twenty feet thick. Empty guard towers rose every few feet along its length.

"Why does the wall curve inward?" I asked.

"It's forces the enemy into the middle," Ki said.

I imagined an invading horde being compressed into a kill zone. While it might work for conventional armies, it wouldn't do squat to eidolons.

IMPRESSIVE AS THE WALL WAS, Camelyn itself was a wonder.

The architecture borrowed heavily from the Roman Empire and Middle Ages. Marble domes mingled with stone buildings and peaked turrets. Most houses appeared similar in size, built in the craftsman style one might expect to find in a fairy tale about seven dwarves. In retrospect, Camelyn was probably where Roman and Medieval architecture came from.

The river ran beneath the looming walls, bisecting the city in a nearly straight line. Dozens of ornate bridges, each one more magnificent than the last, spanned the crystalline waters for over ten miles until the river exited beneath the back wall and into the ocean.

The only thing missing was a giant castle.

Two marble towers rose from the middle of the city, one on either side of the river and connected by an ornate bridge. They were the siblings of the modern towers in Solan, the former meeting place for the three councils. Now they served only Camelyn.

Ki directed us to a plaza. People in sailboats and other watercraft looked up at us with naked curiosity, nearly breaking their necks to watch us go by. We landed in the large plaza outside the east tower and debarked the ship.

252

Ki led us to the balustrade bordering the river. Black marble stairs led down to a walkway along the riverside where moorings held small boats in place. A couple out for a stroll untied a green boat and rowed into the river.

Elyssa's eyes were wide with wonder. "Your city is gorgeous."

"It was the second city of man," Ki said. "Its bones are quite ancient."

"Which one is the first city?" Shelton asked.

"The city and location were lost to history." Ki leaned on the railing. "Some say we migrated here to escape a cataclysm. Others theorize it was destroyed in the great war with Anatopia."

"And the other cities came after Camelyn?" Adam asked.

She nodded. "The council deemed it necessary to spread out geographically in case of disaster. That way we ensured human survival while still managing our population size."

"Smart." Adam took in the sights. "Looks like you guys had it all figured out."

Shelton grunted. "Until disaster struck. Vokan tore you guys a new asshole."

Ki frowned. "You have a fondness for that body part."

"It's amazing humans constructed such a balanced system," Elyssa said. "The noms in Eden are always on the verge of destroying themselves and the environment."

"Yeah, because humans suck, in general." Shelton shrugged. "Too bad it only takes one jackass to ruin a great party."

Ki looked up again. "Hopefully the council members will be here shortly. If not, I'll request a general alarm."

"How do you keep people from being greedy?" Adam asked. "Every kind of economy we've tried in Eden ends up benefitting a few elites while everyone else barely makes it."

"The economy in Camelyn hasn't changed for thousands of years," Ki said. "We have programs dedicated to finding out what people are best at, and ensuring they receive the training for those roles. If they prefer to do something else, then we train them for that."

"Education helps." Adam posed another question. "How many children are born a year?"

"It depends on the number of deaths, Ki said. "We rarely authorize more than ten children a year."

Adam's eyes flared. "Just ten?"

"I'll bet magic helps with utilities," Shelton said. "If the noms in Eden used magic, they could get rid of ninety percent of their bills."

Elyssa gasped. I turned around and gasped. Adam and Shelton joined in the gasp parade. A horse black as midnight spread its huge wings and glided in for a landing.

A spry old man hopped off and bowed. "Commander Ki, it's a pleasure to see you this day."

Ki bowed back. "And you, Magus Agula."

Fine wrinkles danced around his dark eyes when he smiled. "I was informed of your meeting request. How may I be of service?"

"Vokan has assembled a force far larger than anything we've seen before. I estimate just under a thousand gepheron massed outside Morgan's Pass and coming this way."

"This might explain why our other scouting parties have not reported." Agula's eyes wandered toward us and the *Raptor*. "Will you introduce your guests?"

"Of course, magus." Ki gave him our names and told him we were from Eden.

Agula's eyes flared. "How did you arrive here?"

"I'd prefer to save it for the full council," I said. "I'm getting hoarse from telling so many stories."

Agula's smiled returned. "Of course. They should arrive shortly."

Moments later, a flying carriage landed near the black horse, followed by a woman on a flying penny-farthing bike. A petite blonde stepped out of the carriage and jogged over to us.

"What's the emergency?" she asked.

"Friends, this is citizen Daana." Agula motioned to the medium-sized brunette on the bike. "And this is scientist Elaine."

Elaine slid off the bike and brushed off her brown bloomers. "Pleasure to meet you."

"Yes, a pleasure." Daana's admired the *Raptor*. "What sort of vessel is that?"

Agula held up his hands. "First, introductions." He quickly repeated what Ki had told him, then motioned everyone toward the closest tower. "Let's go to the council chambers to discuss this further."

Shelton snapped his fingers. "I know talking is important and all, but we need an alchemist to start work on aether generators."

"Generators?" Elaine exchanged a puzzled look with her comrades.

Ki turned to Agula. "Can you contact magus Cyntha and request her expertise? Our guests have technology that may prove useful to our defenses."

"Of course." Agula tapped his badge. "Jack, please contact Cyntha and ask her to meet us here at her earliest convenience. It is an emergency."

"Yes, Agula." The connection clicked off.

Agula looked at Shelton. "She will drop everything and come at once, I'm sure."

"Is this your entire council?" Elyssa asked.

"It is all we need." Agula started walking toward the tower. "Three from every city were randomly chosen by type for the Grand Council. Those three are responsible for governance of their city. Though the Grand Council is no more, the Camelyn Council is still selected each year."

"Seems like an awfully short term," Adam said. "How do you get anything done in just a year?"

Agula waved a hand and the great double doors of the tower swung open silently. He glanced at Adam before entering. "A year is more than enough time. If I don't finish something, my successor will."

"Sure ain't like Eden politics," Shelton said. "Everyone has a different agenda." His last sentence echoed as we stepped into a large chamber with three triangular tables identical to the ones in Solan.

Agula waved a hand and the tables slid together to form one with enough room for everyone.

Agula sat at the top of the triangle. Daana and Elaine sat to either side of him, and Ki settled down next to Elaine. I opted for a point halfway down from them and waited for the others to seat themselves. Shelton and Adam had just situated themselves when a slender woman stepped inside.

"Ah, magus Cyntha." Agula stood. "That was fast."

"You said it was an emergency." Her words were precise, but not terse.

"Just the woman we need to talk to." Shelton got up. "We need some metalworking done to help you defend your city."

Cyntha looked him up and down. "What sort of costume is this?"

Shelton brushed a hand on his leather duster. "This ain't a costume, honey, it's an outfit."

She frowned. "Honey? The context for that word makes no sense."

Adam groaned and got up. "Magus Cyntha, we can explain everything."

"Please do so outside," Agula said. "We can be more efficient that way."

"As you say." Cyntha bowed. "Pleasurable day, councilors."

"To you as well," Daana and the others replied.

"They're awfully polite," I whispered to Elyssa.

"Manners go a long way," she whispered back.

Shelton and Adam followed Cyntha outside. Then it was just me and Elyssa with the Utopians.

Agula turned to Ki. "Please tell us more about the enemy forces you encountered at Morgan's Pass."

Ki gave him the story, detailing everything Askot said and what his intentions seemed to be. She then backtracked and told them how she first encountered me and how Elyssa rescued us from Askot.

"Elyssa has a sound tactical mind and battlefield experience to back it up. I daresay she has more experience than all of us with military strategies, and we would do well to consider her advice." Ki smiled fondly at my girlfriend. "She also has a great sense of honor."

I stifled a groan.

"Jealous?" Elyssa spoke quietly from the side of her mouth.

"Mary Sue," I hissed back.

She grinned.

Agula turned to Elyssa. "High praise from one of our top commanders. Would you care to tell us more of your story?"

Elyssa gave me a look. "Do you want to?"

I shook my head. "My throat hurts. You do it this time."

She stood. "I'd be happy to." Elyssa launched into a timeline of events dating way back in the grand scheme. She threaded everything neatly together without meandering and brought us to our present situation in Utopia, all in the span of about ten minutes.

Damn she's good.

Ki probably thought I was a real drag on Elyssa's amazing career.

After Elyssa sat down, Agula and the other council members took a moment to discuss and process all that information.

"It is troubling to discover our dire situation is but a footnote in the looming cataclysm," Elaine said. "We have struggled to counter Vokan, but before he took power, we had very few military resources."

"There was no reason for a mighty military," Daana said. "The cities prospered in peace. The few citizens who chose a disruptive path were taken to task by our security or banished."

"I think what we're trying to say is that we welcome your help." Agula smiled. "Commanders like Ki have done a remarkable job training in the art of war, but we need more."

"We are primarily defenders," Ki said. "There is little offense to our forces."

"I'd be happy to help." Elyssa sat back down. "Maybe we could have a strategy meeting about the incoming threat. I need to know all your capabilities."

"Absolutely," Daana said.

"Who's your primary military leader?" Elyssa asked.

"We are." Elaine motioned to herself and the other council members. "Our forces are divided into squads. Each squad commander reports to us."

"Our hierarchy is a bit different." Elyssa told them a bit about the Templars. "We find it more efficient to have a single military leader who then reports to a civilian council."

"I've never heard this distinction between civilian and military," Agula said. "Eden must be in a constant state of war if you separate your citizens in such a way."

"It's not quite like that." Elyssa tapped a finger on her chin. "It's a distinction between the untrained population and the defenders."

I took the moment to raise a point. "I assume the magi also fight and defend."

"Yes, we all contribute," Elaine said. "There is no line between military and civilian when our very existence is threatened."

"Obviously, our cultures are very different," Elyssa said. "Could you familiarize me with your structure from top to bottom along with all your military assets?"

"Gladly," Agula said. "After Vokan nearly overran our walls decades ago, we gave every citizen a sword and trained them to fight the best we knew how. Due to their strength and agility, gryphons became our most reliable allies."

"What about flying horses?" I asked.

Agula nodded. "Pegaasi are excellent for transportation, but not nearly as agile, fast, or sturdy as gryphons."

"How many citizen-soldiers are there?" Elyssa asked.

"Fort-nine thousand and twenty-three." Elaine folded her arms in her lap. "We have fifty-three magi, and eighteen apprentices with some proficiency at magic. Four thousand citizens are assigned support roles. Three hundred and forty-seven gryphons and their riders defend and scout our borders." She took a sip of water and kept on going. "We have ten thousand acres of farmland, and twelve thousand acres of dedicated to livestock."

My eyelids grew heavy as Elaine continued her numbers rampage. When Elyssa finally spoke again, it jolted me awake.

"That's very precise, Elaine. Thank you."

Elaine nodded at her. "I find it efficient to know our capacity."

Elyssa tapped on her phone screen and stared at it for a moment. "If we added the pegaasi to the air force, that would be an additional eighty flying troops. It's not much, but every bit counts."

"The pegaasi aren't accustomed to fighting," Daana said. "They might startle."

"In an emergency like this, we have to take the chance." Elyssa bit the inside of her lip. "Do you have flying brooms or carpets?"

The council members exchanged confused looks. Agula leaned forward. "Why in the world would we have brooms that fly?"

I snorted. "I guess it is pretty ridiculous when you didn't grow up with tales of evil witches."

It was obvious from the tilted heads and furrowed brows they didn't get that reference either.

Elyssa changed tact. "Can you enchant objects to fly?"

"Well, yes," Agula said. "We have flying coaches."

I blinked. "Flying whats?"

"Horse carriages, Justin." Elyssa pursed her lips. "Are they nimble?"

"Not really," Daana said. "They'd be destroyed quite easily by gepheron."

"How many?" Elyssa turned to Elaine.

"Two hundred eighty," the scientist replied. "But what good would even a thousand be?"

"Agula, could you talk with Adam and Shelton about enchanting objects for fast and nimble flight?" Elyssa said. "We can supplement our gryphons and pegaasi with inanimate objects."

"What an intriguing idea." He nodded. "I'd be happy to do so."

"I also have some ideas for the flying coaches. Can they fly without occupants?"

"Yes," Agula said. "That's how they pick up passengers who request them."

"Excellent." Elyssa looked down at her phone. "I'm confident we can defend Camelyn against the gepheron." She bit her lower lip. "But there will be casualties."

Daana sighed. "As repugnant as war is, we have come to accept that we have no choice but to kill to survive."

That reminded me of another important factor. "Agula, do you have any experts on sprites?"

He clasped his hands together. "Yes, I've worked with them extensively. Very intelligent beings, and quite friendly if you can get them to sit still long enough for conversation."

"Then we have a puzzle for you."

Agula tilted his head slightly. "I'm intrigued, young man."

Ki interrupted me. "I formally request we temporarily assign Elyssa as our head commander. This will allow her to make decisions quickly without having to consult the council."

Elyssa blushed. "But I'm not even from here."

"Approved," Agula said. "We only ask that you notify us of your decisions through a liaison."

"Agreed." Daana knocked a fist on the table.

Elaine pursed her lips. "I also vote in favor."

"I mean, you just met us," I said. "Why in the world would you entrust your entire military to us?"

"Because we literally have no idea what we're doing," Ki said. "Our realm had been at peace for thousands of years. Since Eden was constantly at war, we consulted journals and learned what we could. It was not the most effective way, but it was the only way."

"Your swordplay looks pretty solid," I said.

"Yes, but our overall strategy is lacking." Agula nodded at Elyssa. "If Ki has such faith in you, then so do we."

Elyssa gave me a deer in the headlights look. I knew exactly what she was thinking. If these people were willing to hand the reins over to some strangers, their military must really suck.

Bells gonged in the distance and were soon answered by others closer to us. Ki jumped from her seat and ran from the council chambers. Elyssa and I looked at each other then ran after her. Ki ran to the riverside and stared, face aghast.

It didn't take long to see what had shaken her so. The once mighty river had turned into a stream. Within minutes, it reduced to a tiny trickle.

The siege had already begun.

CHAPTER 26

"How is this possible?" Ki looked up and down the empty riverbed. Cries and shouts from stranded boaters echoed from below.

A man tried to climb the mast of a sailboat, but the river was at least forty feet deep in this area. Fish flopped and gasped for water. People climbed from their boats and began tossing fish into the narrow stream —all that was left of the river.

"Man, they're even trying to save the fish," I said. "Are you sure we didn't end up in Canada?"

Dozens of gryphons soared up and down the river. Instead of rescuing people, they dropped off crews to help stranded fish.

"This isn't the reaction they should have." Elyssa turned to Ki. "We need information and scouts at the walls. An attack could be imminent."

Ki tapped her badge. "Commander Ki to the wall defense. What's our status?"

"No enemies present," a man replied. "The river has dried up outside the wall as far as I can see."

"That will be all, thanks." Ki tapped the badge again. "Apparently, this is just Vokan's first step."

Elyssa stared at a map on her phone and calculated distance. "I'm not as great at math as Adam, but I think Askot's forces are still about a hundred miles away."

"Even more, if they stopped to rest," I said. "I traced the river with a finger. As I'd seen on the journey here, it basically ran straight up to Morgan's Pass before taking a sharp turn east. "They could have dammed it up anywhere."

"I'd like to know how and where." Elyssa studied the map. "You can't just toss up a dam to hold back that much water."

"Maybe they diverted it." I pointed to several lakes in the vicinity.

Ki scowled. "Vokan can freeze the water or carve another riverbed to divert it."

I blinked. "You can't be serious. One person can control that much water?"

"You saw what he did with that storm," Elyssa said. "Vokan's drawing on the power of thousands of souls."

"But even he can't put a dent in the magic city wall, right?" I sought reassurance from Ki.

She nodded. "He couldn't the last time he tried."

"Looks like a classic siege situation." Elyssa took her eyes off the riverbed. "Are there other sources of drinking water?"

"We can desalinate ocean water," Agula replied. "Much of the city is supplied from fresh water springs that are separate from the river."

"In other words, cutting off our water doesn't affect us," I said.

Agula nodded. "They cannot starve us out."

Elyssa frowned. "They must know that. So what's their plan?"

"It's better if we go find out instead of sitting back and waiting." I pointed to the *Raptor*. "We can be in and out before they even notice."

"Yeah, that's a good idea." Elyssa punched my shoulder. "Good job."

"Good to know I'm not entirely useless." I turned to Agula. "Here's another puzzle to solve. We have a prisoner on our ship—well, two actually. One is a human being controlled by a sprite. The other is an enslaved sprite."

"A human controlled by a sprite?" Agula forehead turned into one big wrinkle. "I've never heard of such a thing."

"That is not reassuring." I tried not to slump. "Most of Askot's people are not willingly fighting for him. They're possessed by enslaved sprites. Is there any way to emancipate a sprite?"

"It depends," Agula replied. "We don't practice slavery of any kind."

"Decades ago we began a freedom campaign demanding all enslaved sprites of Solan be released," Daana said, "but Vokan attacked, and our priorities shifted."

"Well, we need to figure out a way to free the sprites." I pointed up and away. "For every willing gepheron flier, I'd be willing to bet there's ten who are slaves. If we can free them, Askot won't have squat to fight with."

"This is even more awful than I thought." Daana blinked back tears. "We can't kill the slaves. They are innocents!"

"An important distinction," Agula said. "We should make every attempt to subdue rather than kill them."

"That might be a luxury we can't afford." Elyssa stopped walking and gave them a long hard stare. "Let me make something very clear—if we can't free the gepheron riders without great loss of life, we'll have no choice but to kill them. They already have a huge numbers advantage."

"We could try to kill the loyalists," I said, "but first we'd have to get through all the bodies protecting them."

"Elyssa is right," Ki said. "Trying to subdue the slaves will only get more of our people killed."

"The numbers agree," Elaine said. "Some slaves must be sacrificed for the greater good."

Daana slumped. "There must be a way to save them." She gripped Agula's hand. "Please find a way, magus."

Elyssa stared down the council members. "Knowing what I just told you, do you still want me in charge?"

"Of course," Elaine said. "You are rational, logical, and forthright."

Agula nodded. "I know you will face unpleasant decisions, but nothing you've said has alarmed me."

Daana hesitated. Nodded. "I do not envy your task, or the blood that will coat your hands."

I did a double-take. "A little dramatic, don't you think?"

She didn't look a bit ashamed. "Every life is worth saving."

Elyssa nodded. "Thank you. I'll do my best."

The councilors oohed and aahed at the ship, so we gave them a brief tour and told them about the Mzodi.

"If only we had ships like these," Elaine said. "It would make all the difference in the world."

I pulled Bonehead from the cargo bay and brought him upstairs. None of the councilors even flinched at the sight of a skeleton. Elyssa carried the slave soldier from the healing ward and handed him over to Ki. She slung the unconscious man over a shoulder.

"How did you carry him so easily?" Elaine looked Elyssa up and down. "You're athletic, but you don't look particularly strong."

"I'm a dhampyr." Elyssa explained before they could ask what that was. "I'm like a vampire, but I'm warm-blooded and I don't have an aversion to sunlight."

"Shape-changers, blood drinkers, and half demons?" Agula shook his head. "The mutations among Edenians is astounding."

"Must be something in the water," I said.

Elyssa showed the councilors how to unfasten the sleeper cuffs from the prisoners.

"They'll both try to kill you the moment the cuffs come off," I warned them. "Bind them beforehand."

"I will," Agula said.

Elyssa gave him a thumbs up. "Ki, I need a comm badge to communicate. You'll be my liaison with the council."

Ki's eyes flashed. "I would be honored." She took off her badge. "Take mine. I'll replace it."

We boarded the *Raptor* and left to find out what in the hell Vokan was up to. Elyssa guided us just over the wall and then went straight up.

"What are you doing?" I asked.

"Getting a bird's-eye view of the battlefield." We were nearly as high as the distant mountains when the ship shuddered violently. Elyssa dropped altitude until the vibrations stopped.

"Guess I now know what happens when you take the ship too high." I went outside and looked over the railing. "We're way up here."

Camelyn looked like a miniature model of an ancient city. The wall stretched for miles to the east and west until terminating in vertical cliffs. Nothing but ocean lay to the south. Mountains to the east and west protected the outer flanks. The only clear path was from the north, whether by land or air.

Elyssa took pictures and made notes on her phone. *Ocean assault unlikely. No flanks. Ingress from north. Weather a problem?*

"You're a real military nerd, you know that?"

She chuckled. "Me and everyone in my family. Thomas Borathen pounded it into our heads."

"Luckily for the Utopians." I gazed at the beautiful city below. "It's hard to believe we found a place with mostly good, caring humans."

"It's definitely a society worth saving." Elyssa tucked her phone into a pocket. "Unfortunately, they didn't have the military might to stop Vokan early."

"I doubt it would've done them much good. That soul-sucker relic took an entire city before they knew what hit them."

Elyssa went back to the bridge and thrust the accelerator forward. The ship eased into motion at a miserly pace. "Wow, this thing really does suck at high altitude." She guided the ship lower and the speed increased in direct proportion. The propulsion gems hit equilibrium at about two hundred feet, achieving a maximum speed of three hundred knots, or as Elaine would have said, three hundred and two point four knots. *Talk about a numbers person.*

The sky darkened further north, a black line of storm clouds blotting out the mountains. Since my storm was on the other side of the mountains, either this one was natural, or something Vokan whipped up. My gut told me it was the latter.

"Better update your notes," I said. "Weather will definitely be a problem."

We spotted the first gepheron fifty miles north of Camelyn. There weren't many of them, indicating the bulk of the army hadn't caught up to the advance force yet.

Elyssa gained altitude, sacrificing speed to avoid contact with the enemy, but keeping the river valley in sight. When we reached the part with steep, white cliffs, I did a double-take. A symmetrical wall of stone dammed the river, and the level was rising as far back as I could see.

"The valley has to be a hundred feet deep." Elyssa looked down the length of the forming lake. "Vokan didn't cut off the water supply to starve us out."

Even I saw where this was heading. "He wants to flood the city."

"Exactly." She took pictures from the front of the ship, then went aft and studied the terrain. "The river valley will deliver all that water right into the walls."

"Yeah, but the walls are as tall as the valley. Won't the water just go around them?"

Elyssa bit her lower lip. "The walls might be unbreakable, but the ground they're rooted in isn't."

"You think the water could uproot the walls?"

"Possibly. Even more likely, such a massive volume of water pounding into the wall at once will overflow into the city and flood it."

Neither possibility sounded good. "I know from experience I can't hold back a wall of water that huge."

"Are you referring to the tsunami in Thailand?" Elyssa said.

I nodded. "Still freaks me out just thinking about that tidal wave."

"Maybe the magi can shield the city from water." Elyssa tapped her badge and relayed the information to Ki.

"This is monstrous!" Ki said. "Agula is with me. I'll ask him."

Agula must have leaned into her badge to speak. "Our water magi can't stop that much water. "We'll have to evacuate the northern part of the city."

"How deep underground does the wall go?" Elyssa asked.

"Perhaps forty feet," Agula said. "There were problems enchanting the stone belowground."

Elyssa frowned. "So the parts of the wall underground don't have the same magic or physical resistance?"

"Only the first ten feet," he replied.

She bit the inside of her lip. "How thick is the wall?"

Agula paused a moment. "Twenty feet."

"Better start the evacuation now," Elyssa said. "Vokan could release the dam any time." She tapped the badge and gave me a concerned look. "I don't know if the wall will hold."

"We're screwed if it goes down."

The storm clouds I'd spotted earlier moved overhead, dumping torrential rains as they went. I wondered why Vokan bothered making a thunderstorm, but actually figured it out all on my own. "Vokan is saturating the ground between here and the city, so it can't absorb the water."

Elyssa looked at the clouds, realization dawning in her eyes. "I didn't even think of that. Good catch."

I couldn't help but puff out my chest a little. "Thanks!" I decided not to rest on my laurels and brainstormed how to stop the massive storm and the incipient flood. I certainly couldn't manipulate the earth or the weather like Vokan, and all my brute force was nothing compared to a trillion tons of water.

If there was one thing I'd learned from Fjoeruss and Jeremiah Conroy, it was that a simple nudge can wreck the best laid plans in a heartbeat. Fjoeruss could create tornadoes without breaking a sweat, because he knew how to prod the weather just enough to let it do its own thing. There had to be a way I could nudge Vokan's plans off track.

Fifty miles is a long way to go for a flood. Vokan had chosen this location to place his dam because of the steep cliff walls. With the storm soaking the ground in advance, very little water would be lost to saturation.

"We don't have much time." Elyssa directed my attention to a swarm of gepheron headed our way. "We've been spotted."

"When we head back to the city, can you fly lower and slower? I want to get a good look at the flood path."

"Gotcha." Elyssa spun the ship around and dove toward the ground fast enough to make my asshole pucker.

I grabbed hold of the railing and gave her a dirty look over my shoulder. "Trying to give me a heart attack?"

She flashed a grin. "I thought you needed some excitement."

I stuck out my tongue. The ship slowed and leveled out inside the valley.

"This good?" Elyssa said.

I gave her a thumbs-up. "Just make sure the gepheron don't catch up."

The valley widened a little but narrowed again over the next few miles. I looked for release outlets or places to slow the surge of water, but the hills didn't offer anything in the way of giant boulders or collapsible cliffs. The entire fifty-mile stretch looked ideal for channeling a massive flood right into the city. The bowl shape of the wall would force all that water right into the middle where it would gush over the top.

The constant deluge from the thunderstorm hindered our line of sight, hiding the terrain until we were nearly right upon it. Though we moved slowly, we passed beneath the storm front and entered clear skies. Even then we found nothing of use. By the time we neared the city, I felt thoroughly demoralized.

Elyssa stopped the ship about a mile outside the city walls and turned it to face the oncoming storm. "Nothing?"

I shook my head. "Nothing."

JOHN CORWIN

Camelyn was about to get wrecked.

CHAPTER 27

I really wished I could talk to Jeremiah Conroy. Way back in the day he'd also been known as Moses, aka, the guy who split the Red Sea. If he could do that, it stood to reason he could stop a river from flooding a city.

"How in the hell did he do that?" Moses was an Arcane, not a Seraphim. Had he known elemental magic?

Elyssa gave me a puzzled look. "Do what?"

"Moses and the Red Sea." I put my hands together and split them apart. "If I could do that, our problems would be over—well, at least this problem."

"I don't know what to tell you." She studied the valley. "I don't see how anyone could stop the volume of water about to rip through here."

I couldn't dig a channel through the hills big enough to divert water. I couldn't form a shield large enough to block it. The city wall might be twenty feet thick and a hundred feet tall, but from here, it looked fragile as an eggshell. "I think the base of the wall is going to crack, and when it does, it's going to demolish everything behind it. Then the water will rip a channel straight through the middle."

Elyssa stared at the wall for a moment. Nodded. "I think you're right. Once that happens, Camelyn will fall."

We flew into the city. A steady stream of flying carriages ferried people and belongings to the south side of the city at the far corners away from the river while people flooded the streets in a calm and orderly manner.

Elyssa parked the ship in the plaza next to the council tower. Agula stood on the steps outside talking to people and directing them where to go. Despite the looming threat, the Utopians didn't seem discombobulated.

I went to the magus and whispered in his ear, "We need to talk."

He transferred his duties to another man and stepped away from the crowd. "Let's go up to the council chambers." He led us inside where we rode the levitator up to the top. Agula stepped outside and turned to us, eyes hopeful. "Did you find any way to stop the flood?"

I shook my head. "No, if anything we think it's going to snap the wall off at the base where it's weakest. We won't stand a chance against Vokan's forces once that happens."

"Is there any possible way your magi can divert the water?" Elyssa said. "If we can lessen the load on the wall even a little bit, it might help."

"Given time, we could construct another wall or dig channels in the valley walls," Agula said, "but we don't have the personnel necessary to do that in a few hours, a day, or even a week."

I punched my palm. "I wonder how many souls Vokan burned through to build that dam."

"That leaves us with few options." Elyssa looked worriedly at the distant wall. "It'll take a day or more before the volume of water reaches critical mass. I don't know if blowing the dam early will help or not."

"What prevents Vokan from simply repairing the dam or starting over?" Agula said.

"Nothing, but it buys us more time." She nodded toward the ocean. "Do you have ships?"

"A few fishing boats," Agula said. "Our pleasure vessels were destroyed decades ago. If you're asking for an evacuation by sea, I'm afraid we don't have the means."

I was already brewing a plan for the dam as they continued to bounce ideas off one another. A concentrated blast of Brilliance would open a hole in the base and allow thousands of gallons to flow out without creating a flood. I doubted Askot even bothered to guard the dam. Who would be crazy enough to sneak in where hundreds of gepherons and their riders waited to tear them apart?

I can do it.

"Challenge accepted," I said.

Elyssa and Agula blinked.

"Um, you want to herd all the goats and sheep to the southeast quadrant?" Elyssa said.

I hadn't realized the topic of their conversation when I interrupted. "No, I mean, I can punch some holes in the base of the dam with Brilliance. It'll drain the dam without unleashing a flood. If we do it at night, they may not even realize it until the next day. Either way, it'll buy us time."

"That's not a bad idea," Elyssa said. "But I have to meet with the gryphon riders and other troops to work on our defenses."

"There won't be much to defend if we don't do something about the dam." I looked down at the ship. "Shelton or Adam can take me."

"They're working on the aether generators." Elyssa shook her head. "That dam was pretty thick. You're strong Justin, but are you that strong?"

"By myself, maybe not. With the lens from Argus?" I shrugged. "I think so."

"Dammit, Justin, why does your plan have to make so much sense?" Elyssa sighed. "You're right. We won't have anything to defend if we don't stop the water. I'll get you in and out."

I grinned. "Nothing I love better than covert ops with my baby."

Agula raised an eyebrow. "You enjoy putting yourself in mortal danger? I find this entire ordeal rather terrifying."

"It's not the danger I enjoy, it's screwing with the plans of assholes like Vokan." I cracked my knuckles. "I freaking hate bullies."

A horn sounded in the distance. At first, I thought it was an attack, but then I spotted a handful of gryphons approaching from the northeast, Gemma at the lead. "They made it." I hoped Cinder and Bliss were okay in Solan. Since Vokan was out here causing trouble, they might have an easier time gathering info.

I went back to the ship and took a nap so I could recover my strength for the operation. When Elyssa woke me, it was two in the morning. "Justin, it's time to go." She wore the honeycomb armor of the gryphon riders. The cloth accentuated every luscious curve in her body.

"Damn, you look good." I ran a hand up her leg and grinned lasciviously. "Got fifteen minutes before—"

She put a finger on my lips. "No, babe. Put on your pants and let's go."

I sighed. "Party pooper."

"Hey, you were the one with the brilliant idea for a night assault on the dam." Elyssa leaned down and gently nipped my ear. "But I could definitely go for a victory celebration after."

That got me at full attention. I got up. "Yes, ma'am!"

"I got you some Utopian armor too." She handed me a unitard with an open seam in the front. It hung off my frame like a tent at a clown rodeo. "They didn't have any my size?"

Elyssa laughed. "You're adorable." She reached down to my crotch. My blood grew hot and hormones kicked into full overdrive. Her finger reached inside and tugged. The seam sealed from bottom to top and the armor shrank to a perfect fit.

I released a long breath. "That didn't go the way I thought it would."

"With a one-track mind like that, a lot of things won't." Elyssa winked. "Let's go."

I took out my arcphone and selected a cloaking spell. It was a good spell, but it'd drain the phone fast to keep such a large object as the *Raptor* hidden from enemy eyes. Arcphones recharged themselves from any source of aether, but even they couldn't maintain such a high output for long.

"Do me proud, Nookli." I stroked the screen. "We've been through a lot."

"There are no Indian restaurants nearby, Justin," It replied. "Would you like me to expand the search parameters?"

Elyssa rolled her eyes. "What it is it with your phone and Indian restaurants?"

I shrugged. "I don't know, but it always seems to think that's what I'm looking for."

"I'd risk the diarrhea for some real Indian food right now." Elyssa sighed went to the bridge. "I miss Eden."

"Me too." I went to the stern and checked Argus. Adam had stored the Chalon in his cabin so I could use the lens. He and Shelton were burning the midnight oil to get a working aether generator pieced together. "I think we have everything we need."

I saw a figure coming up the stairs behind Elyssa and blurred inside.

Bliss nearly fell over backward when she saw me coming. "It's just me, Justin!"

"Bliss?" Elyssa took her hand off the hilt of her sword. "What in the world are you doing here? I thought you were in Solan with Cinder."

"He sent me back to warn you that Vokan is on his way to Camelyn." She seemed out of breath. "I only just got back."

I frowned. "We didn't expect you so soon."

Bliss nodded. "Cinder decided to take a route past Morgan's Pass to make sure all the gepheron entered the pass. Not long after that, Vokan's flying citadel appeared. Cinder sent me to warn you as requested."

"Well, I hate to break it to you, but we already know." I filled her in on the most recent events. "We're on the way to put some holes in his dam."

Bliss seemed to take a moment to collect herself then nodded. "It's even better that I am here. I can help you."

Elyssa shook her head. "You look exhausted."

Bliss's shoulders stiffened. "With me along, Justin will have even more power."

It was an offer I couldn't refuse. "You're right. I'll take all the help I can get."

Her shoulders relaxed, as if my words cut an invisible rubber band. "Good. I was afraid you wouldn't let me."

"Well, let's get going." Elyssa piloted the ship up and over the giant wall, and we zipped ahead into the night.

I stood at the bow watching the shadowy landscape blur past. Pre-mission jitters twisted my stomach into knots. It didn't matter how many battles I'd fought, or undercover operations I'd executed, I didn't think I'd ever get used to this.

"I think I see something," Elyssa said. "Hang on." She angled the ship down to the bottom of the valley. My blue-tinted night vision outlined the treetops along the empty riverbed. Elyssa's superior night vision guided us just feet over them. The hum of the levitation gems and the gentle susurrus of the wind against the weather shield were the only sounds in the still of the night.

The flames of several hundred campfires lit the dark landscape ahead. I looked up at the sky, trying to discern flying sentinels from shadows and figments of my imagination. Elyssa spotted two, but they were high above.

I went to the bridge. "Looks like the rest of the army caught up."

"Agreed." Elyssa checked the map. "Turn on the cloak."

I took my arcphone outside and climbed on top of the bridge. I stuck the phone on the surface where it adhered with a click. A flick of my finger toggled the spell code to active. Symbols flashed, and the surface of the ship blurred to match the surroundings. For an instant, my instincts informed me I was standing on thin air though my brain knew otherwise. It still caused a moment of panic and disorientation to see the ship vanish.

I carefully climbed back down. The front deck was invisible along with the bridge. I felt around like a person in the dark. A hand reached from nowhere and pulled me inside the bridge. Bliss looked amused. "You looked lost."

I let go of her hand and smiled back. "Yeah, it's trippy out there."

Elyssa eased back on the throttle and the *Raptor* slowed as we neared the target. "The moment you start blasting with Brilliance, it'll light up this place like fireworks and alert the camp."

I gulped. "In other words, work fast, right?"

"Can I suggest something?" Bliss said.

I shrugged. "Go for it."

"What if we channel Stasis into several points along the base to weaken the stone first, then shatter those places with Brilliance?" She looked back and forth between me and Elyssa. "Was that a stupid idea?"

I stared blankly at her. "It's brilliant."

"Technically it's not," Elyssa said, "and that's what makes it brilliant."

I groaned. "Since when do you make bad jokes?"

"Sorry, couldn't help it." She turned to Bliss. "It's an amazing idea."

Bliss's smile could have warmed the sun. "Thank you."

The *Raptor* hovered a few feet from the base of the dam. Elyssa guided it to the left. I aimed Argus at the base. "Bliss, I need you to bolster me. You need to—"

She put a hand on my back and channeled. A surge of energy rushed into me. "Like that?"

My forehead tightened. "When did you learn that?"

"I learned it from your mother when she came to check on Cinder's progress with Argus." She looked down. "Alysea seemed surprised I could do it, since I'm not real."

"Hey." I turned around and nudged her chin up with a finger. "You're as real as it gets." I faced Argus again. "Let's do this."

Bliss poured energy into me. I added it to my own and wove Murk and Brilliance into a gray thread of Stasis. Argus amplified it into a beam four feet in diameter. Though it was dim, it still cast nebulous light that would be visible from above if anyone gave it a close look. I hoped the campfires on the sides of the river would mask it from the gepheron patrols.

The stone crackled and turned as gray as the beam, but it was hard to tell how deep it penetrated.

Elyssa looked up worriedly. "Maybe you should make a long gash instead of holes. This is taking too long."

I nodded. "Sweep the beam across."

Elyssa swiveled the lens slowly to affect the neighboring rock. Every second ticked by like an eternity. Sweat beaded on my forehead and Bliss's hand trembled on my back. I couldn't tell how far the Stasis penetrated, but it was time to test our handiwork. Elyssa had just adjusted the lens when wings rustled overhead.

Two gepheron landed right next to the beam.

"What is it?" The man wore the black and red armor of the loyalists. He stared directly at us, but the cloak shielded Argus and we stood behind the giant lens.

"It's coming from nowhere," the second man exclaimed. "Something's not right. Sound the alarm."

Elyssa swiveled Argus and the Stasis caught the first gepheron and its rider. They froze like statues. The second rider held what looked like a kazoo to his mouth and blew. Elyssa swiveled the lens toward him, but it was too late. A deep bellow like a fog horn echoed just before the man froze. Shouts and cries rose from the river banks.

"We're out of time," Elyssa said. "Blast the dam!"

I switched to Brilliance. The massive beam lit up the night like a match in a fart factory. Since Elyssa hadn't redirected the lens, the blast shattered the second gepheron rider. She jerked the lens back to the first part of the wall, raking the first rider in the process. He broke apart like glass.

The rock proved tougher. The granite chipped and popped. Cries and shouts of alarm echoed all around us. The flapping of giant bat wings gave the impression the sky was filled with gepheron. The deck blurred back into sight. My phone had run out of juice and the cloaking spell was off. I felt as naked as a blue jay on a Sunday afternoon.

"Come on, dammit. Break!" I felt another surge from Bliss and doubled down with everything I had left. The rock exploded into dust. Elyssa dragged the beam and the neighboring rock cracked and fell away. But one major thing was missing.

"Where's the water?" Bliss said. "Why hasn't it—"

She didn't have a chance to finish her sentence. A gout of water exploded from the first hole and knocked me backward. I slammed into the bridge window. Bliss cried out and grabbed the railing. The ship shuddered and drifted backward. A giant crack ran along the base of the dam about twenty feet in length. Rock shattered and broke beneath the strain of millions of tons of water.

"Shit!" Elyssa crawled beneath the rushing water and got back to the bridge. The *Raptor* lurched sideways out of the water and the weather shield flicked on. Dozens of crossbow bolts rained down, bouncing off the barrier.

Water roared into the valley, but it wasn't enough to escape the river banks. Aside from the huge hole we'd made, the rest of the dam held, just as we'd planned. I helped Bliss onto the bridge. She strapped herself into a chair while I gripped the back of Elyssa's chair.

"Hang on." Elyssa thrust the accelerator forward. The gems hummed to full power and—and nothing. We stayed in place.

"What?" I looked around, but nothing blocked us from going forward. I ran onto the deck and looked around. It didn't take long to find the massive claw of energy holding us in place.

Vokan had us by the balls.

CHAPTER 28

"It's one of those damned energy hands!" I ran to the nearest finger and summoned the last bits of my energy to thread Stasis. I didn't have nearly enough juice left to hit the whole hand, so I tried to think smart. *WWFD? What would Fjoeruss do?*

Lightning lit the sky like day. A massive platform with an ivory tower floated above the dam. Vokan stood at the top of the citadel, arms spread like a god about to smite an insect. "Such arrogance to think you could beat me, boy. Give me your ship, and show me how to use the portal device. In return, I will spare Camelyn and your friends."

I actually considered his offer. I could save an entire city if I just said yes. On the other hand, I'd unleash Vokan on the rest of the realms and we'd be trapped here for good. Instead, I answered him diplomatically with my middle finger. "Why don't you stick your energy fingers up your ass, Vokan?" Speaking of fingers, that gave me an idea. Fingers couldn't grip very well if they didn't have an opposable digit. I ran starboard and slid a little Stasis beneath the thumb.

Just a touch greased up the *Raptor* like a pig. The thumb lost its grip and the fingers couldn't apply any more pressure. Hundreds more crossbow bolts pinged off the shields. Gepheron swarmed around us. But the ship sprang free. We smashed through a squad of fliers. Bodies flew, and bat creatures scattered. Raging waters cut screams short.

Vokan's voice boomed, but I couldn't make out his words through the thunder and rumbling water.

We bolted the hell out of there.

The energy hand faded away. I didn't spot any others, probably because Vokan had to divert his attention to his leaky dam. Despite all his powers, I wondered if even he had the strength to hold back such a massive amount of water while patching the hole.

A tremendous crack echoed and the roar of water doubled in volume. I quickly realized what that meant. Vokan had just flipped *me* the middle finger.

"Oh, shit." I ran back inside the bridge. "Vokan just broke the dam!"

"That bastard!" Bliss gripped the armrests of her chair as if she wanted to tear them off. "All that for nothing."

Elyssa shook her head. "Not nothing. He planned to let water gather all night. That's millions of gallons that won't be slamming into the walls all at once. There's a chance he released the water before it reached critical mass."

"That's still an insane amount of water." I pushed wet hair out of my eyes and looked behind us. "If only we had a giant sponge."

Bliss slumped in her seat. "I feel so powerless."

I sighed and patted her shoulder. "We did everything we could. Now we just have to hope it was enough to keep the walls up."

"What if he makes another dam?" Bliss said. "Vokan could keep doing this until the walls finally fall."

Elyssa grimaced. "She's right. Even if the walls hold this time, there's nothing to stop Vokan from trying again."

I threw up my hands. "Great! Thanks for crushing that last bit of hope I had left." I went through the back door to the aft deck and stared out at the night sky. A mountain of water raced behind us. It would reach the walls in thirty minutes, give or take, and there was nothing I could do to stop it.

"It's inexorable." I'd been saving that word for a rainy day. The war against Daelissa seemed like a walk in the park compared to Vokan. And if I couldn't deal with Vokan, what hope did I have of fighting Baal and Xanomiel? "None at all."

It was one thing to fight with brute force, but something completely different to match wits with a being as ancient as Baal. Vokan seemed smarter and stronger than me. He also had an ego the size of a pregnant yak. If that was his weakness, I hadn't figured out how to exploit it.

Short of controlling the weather myself, I couldn't come up with a single way to prevent the flood. Since Camelyn had no way of evacuation by sea, it meant the city would fall. Vokan would soon control the last city, and Baal's master plan would take another giant leap forward.

I hoped Mom was holding things together back in Seraphina, because I was riding the fail boat straight to the bottom in Utopia.

We reached the city walls well in advance of the flood of doom. It seemed the entire city was still awake judging from the crowd at the council towers.

Agula jogged over to meet us the moment we landed in the plaza. The light of hope faded from his eyes when he saw the slump in our shoulders and the defeat in our faces. "It did not go well?"

Elyssa shook her head and summarized the events. "Our only hope is that the waters didn't reach critical mass. Unfortunately, we won't know until the flood hits."

"You did what you could," Agula said. "For that, we are grateful."

"Even if this flood doesn't break the wall, Vokan will probably build another dam and try again in a few days." I shook my head sadly. "No matter what we do, he'll eventually win."

"Is there anywhere to evacuate the city?" Elyssa said. "Surely there's some contingency plan."

"Even if we loaded every flying carriage with people, and every flying creature took two passengers, we still would be woefully short," Agula said. "And where would we go?"

"Anywhere is better than staying here and dying," I said.

"If Vokan's past patterns hold true, then it is unlikely he'll kill us." Agula's eyes pinched with worry. "It is more likely he'll turn some of us into slaves." He looked toward the wall. "How long do we have?"

"Maybe thirty minutes," Elyssa said. "Is everyone safely away from the northern side?"

Agula nodded. "It is abandoned."

I didn't dare rest my hopes on anything, but I asked anyway. "Where are Adam and Shelton?"

"They relocated to a workshop two blocks south." Agula pointed to a three-story stone building that might have passed for a medieval church. "They seemed to have made some progress."

"What about the sprite problem?" I asked.

"Ah, yes." Agula's eyes brightened. "Vokan's enchantment is complex, but we deciphered all but a critical part of it."

"What's preventing you from deciphering it?" I asked.

"It appears to be demon magic." Agula sighed. "As it is a banned subject, we have no experts."

I groaned. "More bad news. Can't you dispel the part you understand?"

"I'm afraid not," Agula said. "It could kill the host human."

"What about Bonehead? He's not linked to a human."

Agula shook his head. "The demon magic is threaded into the enchantment. Until we understand what it is, we cannot risk extinguishing a life whether human or sprite."

"Like I said, more bad news." I huffed. "I'm going to talk to Shelton and Adam. Maybe they have a little sparkle of sunshine to offer."

Elyssa's brow furrowed. "I'll stay here and see what we can do to defend the city if the flood breaks the walls."

I squeezed her hand. "Don't take any unnecessary risks. I'll be back soon."

She nodded. "I plan to take the *Raptor* up for a view of the flood." Elyssa checked the time. "Meet back here in fifteen if you want to go."

"I'll be here." Despite my magical exhaustion, my physical side had plenty of vigor left. I ran to the building Agula had pointed out and found Shelton and Adam inside watching a group of people working on metal objects.

Shelton's eyes flared with hope. "Success?"

I shook my head. "We're screwed." I told them what to expect.

Adam groaned. "Well, at least I have epic destruction to look forward to."

I nodded at their work in progress. "Any luck with aether generators?"

Shelton shrugged. "A little." He took me to a large black box. "This is the prototype." He tapped his wand against it and the motor hummed to life. Well, it didn't exactly hum. It rattled, shook, and shut down with an explosive exhale of black smoke. "As you can see, it's not working great."

Adam pointed out the other people in the room. "The earth and water magi are adjusting the molds we used to make the prototype. Once they're done, we'll recast the cylinders and engine block."

"What about the aether generating part?" I asked.

"That works fine," Shelton said. "We used some aetherite gems Adam brought with us to magnify the output. If we can get the combustion engine working, we'll have more than enough power to make shields."

"How many generators do we need to shield the entire city?" I asked.

"A hundred at least, strategically placed," Shelton said. "Even if we get a working prototype by tonight, it'll take us weeks to make enough to cover the entire city."

"If only we had some of those car engines from Solan." Adam sighed. "A big block eight-cylinder would really pump out some serious aether."

"Provided we could get them working again," Shelton said. "Most of those cars were real rust heaps."

Adam scoffed. "Dude, anything is better than building an engine from scratch."

"Well, do what you can." I headed for the door. "I'm going to watch the flood hit and pray the wall holds."

Shelton grimaced. "What happens if it breaks through?"

"Then we fight an army of gepheron with what we have." I left them with that grim thought and returned to the plaza to board the *Raptor* with Elyssa.

Bliss walked up the gangway and took a seat on the bridge without a word. She looked as defeated as I felt. Elyssa gazed dully out the window as she guided the ship up and toward the wall, the usual spark absent from her violet eyes. I went to the bow. Water already flowed through the river and into the city, but it was the small amount we'd released with our sabotage.

A distant rumble reached my ears. As fingers of pink spread across the dawn sky, a roiling wall of water roared down the valley. Trees, mud, rocks, and other debris tumbled before the might of the raging flood.

The last mile before impact seemed like an eternity of stomach-wrenching stress. A bitter taste filled my mouth. We were safe in the ship, but what if the wall fell? Would we stay and fight, or flee?

Cold wind rushed against my face. The thunder grew to a deafening crescendo. It felt like Thailand all over again. The defining moment that led to betrayal and banishment from Eden. The start of our odyssey in Seraphina. My fists clenched, and my heart filled with rage and despair.

The flood waters hit.

If the wall had been straight or curved outward, it might have lessened the impact, but the bowl shape diverted the water directly toward the center. The first surge barely reached a quarter of the way up the wall. The second scaled halfway. The third built upon the first two and crested over the wall. Muddy water and debris rushed over the top. Trees speared into buildings.

Terra cotta shingles shattered. Windows broke. The stone buildings withstood the initial abuse. Caught in the cup of the wall, the water had nowhere to go but up and over. Thousands of gallons rushed beneath the wall and through the riverbed, but it did nothing to abate the millions pouring over the top.

Bliss pointed down. "Look at the wall!"

The top shifted noticeably, leaning back a foot. Even more water flooded the streets, turning them to rivers. I covered my ears to drown out the roar. And then, it was over. The flood water caught in the curve of the wall sank back, its momentum arrested and settled into a massive lake. The water found its way around the sides of the wall and the riverbed acted as a drain.

The front half of Camelyn resembled Venice. Few streets were visible beneath the muddy water, but it wasn't as bad as it could have been. Two buildings near the front had collapsed beneath the weight of mud and trees. Most had withstood the impact, a testament to the builders.

"Son of a bitch." Elyssa's jaw tightened. "The river is drying up again."

Sure enough, the water slowed to a trickle not far out from the new lake in front of the wall. "Vokan is prepping another flood."

"The wall barely withstood this one," Bliss said. "The next one might topple it!"

She was absolutely right. We weren't up shit creek without a paddle— we were at the end of the creek in a sinking boat. And there was nothing we could do to stop the destruction.

CHAPTER 29

"We need more time." Shelton took off his hat and ran a hand down his head. "Ain't no way we can come up with enough generating power to stop a damned flood in a few days."

It was the morning after the flood and we'd convened at the top of the council towers to survey the damage and talk options. It would take only three days for the flood waters to reach critical mass behind Vokan's new dam. He might even give it a fourth day if he felt extra spiteful.

Adam and Shelton had managed to make a working generator prototype that didn't sputter and die within minutes, but now another dilemma slapped us in the face.

"Most of our natural and liquid gas were wiped out by the flood." Agula pointed to the wreckage of toppled metal cylinders in the northwest quadrant of the city. "Those were our primary storage tanks."

Ki scowled at the rainbow tint on the muddy waters coursing sluggishly through the city. "It has fouled the water. Our plumbing and sewage is clogged with debris. It will take our water magi hours to cleanse enough water for drinking."

Adam groaned and leaned against the railing. "One working generator. Barely enough gas to fuel fifty, much less the hundred or more we need."

"And we can't even flush the toilets after a big poop," Shelton finished. "I think it's time to consider other options."

"We don't have time to build ships, and not enough capacity to evacuate the city by air," Agula reminded him. "There's nowhere to hide by land."

"No secret caves in the mountains? No forests to hide in?" Shelton waved a hand at the landscape. "It's a big world out there. Why not evacuate while it's dark and find some other place to live?"

"Our citizens are ready to fight," Ki said. "But how can we fight water?"

"Maybe we should make surfboards." Adam scoffed. "At least we could ride the wave of doom."

Shelton chuckled. "That much force would shoot you to the moon."

"At least it would be an entertaining way to die." Adam leaned his forehead on the railing. "It was so much easier when we fought soldiers. Hell, I'd rather fight the gepheron."

I imagined all that water pressing down on the wall. Imagined it crashing through the city and leveling everything. *There's no way to stop it.* Looking at the streams the streets had become knocked loose an old memory, namely Bucky Cuffler's science fair project in fifth grade.

And it reignited a spark of hope. "I've got an idea that's so crazy it might just work."

"Does it involve hot air balloons?" Shelton said. "Because I'll bet we could make enough to evacuate the city."

All conversation stopped.

"Hot air balloon?" Adam looked dumbstruck. "Shelton, that's literally the worst idea you've ever come up with."

"Or the best," Shelton shot back. "I mean, we're all doomed, so let's go out in style."

"Blaze of glory," Adam said, as if the idea appealed to him.

I clapped my hands. "Um, did anyone hear what I said?"

"Yeah, but the cliché kind of got lost in the moment," Shelton said.

Adam raised an eyebrow and waggled it. "There is a theory, but it's never been tried."

I groaned. "No, really, I think this will work."

Elyssa leaned against the wall. "I'm willing to entertain any ideas at this point."

I told them all about Bucky's science fair project and how we could apply it to save the city. It wasn't a homemade volcano, or a potato battery, but something far more practical. And no, it wasn't a submarine.

"First of all," Shelton said, "we'd need some extremely strong materials to pull this off."

"Same enchantment as the wall." Adam sketched out long flat panels on his phone and showed it to Agula. "How long would it take to enchant these with the same resistance to the wall?"

"How many?" he asked.

"Two dozen at least," Shelton said.

"A day perhaps." Agula examined the dimensions. "Are they large enough?"

"What about the debris?" Elyssa said. "Won't rocks and trees jam it?"

"Not if we make a baffle around it," Adam said. "It'd have to be enchanted as well."

"Actually, there shouldn't be nearly the same amount of debris this time," Shelton said. "The first flood wiped the valley clean."

"Oh, good point." Adam pursed his lips. "If we space the panels wide enough, it might not jam anyway."

They tossed design ideas back and forth and finally settled on one that would best survive the flood.

Elyssa and I risked a reconnaissance flight to confirm the existence of a new dam. We paused just over the city walls to examine the mass of trees and rocks piled up outside. Earth magi reduced rocks to rubble while those skilled with air levitated entire trees out of the dry riverbed and stacked them neatly outside the flood zone.

"Pretty cool," I said. "I could learn a thing or two from these people."

"All the realms could." Elyssa steered the *Raptor* away from the wall and we sped along the valley.

Few trees remained standing and most of the foliage was either gone or covered in mud. The next flood would have nothing standing in its way when it roared down the channel. I hoped my plan worked. If it did, I'd give Bucky Cuffler a gold star for his brilliant work.

We reached the dam a few minutes later. It stood twice as tall as the old one, and the reservoir was already half full. A lone gepheron flew toward us. We could easily outrun it, so I wasn't particularly worried.

A young man waved a green flag as he approached. I waited until he was a hundred feet off our bow before telling him to stop.

"I come under a flag of truce," the man said. "Lord Vokan, the Grand Magus of Utopia, extends an armistice that he may avoid the utter destruction of Camelyn and the people within its walls."

"Let me guess. If I give him the ship, he'll spare everyone, right?" I could already tell this guy wasn't a willing soldier, but under compulsion.

"I am not privy to his conditions," the man said. "Come with me as honored guests."

Elyssa rolled her eyes. "Yeah, so he can steal the ship and kidnap us. I don't think so."

Sunlight shimmered strangely in the air about a hundred yards to port. I focused my gaze and watched. It did it again a few seconds later. What it meant sent my heart racing. "Elyssa, get us out of here!"

She didn't need to be told twice. The ship wheeled around and jetted east just as fifty gepheron exploded from behind a camouflage shield. Apparently Vokan's elemental skills allowed him to bend light just like our spells. Except he concealed an entire freaking army. If we'd waited a moment longer, they would have swarmed the deck before we got the shields up.

I cupped my hands and shouted, "Tell Vokan to shove his armistice up his pasty white ass!"

Elyssa took a deep breath. "That was too close."

"Yeah, but it also gives us an edge."

She raised an eyebrow. "How so?"

"Now I know what he's capable of and how to spot it." I dropped into a seat. "Then again, there's not much I can do if he cloaks a hundred gepheron and sends them over the walls."

"He can try, but they won't make it past the perimeter wards," Elyssa said. "Plus, Vokan would have to be within a hundred yards of the wall and I doubt he'd go that close."

"True." I stared at the blue skies ahead and hoped our new master plan would help us withstand the next flood.

The wall was nearly clear of debris when we returned to Camelyn later that day. A silver cylinder roughly the size and shape of a jumbo jet engine was being buried by earth magi in the dry riverbed about a hundred yards from the wall. Another one sat on the river shore. Things had moved faster than I thought possible during our day trip. I hoped that meant the entire project was going as well.

I found the rest of the gang outside the same warehouse they'd used to make the prototype generators. Shelton watched the door like a hawk. Adam fiddled around on his phone. Bliss sat on a half-empty spool of copper and watched the others.

"What's the word?" I asked.

"They locked us out," Shelton said. "Said they need all their concentration to infuse the materials."

"So you're just standing around outside?" Elyssa said.

Shelton shrugged. "Nothing better to do."

Adam grunted. "Except pray fervently that everything works."

I told them about Vokan's surprise for us.

"Man, he cloaked that many gepheron?" Adam whistled. "That dude's got access to way too much power."

"That's for sure." I nodded at the door. "Is Agula in there?"

"No, he's back at the council tower," Adam said.

"Okay. Let me know when they're done." I went outside and walked down the street toward the towers. The water had mostly dried, leaving caked mud and dirt on the once pristine stone roads. Though the most significant flooding happened on the north end of town, the water had reached its tendrils all across the middle of the city.

Elyssa walked next to me, eyebrow arched. "What do you want to see Agula about? I already relayed the info about the dam to Ki."

"I need to talk to him about Vokan." I walked around a pile of mud and rejoined Elyssa on the other side. "I meant to ask him when we got here, but the river dried up and the shit hit the fan."

"No rest for the weary." Elyssa kicked a rock out of the way. "If your plan actually works, then we need to find a permanent solution." Her eyes flashed. "We need to end Vokan."

"Assassination?" I said.

She answered with a curt nod. "Yup."

"I don't know how unless you have a sniper rifle hidden somewhere."

"Vokan is overconfident." Elyssa twirled one of her forked sai swords. "I could infiltrate his camp and"—she drew a finger across her throat —"finish him."

"By yourself."

Her eyebrows arched. "Do you doubt me?"

I put my hands up defensively. "No, but Vokan probably has all sorts of security. It'd be better to take me along."

Her lips pursed. "I'll think about it."

Hundreds of people waited in lines around the tower. They weren't waiting for food or water, but for brooms, pails, and other tools. North of the tower, Utopians worked in groups to clear the streets of large debris while others came behind them and cleaned up the mud.

"Are you for real?" I stopped and stared. "What's the point of cleaning up right now? What if my plan doesn't work and the entire city is wiped away?"

"Well, at least the city will be clean."

I scoffed. "That's like keeping clean underwear in the dash compartment in case of a car wreck."

"Keeping a pair of clean undies around is always a good idea." Elyssa walked around the line and headed inside the tower.

We found Agula at the top. He sat at a table outside with Elaine and Daana.

"Ah, Justin and Elyssa." Agula gave us a curt bow. "Everything is going as well as can be expected." He guided me by the arm and pointed out a group of people guiding a spool of thick metal cable down the street toward the wall. "All the materials should be in place soon."

"That's great." I greeted the other two councilors. "I didn't come here to talk about that, though."

"Oh?" Daana regarded me curiously. "What else is there to discuss?"

"Vokan." I pulled out a chair from the table and sat down. "What do you know about the relic he used to siphon souls into the cantrap?"

The trio looked at me uneasily for a moment before Agula answered. "There are many stories surrounding what really happened, but the truth is rather mundane. It so happened I was on the Grand Council that year, so I witnessed most of this first hand."

I settled into my chair. "Tell me everything, please."

"Three strangers visited the council chambers in Solan during one of our monthly meetings. They brought with them what appeared to be a fossilized embryo." Agula shuddered. "We had many questions, of course. Who are you? Where are you from? What is this thing?"

"Three strangers?" I looked at Elyssa. "I'll bet it was the Fallen."

"Sounds like their modus operandi." Elyssa saw the questioning looks on the councilors' faces. "The Fallen are Seraphim who were banished from Seraphina thousands of years ago. They took up residence on Mount Olympus near Atlantis and apparently spend their time traveling to other realms so they can scatter Relics of Juranthemon around."

Agula nodded. "Yes, they said something similar, though they didn't mention their banishment from their home realm."

"These relics are the ones you mentioned in our first meeting," Daana said. "If too many are put together, it could cause the realms to collide."

I nodded. "Those are the ones."

"The Fallen told us this relic was named the Child of Jura, and that it was vital we hide it and protect it for all eternity." Agula smiled. "We agreed."

"How'd Vokan get it?" I asked.

"Vokan was an apprentice at the time. I only know this because he was scheduled to come before the magus council for another disciplinary hearing." Agula shook his head. "Because of his brilliance, the boy thought he was better than everyone. We suspended him from school for one year. Instead of accepting his punishment, he took the arch to Eden and used his magic to take over a tribe in South America."

"How awful," Daana said. "How could anyone act like this?"

I wondered that myself. Nearly every Utopian seemed to adhere to their social code. What made Vokan such a rebel?

"We arrested him and brought him back for trial." Agula sighed. "He was banished from the cities for life."

"We read some history on him," I said. "He returned fifty years later a full master of all the elements, right?"

Agula nodded. "He simply showed up in Solan during a monthly meeting, showing off his powers like some sort of entertainer."

Elaine scowled. "Disgraceful."

"Indeed," Agula said. "I was not on the council at the time, but we saw the newscast where he fought the entire council. We later examined the video and realized he had the Child of Jura on a chain around his neck."

"How did he get it?" I asked.

"We suspect he used his power to steal it from the underground chamber where it was stored." Agula seemed to gaze into the past. "He must have had it for some time, because he already knew how to use it."

"What about the cantrap?" I said. "Where did that come from?"

"The Child of Jura removes the soul from a being and transfers it to another vessel. You could use it to swap souls between bodies if you so desired." Agula's eyes tightened. "The cantrap is a demonic construct designed to store souls as an energy source."

I grimaced. "It's like a snack pack for demons."

And Vokan had a way to fill it with every soul in this realm.

CHAPTER 30

"The cantrap stores the souls, and Vokan feeds on them as needed." Agula's shoulders slumped. "The remaining free cities elected new council members to replace those soul-ripped by Vokan. The new council lifted the ban on demon magic so we could study how to counter the cantrap. Unfortunately, Vokan conquered Hevia and Ganalon over the next year. We used that time to build the wall and protect ourselves from the eidolons."

"Do you have any texts on the cantrap?" I asked. "I need every shred of info I can find."

"Our texts only describe the cantrap, not how to make one." Agula shrugged apologetically. "Our people banned demon magic thousands of years ago once they realize the perils of inviting such dangerous beings into our realm. The original texts were destroyed. Only vague descriptions exist in the educational texts in schools."

"Yet Vokan somehow overcame those obstacles and learned demon magic." Daana shook her head. "How does one learn something from nothing?"

"Banning demon magic probably saved Utopia from detection," I said, "but Baal eventually found you. I'm almost positive he's the one who influenced Vokan and educated him in demon magic. I wouldn't be surprised if he's the reason Vokan turned out the way he did."

"Father of lies." Elyssa blew out a breath. "He really did a number on Vokan and Utopia."

"So Vokan is not truly at fault for his misdeeds?" Agula's brow furrowed. "This is a terrible injustice."

"Oh, Vokan's still at fault. He gave in to Baal's temptations." I rapped my fingers on the table. "What happens if I somehow destroy the cantrap?"

Agula shook his head. "Your guess is as good as mine."

"If there's nothing to hold them, they go free." Elyssa shrugged. "That's my guess."

I imagined a long tether binding Vokan to the cantrap. Shook my head. *No, that can't be right.* It didn't seem likely he could draw energy from so far away. That meant he had to have a smaller version of the cantrap he could carry with him. "The cantrap kind of reminds me of the soul-stones we used in the war."

"Those things." Elyssa shuddered. "Yeah, I guess there is a similarity, but a soulstone only holds one soul, and breaking it releases the soul. The cantrap looks more like an energy barrier."

I'd hoped knowing more about soulstones might lead to a solution for the cantrap, but it was obviously a dead end. "How does the Child work? Do you have to touch the person to steal the soul?"

Agula nodded. "The relic must touch the skin for several seconds. We believe once the soul is gone, it leaves only raw life force, and a tether between it and the relic. This is how Vokan controls the eidolons. This tether creates an aura around the creatures, protecting them from harm."

"What about the weird mutations?" I asked. "The pouncers, rammers, and others?"

"They did not exist decades ago," Agula said. "It appears the aura mutates some of them."

"Making them even more dangerous," Elaine said.

"All eidolons are dangerous," Agula said. "Because of them, Vokan doesn't need to use the relic to convert more people into his puppets. The tether between the relic and the eidolons allows them to rip the soul from people. When they return to the towers in Solan, they feed the souls into the cantrap."

"That explains how Vokan conquered Solan so easily." I shook my head. "The infection spread exponentially."

"If only it were an infection we could treat," Elaine said. "Unfortunately, it is a state of transition. The subject is not dead or alive, but somewhere in between."

An idea drifted in and out of my forebrain, just long enough to almost, but not quite, grasp it. I finally got a hold of it and dragged it in. "I think I know why you can't decipher the demon bindings giving Vokan control of the sprites." I snapped my fingers. "Where's Bonehead? I need to see him right away."

"He and the other prisoner are in a holding cell below." Agula led us and the other councilors to the levitator and down a few levels.

The holding cells resembled studio apartments, complete with beds and private bathrooms. The Utopians apparently treated their prisoners pretty well. Agula touched a finger to the first door and it slid open. Bonehead the skeleton lay on the bed, wrist bones still bound in sleeper cuffs. I let my eyes lose focus and switched to demon vision. Hazy auras of light drifted around the councilors and Elyssa. The sprite inside Bonehead resembled a pinpoint of light, almost like a distant star. I focused on that light, zooming in so I could see the threads Agula mentioned.

No matter how hard I tried, I couldn't bring them into focus. My physical being wasn't attuned enough to it. I reached for it with tendrils of my own aura. They latched on as they usually did to feed, but the sprite felt cold and alien. I sensed a knot, but nothing more detailed. My efforts were getting me nowhere.

So I turned inward and drew on the support of the rowdy demon half of my soul. *I need your help.*

Consume. Destroy. Give me control.

I sighed. *No.*

Why?

It was the first time in a long while my inner demon had asked a rational question. Dad once told me that the demon part of my soul matured at a much slower rate than the rest of me. He assured me it would be quite a while before it got over wanting to destroy the world.

I took a moment to consider the question. *It's wrong to consume and destroy everything. I need you to help me.*

Why?

Apparently, my demon soul had the mind of a five-year-old. *Do you want to know why the sky is blue too?*

No.

Well, at least there was that. *Look, I need to destroy the control link someone put on this sprite. Can you do that?*

Destroy? It asked hopefully.

Yes, but no destroy until I say okay.

It remained silent a moment before sullenly answering. *Okay.*

It was probably the most constructive conversation I'd ever had with my demon side in years. I let it out of its cage. It was like handing a starving child a tub of ice cream. My demon half surged into my body. I braced myself for swelling muscles and horns. But the physical side-effects never manifested. Instead, my vision shifted and blurred.

I blinked a few times and looked at Elyssa. I shouted in alarm and jumped backward at what I saw. Instead of a person with an aura around them, I saw shadowy outlines filled with ghosts and swirling energies. The ghosts consisted of shifting hues of colors. Shades of blue and red with soft white glows.

This is some next-level shit!

Elyssa's core glowed a soft red. "What is it Justin?" The nearest ghost reached out an ethereal limb and touched my meat shell.

"I'm really freaking out right now!" *Is this how demons see people?*

Meat, soul, life, spirit.

It took a moment to realize what my demon meant. The ghost inside Elyssa wasn't one solid object. It consisted of several overlaid elements, each one symbiotic to the next. I could have stared at the intricate connections all day, but a small voice at the back of my head reminded me that this wasn't important right now.

I turned back to Bonehead. I found the silhouette of the skeleton and examined the sprite within. It pulsed a gentle blue but its aura was sickly yellow. *I need to get closer.* It was as if someone had shoved a microscope in front of my eyes. The sprite swelled to fill my vision. Like the people in the room, the sprite consisted of soul, spirit, and life force, plus other things I couldn't readily identify.

Here. My demon side pointed to a tangled net of energy around the sprite.

Can we untie it?

A ghostly tendril extended from my soul and gently worked at the knots. Time seemed to lose all meaning as I labored. I felt sweat dripping on my physical face. Felt the muscles in my neck tightening. After several knots, I discovered a sickly yellow thread of demon spirit woven into the net. *What now?*

Consume.

I felt my face grimace. *You mean, eat it?*

Yes.

I didn't know how to eat it. *How?*

Demon bro took over. My tendrils latched to the demon spirit and sucked it in like a spaghetti noodle. I could have sworn I heard a ghostly wail as I absorbed the spirit. I felt a brief rush of adrenalin.

What was that feeling?

I sensed my demon smile. *Power.*

Part of me recoiled, but another half, a darker side, relished it. And it scared the hell out of me.

Was that part of a demon?

A newborn caustic spirit.

I recoiled. *Jesus, I just ate a baby demon?*

My demon roared with laughter.

On the bright side, with the baby demon gone, the netting fell apart and dissolved.

Done. My demon retreated back into its cage and shut the door behind it. I blinked a few times as the world resolved once more into physical beings. I staggered back and nearly fell on my ass, but Elyssa caught me.

"Justin, are you okay?" She sat me on the bed. "You literally just stared at Bonehead for an hour. The only reason I knew you were doing anything was because your face kept twitching."

I caught a whiff of rotten eggs. "Did someone fart in here? It stinks."

The others looked at each other. Daana shook her head. "We thought it was you."

I scratched my head. "Must've been the demon in the sprite."

"Fascinating." Elaine sat in a nearby chair with a pad full of notes. "I would love some insight into this phenomenon."

"What happened near the end?" Elyssa asked. "You looked...ecstatic."

"He looked maniacal to me," Daana said. "It was almost frightening."

I took a moment to clear my head. "I can't really explain it." *And I don't really want to.* I tugged at Bonehead's cuffs, but my fingers didn't want to cooperate. "Can you remove those?"

Elyssa opened the cuffs but held the skeleton's wrists. "I'm not taking any chances."

A gentle glow emanated from the eye sockets, flicking on and off as if mimicking a blink. "Where am I?"

"Camelyn," I said. "We took you from Vokan."

Bonehead looked around. "For some reason, I'm not compelled to attack you." He paused. "I feel...alive."

I nodded at Elyssa. "You can release him."

She did and backed off warily.

Bonehead stood. "I have not felt like this in decades. What did you do to me?"

"I removed Vokan's compulsion. You're a free sprite."

His jawbone dropped open. "You, a human helped me?"

"It was Vokan who enslaved sprites, not us," Agula said. "We are firmly against such policies."

"We are sorry for your maltreatment," Daana said. "Though we may not have much time left as free citizens, consider yourself in our sanctuary."

"This is somewhat unsettling." Bonehead walked around as if taking his first steps as a free sprite. "Does this mean I can manifest however I want?"

Elyssa raised an eyebrow. "You don't have to be a skeleton anymore if that's what you're asking."

"But it does look really cool," I said.

Bonehead nodded. "Does this mean you can free other sprites?" He abruptly laughed and danced. "I can talk about freeing others without agony!"

I sat back down on the bed, still sweaty from my earlier endeavors. "Yes, I can free more sprites, but it'll take a while. I'm still learning the process."

Bonehead put a hand on my shoulder. "You have my eternal gratitude." He looked toward the open door. "Can I leave?" He answered himself before anyone else could. "Of course you can. You're free!" The skeleton crackled and rolled in upon itself until only an orb of light twinkled in its place. It streaked away and vanished.

Daana and Agula had tears in their eyes.

"How beautiful," Daana said. "To be free after so many years." She squeezed my hand. "Thank you, Justin."

"Yes, indeed." Agula touched my shoulder. "You are a good man."

Elaine smiled. "You have shown me scientific wonders today. I am in your debt."

"I appreciate the sentiment, but we have a long way to go." I took a deep breath and offered a smile. "Let's move on to the other prisoner."

We went to the next room. The man possessed by the enslaved sprite slumbered peacefully. I called upon my inner demon. *I need you again.*

I will help for trade.

"Here it comes," I muttered. *What do you want?*

Full control.

I knew he'd demand something like that. *I'll give you full control for thirty minutes.*

No. A day.

So you can rape and pillage everything in sight? No. I silently cursed my inability to control this part of me. Dad had mastered it, but he'd once been a pure demon that merged with a human. He told me that Daemos eventually mastered their inner demons, but it could take decades. I was still just a kid by that standard.

A day.

Why do you want to destroy and consume? Why can't you use all that pent up energy to build a house or do something constructive?

Not what I want. I want power.

You do realize that we're tiny little peons compared to Baal, right? You understand he could squash us like bugs in Haedaemos.

My inner demon went silent for a moment. *We consume Baal. Become more powerful.*

There was just no getting through to him and his one-track mind. I had no choice but to give him what he wanted.

CHAPTER 31

I'd give him control, but it definitely wouldn't be for a day. *I will give you one hour. Final offer. Take it or leave it.*

He didn't answer for such a long time, I thought he'd abandoned me. It was so confusing dealing with the demon part of me. We were two halves of a whole, but it felt like I had multiple personalities fighting for control. I'd beaten my demon side into submission long ago. He knew I could cage him at will and that he'd never get out without my participation. So why wasn't he taking my deal?

Offer taken.

The answer jolted me from my reverie. But before I answered, I sensed something I'd never detected before. My demon was amused. More than that, he was overjoyed. Why would he be so happy when I just down-sized his offer from a day to an hour? Was it healthy to talk about a part of myself in third person?

I didn't have any answers. On the upside, I did have a loophole to play with. I'd promised my demon bro an hour of full control, but I hadn't said *when.* I wondered if he could hear my thoughts, or if I could exclude that part of me.

Again, no answers.

Help me with this sprite.

Once again, I shifted into true demon vision. I instantly zeroed in on the sprite and the thread of caustic spirit. Without even touching the other knots, I swallowed my rising gorge and ate the baby demon spirit. The net of compulsion dissolved.

My sight shifted back to normal and I looked at Elyssa. "Release him."

"That was much quicker," Elaine said. "Did you master it?"

I hadn't mastered anything. Apparently, my demon knew exactly what to do now. "Practice makes perfect, I guess."

Elyssa removed the sleeper cuffs. A tiny orb of light flew from his eye and expanded. A tendril snaked from it and touched me. *I am free. Thank you.*

How long were you a prisoner?

We were taken long ago and bound to humans. Can you help the others?

I nodded. *I'll do my best.*

The ball of light bounced around as if doing a happy dance. Then it zipped out of the door.

"They don't seem to be able to go through solid objects." Elaine took more notes. "They are energy, but solid."

"Help!" The man jumped up from the bed and tried to run.

Elyssa caught him and pushed him against the wall. "You're safe. You're free."

The man gasped and looked wildly around the room. "Free?" Tears streamed from his eyes and he sank to the ground, sobbing. "I never imagined being free again."

Daana sat beside him and put a comforting arm around his shoulder. "You're safe with us now."

For now, anyway. Vokan would soon unleash the flood waters and our survival depended on our adaptation of a science fair project.

"Do you remember everything from the time you were enslaved?" Elaine asked.

"I remember." The man looked up, tear-streaked face heavy with grief. "Sometimes I had control of my body, but I always felt the chains around my limbs. When Askot or one of his lieutenants gave an order, I lost control of my body."

Elaine nodded and wrote it down. "Did you see the process they used to bind you?"

"There is a building in Solan filled with, I don't know, glass prisons." His gaze grew distant. "It could have been something else, but I'm no magus."

"What was in the prisons?" Elaine asked.

"Thousands of sprites." His tone grew heavy. "I've never seen so many." He blinked as if coming from a trance. "Askot's loyalists took us one-by-one and bound us to a table. Vokan somehow compelled the sprite to enter our eye. When he was done, the new slave was released to join the ranks."

"How do they enter the eye if they can't go through solid objects?" Elaine seemed to ask the question to herself. "Perhaps organic tissue is different?"

"Perhaps," Agula said.

Elyssa asked the important question. "How many slave troops are there?"

"Over four hundred," he replied. "There are eighty loyalists, including

Askot." His eyes widened, and a vengeful smile curled his lips. "Askot spoke freely in front of us, and I remember it all."

"As in his plans to attack Camelyn?" Daana asked.

The man nodded. "Yes. Vokan means to flood the city."

"Well, he's already done it once." Agula sighed. "The question is, can we survive the second flood?"

The man wiped away his tears and rose to his feet. "I will fight this tyranny. Let me help."

"Soon enough," Agula said. "For now, enjoy your freedom. Eat some food." His eyes brightened. "Live a little while you have the chance. If we survive what comes next, then be ready."

The man threw himself at Agula and hugged him. "Thank you for my life."

Agula patted his back. "The one you should thank is Justin."

I held up my hands to ward off a hug. "Happy to help, really. Now, go get some food."

"I will escort him," Elaine said. "I have several more questions." She motioned to the door and the pair departed.

"You have markedly improved the lives of three entities today, Justin." Agula sighed with contentment. "It is a wondrous thing you have done."

"I've barely scratched the surface." I tried not to sound glum and failed. "There are hundreds more to go."

"You really handled the last one fast." Elyssa tilted her head slightly. "Was it easier with the human, or did you just know what to do this time?"

"Definitely easier." I took her hand. "I could use some food."

Her left eyebrow twitched the way it usually did when she saw through me. "Yeah, let's go." We said our goodbyes to Agula and Daana and headed to the levitator. Elyssa gave me a look when we started our descent. "What do you want to talk about?"

I told her everything about my negotiations with my demonic side. "I have this feeling he's playing me."

"He doesn't sound that smart." Elyssa pursed her lips. "It feels really odd to talk as if there's an entirely separate personality inside of you."

"That's almost exactly what it's like," I said. "I keep those demonic urges blocked off most of the time unless I need to manifest or feed."

Elyssa grunted. "Doesn't the demon half of your soul exist in Haedaemos?"

The levitator stopped at the bottom. We got off and headed for the dining hall where dozens of displaced evacuees ate. "Yeah. Dad calls it the window of our soul. That's how we summon hellhounds and other spawn."

Elyssa bit her lower lip and stopped walking. "Justin, do you think it's possible Baal can access your demon half?"

My jaw dropped. "I never even considered it. My god, he could spy on everything I do if that's possible."

"I don't know about everything," Elyssa said. "Baal probably would have won every engagement if he knew exactly what we were doing."

"True." But I couldn't shake the uneasy feeling. "Hang on." I turned inward and woke my demon half. *Have you been in contact with Baal?*

No.

I sensed the truth just as I'd sensed its joy earlier. I didn't know if it could lie to me, or if that meant I'd actually be lying to myself. It was all so confusing I hardly knew what to think. So I let sleeping dogs lie and returned to the outside world. "It says it hasn't, and I feel pretty certain that's the truth."

Elyssa folded her arms. "You can tell if it's lying?"

"Well, technically it's part of me, so yeah, I get a pretty strong sense."

She shook her head. "It's so weird."

"Yeah, it's pretty messed up when you can literally talk to yourself." Feeling a little better, I went into the dining hall. "Makes me feel delusional sometimes."

"You're definitely delusional when it comes to naming things." Elyssa stuck out her tongue and grabbed a plate.

"So mature." I grabbed her from behind and kissed her cheek.

She giggled. "Justin, people are watching."

I looked around, but everyone was minding their own business. "These Utopians are so damned considerate." I really hoped we could save them.

NEARLY EVERYTHING LOOKED SET the next morning. The debris from the first flood had been cleared, and the earth magi had built wide channels on either side of the wall to facilitate runoff.

Shelton and Adam accompanied me and Elyssa aboard the *Raptor* to oversee the final preparations.

"They just finished putting it together last night." Shelton looked over the side at the gleaming spectacles. "We need to test them somehow."

"It works mechanically," Adam said. "But we don't have nearly enough pushing power to actually test it."

"What about the spell side of things?" I asked.

"We hooked up an arctablet," Adam said. "That part works. The only question is will this?"

Shelton opened his mouth, but horns wailing in the distance drew our sights north. Gryphon riders appeared out of dense fog gathering beneath new storm clouds. Not long after that, I felt the tremble of earth beneath my feet.

The workers in the riverbed ran for flying carriages in an orderly fashion without even crying out in fear.

"Man, they know how not to panic." Shelton watched the carriages ferry the workers to safety. "These people can't be human."

"The riverbed is clear." Elyssa spun the *Raptor* on its axis and guided it to the wall.

Cool wind hit my face. The weather shields were off, and I was fine with that. Even from this height, I felt the rumble building in my bones. Minutes later, a wall of water twice as high as the last one exploded from the fog. I looked down at our contraptions. They looked like delicate pinwheels from this height, but enchanted to withstand magic and physical forces like the wall, they should hold.

The river struck the first waterwheel and it vanished from sight. Seconds later, the second one disappeared. The great flood roared across the remaining hundred yards of river toward the wall.

"Oh, crap." Elyssa stood next to me. "It's not working."

Adam stared at his arcphone screen. "I can't remotely connect to the arctablet. Something's wrong."

"Ya think?" Shelton cursed a blue streak. "Welp, goodbye, Camelyn, it was nice knowing you."

The water slammed into the wall. Rock groaned and cracked. Millions of gallons flooded over the top. A black swarm of gepheron funneled out of the fog behind the flood, hovering in anticipation. The center section took the brunt of the blow. Though the top part of the wall was nearly indestructible, the last twenty feet below the surface couldn't take the pressure.

As if in slow motion, the middle sections of wall toppled inward.

"No, no, no!" Adam dropped to his knees and watched over the railing. "It didn't work."

Despair gripped my heart. "We failed them."

The wall came crashing down, and with it, the last free city of Utopia.

CHAPTER 32

"N o!" Adam's fingers blurred across the phone screen. He tapped ferociously, muttering under his breath like a madman. A loud hum echoed even above the roar of water. The air flickered, and a fluorescent green shield crackled into existence in front of the wall.

"We didn't have the spell primed." Adam looked ready to cry.

"Son of a biscuit eater." Shelton slapped his hat off so it hung by the stampede string. "That's why it didn't turn on right away?"

"I hoped we wouldn't need it, but the spell literally had to charge to full power before it could activate." Adam slumped. "We didn't code an incremental activation."

I stared at the dome shield, powered by the massive hydroelectric generators which in turn were driven by the flood. The shield curved outward like a bubble, diverting the water to the sides of the wall where it flowed through the guide channels and would eventually reach the ocean.

The shield hummed louder and glowed brighter. I sighted the lead gepherons and zoomed my view to Askot's shocked face. Behind him floated the citadel. Vokan stood at the edge, his lips peeled back into a snarl.

But not all was roses and sunshine. The middle of the wall had collapsed, crushing several buildings. Millions of gallons of water once again flooded the streets. At least this time they hadn't brought tons of debris with them.

Shelton nudged Adam. "Did the batteries work?"

Adam nodded. "They're charging." He looked out at the volume of water still streaming in. "If Vokan doesn't block the river again, they'll fully charge in a couple of hours."

"How long does a charge last?" I asked.

"A day at most, provided we turn down the power level on the shield." Adam sighed. "If the river keeps running, the shield stays powered. We just have to hope Vokan doesn't realize how we're generating so much aether."

"If he doesn't try to block the river again, we'll never run out." Shelton spat in Vokan's general direction. "The wall might be damaged, but the shield ain't going nowhere."

"Amen to that." Adam wiped sweat from his forehead. "I almost had a heart attack when it didn't work."

I put a hand on his shoulder. "Keep calm and don't crap your pants, okay?"

Adam groaned and slumped against the railing. "Might be too late for part of that."

Shelton pinched his nose. "I can guess which one."

The hydroelectric aether generators would power the shield spell keeping Camelyn safe for the foreseeable future. But that didn't stop the looming threat of Vokan. So the question remained: What now?

319

Apparently, Vokan wasn't sure of the answer either. His flying house drifted outside the river valley and settled down on a nearby mountain. Askot's gepheron riders settled down on the plateaus on either side of the valley and began setting up camp. The gray clouds hovering over them began to drizzle.

I was willing to bet the weather directly reflected Vokan's current state of mind. Somehow, I had to capitalize on it. I must have smiled, because Elyssa's expression grew concerned.

"Did you just come up with a plan?" she said.

I nodded. "It's not a great plan, but it might work."

"Can't be much worse than using a science fair project as a blueprint for a magical shield," Shelton said. "Spit it out."

"It's not tricky or anything." I waved a hand at the forming enemy encampments. "But it does prey on their weaknesses."

Adam's eyelids fluttered. "Weaknesses? And that would be?"

"We're turtling behind a dome shield. They have superior numbers, but no way to reach us."

Elyssa's eyes flared with understanding. "They think we're in here for the long haul. But we're going to sneak out, aren't we?" She cracked her knuckles. "Assassination."

I shook my head. "Hang on, cowgirl. That's not what I'm thinking." I pointed to the gepheron on the opposite side of the valley from Askot. "I'm going to sneak into their camp and start freeing sprites and humans left and right. Then we're going to bring them inside the city."

"You're gonna what?" Shelton's jaw went slack. "How do you expect to waltz in there and free two hundred people before they take you down?"

I grinned. "Elyssa saw how fast my demon worked last time. It literally took him seconds to exorcise the demon controlling the sprite. Once that happened, both the human and sprite were freed."

"Yes, but won't people notice all the glowing balls of light flying away?" Adam said. "Won't the humans yell or act surprised when they're free?"

I nodded. "Maybe, but I think we can do it."

Elyssa blew out a breath. "Wish I still had lancers. We could knock out a couple dozen people and put them on the *Raptor*. If we start freeing them willy-nilly, how are we supposed to calm them down and evacuate them before the rest of the enemy responds with deadly force?"

"Good question," I admitted. "Unfortunately, I don't have an answer for that."

"Maybe we should have the gryphon riders on alert just in case," Elyssa said. "That way if we need to make a retreat under fire, they can cover us while we get the prisoners to safety."

"Prisoners?" Adam grunted. "Yeah, I guess the sprites and humans under Vokan's compulsion are prisoners."

"More like hostages," Shelton growled. "It's no wonder Vokan rolled over the other cities. Can you imagine all your loved ones being turned into puppets? The regular citizens probably gave up without a fight."

"Here's another question," Adam said. "Supposing you release a hundred people, how in the world would we evacuate that many? We can't cram more than thirty people on the *Raptor*, and it's too dangerous to have gryphons flying sorties."

It was Elyssa's turn to smile slyly. "I think we can get everyone safely out without putting more than a few on the Raptor."

Shelton's eyebrows reached for the sky. "This I gotta hear. You have a teleportation spell I don't know about?"

Elyssa jabbed a finger toward the flocks of gepheron settling all around the camps. "Every single flier already has a ride."

Shelton ran a hand through his hair. "Well I'll be a monkey's uncle."

JOHN CORWIN

I took a closer look at the camps. "It looks like the riders keep their gepherons next to their tents."

"We reduce Vokan's army while building our own." Elyssa clapped her hands and spread them apart. "Easy, peasy."

"Do you think Vokan will expect us to try anything?" Adam asked.

I went into the ship cabin and grabbed a spyglass since it was too far for me to clearly see Vokan's camp. I spotted Askot arranging dozens of riders around Vokan's flying house. Most of them had the dull gazes of people under compulsion. Nearly all of them wore gray or black tunics while Askot wore dark green armor similar to the type Ki and her people used.

Only a couple dozen other people wore the same armor as Askot. "I know how to tell the loyalists from the prisoners." I handed the spyglass to Elyssa. "The armor."

Elyssa scanned both sides of the valley. "There's about one loyalist for every two camps. We need to take them down first before freeing the campsite."

"Sounds like a job for the Super Friends." Adam swooshed back and forth as if flying.

Shelton snorted. "I think the pressure finally snapped his fragile little mind."

"Pew, pew, pew." Adam made finger lasers at Shelton. "Don't make me use my super powers on you."

Elyssa squeezed her eyes shut and opened them slowly, as if to make sense of everything. "Did you seriously flip your lid, Adam?"

"Well, it is a job for the super friends." I patted Adam and Shelton on the shoulders. "That means all of you."

Shelton slapped his hat back on. "Then let's saddle up, partner."

Adam flipped the middle finger toward Vokan's flying house. "Let's do this."

We landed the *Raptor* in the plaza to cheering crowds. Agula was the first to greet us when we stepped outside. "You did it!" He gave each of us a bone-crushing hug. "Camelyn is injured, but she will survive."

Elaine stared up at the shield. "What a breathtaking marvel of science and magic. This arcnology of yours is certainly worth further study."

"Sure is," Shelton said. "Maybe even better than all that elemental jazz."

"Give me a break, Shelton." Adam rolled his eyes. "I think we could all learn something."

I waved at the happy Utopians and allowed myself to feel optimistic about our chances of executing our rescue operation.

Bliss emerged from the throng, face flushed with excitement. "You did it!" She stopped a few feet away, hesitant to come closer.

I held open my arms. "We did it." I gave Bliss a long hug.

She sighed with contentment. "Hugs are my favorite part of being alive." She backed away, eyes wet. "I really like this world, Justin. Do you think we can save it?"

I nodded. "Just so happens we have a plan."

Her smile faltered, and she looked down. "I hope Cinder is okay. I tried to talk to him with the comm badge, but the range isn't far enough."

"I'm sure he's doing fine." I tried not to let my own worry show. I hoped he wasn't pinned down by eidolons or something worse. Then again, with Vokan's attention on Camelyn, Cinder might have the run of the city. I cleared my throat. "We're going to plan the next phase of attack. I think you could be valuable to the plan."

Bliss's eyes brightened. "I'd love to."

We enjoyed a few more minutes of cheers, then excused ourselves up to the council chambers where we told the councilors about our night raid.

"Very risky," Daana said. "But it does seem like our best chance to drive Vokan away from our walls."

"The gryphon riders will be happy to assist," Agula said. "Just tell us what to do."

Elyssa, of course, had already jotted out a sound plan that made my initial offering sound like something a kindergartener drew on the wall with crayons. It was still very risky, but it sounded like it had a better chance of success than just rushing in.

"We have limited supplies of the items you require," Elaine said. "I will make them all available to you."

"Thank you." Elyssa closed the holographic map on her arcphone. "If we're successful, Vokan might have no choice but to leave."

"I'll go prep the shield," Adam said.

Shelton followed him out. "See you kiddos later."

I excused myself and found a quiet room to prepare myself for the mission. I hoped I had enough time for a nap afterward.

It turned out, I did.

I MET the others back at the *Raptor* as the sun was going down. Adam had modified the shield spell so the dome was nearly transparent and didn't give off any light. Once the sun was down, it would be impossible to know if it was on or not unless someone tossed pebbles at it.

Shelton gasped and jumped away from the gangway as I led my menagerie of lesser demon spawn onto the ship. The hellhounds were smaller than usual by design, miniature black greyhounds. Sleek hellcats slinked up the ramp, fur black as pitch, bodies built like cheetahs for speed.

Elyssa's eyes flared. "Beautiful cats."

Shelton waved a hand in front of his nose. "Yeah, but they stink like sulfur."

I shrugged. "Hellcats gonna be hellcats, man."

"Do you think the bad guys will smell them?" Adam asked.

"Won't matter by the time they do." I turned to Elyssa. "Got the stuff?"

She nodded. "Should be plenty." Tilted her head. "Is Fred ready?"

I nodded back. "He seems pretty eager."

Shelton grimaced. "Should I be worried you named your demon half?"

"Maybe. On the other hand, it saves time to just give him a name."

"Fred." Adam chuckled. "Man, that is an awful name for a demon."

"It's like Justin just gave up trying to come up with names." Shelton sighed. "Sad."

Elyssa stroked the fur of a hellcat. The demonic feline coiled around Elyssa's legs, purrs rumbling in its chest. "I've always wanted a cat."

"These ain't exactly kitty cats," Shelton said.

She knelt and fitted a harness around the hellcat's chest. "Still kinda cute though."

The hellcat mewed and rubbed its head against Elyssa's.

"Aww, so sweet!"

One of the hellhounds growled. Some lesser spawn could speak tele-pathically. None of these had the capacity, communicating with images instead. The hellhounds were jealous Elyssa was giving the hellcats all the petting. I tried not to get attached to summoned minions since I usually sent them back once the mission was complete. The only excep-tion was Cutsauce, my pint-sized pooch and the first hellhound I'd ever summoned. Unfortunately, he was back in Eden.

After Elyssa fitted all the hellspawn with their harnesses, she went to the bridge and piloted the *Raptor* up into the air. Adam opened a small portal in the shield to let us through and we zipped out into the night.

Elyssa maintained low altitude next to the eastern cliff and threaded us through a narrow valley. We flanked the eastern encampment and set down out of sight of the campfires. A quick sweep with night vision spells found no enemies, so we crept up the side of the hill and peered over at the dancing shadows cast by hundreds of campfires.

Shelton and Adam took out their wands and staffs. "We'll be here if you need us."

I took a deep breath and tried to quell the rising fear. The odds were hundreds to one if we didn't pull this off flawlessly. If this gamble didn't pay off, it would cost us dearly.

CHAPTER 33

I imagined the armor Askot's people wore and sent the image to the hellspawn. *Seek and bite.* Black forms blurred into the night. I closed my eyes and viewed the world through the eyes of a hellhound. It dashed past tents, pausing to look inside each one. The enslaved gepheron riders glanced around, faces dull, eyes night blind from staring into the campfires. If they caught a glimpse of the enemies running through the camps, they gave no indication.

My hellhound found three of Askot's loyalists eating around a table just outside a tent. The nearest slaves were at a campfire a hundred feet away. The hellhound summoned help. Black forms melted from the shadows, red eyes glowing. Together, they pounced. Jaws tightened around necks. The drugs laced into their saliva from the harnesses quickly subdued the loyalists, rendering them unconscious before they could sound an alarm.

The hellspawn dragged the sleeping forms out of sight into the forest. I blinked out of the hellhound's mind. "We can start."

Six slaves sat outside the nearest tent. I crept closer, Elyssa watching my back. Thirty feet. Twenty. Ten. I stayed behind the tent and let Fred do his thing. Questing tendrils latched into three people at a time. I sensed the sprites and the demon spirits enslaving them. It was like viewing them through three different sets of eyes. A wave of disorientation washed over me.

I felt Elyssa's hand steady me. "Are you okay?" she whispered.

I focused harder and brought the objectives back into focus. *Consume.* Three demon spirits vanished, and euphoria rushed through my veins. Newly freed sprites burst from their prisons and danced around the campfire. The slaves collapsed. The other three slaves watched in confusion. They struggled to rise but seemed bound in place.

"The loyalists must have commanded them to sit," Elyssa said. "They can't move."

I quickly latched onto them with my demonic essence and consumed the demon spirits. Fire raced across my skin. More sprites joined their free companions.

One of them linked to me. *You saved us. Why?*

I'm here to help. The nearest camp of slaves watched us, faces tight with worry and fear because they were bound in place. *Can you help me?*

Of course. The sprite danced in place. *What do you wish?*

I've got a whole camp to free. Can you make sure the sprites don't make too much light? I don't want to alert anyone.

The sprite immediately dimmed as did the others nearby. *Yes. We will help.*

Shelton, Adam, and Bliss ran up behind us and started helping the woozy gepheron riders to their feet. Elyssa and I moved on to the next camp. The slaves' eyes widened at the sight of enemies. Their mouths trembled with the effort to speak. Their bodies tensed but they couldn't move. Their masters had turned their bodies into prisons. But their last commands had given us the key to freedom.

It took less time to devour the demon spirits. The free sprites helped their comrades and the tiny spheres of light dimmed and stayed low so the other camps didn't see them. I felt dizzy from the rush, but stronger than ever. Fred gloated like an evil mastermind whose master plan was coming to fruition.

Why are you so happy? I asked.

I live to devour. He sounded stronger, more sure of himself than ever. And it kind of frightened me. Unfortunately, I didn't have time for a heart-to-heart talk. I'd only freed twelve slaves and had a lot more to go.

I switched to hellhound view and checked their progress. A dozen loyalists were down and the hellspawn were tracking two more. This end of the camp was clear of anyone who could release the slaves from their last command.

Shelton and the others came to the newly freed camp. "The first group is waiting near the gepherons. They'll be ready to fly when you give the word."

"Good job." I moved on to the next camp and the next. The heady feeling of consuming demon spirits turned to nausea, like eating one slice of pizza too many and getting an upset stomach.

Is this normal? I asked Fred.

Caustic demons are foul, he replied. *They take time to assimilate.*

Fred's communication skills had markedly improved, or else he'd just been faking the dumb brute act. Then again, something else had changed. I'd devoured other demons. This was how demons in Haedaemos gained more power. Dad had never mentioned it doing the same thing to Daemos or their demon souls.

No wonder Fred gloated. He was getting stronger and more powerful with every spirit I took. I didn't know if that was good or bad. Unfortunately, it was necessary if I wanted to save lives. I swallowed the gorge rising in my throat and went to the next camp. I hit all six slaves at once. Sprites rose and bodies fell.

Bliss ran from her hiding place and calmed the frightened, roused the unconscious, and told them the plan. Some were too disoriented, but most grasped what to do and helped Bliss. Elyssa and I went to the next camp and started again.

Each camp blurred into the last. I felt feverish and the urge to vomit nearly overwhelmed me with every step. Elyssa guided me into a hiding place and peered at me with concern. "Your eyes have streaks of yellow in them, Justin." She put a hand to my head. "You're burning up!"

"Caustic demons." I gagged. "Nasty."

"You need to rest."

"How many?" My words slurred together. "How many saved?"

"Sixty," she said. "Ten camps."

I nodded and leaned my head back. *How long does assimilation take, Fred?*

Not long for tiny spirits. I sensed his joy. *They become part of us. Make us stronger.*

They make me want to puke.

Growing pains, he replied.

I didn't want to take a long break, but I really couldn't stand the thought of consuming one more demon. Shelton sneaked over to us. "Something wrong?"

I told him the situation.

He nodded. "The hellhounds are still dragging loyalists into the woods. I think they got about half of them subdued by now. We got sixty free souls ready to fly back to Camelyn. Maybe that's as good as it gets."

I shook my head. "I want everyone on this side free."

Shelton pursed his lips. Looked at Elyssa. "Talk some sense into him?"

She squeezed my arm. "Shelton's right. We saved a lot of lives tonight."

I closed my eyes and took a deep breath. The nausea slowly subsided, like filthy water in a clogged sink. Another fifteen minutes of rest and I might be able to go another sixty spirits. *I can do this.* "Most of the loyalists are down. There's no alarm, and the slaves are under orders to stay seated. We've got time for me to rest."

Elyssa looked around warily as if confirming my assessment and nodded. "Take the time you need." She turned back to Shelton. "Let's keep going as long as he can."

Shelton looked at me for a long moment. "Don't kill yourself, man. We still kind of need you."

I chuckled. "I'll do my best." I closed my eyes and waited until it felt like I wouldn't lose my lunch. Then I gave myself another couple of minutes. It probably wasn't enough, but it would have to do. Every minute we tarried was another minute for something to go wrong.

After freeing the next two camps, the vomit meter hit half-staff. I pushed on and got three more before it was too much to bear. I sat down, back against a tree to recover, but someone had other plans.

A horn sounded. I flicked into hellhound view and saw a dozen alarmed loyalists staring back at me. My hellspawn had been spotted and the gig was up.

"What sort of dog is this?" one of them shouted. "Where did it come from?"

"The enemy must be using them as spies. Kill the—argh!" His command was cut off as a hellcat pounced him from behind. The rest of my pack went for the jugulars and before long, the loyalists were down. But it was too late. Horns echoed from the other side of the valley. It wouldn't be long until they swarmed our position.

I forced down the nausea and freed another camp, and another. I dropped to my knees and emptied my stomach. It didn't make me feel any better.

"We've got to go, Justin!" Elyssa watched Bliss lead away the latest group of freed people. "You've done all you can."

I looked at the remaining camps. There were men, women, and children crying to be free. After tonight, I wouldn't have that chance again. Vokan would no doubt tighten security, and that would be that. I couldn't let that happen. "No. Help me."

"Damn it, Justin, you're going to get us all killed." Elyssa slung my arm over her shoulder and dragged me to the next camp. "And your breath is awful."

It took all my concentration to free the next camp. Those six extra demons were like boulders, dragging me to the bottom of lake of slime. My guts squirmed, filled with the caustic maggots.

I couldn't move. Couldn't speak. The world faded away.

SEARING heat raced along my skin. Something struck my midriff. I blinked awake and staggered in darkness. Strong hands grabbed me. "Run!" Elyssa shouted. She jerked me along behind her.

Hundreds of lightning bolts stabbed the earth. Tornados ripped through the trees. Massive energy hands clawed the night sky. Fiery meteors and hailstones rained down. People screamed and fell. Shrieking gepheron spiraled to the ground.

"What in the hell is happening?" I asked.

Lightning splintered a sapling and a twister ripped a furrow in the ground a hundred feet away. I shielded my eyes from the debris and spat dirt out of my mouth. Night blind and disoriented, I turned and nearly ran into the *Raptor*.

Elyssa yanked my arm and practically tossed me up the gangway. Shelton, Adam, and Bliss sheltered on the bridge.

"Jesus Christ on a pogo stick!" Shelton stared at the destruction raining down. "Vokan's lost his damned mind!"

Elyssa grabbed the control stick and lifted off. She dodged tornados and ducked beneath grasping energy hands. Before long, we reached the city shield. A few gepheron riders waited on the ground below and flew up to meet us. Lightning claimed two of them before we made it through the shield.

Bliss stared at the warring skies behind us, tears pouring down her cheeks. "That monster!"

I shook the grogginess from my head. "What happened?"

Elyssa blew out a shuddering breath. "You passed out. I told Shelton to get the slaves out of there. Askot spotted them and must have realized we'd freed them."

"Then Vokan unleashed all hell on everyone." Shelton shook his head. "Man, the poor people in the camps below us—he just blew the place apart."

"He didn't care who he killed," Adam said. "Slaves or freed, it didn't matter. He scorched the earth."

I slumped into a chair, shocked. "How many made it out?"

"Maybe thirty." Elyssa looked at the winged forms following us. "I just don't know for sure."

We got a better count when we landed. Thirty-eight freed survived. God only knew how many slaves Vokan killed in his rage. It should have been a victory, but it tasted like defeat.

The freed riders mobbed us when we left the ship.

"Thank you, thank you, thank you." I found only gratitude where I expected words of regret and anger at the loss of lives.

"I would rather die than live another moment as a slave," was a sentiment many expressed.

"I was trapped in a prison of my own body," another said.

Their words made me feel slightly less awful, but I was far from feeling good. My plans of salvation had fallen far short of the goal. *If only I'd been stronger.* It should have taken me less than two hours to clear that entire encampment. But I'd let weakness get in the way. My demon side wasn't strong enough to deal with such an influx of caustic spirits. Rage simmered in the pit of despair hollowed out in my stomach. I wanted to kill Vokan more than anything else in the world.

Agula and the other councilors greeted the freed riders and assigned them homes to stay in, while others took the gepheron to the gryphon stables.

"Why didn't you call on us to come?" Ki asked Elyssa. "We were ready to fight."

"You can't fight the weather." Elyssa shook her head. "I won't throw lives away."

I slipped away and walked down dark streets to the north. I just wanted time to be alone and think. *How did it all go so wrong?* My dark brooding led me back to the damaged parts of the wall. I climbed on one of the fallen sections and looked out at the valley. Somewhere out there, Vokan simmered in his own rage.

I wanted to beat the ever-loving shit out of him.

Elyssa contacted me on the comm badge some time later. "Justin, I know you're upset about tonight, but it's not your fault."

I closed my eyes and sighed. "That doesn't make me feel any better."

"Well, suck it up. We need you."

Her brusque words rubbed me the wrong way, but she was right. Sulking wouldn't win this war. "Fine."

"Oh, and one more thing."

"Yes?" I said.

"Cinder is back."

CHAPTER 34

I arrived at the plaza just as Cinder landed his gryphon. Bliss was the first to greet him. She hugged him and kissed his cheek. Tears of joy glistened in her eyes.

Cinder manifested a smile and gave her a wooden hug and kiss. *Poor guy is trying so hard.* He wanted to understand emotion. He wanted to be human. He still had a long way to go.

Bliss hooked her arm in his and walked with him, a bright smile on her face. *She really does love him.* I guess we all did, in a way, but not like Bliss. I remained shrouded in darkness just at the edge of the plaza, hiding my shame. I'd hated Bliss for what she was instead of accepting her for who she was. Three years I'd avoided her as much as possible. I'd treated her like a thing, an impostor.

Nightliss would disapprove.

I closed my eyes and envisioned her petite frame, olive hair, and lively green eyes. I still wanted to cry every time I thought of her. I didn't think I could ever say goodbye to someone who so deeply touched my life. But I could accept that the good in her still lived on in Bliss, and maybe even Issana and the other dolems.

It would take time, but maybe I could truly feel kinship with Bliss.

I stepped into the light. Cinder saw me at once and walked over. I gave him a firm hug. "Man, we were worried about you."

Cinder patted my back. "It is good to be back."

Bliss couldn't stop grinning. "He got inside the towers."

"Yeah?" I looked around for the others and saw them standing on the deck of the *Raptor*. "Well, let's hear it."

We boarded the ship and sat on the back deck. Cinder cut to the chase. "There is more than one cantrap. The largest is in Vokan's tower in Solan. When he travels, he takes a smaller version in his flying citadel."

"How do you know there's one in his citadel?" I asked.

"Because he has three other flying platforms with citadels," Cinder replied. "I assume the one he has now is similarly equipped."

"Where does he keep the citadels?" Adam asked.

"They're just outside the towers." Cinder projected images of the towers from his arcphone and circled two structures near the plaza. "They are hidden in plain sight, so to speak."

"Wow, you really had the run of the city," Shelton said. "Did the eidolons give you any gruff?"

Cinder raised an eyebrow. "Gruff? No, they ignored me. I don't know if it is because I am a golem and not alive, or because Vokan was not present to control them."

"Probably the second," Bliss said. "Because you're definitely alive."

Cinder smiled ever so slightly. "I also discovered detailed journals that fill in the missing pieces of his history."

Shelton rubbed his hands together. "About damned time. Let's hear it."

"Vokan is rather self-absorbed, as you may have observed," Cinder said. "He wrote in great detail about his life, so I will have to summarize."

Adam scoffed. "That dude is narcissistic to the max."

Shelton made jazz hands. "Amen."

"Vokan's parents were influencers stationed in Eden during the late fifteenth century England, their mission to subdue the power of the church and shift Eden toward a secular society." Cinder projected a slide show with pictures taken from the journal. Since Utopia was magically and technologically centuries ahead of Eden at the time, they took photographs. "Accused of witchcraft, the locals executed them by dismemberment in front of their child. Vokan was put in the care of the church. He learned his first demon magic from a group of priests who regularly used it to produce miracles and increase the following of the church."

Shelton barked a laugh. "Jesus, what a bunch of hypocrites!"

"Utopians rescued Vokan from his indentured servitude and returned him home. But his brush with demon magic opened him to influence from Haedaemos." Cinder displayed several demon diagrams, each one more complex than the last. "He made contact with a powerful demon and gradually worked his way up the chain until he caught the attention of Baal two centuries ago. Baal expressed an interest in Utopia and they formed a partnership."

"Two centuries of plotting and planning." I shook my head. "We're so far behind the curve it's not even funny."

"Vokan decided he was powerful enough to rule Eden, which led to his ill-fated venture in South America. The Utopians found him shortly after he declared himself ruler of a tribe and took him back for judging and sentencing. After he was banished from the four cities, he moved to the far southwest." Cinder displayed a crude hut on a beach. "He renewed his partnership with Baal. Though there are not many details of his education, demon magic enhanced Vokan's ability to retain information. This is how he mastered the four elementals."

Elyssa stared at the picture of the hut. "That's when he returned to Solan, right?"

Cinder nodded. "Using demon magic, he created a cantrap and captured his first souls."

"Were there any details about how Baal tricked us here?" I asked.

"Baal did not share many details with Vokan," Cinder said. "Vokan noted that Baal wanted him ready for the day people fitting our description entered his realm. Two years later, we did."

"Well, at least it took us two years before falling into this trap." Shelton huffed. "Man, talk about playing the long game."

"While the background is interesting, I believe you will find the information from Vokan's spell book most useful." Cinder switched to a spell blueprint for a cantrap.

A complex pattern summoned a demon spirit and used it as a vessel to store souls. It was a marvel of demonic ingenuity. I wondered if I could break it. "Do we break the pattern to release the souls?"

"Breaking the pattern would send the souls to Haedaemos with the demon," Cinder said. "I know little about the afterlife, but I believe this would doom the souls."

Elyssa shuddered. "We can't allow that."

"Then what's the solution?" I asked.

Cinder shook his head. "I do not know. Vokan did not document how to free the souls."

"How does he link to the cantrap?" Adam asked.

"Vokan can tether to the pattern and utilize the souls and control the eidolons so long as he is within a few miles of the cantrap." Cinder scrolled to another diagram outlining the tethering technique. "Theoretically, anyone with the proper training could utilize the cantrap."

"In other words, I could tether to it and amplify my powers," I said.

Cinder nodded. "Souls are self-replenishing so long as they are not used up too quickly. I discovered enough dead eidolons in the city to indicate Vokan has acted without restraint lately. He has burned through hundreds of souls in his attempts to capture us."

Tears pooled in Bliss's eyes. "He's a monster."

"How do we disable the cantrap without damning the souls?" I searched for answers in the blueprint, but nothing stuck out to me. I sensed a figurative tap on my shoulder coming from that other side of me. *Do you know how to break the spell?*

Break the pattern, lose the souls. Consume the demon, save the souls.

I stared at the cantrap blueprint. The bigger the size, the more demons it required. The massive one in the tower used ten patterns. *I have to absorb ten full-size demons?*

Only three, Fred replied. *The rest cannot hold. The vessel will break, and the souls will be freed.*

I couldn't help but feel suspicious. *How do you know this, and why didn't you tell me sooner?*

You fed me. I am stronger, smarter.

All those baby demons improved you?

I sensed a nod from Fred. *Our demon spirit has grown.*

Ours? It felt separate from me and yet Fred and I were two halves of the same soul. *Damn this is confusing.*

Fred seemed amused by my musings.

Where will the souls go once freed?

I do not know.

Well, at least he didn't have all the spiritual answers.

I noticed Cinder and the other staring at me and realized I must've been talking to myself. I cleared my throat. "Yes?"

"You said something about eating demons," Elyssa said. "Were you talking to Fred?"

"Yeah." I already felt ill just thinking about stuffing those nasty caustic demon spirits down my throat. "The big cantrap is made from ten demons. I need to eat three of them to break the vessel and free the souls."

Bliss's eyes widened. "What happens to them then?"

I shrugged. "No idea."

"I cannot say where souls with no bodies go," Cinder said. "I believe that once unbound, they might go to an afterlife."

Adam stood in front of the holographic blueprint. "What if I told you we could potentially return all those souls to their bodies?"

That perked my ears. "How?"

"Theoretically, when a body dies, the soul is free to move on." Adam scrolled through the blueprint. "The problem is, the bodies for these souls are still alive. Even though the Child of Jura moved them from one vessel to another, they're still bound to the original body."

"So once we break the cantrap, the souls should go back to their bodies?" Shelton said.

Adam shook his head. "No. The Child tore them out. It's the only thing that can put them back in."

"Ain't no way in hell we can steal that thing from Vokan," Shelton said. "We couldn't get within a hundred yards of his flying citadel before he incinerates us."

"That is not necessarily true now," Cinder said. "Vokan used an incredible amount of energy last night. I believe he has burned through the souls he brought with him."

Bliss shuddered. "How awful."

"Awful but good." Shelton cracked his knuckles. "I see where you're going with this. Vokan doesn't have spare batteries with him. He's weak until he goes back to home base for more souls."

"Provided I am correct in my assumption," Cinder said. "The cantrap in his flying house holds a hundred souls. If you consider everything he has done in the past few days, I think it likely he has very few souls left."

I still didn't like the idea. Askot had plenty of gepheron riders left, and Vokan was plenty powerful even without souls to amplify his powers. "What's to stop us from flying to Solan right now and breaking the cantrap?"

"If we free the souls now, they will either be free, or forced to remain as ghosts, unable to enter their original bodies," Cinder said. "Even if we acquire the Child of Jura later, it will be nearly impossible to locate the displaced souls and return them to their bodies. If we secure the Child now, we can return the souls to the bodies and then break the cantrap once it is done."

"If Vokan has even a few souls left, he'll blow us to pieces," Shelton said.

"Or will he?" Adam tapped a finger on his chin. "He'll probably conserve them as much as possible knowing he's got no backup if he tries to destroy us and fails."

"He'll be far more cautious," Elyssa said. "Despite all his rage—"

"He's still just a rat in a cage?" Adam said.

"Huh?" Elyssa frowned. "Look, he threw everything at us and we survived. The *Raptor* can hold up under everything but the energy hands."

"I can keep those off us," I said.

"Vokan may not even commit the energy hands," Cinder said.

Elyssa tapped a finger on her chin. "We need to see what he's got and what he's willing to use to stop us before he rushes back to Solan."

Adam raised an eyebrow. "And we can't let him do that, right?"

"Exactly." Elyssa took a deep breath. "We have to attack as soon as possible. The gryphons are already on standby. The flying carriages are ready to go. Askot is down to half his forces, and Vokan may or may not have the souls to fight us."

I nodded. "Then let's get the council."

Agula, Daana, and Elaine were cautious but excited about the plan. Ki summoned the gryphon commanders, and had the flying carriages brought into the plaza. By the time the ass crack of dawn appeared on the horizon, we were tired, but ready to fight.

"What do we do about the slaves?" Shelton said. "I hate to kill the poor bastards, but I ain't about to let them kill me first."

"Target the loyalists first," Elyssa said. "With their better armor, they'll stick out from the slaves."

"Easier said than done," Shelton grumbled. "I guarantee those cowards will be at the back of the fight."

"We have spoken at length about this," Agula said. "It pains us, but we believe the slaves would be willing to give up their lives to free all of Utopia from the bonds of Vokan."

Daana nodded somberly. "The sacrifice of hundreds is worth saving thousands."

Elyssa slumped a little. "I don't like it, but I agree."

The councilors left the ship and took refuge in the tower.

"Open season, I guess." Shelton unsheathed his staff and extended it.

"Damn, I hate to kill people who aren't even in control of their own bodies."

"Just be careful, okay?" I clapped Shelton on the back. "I don't want to have to clean your blood off the deck."

Shelton grinned. "Be more crap than blood. I'll make sure of that."

Adam gagged. "Dude, you're nasty."

"Humans frequently defecate at the time of death, Adam." Cinder tried to look concerned. "I assure you, it is perfectly natural."

Bliss laughed. "Natural or not, it's smelly."

Elyssa went onto the bridge to prep the *Raptor*. The holographic display flickered on for a moment, then vanished. She frowned at the console and came back outside. "Something's wrong."

Adam tried the controls. "Nothing's responding." His eyes tightened. "Oh, no."

"What is it?" I said. "Flux capacitor die?"

We piled down the ramp and into the generator room. Black dust swirled around the room. The aetherite that powered the ship had burned out.

CHAPTER 35

"**S**on of a bitch." Shelton opened the compartment and pulled out the spare gem. "Let's hope this works." He held it between the conducting crystals. After a few seconds the crystals pinched the aetherite between them.

A soothing voice spoke. *Calibration started. Four hours remaining.*

"You've got to be kidding me!" Shelton face-palmed. "How are we supposed to get to Vokan without the *Raptor*?"

"We have to go now before Vokan decides to return to Solan for more souls," Elyssa said.

I blew out a sigh. "We can take the gryphons instead."

Elyssa shook her head. "There aren't enough."

Bliss held up her hand. "What about the gepherons?"

Elyssa pursed her lips. Nodded. "That might just work." She blurred away without another word.

I blinked a couple of times before realizing she'd gone. She returned leading several gepherons by their leashes. The feline-bat hybrids squeaked and looked curiously around.

"Um, do you know how to ride one of those things?" I asked.

"A pair of freed slaves showed me what to do. They're similar to the gryphons but not as intelligent." Elyssa handed reins to me and hopped into the saddle of hers. She stood in the stirrups as if judging the balance, then practiced drawing her light bow and swords. "Yeah, this will work."

Shelton got on one and wobbled in the saddle. "Man, I'm not too sure about this."

"At least if you die, we don't have to clean your poo off the ship," Adam said.

Shelton bared his teeth. "I'll make sure I land on you, Nosti."

Bliss and Cinder took two more gepherons. Once we were all situated, Elyssa showed us how to control direction and altitude with the reins. It took some practice, but before long, we were able to make laps around the tower without issue.

Adam gave the *Raptor* one more inspection, but the new power gem still hadn't calibrated. It was the gepheron or nothing.

We flew our steeds to a wide field where the rest of our forces rallied. Nearly three hundred and fifty gryphons stood in neat rows. Behind them were dozens of magi on pegaasi, and behind them were the flying carriages.

"Utopians, form up!" Elyssa held a fist in the air and a great roar went up from the soldiers. Wings beat the air and the gryphons formed into squadrons. The magi directed their flying horses behind the front gryphons, and the carriages drifted to the front lines. Elyssa thrust her hand forward, and we glided toward the wall.

Vokan's flying citadel hovered over the valley a half mile away and already flying north. Black clouds of gepheron guarded both flanks.

"He's already leaving," I shouted above the wind. Unlike the gryphons, the gepheron had no magic to block wind or sound. "How fast can that thing go?"

"By itself it is not fast," Cinder said. "I believe Vokan uses wind currents to drive it faster."

"With such a big head start, we might not catch him," Adam said.

The wind blowing against us abruptly shifted. The gepheron and gryphons spread their winds and glided, carried faster by the new currents.

"We have our own magi to help us," Ki said.

We began to close the distance. The citadel rotated to face us and set down on a plateau. The massive platform crushed trees and everything beneath it. The gepheron formed a barrier before it.

"Looks like Vokan's gonna fight." Shelton's brow furrowed with suspicion. "Is he really that sure of himself?"

"Classic narcissist," Elyssa said. "He's so used to being the bully he's forgotten what it's like to lose."

"So let's teach him." I cracked my knuckles and began picking out loyalists among the gepheron riders. While the rest of our forces took on the slaves, I'd focus on the ones controlling them. Unfortunately, there seemed to be no easy way to avoid killing the slaves.

True to form, the loyalists remained near the citadel while the slaves met our first wave. The flying carriages plowed through their ranks, heading straight for the citadel. Crossbow bolts cracked into the wood with no effect. Askot and the loyalists attacked with energy axes and swords, cleaving through the carriages until the levitation enchantments had nothing to support.

Despite their efforts, six carriages rammed into the citadel and exploded. Stone crumbled and cracked, but the explosives weren't enough to take it down. An energy arrow speared into the chest of a loyalist. He fell clutching the wound in his chest and bounced off the citadel wall. Elyssa speared another and dodged the attacks of a cross-bow-wielding slave.

I swooped close and nailed the man in the neck with a dart. The crossbow dropped from numb fingers and the slave slumped in the saddle. Without guidance, the gepheron flew onward and out of the battle.

Elyssa's gepheron took an arrow in its haunch. It squeaked in pain but continued to fight. Bliss swept in and shielded her flank from another volley as Elyssa picked off two more loyalists with pinpoint precision.

A gryphon rider cried out and fell from her beast, two crossbow bolts sticking from her chest. The wounded gryphon roared in anguish at the loss but remained in formation to help the others.

Elyssa fired a red arrow straight up and two squads of gryphon riders responded to the flare. Gemma roared a battle cry and led her riders from the eastern flank while Ki led her forces from the west. They fired volleys of drugged darts at the slaves, taking them out of the fight one way or the other.

We unleashed salvos on the slaves in the middle. Leather belts kept most of them from falling to their deaths. Utility squadrons flew in and guided the rudderless gepherons out of the fight. Unfortunately, we had only a limited supply of darts. Once we ran out, there wasn't much we could do but fight.

Despite our numbers, there were still nearly twice as many gepheron. We would have a lot of innocent blood on our hands.

Elyssa speared a slave. The woman died without a sound. Elyssa cringed. "God, I hate this."

Shelton leveled his staff. Flak exploded in front of a wave of gepheron, sending them scattering. "I'm with ya. I thought I could do it, but I'm going to hate myself if I slaughter these poor bastards."

"What the hell?" Adam reared back in his saddle. "Is that a sprite near your head, Justin?"

I hadn't seen the orb of light in all the confusion. It came closer and I flinched. "Vokan's trying to possess me!"

A familiar voice sounded in my mind. *No, this is Bonehead.*

"Bonehead?" I was confused. "I thought you went back home or wherever it is you live."

I did. So did dozens more sprites you have saved. We decided it was in our best interests to help you free others, so we returned.

"Can you free the other slaves?" I asked.

No, but we can help remove them from the fight. We will keep them busy while you fight the true evil.

"Thank you," I said, but Bonehead had already flitted away. He intercepted a gepheron rider on an attack vector for us.

The slave flailed and spasmed. The gepheron flew past us, its rider convulsing. Hundreds of balls of light lifted from the trees, stars returning to the skies. The sprites intercepted the slaves and it was seizure city in the unfriendly skies of Utopia.

Shelton slapped his knee. "Well, I'll be a three-legged donkey in a Siberian video game store. They're doing it!"

Adam gave him a confused look. "A what in a what?"

"We're not done yet!" Elyssa continued her assault on the fifty loyalists still left. Askot rallied them and charged her position.

"Oh, this is too easy." Elyssa bared her teeth and rushed to meet them.

An arrow slammed into my shoulder. Anger heated my face. I jerked it out with a scream of pain. Another arrow narrowly missed my face. Rage simmered to a boil. "You're dead, Askot!"

Bliss and I formed up to the sides and met the attacks head-on. Bliss fried two loyalists and slammed another from his saddle with a volley of Murk. I channeled a blazing sword and slashed crossbow bolts from the air. With a cry, I leapt from my saddle and landed on the back of Askot's gepheron.

He shouted in alarm and slashed at my legs. I lopped off his hand at the wrist then separated his head from his body. Another slash cut the saddle belt and his body tumbled to the ground far below.

The rest of the loyalists turned tail and ran. They deserved no mercy and I gave them none. I steered Askot's gepheron after them and shot webs of Murk to tether them so they couldn't get away.

"Destroy!" I roared and leapt to the next gepheron. Two slashes ended the loyalist. I kicked his body. It slammed into another loyalist and knocked him out. Cold and heat sliced through my shoulder blades. Blinding pain pounded my skull. The pain vanished in the blink of an eye. Heedless of the risk, I launched myself after the next loyalist, jetting through the air on my own wings.

He screamed and flailed frantically with his sword. "Die!" I roared. My blazing sword of Brilliance burned into his chest. Blood sizzled and the wound cauterized. The blade turned from white to crimson. I reared back my head and cried, "Destroy!"

Another high bound took me to the last loyalist tethered to his dead master's gepheron. He threw up his hands. "Mercy!"

"Never!" I slashed his saddle belt and kicked him into the sky.

A lone figure stood atop the citadel. *Vokan.*

"Did you really think you could beat me?" Vokan's voice boomed supernaturally loud. Thunder rumbled in the background. "I have the powers of a god."

Dark clouds swirled overhead. Dozens of dark funnels dropped from the skies and churned against the earth. Dust and debris filled the air. Still standing on the saddle of the last loyalist I'd killed, I turned and looked. Tornados swept entire wings of gryphons out of the air. Lightning struck down others.

I couldn't find Elyssa, Shelton, or any of the others.

The scent of ozone filled my nostrils. The hairs on my neck pricked. I channeled a dome overhead just in time to intercept a lightning bolt. Two tornados shifted course and came for me. Flames flickered in my vision and my muscles swelled. I locked my infernal gaze on the one place the tornados wouldn't go.

Vokan's tower.

I gripped the reins and urged the gepheron to full speed. The creature squeaked with fear as I led it around the debris field of a tornado, weaving a cloud of Stasis. The tornado sucked it in and unraveled like a ball of yarn, its fuel neutralized. Another lightning bolt struck the gepheron in the wing. Before it went down, I ran along its back and launched myself at the citadel.

Vokan flung out his hands but I fired a volley of Murk at him and forced him to take cover. It gave me the seconds I needed to reach the roof. I landed on my feet and rolled in case he had another attack ready.

Vokan glared at me with infuriating condescension. "So, you have brought out your demon side for the fight. You are sadly mistaken if you think you can win."

I looked down at my hands. My hands were huge, my skin blue, my fingernails black claws. I had manifested into demon form without even realizing it. My wings unfurled to the sides, burning as crimson as the energy sword in my hand. *What in the hell?*

The thought evaporated in the heat of my rage. "I will destroy you, Vokan." I stepped toward him. "You have few souls, if any, left to fuel your magic."

"Few?" Vokan laughed. "The cantrap in this citadel holds over a thousand, demon boy. I am not even halfway through my supply." Giant hands of energy descended from the sky. A net of lightning formed over the rooftop. "Baal was right. You are powerful, but foolish. With his tutelage, you can become as powerful as me."

"Why would I want Baal to teach me anything?" I roared.

Vokan laughed. "Boy, you are part of his master plan. You will be one of his horsemen."

I tried to think of a witty comeback but spat out something that made no sense. "I will never groom his horses." *What kind of stupid response is that?*

"A horseman of Baal's apocalypse, you idiot." Vokan shook his head slowly.

"A horseman of the apocalypse?" The idea strangely appealed to me. "There would be great destruction. Souls to consume." I nodded. "But I will never be second to you." *What in the holy hell am I saying and thinking?*

Glowing eyes appeared in the stairwell door and eidolons flooded onto the rooftop, encircling me. I swept my tail and spilled dozens over the side of the citadel. Using Murk, I blasted another group out into the air. If they grasped me, it was over. They kept pouring out of the door in an endless wave, voices humming, eyes glowing with unsated hunger.

I roared and spilled another wave of them over the side. I'd seen no door at the base of the citadel. Presumably, Vokan flew himself up to the top to get in. That meant the eidolons couldn't get back inside.

AN ENERGY HAND grasped at me. I rolled to the side and funneled Stasis. The energy lost cohesion and drifted apart. Two more hands replaced it. I neutralized one and dodged the other all while slamming eidolons off the roof with my tail. But for every hand I destroyed, two more replaced it.

Two rammers exploded from the stairwell, streaking toward me at inhuman speeds. Another energy hand blocked me in. Instead of neutralizing it, I ran at the oncoming enemies. Electronic roars hummed from their glowing mouths. They thought they had me.

I channeled Murk and jetted myself sideways at the last instant. The energy hand scooped the eidolons from the roof and catapulted them out into the air. I spun, ready to face more eidolons, but the doorway was empty. Either they were all outside the citadel or I had a brief respite. Now was my chance. I had to neutralize Vokan, so I did something I hadn't done in a long while.

I channeled Murk and Brilliance with my hands and spun it into Stasis, then fired rays of Murk and Brilliance into the orb of Stasis. A clear beam of Clarity speared straight into Vokan's chest.

Let Vokan see who he really is.

Vokan stiffened and the energy hands faded. His eyes brightened, and his lips spread into a maniacal grin. "Yes, I truly am the greatest. I am the right hand of Baal himself!"

That is not what I was going for. Clarity had opened Vokan's mind and revealed his true nature. When faced with the naked truth about herself, Daelissa felt shame and remorse for the first time in millennia. It revealed the depths of her depravation and insanity. The shock killed her.

Apparently, Vokan relished his true nature, and I had just bolstered his ego exponentially.

It really pissed me off.

I released Clarity and focused beams of Brilliance on the magus. A lightning shield blocked my attacks. Howling winds blew me backward. My feet lost their purchase, and energy hands swooped to secure me. I had only one chance. I spread my wings and let the wind carry me backward. My claws latched onto the stairwell doorway.

I dragged myself inside and leapt down the center of the spiral stairwell.

Seven stories blurred past. My wings flared at the last instant and arrested my momentum. My huge hand ripped open the door at the bottom. I wanted to take a moment to understand how I'd manifested without thinking about it, but I stepped through the door and saw the target.

Unguarded by eidolons, the cantrap stood two stories tall in a lavishly designed throne room. Rich carpeting ran from wall to wall. Great portraits of Vokan hung above the throne and on the sides. Tapestries hung from the domed ceiling. Capping it off was a massive mosaic of Vokan overhead.

It was a lot smaller than the main cantrap in Solan, but it was still huge. I crossed the space between me and it. Without asking Fred, tendrils of my essence spread out and latched onto the demon spirits holding the souls captive. At the last instant, I thought about what freeing them meant. The souls would be stuck in limbo, trapped between here and whatever afterlife might exist beyond this one.

Fred didn't care, and he didn't hesitate. Devouring these demons was nothing like the tiny spirits enslaving the sprites. Those had been appetizers before the main meal. And these weren't easy prey. Even trapped as they were by the patterns and the cantrap, the caustic demons fought back with everything they had.

Where the baby demons had been like wriggling worms, the older ones slithered like snakes in my grasp. Constricted to one form, trapped by singular purpose, they couldn't adapt to Fred's assault. I absorbed the first one. It felt like a giant lump passing into my psyche. The rest adapted, keeping the cantrap whole. But this construct was only held together by five demons. I consumed the next one and the cantrap could not hold.

The demons wailed. The patterns lost cohesion, and the surviving demons vanished back to Haedaemos. The glowing vessel flared with a blinding light, and the souls within vanished into the ether just as Vokan burst into the room.

CHAPTER 36

"No!" Vokan screamed like a wounded animal and ran at me. The floor of the citadel rose, blocks of granite forming a great rock beast. A giant fist slammed into my face.

I was vaguely aware of flying through the air and smashing into a wall. Before I could rise, more creatures formed from the stone of the citadel and pummeled me. Vokan was still powerful even without souls.

Fury exploded. Black spines spiked from my back and my frame swelled to twice its size. I slammed the nearest stone monster and crushed it into rubble. I met the next one with my horns and rammed it into another wall. Vokan roared with rage and hurled more and more of his golems at me.

The entire citadel rumbled. Walls crumbled. Without the missing stones, the building couldn't hold. Even in my enraged state, I saw this and realized I couldn't stay here to fight. Tons of falling stone would crush me like a bug. I fought off the next monster and found a weak spot in the wall. My fist punched through to open air. I dove outside and rolled across stone platform.

The citadel wobbled back and forth. It toppled slowly away from me, its

355

death knell like rolling thunder. I leapt to my giant feet and looked around for Vokan. The tornados and storms he'd summoned were gone, the last nimbus clouds fading to blue skies. Piles of bodies lay around the citadel. Once the eidolons fell off the building, Vokan had stopped giving them orders. Some stood while others lay on the ground, glowing eyes staring up at the sky.

I saw nothing of the magus and roared in frustration.

"His blood was mine to spill." I grabbed rubble and threw it carelessly away, digging for the prey I couldn't let escape.

Something is terribly wrong with me. These thoughts seemed like something Fred would have, not me. I focused inward.

"Justin!" Elyssa's cry drew my eyes skyward.

Shelton and the others glided in on their gepheron, landing all around me. Pain wracked my body. My back cracked. Bones and sinew unthreaded and shrank. Horns snapped from my forehead and clattered on the stone. My body melted back to its normal size and left me panting and sweating in torn pants that barely covered my tender bits.

I blinked and cleared bleary eyes. "Ouch."

Elyssa helped me up. Kissed my forehead. "Baby, what happened?"

"Jesus, you went full demon, Justin." Shelton chuckled. "Looks like you tore Vokan a dozen new assholes."

The fury I'd felt earlier was a vague memory. All I could think of was all those souls I'd released. How many were left? How many had Vokan burned through? Had I doomed them to an even worse fate than oblivion? I felt sick to my stomach. I jabbed a finger toward the rubble. "Vokan."

"He's in there?" Shelton readied his staff. "Nosti, let's clear some space."

Bliss and Cinder landed on the platform and ran over to me.

"Justin, are you okay?" Bliss looked at the giant curving horns that moments ago adorned my demonic head. "I've never seen you do that demon thing before."

"Yo," Shelton shouted. "We need to find Vokan in all this mess. Give us a hand?"

Bliss nodded. "Y-yes, of course." She channeled Murk into a scoop and began scraping rubble off to the side.

"I am glad to see you're okay." Cinder patted my shoulder. "You should be more careful, Justin."

I flashed a weary grin. "Yeah, I don't know what came over me."

Elyssa's brow furrowed. "We noticed."

Adam took out his arcphone and activated a spell script. Green light waves emanated from the end, turning rubble into dust. But even that barely put a dent in the massive pile. "This is gonna take a while."

"Over there!" Bliss streaked across the platform.

Elyssa's eyes flared, and she ran after her.

At first, I saw nothing. Then I realized the slight blur in my vision wasn't from exhaustion, but a camouflage spell. Cinder was closer than the others. He turned around and dove at the shimmering air.

Vokan appeared as if a curtain had fallen away. He was bloodied and bruised, but otherwise intact. A pile of stone clacked together into a giant stone golem. A fist slammed Cinder to the ground. The stone golem raised giant fists, ready to crush him.

"No!" I sprang to my feet, but even with all my speed, there was no way to reach him in time. The fists crashed down. Dust filled the air. Vokan faded from sight.

"Cinder!" Adam and Shelton scrambled around the fallen citadel. I streaked past them and found our friend.

He lay on the ground not far from the stone fists of the now-dormant golem. Cinder looked around, confused. In one hand he clutched a chain with something resembling a fetus dangling from the end. It was the Child of Jura.

"Oh my god, I thought—" My words lodged in my throat at what I saw in the clearing dust. Terror pierced my heart. "Elyssa!"

"I'm here." She staggered from the other side of the fist, blood streaming down her forehead.

I looked down. "Then who—" I suddenly knew. "Help me!"

Cinder's eyes flared with genuine surprise. He crawled on his knees to the still form. Bliss's legs and the lower half of her torso vanished beneath the stone fists. She lay face down, hands outstretched in front of her.

"Bliss." Something approaching fear wavered Cinder's voice. He knelt next to her. "Bliss, please."

Shelton rounded a pile of rubble. "Oh god." His face blanched. "Oh shit."

Bliss turned her head feebly. Blood foamed in her mouth, but she smiled. "I'm glad I met you, Cinder." Blood bubbled on her lips and she went still.

Cinder stared, frozen.

"Get the damned stones off her!" I shouted. "Do it now!"

Tears streamed down Elyssa's face. "Justin, it's too late."

"No, she's a dolem! We can preserve the spark!" I gripped one side of the giant fist and hoisted it up a few inches despite how tired I was. "Pull her out!"

Elyssa pulled out what was left of Bliss's body. Her legs and hips were crushed. The demon flesh wouldn't rot, but it would eventually dissolve into goop. I turned Bliss onto her back. Her eyes stared, glazed and lifeless.

Tears burned my eyes. I channeled a blazing dagger to carve open Bliss's chest. "We can take out the soul sphere. I know we can preserve the spark somehow." Cinder didn't say a word. He stared as if comatose. As if his mind couldn't handle what had just happened. I knew the feeling all too well. I'd nearly lost Elyssa once and that had almost killed me. Losing Nightliss had been nearly as bad.

It felt like I was losing her all over again. All I could see was the face of my beloved friend.

"Let me." Adam pushed me gently aside. He steeled himself with a deep breath and used his wand to carve open Bliss's chest. I forced myself to watch, hard as it was seeing someone I knew carved open like an animal.

The soul sphere slid out between the ribs. The spark dimmed, and the soul shard began to fade. Adam took out his phone and activated a spell script. The aether maintaining the soul shard glowed softly. Adam blew out a breath. "The soul sphere is intact, but I don't know how long it'll maintain the spark without a vessel. We need to summon a demon body that can hold it. For that, we need all sorts of demon magic none of us can do."

Cinder stroked Bliss's hair one last time and closed her eyes. He stood woodenly and clutched at his chest, genuine confusion furrowing his brow. "This is pain?"

Elyssa put a hand on his shoulder. "Yes, Cinder. This is the worst kind of pain."

He held out his hands toward the soul sphere. "May I?"

Adam nodded and handed it to him. "I'll do what I can to preserve her spark, but I'm afraid it isn't much."

"Why can't you just feed it more aether?" I said. "Wouldn't that keep it powered?"

"A regular golem spark can survive without a body," Adam said, "but these soul spheres are different. The soul needs a body. Without it, the spark can't hold the soul."

All that talk of souls reminded me of what I'd done to defeat Vokan. "Oh, shit."

Shelton's eyes tightened. "What?"

"I ate the demons in the cantrap." I looked around as if I could see ghosts. "The souls flew free."

Cinder handed me the Child. "I cannot use this. Perhaps you can."

The relic felt like ice to my bare flesh. I sensed a presence burrowing into my mind and the urge to throw the cursed thing nearly over-whelmed my common sense.

You are the demon eater. The soul taker. Sate your hunger, Kalesh.

I yelped and dropped it on the ground. "Holy shit. That thing's talking to me."

"It's what?" Shelton leaned down and poked it like a dead snake. "Cold as hell." He grasped it. His eyes went blank and his body grew still. As if waking from a trance, he threw it on the ground. "Yeah, I'm not about that life."

"Did it talk to you?" I asked.

"Told me to use souls to increase my powers." He shuddered. "Man, I can't imagine having that thing in your mind. No wonder Vokan gave no shits about burning souls for his own power."

I took a deep breath and picked it up. "It's time to make this thing work for good."

The whispers started again.

Who is Kalesh? I asked.

I sensed Fred stirring. *It is our demon name.*

360

I shuddered involuntarily as the Child flowed in my mind. *How do I use you?*

Seek the souls.

I didn't know what it meant, so I just concentrated on finding souls. It was like opening my eyes to a constellation of stars. The souls I'd released drifted lazily overhead in a shimmering cloud. Some of them drifted free of the mass, dropping lower.

Shelton stepped around a pile of motionless eidolons. "What do we do about those things?"

I reached toward one of the floating souls. It flew to me, a vaguely humanoid shape. *Devour it and become powerful,* the Child whispered in a tiny voice that could have been male or female. It was creepy as hell.

Fred growled hungrily but made no move to take it. As the soul came closer, I sensed a faint tether running from it to one of the nearby bodies. I directed the Child to let it pull the soul back inside the body.

A woman gasped. She rolled off the pile of people, a scream tearing from her throat. Elyssa grabbed her. "You're okay now. We've got you."

"Cold." The woman shivered. "So cold!" The glow from her eyes and mouth faded, revealing the organs still in their correct places.

"We're gonna need a shrink for these poor people," Shelton said. "They've been stuck halfway between here and the afterlife for three decades."

"Help!" The woman screamed and grasped at Elyssa. "Please."

"You're safe." Elyssa hugged the woman and that seemed to quiet her for the moment.

I looked around for the next soul and saw Cinder sitting on a stone, Bliss's soul sphere in his lap. He stroked the transparent casing and talked to it, as if Bliss might be able to hear him. I wanted to talk to him, to console him, but there were too many more souls to save right now.

It took hours to send all the souls back. The Child didn't like it. The unborn child of Saila was evil incarnate, whispering black deeds into my mind, chipping at my resistance. Fred licked his chops but didn't interfere with my operations. If anything, he seemed amused, and it scared the hell out of me.

The citizen of Camelyn flocked to the broken citadel to help their fellow Utopians. Most of the former eidolons weren't ready to be back in their bodies. Every last one of them spoke of being cold, of being in a between place. Some spoke of visions, of seeing other spirits and creatures.

Those who'd been rammers and pouncers kept their strange physiques. The healing magi thought they'd keep those traits for the rest of their lives without intense magical therapy. By the time it was all said and done, we had over four hundred humans in need of psychologists.

"I have one more patient." Agula held a glowing female in his arms. Her face was contorted, as if Vokan relinquished his control of her in the middle of a scream.

"A wraith," Ki said softly. "At least that's what we called the ones who glow like her."

"Her name is Magus Anya," Agula said. "I remember her from magus school."

I reached out with the Child and found her soul drifting aimlessly near the edge of the citadel platform. I'd learned the relic could detect souls within a wide radius, which made it harder to find something specific with a lot of people around until I'd learned another trick. Souls inside bodies felt warm and gooey to my mind, while separated ones felt like clouds of ice.

I sent Anya's soul back inside. She sucked in a breath. Her eyelids fluttered open. The glow from seemingly empty eye sockets dimmed until green eyes became visible. She blinked and looked calmly up at her surroundings. "I am corporeal again."

Agula looked surprised. "You're rather calm."

"Calm?" Anya sat up and examined her still-glowing skin. "I feel like screaming. I felt frozen for so long only to be burning up now." She felt her forehead. "How bizarre." Tears glistened in her eyes. "I feel trapped in my own flesh."

Agula gently held her shoulders. "It will take some getting used to, but you'll be fine."

"I saw so much." Anya trembled. "I saw existence held together by slender threads in a shattered world. Spirits danced between the worlds, pulling at the strings, drawing them together."

Agula's forehead pinched. "Visions or bad dreams?"

"I don't think she was dreaming," Elyssa said. "It sounds like she glimpsed the realmverse."

Anya had seen Baal pulling at the strings of our existence.

CHAPTER 37

Crews spent the day searching for Vokan. Even the sprites joined the hunt, eager to exact justice on one who had abused them for so long.

Over a hundred gepheron riders waited back in the tower plaza in Camelyn. They stood or stayed where the sprites left them, puppets without a master to tug their strings. I still felt queasy from devouring the demons in the citadel, but I couldn't waste time. We had to get to Solan before Vokan did.

While he couldn't control the souls without the Child, he might be able to destroy them or release them into the world. It had taken forever just recovering a few hundred souls. I couldn't imagine how it would be with tens of thousands.

I took time to recover after every ten baby demons. The sprites greeted their newly freed comrades while the humans took care of theirs. Agula spoke at length with several sprites in the hopes of striking up relations.

Bone weary and sick to my stomach, I freed the last slave and leaned on Elyssa for support. "We need to get to Solan."

She stroked my hair. "It can wait a day. Vokan only had one flying citadel with him. It'll take him a month to walk back to Solan."

"We need to mobilize recovery teams as well," Agula said. "There will be thousands of distraught citizens to counsel."

I knew they were right, but I still felt a profound sense of urgency. "There are more sprites to free in Solan."

Agula nodded. "The sprites are aware of this and several will travel with us to aid in their recovery."

The task seemed absolutely monumental. How many thousands of house sprites were there in Solan? How would we track them all down? I didn't even know where to begin.

Agula patted my back. "You look overwhelmed, Justin. Please, let us help you. We can use the Child to restore souls and take a burden off your shoulders."

"The relic is evil. It will try to make you do terrible things."

He smiled. "I believe I can resist the temptations."

I slumped. "Yeah, I think you can too."

Elyssa led me back to the ship to rest. But when I saw Shelton, Adam, and Cinder gathered in the plaza, I knew it would have to wait.

Cinder held a small crystal box. "I cremated Bliss," Cinder explained. "It seemed disrespectful to let the demon flesh melt."

"I'd be surprised if the ashes don't turn to goop," Shelton said.

"I thought it appropriate to hold a brief ceremony in her honor," Cinder said. "I believe she would appreciate it."

Salty tears stung my eyes. "I think so too, Cinder."

We flew the *Raptor* out over the ocean for a clear view of the setting sun.

"Perhaps we could all speak of a fond memory of Bliss." Cinder set the box on the railing.

"I'll start." Adam cleared his throat and wiped his eyes. "I remember how angry she was at herself all the time. She'd been a slave to her creator and hadn't even realized it. Bliss told me that Cinder always treated her like a real person from the first day they met. She never really talked a lot about herself, but I think you meant the world to her, Cinder. I think you gave her a sense of purpose."

Cinder nodded. "Thank you, Adam."

Shelton went next. "Bliss used to hate the idea of eating meat, but after I got her to try one of my hamburgers, she couldn't get enough." He chuckled. "She wasn't afraid to try anything once."

"Bliss came to me for instruction in Templar fighting techniques," Elyssa said. "I got to know her better and respected her as a warrior. She never backed down from a fight and was fiercely loyal." Elyssa turned to me. "Bliss wanted to be a hero like you, Justin. She wanted to redeem her existence in your eyes."

The lump in my throat swelled. "Bliss was a hero. I regret that I didn't see that in her a long time ago. I regret that I didn't see past her shell to a soul that she made her own." I wiped the tears from my eyes. "Nightliss would have been proud, and I'm proud, very proud, to have called Bliss my friend."

Cinder took the box. "Bliss made me truly feel emotion for the first time. I now feel as if a hole has opened inside me that cannot be filled. I believe this means I loved her." He held the box over the side of the ship. "I love you, Bliss."

The box fell into the water with a gentle splash and disappeared.

"She's not entirely gone yet." Adam squeezed Cinder's shoulder. "Maybe we can save the spark and the soul shard somehow."

Elyssa wiped red eyes. "Can we use the Child?"

"I can move the soul shard with the Child." I took a breath to soothe my aching heart. "But I can't put it in a body with a soul. Since it's not an entire soul, it won't last long without a body."

Cinder turned away from the railing. "Thank you for your words and your help. I think I will go sit somewhere quiet for a while." He went below decks.

The rest of us stared out at the ocean for a while longer before returning to town.

EVERY AVAILABLE GRYPHON and gepheron left Camelyn the next morning with hundreds of volunteers and soldiers bound for Solan. Agula and several other magi rode aboard the *Raptor* since we'd arrive there well before the others. There was plenty of prep work to do before we started joining souls to bodies, and we wanted to be ready.

We arrived in Solan late in the afternoon and landed on the tower with the cantrap. When I grasped the Child, I understood what Vokan felt.

Heat flashed across my skin, searing me to my bones. The eidolons felt like extensions of me, flush with power of their own. I could flick instantly from one to another, use their eyes as my eyes, their legs as my legs. It reminded me of the real-time strategy video games I'd once loved.

Except my micro would be ten times better.

With this army, I could control cities. With the power of the cantrap, I could control worlds. Another source of souls pulled my gaze.

Use them. Increase your power.

The siren call of the Child was almost too much to bear. The shells around the souls were just meat, new slaves to bring under my command. I could defeat Baal. I could defeat Xanomiel. The realms could be mine.

Sharp pain jabbed my chest like a knife. But it wasn't metal that pierced me, but my conscience. *Dude, you're going insane.*

My friends weren't mere meat cases for souls, and I had no desire to rule the realms. I gently pulled the strings of the eidolons and told them to come to the towers. It was time to restore the citizens of Solan to life.

I started the process slowly, giving Agula and his people time to treat the trauma the Solanites had suffered. Not only would they have to come to terms with their long separation from their bodies, but with the deaths of loved ones whose souls Vokan had consumed for his power. Where Vokan had reduced the population of Solan to eidolons in days, it took us weeks simply to return them all to their bodies.

We sent the other flying citadels to Camelyn to ferry in thousands of citizens who wanted to help Solan recover. I didn't know if Utopia would ever be the same after the horrors inflicted on it. But Agula and his people worked hard and the Solanites began to adjust to real life again.

Miraculously, most of the councilors who'd faced Vokan that first day were still alive, souls bruised but intact. Nearly every magus returned to their bodies had experienced visions during their time as a disembodied soul. Most of them had glimpsed the realms and the gravitational lines connecting them to the Anchor Stone in the Glimmer.

Over the past few years, the lines had grown thicker. We suspected it meant the pull of the Anchor Stone had increased, but there was no way to tell if it had effectively pulled the realms closer without visiting the Glimmer.

The house sprites were another matter I had to take care of. It turned out demon spirits didn't control them like the gepheron slaves, but used a compulsion enchantment. Shelton, Adam, and Cinder formulated a counter-spell, but it had to be applied individually to each and every sprite. Agula organized every magus at his disposal, including those Solanites restored to their bodies, to help with the tremendous undertaking.

Solan was just the beginning. Loyalists still controlled Hevia and Ganalon. We hadn't changed any of Vokan's propaganda broadcasts or spread the word of his defeat so they wouldn't be on alert. Without gepheron or slaves to fight, the cities fell easily into our control. Barely a handful of loyalists had controlled the populations. Most surrendered without incident. Some committed suicide. Others ran, but none escaped.

We found no trace Vokan had visited either of the other towns. Since he had no flying platforms or beasts, it seemed likely he was on foot, probably somewhere in the vicinity of Camelyn. The area was heavily forested outside the valley, so flying patrols had no luck tracking him down.

It seemed unlikely he would go to the place he called home during his long banishment, the hut mentioned in his journal, but we took the *Raptor* there anyway. The hut was nothing but a pile of rotting sticks when we found it, but we searched the surrounding beach and forest anyway.

Shelton was the first to find something. He appeared from the forest, face ashen.

I did a double-take when I saw how white he looked. "What's wrong?"

"You gotta see this." He led me and the others into the forest. The thick foliage ended in a field of rotting trees and dead bushes. It was soon evident why. Faded demon patterns of all shapes and sizes were etched into the hard-packed earth, each one blackened with old blood.

Piles of human bones sat in some patterns. We skirted the barren field and found a mass grave filled with the remains of species we had trouble identifying.

Adam knelt next to a human skull twice the normal size. It seemed to belong to the huge ribcage and long leg bones next to it. "Call me crazy, but if I had to guess, this thing had a human torso and a horse body."

"You're telling me it's a centaur?" Shelton stared at it for a moment. "Hot damn, I think you're right."

"Some of the human remains are just weird." Elyssa pointed out a skeleton that might have belonged to giant, and another to a midget. "Do you think there might be other species living in this place?"

"Whoever or whatever they were, they died gruesomely," Adam said. "I think Vokan sacrificed them to demons."

"And killed the earth in the process." I kicked up the black dirt. "He must have really poisoned it if nothing has grown here in decades." My foot landed on one of the patterns. A nauseating feeling wormed its way up my esophagus.

Blood splashes. An inhuman scream pierces the air. Infernal fire explodes from the earth.

I gasped and jumped back. "Holy shit."

Elyssa's eyes lit with concern. "What happened?"

"I stepped on a pattern." Despite my disgust, I sensed joy coming from my demon half. Fred liked this place.

Kalesh. Fred apparently didn't like the name I'd given him.

Sounds pretentious, I told him.

My name is Kalesh.

I didn't like his use of singular possessive. *Don't you mean our name?*

Mine.

His response was not reassuring, so I did the smart thing and ignored him.

We walked back around the field toward the beach. "If Vokan came this way, it would take him weeks arrive." Elyssa looked at the map on her arcphone. "Hopefully, we won't be in this realm by that time."

370

"Pray to freaking god." Shelton made the sign of the cross. "Never thought I'd miss Seraphina so much."

"Technically, you miss Bella." Adam nudged him. "Am I right?"

Shelton slumped. "Man, I can't take another day without her." He glared at me. "You're a lucky son of a bitch to have Elyssa along all this time."

I grinned. "Maybe she's the lucky one."

Elyssa groaned. "Oh, so lucky."

Our route took us past a rocky formation we hadn't passed the first time. Elyssa noticed the black maw leading inside. I summoned a sphere of light and walked inside. The tunnel curved for a hundred feet and terminated at a black pit with no discernable way down. Something glowed softly in the sea of pitch.

I snuffed my light.

"What the hell?" Shelton grabbed my arm. "Warn me before you do that when we're right next to a pit of doom, man!"

"What's glowing down there?" Elyssa said.

I was too curious to walk away. "I want to find out." I channeled a beam of Brilliance to light the depths.

Shelton shouted. "Dammit, now I'm blind!"

The pit looked a couple hundred feet deep, but my shaft of light found rough stone stairs leading down the side. They looked as if they'd been neatly carved out of the wall using earth magic. About twenty stairs from the bottom, I no longer needed to use my magic to light the way because of the spectacle waiting below.

A chorus of gasps went up from all of us. Even Cinder might have gasped if he hadn't remained in Solan to help with the recovery efforts. A petite woman hung suspended inside a cantrap. Aside from being a perfectly proportioned female of only three feet tall, gossamer wings curled around her. The glow seemed to emanate from her skin.

Shelton gulped. "Holy farting fairies."

Adam looked on with wonder. "For once, I think you might be right."

"It looks just like a fairy," Elyssa said. "Doesn't it?"

I nodded. "Yeah, it does."

Apparently in Utopia, fairies were real.

CHAPTER 38

"Uh, guys." Shelton lit the end of his staff and shined it into a shadowy corner. A dark vessel held another fairy, this one with amber wings.

I reached out with my senses and counted only two demons holding the first fairy. It probably wasn't a good idea, but I consumed one of them and broke the cantrap. I fought down the urge to vomit as the caustic demon slithered through my psychic guts. Fred wolfed it down like a raw steak and loved it.

The fairy fluttered to the ground. I knelt next to her and touched her neck. Her skin was warm, but I found no pulse. Before I could adjust my fingers, I felt a beat against them. I released the other fairy as well.

Elyssa picked her up and pulled her into the corona of light coming off the other one. The glowing fairy's eyes flashed open. She tried to leap to her feet but failed. Angry words in an alien tongue flowed from her lips. Despite her diminutive size, her voice was as deep and rich as a grown human female's.

"What are you saying?" I held out my hands to show they were empty. "We come in peace."

The fairy pushed herself into a kneeling position, wings fluttering weakly, and regarded us for a moment. She spoke with a thick accent. "You are not the one who took me."

I shook my head. "An evil man named Vokan took you. We just found you and released you."

"What's your name?" Elyssa asked.

"I am Pyra, emissary of Pangaea." She looked down at the tattered clothes she wore. "We recovered a dangerous Unfae who escaped to the human lands, but on our return journey, the tides brought our ship here and crashed it upon the shore. The evil one who captured us imprisoned me." She looked around confused. "Where are my people?"

Elyssa grimaced. "Pyra, you've been a captive for decades."

I thought of the mass grave beyond the field. "I'm so sorry, but I think your people were killed by Vokan."

"No!" Pyra shrieked. "What monster would do this?"

"Um, guys." Shelton looked around confused. "Where did the other fairy go?"

Pyra's eyes widened. "Was there another like me imprisoned here?"

I nodded. "I mean, she looked similar, but she didn't glow."

"The Unfae." Pyra growled. "She is free and there is nothing I can do." Tears sparkled down her cheeks. "My crew is dead."

"Maybe we can help you track her down," Elyssa said. "We have a ship."

Pyra shook her head. "No. We have no nulls to negate her magic, and I will not see others killed."

"We're not exactly helpless," I said.

"I must return to Pangaea and report to the queen."

I projected the holographic map from my phone and pointed to Anatopia. "Is this Pangaea?"

Pyra frowned but nodded. "We have never cared for the name the humans gave us, or the humans in general."

"The humans here are actually pretty nice," I said. "Have your people been spying on them? Is that how you learned their language?"

Her brow furrowed. "We use magic, of course."

"Oh, of course." Shelton rolled his eyes. "Guess no one has to learn anything else these days."

I turned to our resident genius. "Adam, how long would it take us to reach Pangaea and get back?"

Adam tapped on his phone. "At top speed, a day and a half each way, provided her city is on the closest coast."

"That is as far as you may take me." Pyra jabbed a finger at the north-western edge of Pangaea. "We have a city there. You will have to stop offshore. From there, I can fly."

I blinked. "We're taking you all that way and can't even see the city?"

"No humans." She put her hands on her hips and managed to look rather menacing despite the height difference. "We escaped the evil of humans in Eden long ago and swore we would never deal with them again."

"Whoa." Adam staggered back. "You mean that's what happened to all the fairy tale creatures?"

Pyra scoffed. "The Fae are not tales and we do not abide humans."

Elyssa scoffed right back. "Not even the nice ones offering to take you across the world so you can get home?"

The fairy quirked her lips. "I will abide you if I must."

"Damn, talk about a tough crowd." Shelton directed an orb of light around the pit. "Do we need to worry about that Unfae killing us?"

"Cowardice rules that foul creature." Pyra fluttered her wings and lifted off the floor a few inches. "She will scurry to a hole and hide. Never fear, we will return and dig her out again."

"What did she do that's so bad?" I asked.

"That is none of your concern." Pyra lifted higher. "Come now. Take me to your ship. I wish to put the human lands behind me."

"Gotta be kidding me," Shelton grumbled. "Save her life and now she's commanding us around like we're her servants."

"We know where your crew are buried," Elyssa said. "Would you like to see them?"

"I have no time for the bones of the dead." The fairy folded her arms across her chest. "I must return to Pangaea."

"Why do I feel like we just opened a new can of worms?" Shelton said.

Adam gazed warily at Pyra. "Because we have."

We led the fairy to the *Raptor*, all of us on guard in case the Unfae decided to pull a fast one on us.

"This ship will cross the ocean in a day and a half?" Pyra scowled. "It doesn't even look as if it will float."

Shelton wiggled his fingers. "Because it uses magic."

She turned her scowl on him. "Do not make me use my magic on you, human. I assure you, it will quiet your lips."

Shelton backed away from her very slowly and quietly.

Pyra sniffed and flitted up the gangway. "I require quarters and solitude."

"I thought we could talk, maybe exchange stories," I said. "There are some pretty monumental things going on that might be of concern to your people."

"Human concerns are of no concern to us." She hovered in place. "Quarters."

The *Raptor* sped us across the ocean, south of the equator to the only other continent of Utopia. Pyra remained in her quarters the entire trip, not even coming out to eat. She refused to answer any questions or even speak with us.

As we neared Pangaea, I finally decided to cut the bull and make her listen. A knock on her door got no answer as usual, so I pressed the gem and the door misted away. Pyra sat on her bed. Her eyes flicked open the moment I stepped inside.

Light sparkled and danced on her fingertips. "Leave me, human, or I will make you leave."

"Not until you hear me out." I stood in the doorway. "Do your people know about the other realms besides Eden?"

"Of course."

"Do you know of the Apocryphan?"

Her eyes tightened. "We know the tales of the Breaking, when Gaia was split asunder. It was then we ancient races decided to leave the humans to their own. Had we known some would follow us here to this realm, we would have wiped them out long ago. Humans are a plague to any place they touch."

"Um, okay." Her distrust of humans was too ingrained to overcome, but I'd found a weak point. "Xanomiel, one of the Apocryphan, wishes to recombine the realms back into one Earth so he can rule over all. Does that sound like something you want to happen?"

Pyra looked uncertain for the first time. "How do you know of this?"

"That's a long story. If you'd let me tell you, it would all make sense."

"What do you wish of us?"

I took the opening. "We need your help. We need the ancient races to ally with humans so we can defeat Xanomiel and his competitor for dominion, Baal, Grand Overlord of Haedaemos."

Pyra bared her little teeth. "Baal's influence stretches far and wide across the realms. He will not be easy to defeat."

Across the realms? "You speak as if you have some insight as to what happens across the realms."

"We have those who can peer into other realms." Pyra pursed her lips. "I will grant you this audience, human. Tell me the story and I will pass it on to the queen."

I had just enough time to fit in the important details before we arrived at the northwestern shores of Pangaea.

"Do not approach shore," Pyra ordered Elyssa. "I will fly the remainder of the way."

Elyssa gave her a mock salute. "Yes, sir."

The *Raptor* stopped a quarter mile offshore. Sugary white sand sparkled on the beach. Massive trees with trunks as large as redwoods rose in the distance. A sapphire waterfall plunged from a cliff and into the calm ocean waters. Pangaea looked like a Caribbean paradise.

I stepped in Pyra's way before she left. "We could really use your help. Please talk to the queen."

"I keep my word, human." Pyra flitted over the railing and zipped over the water to the shore. In the blink of an eye, she vanished into the forest."

"What an ungrateful bitch," Shelton muttered. "Man, I wish she would've tried some fairy magic on me. I would've shown her some real magic."

"She probably would've turned you into a frog," Adam said. "Then Bella would have to kiss you to turn you back into a jackass."

I looked at the forbidden continent a moment longer then made a circle in the air with a finger. "Let's get out of here."

Elyssa patted my shoulder. "Hey, we tried. Maybe something will come out of this."

"God knows we'll need it." Bright yellow fish darted below in the crystal clear waters. Something huge and dark sent them scattering. "We can barely fight Baal. Xanomiel might be impossible without some major help."

The *Raptor* delivered us back in Solan a couple of days later, just in time to say our goodbyes to the Utopians. We met them outside the house on Juniper street where the gray fog of Voltis already hung thick in the air.

Agula hugged each of us. "Your sacrifices and kindness will not be forgotten. Once we have restored our communities, rest assured we will join you in the fight against Baal and Xanomiel."

"Agreed." Daana shook our hands. "We will soon hold a drawing for the next council. Until then, the three of us will lead the best we can."

Elaine held Cinder's hands. "Brave golem, I am devastated by the loss of Bliss. She will be commemorated for her sacrifice."

"Maybe build her a statue," Shelton said.

"Such edifices are not allowed," Daana said. "A statue is only a sign of hubris, and we believe Vokan exhibited enough hubris to last us another millennium."

"Thank you for your excellent leadership, Elyssa." Ki took Elyssa's hand and gently kissed it. "You are a wonder."

Elyssa's face flushed. "Thank you, Ki. Your people fought bravely and won the day. I look forward to seeing you again soon."

Shelton chuckled. "Aww, ain't that cute."

Elyssa elbowed him in the stomach so hard he doubled over.

Seraphina, here we come.

I channeled through Argus. A portal ripped open the air. Stormy skies greeted us on the other side.

"Safe travels!" Agula called.

"I'll miss you," Ki said.

There was no doubt who she was talking to.

Elyssa flew us through the gateway and back to Seraphina at the exact place we'd left from two months ago.

"We're home!" Shelton danced in a circle. "Finally!"

"Well, second home," Adam reminded him. "It's still not Eden."

"I really need to communicate with my father." Elyssa zipped us out and away from Voltis. "Let me see if I can raise the *Uorion*."

"Man, four months we've been gone in Seraphina time." Adam shook his head. "They probably thought we died."

"Two days, give or take, for every day we spent in Utopia?" Shelton shook his head. "Thank god Bella is the immortal one."

The ship slowed to a stop and Elyssa rushed out onto the forward deck. "Are those Mzodi ships?"

I followed her gaze and spotted a dozen of the smaller frigates barreling our way. Silhouettes danced against the orange skies on the horizon. Dozens, no hundreds, of winged reptilian forms pursued the ships.

"Holy smokes." Shelton pressed against the railing. "There must be two hundred full-grown dragons behind them."

Adam held the spyglass to an eye. "The ships will be here any minute."

As promised the first frigate whooshed past, the levitation foils glowing bright against the sleek black hull. The crew on the deck spared us a confused look as they flashed past toward Voltis. The next two ships were slower, their organically curved hulls scarred with giant claw marks and burn marks.

The last ship slowed, and a crew member called out to us. "Get back inside, you fools. There are too many to fight!"

"Inside where?" I asked.

"Atlantis!" He chopped his arm forward and the ship picked up speed.

"I'm confused." Adam looked back at the dragons. "You know, they're flying pretty damned fast. Maybe we should—"

"On it." Elyssa wheeled the *Raptor* around and sped after the last ship.

A gem on the prow speared a giant beam into Voltis and a portal opened big enough to drive a ship through. We followed the frigate and emerged on the other side over calm, blue waters.

Massive stone columns jutted from the ocean floor, each one outfitted with gem turrets. Several more of the black ships hovered behind the turrets, the crews running around the decks at full alert. A crystalline sheen spread across the sky behind us, a massive shield the likes of which I'd never seen.

"What in the hell?" Shelton turned in a circle. "None of this was here the last time." He turned to Cinder. "Was it?"

Cinder shook his head. "I have never seen such Mzodi ships or these turrets." He looked up at the shield. "Fascinating."

A silver ship shaped like a giant manta ray glided toward us. It looked like a single-decker, something not meant for long-distance travelling. The captain called out over the railing. "Who are you? We didn't authorize your ship to leave Atlantis."

Elyssa stepped forward. "What do you mean, who are we? I'm Elyssa Borathen. This is Justin Slade."

The woman's eyes flared wide. "By the gods of Atlantis, you're here?"

Shelton scoffed. "Duh."

"Come with me at once." The woman circled her finger above her head and the manta ship spun around. "Your father will want to see you."

"Duh again." Shelton shook his head. "Damn, you'd think we've been gone four years instead of four months."

An uneasy feeling formed in the pit of my stomach. "Something is horribly wrong here. Nothing is the same as we left it."

And why were there so many Mzodi in Atlantis?

CHAPTER 39

"T his doesn't make any sense. The Mzodi didn't have so many ships stationed in Atlantis." Despite her concerns, Elyssa piloted the *Raptor* after the manta ship.

A few miles inward, we passed through a haze and Atlantis popped into view. The city rose from sea level up nearly a thousand feet to the top of a mountain where a massive statue of Poseidon aimed his spear at the sea. Beautiful marble buildings rose along the flat lands at the base and dotted the mountain all the way to the top.

Out of sight, Mount Olympus rose to the east of Atlantis. It was the former home of the Fallen, ancient Seraphim banished from Seraphina. They possessed the secret of traveling anywhere from within Voltis but had left for parts unknown and never returned.

Manta ships zipped to and fro across the busy seaport of Atlantis. The docks were at least ten times larger than I remembered, as busy as the dockyards of Cabala. More of the black frigates sat on the docks, most of them undergoing repairs by crews with fabrication gems.

"Why are the Mzodi in Atlantis?" Adam couldn't take his eyes off an

Mzodi cruiser lifting off. "Is it me, or do their ships look completely militarized?"

Shelton blew out a breath. "Yeah, they looked ready for war."

We followed the manta ship toward a large round pier in front of a large domed building. A large contingent of people waited near the dock. It had been two months since I'd seen my parents, but over four months for them. Despite my apprehension, I was excited to see them.

I leaned over the railing, scanning for familiar faces. I found Dad, but his trademark amused grin was uncharacteristically absent as he led Mom to the front of the crowd.

Cinder looked down. "I hope Issana will not take Bliss's death too hard."

"Her soul sphere is still intact," Adam said. "Maybe Justin's dad can help us get her a new body."

Cinder nodded mutely. I hated so much that the first emotion he learned was the pain of loss and sorrow. If he'd been human, it probably would have wrecked him.

Elyssa landed the *Raptor*. I rushed down the gangway and hugged my parents.

"Justin, is it really you?" Tears trailed down Mom's cheeks. "We thought you'd died."

Dad wrapped me in a rough embrace. "Damn, son, couldn't you have at least called?"

"I'm sorry, I really am." I sighed. "We ended up trapped in the wrong realm and had to overthrow a tyrant. You know, the usual."

"It's my bro!" A flash of platinum locks nearly bowled me over. I staggered back and stared in confusion at the familiar face. It took the space of several heartbeats before I managed to speak her name.

"Ivy?"

She laughed and hugged me. "I'm here! We just got here a few months ago, and it's been super crazy. You couldn't believe where I've been all this time."

"How—how did you get here?" I was so shocked I could barely think.

"Long story, but totes worth it." Ivy struggled to free herself. "Too tight."

"Oh my god, I can't believe you're here!" I swung her around and put her down. "Ivy, what happened to you? Are you okay?" I looked her over and realized she'd hardly aged a day since I last saw her.

"Ivy!" Elyssa embraced her before she had a chance to recover from my enthusiastic hugs. "We were so worried!"

Ivy giggled and freed herself. "You can thank Conrad for saving me."

"I want to hear everything." I kissed her cheeks. "I'm so relieved you're okay."

"Well, if you're surprised by me you'll never believe who else is here!" Ivy clapped her hands and jumped in place.

Issana stepped out of the crowd, eyeing me warily. She looked even more like Nightliss than I remembered. Except, Issana wasn't so short and petite. This wasn't her—it was another dolem that was nearly identical to Nightliss. I swallowed the sadness and anger rising in my chest.

"Justin?" Tears pooled in her eyes.

I took a step back. "Where did you find another dolem that looks just like Nightliss?"

"What's a dolem?" Ivy asked.

"A demon golem made with demon flesh, a soul shard, and a golem spark."

"Oh, you mean an infernus." Ivy laughed. "Silly bro, that's not an infernus. That's the real Nightliss."

I stared blankly unable to process what she'd just said. "The real Nightliss?"

"Yeah. Victus replaced her with an infernus and faked her death." She giggled as if the entire thing were hilarious.

My knees went weak and I staggered. I couldn't think, couldn't talk. *This can't be real.* But it was. My sweet friend was alive! "Nightliss!" I wrapped my arms around her and kissed her cheeks. Hot tears blinded me. I laughed with almost manic joy. "You're alive! You're alive!"

"Yes!" She laughed and hugged me harder. "I'm so sorry you thought I was dead all this time."

I backed away so I could look her over. "When did Victus take you?"

"When I took the escape capsule with the bomb up into the sky, one of Victus's ships caught it and took it inside a hangar. Another identical capsule left the hangar and took its place. My infernus clone was on it. Before I could do anything, gas inside the ship knocked me out."

I couldn't stop sobbing. "You're alive and that's all that matters."

"Wait, I got tons more surprises!" Ivy jumped with glee. "Conrad killed Victus and practically saved the Overworld."

Ivy was here. Nightliss was alive and well. Victus Edison, the bastard who'd trapped us here, was dead.

It was one of the best days of my life.

There was only one other thing missing. "Where's Cutsauce?"

Ivy's grin faded. "You know, I completely forgot about your little doggie. I don't know where he is."

"He's such a sweet little hellhound." I missed Cutsauce, but as a hellhound, he wasn't in much danger of dying unless a bigger demon ate him.

Ivy shrugged. "You've been gone a long time, Justin. Cutsauce probably ran away with a poodle or something."

After our happy reunion, Ivy introduced the people who'd gotten her here. A tall, skinny boy with brown hair stepped forward. I saw hints of Victus in his face, but more of Delectra in his eyes. I'd met this boy before, years ago.

Eyes bright, he held out his hand. "Justin, I'm Conrad Edison."

I squeezed his hand and shook it. "Wow, you've really grown."

"Oh my god, Max, just kiss him already!" The brown-haired girl behind Conrad rolled her eyes. "You're simply too much."

A tall blond boy stared at me with wonder in his eyes.

I stepped toward him. "Are you Max?"

"Huh?" He snapped from his trance. "Did—did you talk to me?"

"Yes." I chuckled. "Are you okay?"

"It's Justin bloody Slade!" Max gripped my hand. "My god, I'm touching a hero of Eden!"

"I'm a hero of Eden too, Max." Ivy frowned. "Guess I'm not as good as my big bro, huh?"

"I can't believe it!" Max stared down with wonder at our hands. "We did it, Conrad. We really did it!"

I turned to the girl. "And you are?"

"Ambria Rax." She held up a hand. "Yes, I'm related to Cyphanis Rax, but he's dead and I'm not evil."

"Um, I wasn't even gonna go there."

"Well, everyone does eventually." She sighed and shook my hand as if it were a distasteful duty. "Pleased to meet you, Justin."

I mocked her British accent. "Delighted, I'm sure."

"We've got to tell Justin how we got here." Ivy grabbed Conrad's hand. "I know he hates Victus as much as I do."

"Well, yes, but I'm sure he'll want to catch up with family." Conrad nodded at me. "I can't tell you how good it is to finally meet you. When you vanished all those years ago, the Overworld sank into a terrible decline. We really need you back in Eden."

My eyes flared. "You can get us to Eden?"

"Of course. We're working on a larger scale portal device, but our ship can take us any time."

I pumped a fist in the air. "Yes! Pizza time!"

A silver-skinned girl stepped from the edge of the crowd. I only knew one girl who looked like that. Evadora had grown since I'd last seen her all those years ago, but the odd skin gave away her identity. My heart nearly froze with shock when I recognized the orange-haired woman behind her.

"Cora?" I stepped closer. "My god, the last time I saw you, an interdimensional bubble swallowed you."

"Yes, after I rammed the *Evadora* into Cephus's crimson arch." She shivered. "I ended up in Eden where I eventually found Conrad again. I was his foster mother for a time before I died."

I blinked in confusion. "You died?"

She nodded. "From cancer. But Conrad used my mirror image to resurrect me." Cora smiled. "It's a rather complicated story."

"Everything's bloody complicated around here," Ambria said.

I couldn't wait to find out what happened.

Elyssa frowned. "Where are my parents?"

Dad nodded his head toward an imposing gray marble building. "He was pretty busy in a war council, but I know he'll break away, especially since you've been gone so long."

I waved a hand at the small armada of Mzodi ships in the harbor. "What in the world happened in the four months we were gone?"

Mom's eyes flashed and met Dad's.

"Four months?" Dad shook his head. "Son, you've been gone much longer than that."

Adam gulped. "But I calculated the time dilation was about two days here to each one in Utopia."

Mom took my hands and squeezed. "Son, you've been gone over six years."

"What?" My knees turned to jelly and nearly brought me to the ground. Today was just one shock after the other.

"It's no wonder you thought we were dead." Shelton face-palmed. "You messed up, Nosti! Bella is gonna kill me!"

A blur of yellow flashed through the crowd and smacked into Shelton. "Harry, my beloved!" Bella peppered his face with kisses.

Shelton didn't hold back, quickly turning their reunion into an awkward moment for everyone in a one-mile radius. "Hot damn, woman, I missed you!"

"Six years!" Bella shoved him away. "How could you vanish for six years? I thought you were dead, papi!"

"Damned time dilation." He sagged. "Looks like Seraphina went to hell in a hand basket while we were gone, too."

"That would be accurate." Thomas Borathen stepped through the crowd, flanked by the rest of his clan.

"Dad!" Elyssa traded hugs with everyone.

"Thought you were gone for good, Ninjette." Her hulking brother Michael mussed her hair.

Mom smiled at me. "I told myself to let you go so many times, but a part of me wouldn't give up hope."

"Tell me what's happened since we've been gone." I looked at the far horizon. "Why did you abandon Seraphina?"

Thomas stood next to Mom. "Baal controls Azoris and Sazoris. Pjurna is next. We simply didn't have the capacity to fight him, so we evacuated as many souls as we could and found refuge in Atlantis."

"I don't think we're safe in here," I said. "Baal's influence is spread all across the realms, even in Utopia."

"Yes, I don't doubt it." Thomas folded his arms across his chest. "Shortly after you and Elyssa left, Baal destroyed the shipyard in Cabala. The Mzodi haven't been able to make ships fast enough, and we don't have enough Daskar or archangels to fight airborne dragons."

"Sounds hopeless." Shelton leaned his forehead against Bella's. "Guess we're gonna die after all."

It felt like the start of the Second Seraphim War all over again. Outgunned and backs to the wall, it looked like Daelissa was going to take over Eden. In this case, Baal had a dragon army and had nearly taken over all of Seraphina. But there was a lot more to the realms than I'd ever imagined, and we'd barely scratched the surface. What if we could gain allies like Pyra? Surely not every dragon from Draxadis was on Baal's team, and where did the Sirens stand?

"David, may I ask you a personal favor?" Cinder's question snapped me from my thoughts.

Dad raised an eyebrow. "What do you need?"

Cinder held up Bliss's soul sphere with the fading spark. "Can you make a new body for Bliss? She perished while saving my life."

Conrad stared at the transparent globe. "Bliss was an infernus?"

"Yes. She was special to me."

Regret filled Dad's eyes. "Cinder, I might be able to build a demon foundry, but it'll take me weeks. Can her spark survive that long?"

"I'm afraid not," Adam said. "The soul shard needs a body. I'm surprised it's lasted this long."

Nightliss stepped closer and peered inside. "That is part of my soul?"

Cinder nodded. "A very good part."

The ghostly gray matter of the soul pulsated brighter and drifted to the side with Nightliss. It seemed to strain against the container.

"What in the world?" Adam leaned closer. "It's almost like it knows where it came from."

Cinder looked back and forth between Nightliss and the soul sphere. Something like understanding dawned in his gray eyes. He placed the sphere in Nightliss's hand. The soul shard seeped through the container and vanished.

Nightliss gasped and her eyes flared. She looked at Cinder and smiled fondly. "Bliss and all her memories are with me now." She pressed her hand to his cheek. "She loved you very much."

Cinder's forehead pinched with pain. "Will you tell her I love her too?"

Tears sparkled in Nightliss's eyes. "She knows, dear. She knows."

"Incredible." Conrad smiled. "I can't imagine an infernus being capable of overcoming their original programming and becoming their own person."

"Or an emotionless golem falling in love." Shelton wiped his eyes. "It's a Christmas miracle."

A surge of hope rushed through me. "We've faced these kinds of odds before, people. Baal thinks he's smart. He thinks he's won. Baal doesn't know squat." I pumped a fist in the air. "We will find allies, and we will fight. Not even the Grand Overlord of Haedaemos can stand in our way!"

Cheers roared through the crowd.

Baal seemed unstoppable. We were refugees, hiding in the last fragment of the original Earth. But the war of the realms was only getting started. I would find allies and somehow, I would find a way to send Baal straight back to Hell.

BOOKS BY JOHN CORWIN

THE OVERWORLD CHRONICLES

OVERWORLD UNDERGROUND

OVERWORLD ARCANUM

Conrad Edison and the Broken Relic

Conrad Edison and the Infernal Design

Conrad Edison and the First Power

STAND ALONE NOVELS

Mars Rising

No Darker Fate

The Next Thing I Knew

Outsourced

For the latest on new releases, free ebooks, and more, join John Corwin's Newsletter at www.johncorwin.net!

ABOUT THE AUTHOR

John Corwin is the bestselling author of the Overworld Chronicles. He enjoys long walks on the beach and is a firm believer in puppies and kittens.

After years of getting into trouble thanks to his overactive imagination, John abandoned his male modeling career to write books.

He resides in Atlanta.

Connect with John Corwin online:
Facebook: http://www.facebook.com/johnhcorwinauthor
Website: http://www.johncorwin.net
Twitter: http://twitter.com/#!/John_Corwin